IN THE MOUTH
OF THE WHALE

PAUL McAULEY

IN THE MOUTH OF THE WHALE

GOLLANCZ
LONDON

Copyright © Paul McAuley 2012

The right of Paul McAuley to be identified as the author
of this work has been asserted by him in accordance
with the Copyright, Designs and Patents Act 1988.

First published in Great Britain in 2012 by Gollancz
An imprint of the Orion Publishing Group
Orion House, 5 Upper St Martin's Lane,
London WC2H 9EA

An Hachette UK Company

A CIP catalogue record for this book
is available from the British Library

ISBN 978 0 575 10073 2 (Cased)
ISBN 978 0 575 10074 9 (Trade Paperback)

1 3 5 7 9 10 8 6 4 2

Typeset at The Spartan Press Ltd,
Lymington, Hants

Printed and bound by CPI Group (UK) Ltd,
Croydon, CR0 4YY

The Orion Publishing Group's policy is to use papers
that are natural, renewable and recyclable products and
made from wood grown in sustainable forests. The logging
and manufacturing processes are expected to conform
to the environmental regulations of the country of origin.

www.unlikelyworlds.blogspot.com
www.orionbooks.co.uk

For Georgina
and for John and Judith Clute

Man has only one life, and must live it so that he does not recall with pain and regret the aimless lost years, and does not blush with shame over his mean and trivial past, so that when he dies he can say, 'All my life has been devoted to the struggle for the liberation of mankind.'

Nikolai Ostrovsky, *How the Steel Was Tempered*

It seems ridiculous to suppose the dead miss anything.

Marilynne Robinson, *Gilead*

PART ONE
BOW SHOCK

1

When the Child was a child, a sturdy toddler not quite two years old, she and her mother moved to São Gabriel da Cachoeira, in the north-west corner of the Peixoto family's territory in Greater Brazil. It was an old place, São Gabriel da Cachoeira, an old garrison town on the Rio Negro, serving an army base and a depot for workers in the Reclamation and Reconstruction Corps. Civilians, mostly descendants of Indians and early settlers, lived in a skewed grid of apartment blocks and bungalows beneath the green breast of the Fortaleza hill. Senior army officers, supervisors, and government officials rented villas along the Praia Grande, where in the dry season between September and January a beach appeared at the edge of the river. There was an airfield and a solar farm to the north, two schools, a hotel and half a dozen bars, a scruffy futbol pitch, a big church built in the brutalist style of the mid-twenty-first century, and a hospital, where the Child's mother, Maria Hong-Owen, had taken up the position of resident surgeon.

Maria's husband had been a captain in the army's intelligence service, killed when the plane in which he'd been travelling, a routine flight between his base and Brasília, had crashed after being caught in a lightning storm. The Child knew him only through pictures and clips. A handsome young man posing stiff and unsmiling in uniform. Standing bare-chested on a sunny lawn, a halo burning in his cap of blond hair, his face in shadow. Riding a bicycle down a dusty white road, the camera turning as he passed it and dissolved in a flare of light.

We do not know why Maria, a widow at twenty-eight with a young child to care for, quit her comfortable position in the teaching hospital in Montevideo and took up work in a half-forgotten town in the upper reaches of the basin of the Rio Amazonas. She was a devout Catholic – it was one of the reasons why her daughter severed all contact with her years later – so let us suppose that she decided to dedicate her life to a good cause. To atone for some real or imagined sin that had opened the hole in the world that swallowed her husband. Every day, she attended early-morning Mass and then worked long hours in the hospital, walking the rounds of the wards, helping out at the day clinic, delivering babies, treating fevers and parasitic infections and all kinds of cancers, repairing the cleft palates common amongst the children of the local Indians, dealing with the machete wounds, shattered bones, and other injuries of workers in the sugar-cane, pharm-banana, and tree plantations.

In short, she had too little time for her daughter, who was educated by a generic AI teaching package and cared for by her nursemaid or ama, Paulinho Gonzagão Silva. We know almost nothing about Ama Paulinho. She is one of the many players in the Child's story whose life was written on water: we must reconstruct her by approximation, stochastic sampling, and best guesses. So let's say that she was a full-blooded member of the Ianomâmis tribe, a stocky nut-brown old woman from a large family of some importance in the town, a widow like Maria Hong-Owen.

The Child quickly came to love Ama Paulinho as much as she loved her mother. They went everywhere together. See them in the jostling market, the pale child riding in a cloth pouch on her ama's back, clutching the old woman's woolly grey hair and looking around with an imperious gaze. See the Child sprawled on her tummy on the thread-bare lawn in the hospital compound, studying one of her AI teacher's exercises while Ama Paulinho sits in the shade of a tree, a tablet in her lap, following her chosen thread in a saga. See the Child standing in her ama's skirts at the edge of a street, the two of them watching army trucks rumble past in a blowing envelope of dust.

Bright moments shining like stars in a dark and backward abyss. Constructed from file images and fragments of an audio clip discovered in a memory box that the Child created fifteen centuries ago.

So much has been lost, and we lack the skill and knowledge to retrieve or resurrect most of it. All we can do is string what remains into some kind of order and pattern. Weave informed guesses and extrapolations based on heuristic sampling of historical records into a narrative that, if not accurate, is at least self-consistent. So we proceed, second by second. So the Child, our dear mother, twice dead, twice reborn, dreams herself towards her destiny.

Ama Paulinho told the Child stories about the people of the town and its history, recounted the legends of the long ago. Once upon a time, a giant snake lived in the Rio Negro, swallowing any who tried to cross the river, until at last two heroes tricked it into coming ashore, where it was turned to stone by the heat of the sun – it could still be seen, a long and disappointingly mundane bump in the avenue that ran through the middle of the town. Once upon a time, a beautiful woman was seen bathing in the shallows of the river by two friends who both fell in love with her at first sight and fought over who would have to right to approach her. Frightened by their ferocious rivalry, the woman struck out for the far shore but was caught in a strong river current and drowned; the two friends swam after her, and when they reached her body it turned into the island Adana, and they became the streams of water passing by on either side.

At the western point of the town's promontory was a grassy rise where the trenches of the ancient fort of Morro da Fortaleza could be traced. To the east, the peaks of the Serra da Bela Adormecida mountains sketched the profile of the fairy-tale princess waiting for a handsome prince to kiss her awake. To the north-west was the Neblina Peak, whose slopes ran with icy springs that fed the river, and all around volcanic cones stood up from the patchwork of renewed forest and dry grassland. In several of these, according to Ama Paulinho, dinosaurs, giant sloths, spotted tigers with teeth like knives, and other fabulous animals still lived. Products of the blasphemous technologies that had caused the Overturn. Wildsiders lived there, also. Animals who looked like men; men who looked like animals. River Folk whose sweet songs could cloud the minds of men. Bat people who fed on the blood of cattle and children. Ground sloths who captured unwary travellers and forced them to work in underground galleries, cultivating fungus on fields of rotten wood.

Ama Paulinho had her own story, her own mythos. She'd been married, once upon a time, although she said that it was so long ago that it might as well have been in another life. She and her husband had both been very young. Fifteen and sixteen. Little more than children. Her husband had worked as a general labourer for the R&R Corps. One day, while he was helping the big machines plant trees in a valley folded between two mountains, he had stepped off the road to urinate. When he finished, he saw a beautiful young woman staring at him from the green shade of an old tree that had somehow survived the hyperstorms and droughts and general ruin of the Overturn. She had large dark eyes and her tawny skin was dusted with golden freckles. He started to apologise, she laughed and ran off, and he chased after her, running up the side of the valley through a tract of old-growth forest, running faster than he had ever run before, running with such speed that he outran his human form and found that he had become a jaguar. He was so astonished that he stopped running, and he had been going so fast that when he stopped he tumbled head over tail (whenever she told the story, Ama Paulinho always widened her eyes in mock astonishment at this point, and the Child always laughed). The young woman came back and circled him and in the green light of the old forest he saw her true form: he saw that she was also a jaguar. And so they ran together through the tall and ancient trees, and he never again thought of or remembered the wife he had left behind, except in dreams.

'And that is how I know what happened to him,' Ama Paulinho said. 'Because I shared his dreams, for a little while. And because he lives still, I have never looked for another husband, and that is why, little one, I am able to look after you. So you see, it is a sad story with a happy ending.'

Ama Paulinho's family possessed a deep knowledge of the forest, handed down from generation to generation. Her uncle and two of her cousins were ethnobotanical advisers to the R&R Corps, which in the past century had made great advances in repairing the ecological damage caused by the Overturn to the forests along the Rio Negros and the Rio Uampés. Her father, Josua Mão de Ferro Almeida Gonzagão, had served on the front line with the R&R Corps for more than forty years. He lived in a rambling single-storey house that was as familiar to the Child as her mother's bungalow in the hospital compound. A fabulously old man, gaunt and leathery and bald as a turtle, who spent most of his time on a couch in a back room, watching a screen that was always streaming news, and receiving visitors. Old R&R comrades who drank maté with him and talked about the good old days; townspeople who came to ask his advice on business or personal matters, or to ask for small loans, or to pay off the interest on loans he had already given them. The household was run by his sister, widowed like Ama Paulinho. Her son and his wife and daughter lived there, too. The Child played with the daughter and her cousins and friends, and she was fond of Josua Gonzagão, who asked her opinion about various

6

items of news, listened to her talk about her studies, told her that she was destined for great things (which she liked), told her that she should listen to her mother and her ama (which she didn't), and talked about his work in the R&R Corps, and the properties of trees and lesser plants of the forest, and the lives and uses of its insects and animals. And so the Child began to be shaped into what she would – what she should, what she must – become.

Maria Hong-Owen's position in the hospital gave her considerable status, but her manner was severe and abrupt, she showed little interest in gossip, and was innocent of tact. Those who believed they mattered in the town thought her a typical barbarian from the Spanish-speaking south. At first, she was invited to parties and formal dinners and introduced to everyone who was anyone, but the wives were jealous of her independence and feared that she would steal their husbands, and the husbands did not know how to deal with a woman whose professional accomplishments gave her the kind of independence they jealously reserved for themselves. It did not help that, quite soon after her arrival in São Gabriel da Cachoeira, Maria had a very public row with the supervisor of the sugar-cane plantation. A pipe in the plantation's mill fractured; pressurised steam scalded three workers; Maria saved their lives and reconstructed their faces and hands with grafts of cultured skin and collagen, and presented a strongly-worded letter of complaint about work practices in the plantation to the members of the town's council. They rejected it out of hand, of course, being friends and business associates of the plantation's supervisor, Vidal Rahai Francisca, but Maria's headstrong action had an effect she couldn't have anticipated.

Unlike most of its important citizens, Vidal Francisca had been born in the town. His father had been a teacher in its school; Vidal had studied at the agricultural college in Manaus and returned to take charge of the plantation, which was owned, like much of the town, by a minor scion of the Peixoto family. His beautiful young wife had died suddenly of an aneuryism ten years ago and he hadn't remarried, although it was rumoured that he kept a mistress in an apartment in Manaus. A clever, vain man, he'd taken on the role of ringmaster to the town's tiny social set. He had organised several famous events – a firework display the size of a minor war, a boat race, a polo match on the futbol field, especially returfed for the occasion, a performance of

Turandot by a touring opera company – and every Independence Day held a celebrated and much anticipated barbecue at his large house.

After his spat with Doctor Hong-Owen, he had felt insulted at first, and then intrigued. He saw in the woman's dedication and un-compromising manner something of his younger self, and he sym-pathised with her plight. Her widowhood and, so he supposed, her loneliness. So he was disappointed when she sent him a polite message declining his invitation to that year's Independence Day party, excusing herself on the grounds of pressure of work.

Her absence was noted, of course; most people agreed that she was a ball-breaker too proud and snobbish to associate with people she believed to be no better than country bumpkins. Vidal Francisca found himself defending her on more than one occasion. 'I know how it is, to lose a loved one, and to raise a child alone,' he said, at a dinner party. 'It leaves you with little energy for anything else. And if that is not enough, she is a capable woman very dedicated to her work.'

'If she had any love of her work she should know who pays her salary,' someone said.

'Do we pay her to abase herself before us,' Vidal asked, 'or to do her work?'

'Vidal is in love,' someone else said, to general laughter.

Vidal Francisca managed to change the subject, but more and more he found his thoughts turning to the young doctor and her precocious daughter.

Because her mother was more or less frozen out of the town's social set, the Child did not mix much with children of her class. She was tutored in mathematics and physics by the teenage son of the hospital director, but that was about it. At first she was too young to know any different, and later she pretended that she did not care.

Imagine the Child growing up in that small and sleepy outpost, blonde and light-skinned like her father, secretive, sunburned, lanky. She learned how to trap birds with sticky sap and poison fish in a pool with a mash of berries, where edible fungi grew and at what season, which trees had kindly spirits and which were possessed by angry spirits that must be acknowledged and pacified, or else they might drop a branch on your head. She learned to read some of the signs with which the Ianomâmis marked their sacred places, and she collected and catalogued beetles and moths, and discussed the pharmaceutical properties of forest plants and mosses with her mother. And so she passed back and forth between two irreconcilable worlds: the numinous world of her mother's God and of Ama Paulinho's ancestral beliefs, where spirits animated the forest, men could shrug off human form, and death was not a full stop but a transformation; and the world of her mother's profession, where logic unpicked mystery and revealed the common principles and laws by which reality could be tamed and manipulated, where disease was driven back by antibiotics and gene therapy, cancers were defeated by tagged antibodies and engineered viruses, and only death remained unconquered.

The Child had an early familiarity with death. She kept a small menagerie of animals collected from the wild places inside the town limits or bought in the market. She had a tank of terrapins, several tanks of river fish. She had an ant farm sandwiched between two plates of glass. She collected several species of stick insect from the forest, and bought a baby sloth from a mestizo boy in the market, but it died because she couldn't figure out how to wean it. Most of her animals died, sooner or later. One day her fish would be all alive-o in their tanks; the next they'd be floating belly up. The ants deserted their maze. One by one, the stick insects dropped to the bottoms of their wire-mesh cages, as stiff and dry in death as the twigs they had emulated in life. Only the terrapins did not die, no matter how often she forgot to feed them, or how fetid the green soup of their little pond became.

And because she made herself useful around the hospital, working in the lab, running errands for the nurses and doctors, fetching water and food for patients, and so on, the Child was also familiar with the deep and powerful mystery of human death. One day she'd be chatting with an old woman; the next, the woman's bed would be empty and stripped to its mattress. Late one sultry night, the Child delivered a bite of supper to her mother as she kept watch on a dying patient in a little room off one of the wards. She saw the man start in his solitary bed and try to rise on his elbows, toothless mouth snapping at the air, his eyes wide and fixed on something far beyond the limits of the room, the hospital, the town, the world. She saw her mother ease him down and talk to him soothingly and fold his hands around a rosary, saw him try to take a breath and fail, and try and fail again, and that was that. Her mother called the Child to her side and they said a prayer over the body. Then her mother rose, her shadow wheeling hugely across the wall and ceiling, and flung open the shutters of the window as if setting something free.

9

Yes, the Child had an early education in death, but to begin with she was only mildly interested in it. Animals died, and it was disappointing because it meant that she had failed in some part of their care. People came to the hospital to get better, but sometimes, especially if they were old, nothing could be done for them, and they died. She did not think that it was something that would ever happen to her until she saw the drowned boy.

She was eleven, that summer. We had at last passed through Fomalhaut's Oort Cloud and were approaching the bow shock of its heliosphere. After almost one and a half thousand years, we were poised to enter the rarified climate of our destination. And the weather that summer in the little town of São Gabriel da Cachoeira and in the vast Amazonia region all around was unusually hot and dry. The wet season ended a month early, and after that no rain fell for day after day after day. The sun burned in a cloudless sky bleached white as paper. The lawn in the hospital compound withered. The streets were silted with silky dust and dust blew into houses and apartments. The R&R Corps stopped planting out new areas of forest. The artesian well that watered Vidal Francisca's sugar-cane plantation dried up; he had to run a pump line two kilometres long from the river. And the level of the river dropped steadily, exposing rocks and an old shipwreck unseen for decades.

It was a return of the bad days, Ama Paulinho said, and told the Child tall tales about great droughts in the long-ago. People prayed to Gaia at every Mass, but no rain came. During the day they stayed indoors as much as possible, sheltering from brassy hammerfalls of heat and light; in the evening they gathered along the beach below the Praia Grande, to enjoy the breezes that blew over the cool waters of the river. Families brought food or cooked there, men drank and talked at a couple of bars set up on the sand, and children ran everywhere.

Maria Hong-Owen was too often busy with her duties at the hospital to visit the beach, but the Child went there almost every evening with Ama Paulinho, where they ate with the old woman's extended family, everyone sitting around a blanket spread with bowls and dishes of salad, rice and beans, fried fish, farofa, hard-boiled eggs, and fruit. Afterwards, the Child liked to walk by herself, watching fat tropical stars bloom in the humid nightblue sky, watching bats dip and skim across the river, watching people moving about. Children chased up and down the beach in little packs, or played the game that was the rage in the town that summer, involving throwing little shells into the air and catching them on the back of the hand while chanting nonsense rhymes, but the Child believed that she had grown beyond those childish things. She was no longer a child nor yet an adult, but something else. A changeling, perhaps, like one of the lonely creatures in her ama's stories. Living amongst people, disguised as one of them, but watchful and apart.

One night, she was walking along the water's edge when she noticed a flurry of activity a little way ahead. A small group of children shouting and pointing at something in the river; two men running towards them, splashing into the shallows. The Child walked towards them over sugary sand still warm from the day's sun. More adults were coming down the beach. Then a woman screamed and ran towards the two men, stooping between them and lifting up the wet and naked body of a little boy. She staggered out of the water and sat down hard, pressing the body to herself, shaking it, kissing its face, looking around at people who would not meet her gaze, asking the dear Lord Jesus Christ the same question over and again. Why? Why had this happened? Why why why?

The Child knew the boy from the market, where he helped his father sell watermelons, but she did not know his name until the woman began to say it, calling to him over and again in a cracked and sobbing incantation, rocking his body, stroking wet hair back from his face. Two small girls were crying, hugging each other, convulsed by huge shivers. One man said that the boy had got out of his depth in the river. Other people talked in low voices. No one dared disturb the terrible eloquence of the woman's grief. The Child stood amongst the crowd, watching everything.

At last, one of the priests, Father Caetano, came along the twilight beach in his black soutane. Two paramedics from the hospital followed him, hauling their gear. They prised the drowned boy from his mother and worked on him for some time; at last they looked at each other across his body and one of them shook his head. The boy's mother shrieked, pushed away a woman who tried to comfort her, was caught and held tight by another. Father Caetano knelt, recited the Prayer for the Dead, and took out a small vial of oil and with his thumb drew a cross on the boy's forehead. Then the paramedics lifted the body on to their stretcher and covered it with a blanket and put their equipment on its chest and carried it up the beach, followed by Father Caetano and the boy's mother and a ragged tail of onlookers.

The Child lingered at the river's edge after everyone else had gone.

Watching the dark water slide past, head cocked as if listening for something.

Late that night, Maria returned from the hospital and looked in on her daughter and found the bed empty. She checked the other rooms in the bungalow and went outside and woke Ama Paulinho. The two women went to the shed where the Child kept her menagerie, and then they searched the rest of the compound. The private gate was locked; the watchman at the public gate at the front of the hospital apologised and said that he had not seen the doctor's daughter. With the help of two night nurses, Maria and Ama Paulinho searched the wards and surgical rooms, the kitchens and storerooms, the offices and the pathology lab, the pharmacy and the out-patient clinic. They found the Child at last in the mortuary, asleep on a chair near the rack of refrigerated drawers where those who had died in the hospital or in accidental or suspicious circumstances were stored before being autopsied.

The Child said that she'd wanted to keep the dead boy company, and despite close questioning by her mother would say nothing else. She never told anyone the real reason why she'd kept watch over the body: that she had believed the boy might have been seduced by the River Folk, that his death by drowning had been the first stage in his transformation. In her mind's eye, she'd seen him waking in the cold dark of the mortuary drawer, had seen herself freeing him, helping him back to the river, earning the gratitude of the River Folk. A fantasy that seemed foolish the next morning, but left her with one unassailable conviction. Green saints and gene wizards could extend their lives by a century or more, and people cheated death time and again in her ama's stories. She was certain that she would find a way to cheat it too.

2

I was on my way to harrow a hell when everything changed. This was on Maui, a no-account worldlet at the trailing edge of the Archipelago. The Trehajo clan had turned it into a resettlement centre for refugees who had fled the last big push by the Ghosts, some hundred megaseconds ago. A family of ice refiners had stumbled upon an active fragment of the old Library, and before informing the resettlement authority they'd taken a peek inside, no doubt hoping to uncover a tasty chunk of data that they could sell on the grey market. They'd woken a minor demon instead, and it had turned them. Luckily, the resettlement authority had realised what was happening, and had moved on the family's tent habitat before things got out of hand. I'd been tasked with the final clean-up.

Maui wasn't much different from the farm rock where I'd spent my early childhood. A dwarf planet about three hundred kilometres across, just large enough to have been pulled into a sphere by its own gravity: a rough ball of water ice accreted around a core of silicate rocks, contaminated with pockets of methane and nitrogen ices, coated in layers of primordial carbonaceous material and spattered with craters, one so big that material excavated by the impact covered half Maui's surface with a lightly cratered debris shield. Two fragments lofted by that impact still circled Maui's equator, a pair of moonlets kindled into sullen slow-burning miniature suns by Quick construction machines during the short-lived world-building era immediately after their seed-ship had arrived at Fomalhaut.

The Quick machines had extensively gardened the worldlet too, planting vacuum organisms in seemingly random and wildly beautiful patterns utterly unlike the square fields of my foster-family's farm.

Huge tangles of ropes, crustose pavements, clusters of tall spires, fluted columns and smooth domes, forests of wire. Mostly in shades of black but enlivened here and there with splashes and flecks of vivid reds or yellows, sprawled across crater floors, climbing walls and spilling their rims, spreading across intercrater plains, sending pseudohyphae into the icy regolith to mine carbonaceous tars, growing slowly but steadily in the faint light of Fomalhaut and Maui's two swift-moving mini-suns.

Once, when the Quick had been the sole inhabitants of the Fomalhaut system, these gardens had covered the entire surface of the worldlet, inhabited by only a few contemplative eremites. Now, they were scarred by tents built to house refugees, the monolithic cubes of fusion generators, landing stages, materiel dumps, missile emplacements, strip mines, refineries, and maker blocks. My transit pod was flying above a region scraped down to clean bright water ice when my security delivered a message. *Report to the Redactor Svern when you are finished.*

'Report?' the Horse said. 'As in talk? As in face to face?'

The Horse was my kholop. We were crammed thigh to thigh in the pod, dressed in pressure suits, our securities overlapping.

I said, 'I don't know of any other way of talking to him.'

'Then you're going home. *We're* going home.'

'It may not mean anything.'

'It may mean your exile is over. That you've worked out your penance. That we're done with minor demons and their petty little hells. We're done with cleaning up other people's mistakes—'

'I doubt it.'

'It has to mean something.'

'It probably means that he's found an assignment so crufty it will make fighting a horde of demons seem like a picnic in paradise. We'll find out soon enough. Show me the dispersal pattern of those walkers.'

'It's the same as all the others,' the Horse said. 'Generated by a pseudo-random drunkard's walk algorithm. If demons ever started learning from the mistakes of their brothers we'd be in real trouble.'

'Show me,' I said.

The close horizon tilted up as we worked the data, growing into a ridge that cut off half the sky. It was the rim wall of the big crater that put a serious dent in the worldlet's northern hemisphere. We flew straight towards it, skimming the smooth contours of its crest and flying out above chiselled cliffs twenty kilometres tall. The pod spun on its axis and shuddered, firing up its motor, braking, falling in a long arc towards a shattered plain spattered with secondary craters and patchworked with vacuum-organism thickets, landing close to a military pinnace on a rise two klicks north of the ice refiners' tent.

'For once, I'm eager to see what fresh hell this is,' the Horse said as the restraints of our crash couches snapped open. 'I know you think me a fool, but I have a good feeling about that message.'

We crossed to the pinnace for a brief conference with the shavetail lieutenant in charge of perimeter security. She was young and scared, and very unhappy about the Horse's presence; the Trehajo clan, old and highly conservative, had no time for Our Thing's new-fangled idea that the Quick might be something more than property. I assured her that he'd been raised as a demon-killer and hated them as much as any right-thinking True, checked the sitrep that her security blurted to mine, and explained what we were going to do.

No harrowing was ever routine, but this one seemed straightforward. My clan had been restoring and curating the Library of the Homesun for more than six gigaseconds. All of the major segments had been discovered and integrated long ago. Most of what was left out in the wild was badly borked and heavily infected, and the fragment discovered by the ice refiners was no different. It had been cached in the dead mind of an ancient gardening machine that the refiners had dug out and dragged back to their tent. The machine was still in the tractor garage; I told the lieutenant she could safely destroy it.

'When you're finished, we're going to level the tent and everything inside it,' the lieutenant said. 'Zap it from orbit with a gamma-ray laser. Make sure every trace of that thing is obliterated.'

'We'll deal with the demon and trace and seal any back doors and relays. That's the only way to be really sure,' I said.

The tent had been badly damaged by the firefight between the turned refugees and the resettlement authority's troops, and lay open to the freezing vacuum. Sealed in our pressure suits, the Horse and I loped across dead, brittle meadows in the stark light of lamps floating beneath the tent's high ridge. Shards fallen from the broken roof lay everywhere amongst scorched craters and the carbonised skeletons of trees ignited by energy weapons. Houses like random piles of cubes, all scorched and broken, were strung along the shore of a lake that had boiled dry when the tent had been ruptured.

The locus of the infection was inside the largest house, guarded by a phalanx of drones primed to blast anything that looked or behaved strangely (including us). The demon had infected the local comms, as usual, and when it couldn't get past the security it had turned the ice refiners. They'd torn out most of the infrastructure of the tent, scavenged metals and rare earths, and fed them into a modified maker that had painted a skin of computronium across the internal walls of the house. Then they'd scooped out their eyes and installed transceivers that jacked into their optic nerves, turning them into a hyperlinked hive-mind controlled by the demon, which had migrated into the computronium skin. When the authority realised what was going on, the hive-mind had been making and releasing walkers intended to sneak demon-seed into other settlements. Slamhounds were still tracking down the last of them.

Luckily, a couple of the hive-mind's human bodies had been preserved. The Horse had already cracked the encryption in their transceivers, and now we used them to access the hell. We sent in a standard set of probes, processed the results of their interaction with the computronium, tailored our interfaces and avatars accordingly, and opened a gate.

Like most of its kind, the demon was insanely smart, but lacked imagination and creativity. Vast heaps of doorless and windowless cubes the piss-yellow colour of old snow on an industrial worldlet stretched away under racing laceworks of black cloud. An anthill city inhabited by creatures roughly human in shape and size, crawling on spidery limbs over jagged slopes, their eyeless faces sloping straight back from the clattering beaks of their mouths. Zombie avatars, sampled from the demon's victims and duplicated and reduplicated, their neural maps supporting most of the hell's low-grade processing. They crawled in and out of openings that puckered in the faces of the cubes, wrapped around each other in listless parodies of lovemaking, knit loose balls around unfortunate individuals who were slowly and systematically consumed alive.

The Horse and I were invisible to the zombies because one of our probes had sampled and synthesised the hive-mind's antpong, but we cast a prophylactic circle around ourselves just in case the demon mobilised them against us, then set loose a standard set of exorcism algorithms. They darted away in every direction, feeding on the lacework computational clouds, swiftly growing into silvery networks that spread out across the sky. The demon was dumb enough to respond with a direct attack. The cubes all around us lit up with the same image, an eye burning blood-red in the centre of churning wisps of fog, and a smoky wind got up around the perimeter of the circle in which the avatars of the Horse and I stood, a whirlwind of bits that coalesced overhead into a gigantic version of the city's myriad eyes. I countered its feeble attempts to crack our perimeter security with a futile-cycle algorithm that ate up most of its computational power and after a little to-and-fro managed to transform it into a mouse-like creature that ran counterclockwise around our perimeter, cheeping like a bird, until the Horse snatched it up and jammed it inside a Klein trap.

Everything froze around us then, and within a few tens of seconds we were able to confirm that this was a finitely bounded hell with no external links, which meant that none of the walkers had managed to lodge a seed in any place where duplicates could grow. It took only a little longer to expose the kernel – a disappointing spew of disjointed information just a few hundred thousand terabytes in size, nothing the Library didn't already possess or hadn't already discarded – and dump it into a sandbox and shut everything down.

It was a routine harrowing, nothing out of the ordinary, but the Horse was shaken and angry for some reason. As we trudged through the frozen ruin of the tent, he told me that I'd let the demon get too close before I'd neutralised it.

'It had a few moves,' I said. 'But none of them were worth anything in the end, and that's what counts.'

'I had to intervene at one point. In case you didn't notice.'

'Are you looking for praise for doing your job?'

'I was doing yours,' the Horse said. 'I'd like to think you're distracted by that message. And I wouldn't blame you if you were. But this isn't the first time I've had to step in and save our souls.'

'I'm not distracted because it won't turn out to be anything. The Library has a long memory, and it doesn't easily forgive.'

'And besides, you don't deserve forgiveness. You want to be punished.'

'And you think it's unfair that you have to share my punishment. But you were there too. You were part of it.'

'You know what would be truly unfair? Having to explain why you got yourself killed because you weren't paying enough attention to a demon's tricks and traps.'

'We've been doing this work for, what? Forty megaseconds now. We'll be doing it a lot longer than that. Get used to it.'

17

'Thirty-seven.'

'What?'

'It's only been thirty-seven megaseconds.'

I said, 'I didn't know you were counting.'

The Horse said, 'Someone has to keep track.'

3

It began like every other day. Ori climbed into her immersion chair and plugged into her bot, trundled it out on to the skin of the Whale, and helped her crew shepherd a pair of probes from their garage to the staging post. Fuelling and charging them, running final checks before they set off on their long journey down the cable. Important, demanding, finicky work, but nothing out of the ordinary.

The staging post was near the base of the Whale's vertical cylinder, at the lip of the conical end cap that tapered to the cable's insertion point. Immediately above, a marshalling yard spread like ivy around a tree trunk, bustling with purposeful movement. At the upper end, hoppers stuffed with a variety of raw construction materials scooted down rack-and-pinion tracks towards tipplers that lifted them up and turned them upside down and mated their hatches with the hatches of bulbous freight cars. The hoppers shed their cargo with quick peristaltic shudders, were swung right-side-up and set down on return tracks on the far side of the tipplers, and zipped back to the refinery. Further down the yard, loaded freight cars assembled themselves into long strings that trundled away along one of the four parallel magrails that crossed the inverted hill of the end cap and converged on the cable, rolling over flying bridges at the insertion point and gathering speed as they descended the cable towards the deck of fluffy white ammonia clouds that sheeted the sky from horizon to horizon, passing strings of empty cars climbing in the opposite direction.

Ori had a few moments to take in this familiar view while she waited for her crewmate and bunky, Inas, to sign off the go-list for the ignition system of one of the probe's separation motors. The strings of freight cars, descending and ascending. A crew of bots prinking about the edge of the vacuum-organism farm that patched the curve of flank above the marshalling yard with a couple of square kilometres of dull red fibrous tangles. The bulk of the Whale looming beyond like a moon-sized thunderhead. Her world entire: a fretted cylinder ten kilometres tall, hung in the upper troposphere like a stylus balanced on its point, packed with hot hydrogen ballonets, fusion generators, try works and refineries, accommodation modules, garages, workshops, and the great engines that kept it stabilised in the winds that roared around Cthuga's equator.

Out in the wide green-blue sky, a small formation of ramscoop drones was heading inward, laden with organic material collected from plumes that trailed downwind of upwelling festoons at the northern edge of the Equatorial Zone. And higher still, at the limits of the resolution of the optics of Ori's bot, a black fleck moved through the diffused glare of the sun's white point. A shrike-class raptor orbiting the upper levels of the Whale.

She often wondered what it would be like to fly one of those sleek, powerful machines. Fly, not ride. That was the thing. The True pilots didn't control the raptors from an immersion chair safely lodged inside one of the Whale's accommodation modules. No, their fierce pride and honour demanded that they put up their lives every time they flew, testing themselves against the storms and hurricane winds of Cthuga, bringing the war directly to the enemy.

Ori had come a long way in her sixteen years, working her way up from general-purpose swabbie to refinery loader, machinist, and finally bot jockey. Working hard to prove her worth, abasing herself when she had to, showing initiative whenever she could, finally making it all the way to the outside. Why not higher still? Maybe she could try out for mechanic one day. After all, keeping raptors sweet couldn't be that much different from running system checks on probes. And if she did well at that, perhaps she'd be allowed to fly one of the drones that accompanied raptors during long-range patrols . . .

The raptor's tiny thorn swung away around the bulk of the Whale. Inas jogged Ori, saying, 'No time for dreaming, kid.'

'They don't usually hang around the Whale. Raptors.'

'The phils want to start rolling this bird yesterday, and we still have to run through the rest of the go-list.'

'You ask me, something's up.'

'I'm asking you to give me some help here.'

'We're still ahead of everyone else.'

'By a bare second. Let's swing.'

'Aye-aye.'

'You want to fly, you need a spotless rep.'

Inas knew all about Ori's ambitions, and cared enough to encourage her.

'Or I could just let go,' Ori said, raising up and hanging from just two limbs for a moment, dangling above the vertical length of the probe, the long drop past the inward-angled slope of the end cap, and the even longer drop beyond, ten klicks to the top of the cloud deck, another hundred and fifty through layers of ammonia-ice, ammonium sulphide, and clouds of water-ice where lightning storms flickered . . .

'Falling isn't flying,' Inas said.

'Sure it is. Except when you're flying, you're in control,' Ori said, and came down to a squat beside her bunky's bot and started the tedious work of checking each function of the separation motor's simple nervous system.

The probe and its twin sat side by side in launch cradles on flatbed rail cars, attended by a small crew of bots that clambered over and around them. The bots were flexible, radially symmetrical machines that looked a little like brittlestars: ten long and many-jointed limbs set around central discs edged with the glittering buttons of optical, microwave, and radio sensors. All engaged in an intricate ballet of hesitations, negotiations and sudden bursts of decisive activity, all talking constantly to each other. Updates on what they planned to do, what they were doing, and what they had just finished doing, interlaced with gossip and jokes and banter. A familiar and comforting polyphonic work song.

Ori and Inas were responsible for checking out the little solid-fuel motors that would fire as the probe approached the cable terminus, separating it from its cradle, boosting it past the very end of the cable and correcting for yaw and spin imparted by the cable's pendulum-like swing. After that, the probe's primary-stage motor would ignite, a brief fierce burn driven by antimatter fusion that would punch the secondary stage through a thickening fog of liquid hydrogen; when it reached the edge of the transition point where the fog turned into a vast deep sea, the shaped charge of the secondary stage would consume itself in a single violent moment and inject the bullet of the payload into the sea's currents, where it would drift down towards the dense hot sphere of superfluid metallic hydrogen at the planet's core.

The payload had already been inserted into the probe: microscopic yet potent amounts of degenerate matter, raw quarks and strange solitons, each suspended in pinch fields stitched into lattices of flawless diamond micropellets that were cased in rhenium carbide and yttria-stabilised zirconia felt. When the casings and diamond micropellets eroded, violent interactions between their cargoes and the superfluid would help to map and anatomise the place where reality itself broke down. Or so the theory went. In practice, only a few payloads ever reached their target. The sea of liquid hydrogen wrapped around Cthuga's core was tens of thousands of kilometres deep, squeezed by pressure that could stamp the Whale flat as a sheet of paper in an instant, reaching a temperature of more than five thousand degrees centigrade at the boundary with the metallic hydrogen core. After more than a century, the True philosophers had scarcely begun to unravel the mysteries of Cthuga's core. And now the gas giant was swinging around in its long orbit towards territory occupied by the Ghosts. War – real war, not skirmishes and scouting fly-bys – was imminent. Time was running out. The phils were sending down pairs of probes as fast as the manufactories could assemble them. At least one pair every day, sometimes more. And still it wasn't enough.

Ori was so absorbed in her work that she didn't at first notice the alarm, reacting a sluggish thirty milliseconds after it began, skimming the top layer of the fat burst of raw data, dumping the rest. Far below the cloud deck, something had struck the cable with enough force to snap it like a whip: residual energy was propagating up its length in a sine wave whose peak was just fifty kilometres away and closing fast. It was the real thing, no drill. No time to return the probes to the garage. Barely enough time to lock everything in place and hope for the best.

She looked all around, hoping to spot some trace of the enemy, seeing only empty sky. High above, a string of freight cars had halted near the exit of the marshalling yard. Beyond, bots were scrambling amongst hoppers and tipplers. Fierce little sparks blooming everywhere as hoppers were welded to their rack-and-pinion tracks. Inas and the rest of the crew were working at the base of the flatbed car, welding it to the skin at brace points, uncoupling power and transmission cabling, clearing clutter from the staging post's platform. Ori swung over the curved flank of the probe, and froze as something blurred past three klicks out. A sleek shape driving straight down towards the cloud tops far below, dwindling away to a bright point seconds before the roar of its afterburners reached her.

Ori called to Inas. 'Did you see that?'

'See what?'

Ori threw a picture. 'The raptor. Every weapon pod everted. Told you something was up.'

'Are you done skywatching? Because I could use some help.'

'It was ready for combat,' Ori said. 'It has to mean the enemy hit the cable.'

'It doesn't mean anything. It could be an eddy. Wind shear. Any kind of extreme weather. All I know is what I'm told. And all they're telling us is it's coming fast,' Inas said.

'I hear you,' Ori said, and swung around and down and started welding the other side of the brace point that Inas was working on. For all the good it would do. The flatbed car was already locked down on the magrail; if that gave, a few welds weren't going to hold it.

She kept half her eyes focused on the distant cloud tops while she worked, half-hoping to see some trace of combat. If it was an attack, it would be the fifth in less than a hundred days. Three had been routine engagements with infiltrator drones far downwind of the Whale, but the last had been just a hundred klicks north and east, a whole wing of raptors streaking out to engage a package that had drawn a thin violet contrail as it slanted through the troposphere, vanishing beneath the cloud deck as they chased hard on its tail, the clouds lighting up a few seconds later as if struck by a localised thunderstorm. Controlled falling. Absolutely.

Bots worked with graceful haste around the two flatbed cars. In under a minute they had done all they could and all movement ceased everywhere. Inas' bot wrapped its limbs around the post of a power point and the bots of the rest of the crew clung limpet-like to various protrusions or squatted inside hastily spun nests of elastomer fibrils. Hunkered down. Waiting for the uprushing wavefront of the quake to hit.

Ori clambered back on to the flatbed car and clung to the edge of the cradle, so that she had a good view up and down the length of the Whale. For a few heartbeats nothing happened. Then the cable humped and buckled at the point where it pierced the cloud deck, and sprites suddenly stood on every sharp edge of the flatbed cars and the equipment scattered around them. Crackling coronal discharges that

23

danced and swayed like flames, blue at their cores, shelled in pale yellows and greens that spat spiky fractal sparks.

One burned so close to Ori that her optical sensors whited out for a moment. When they came back on line the sprite was gone, but tens of others were dancing all around, jumping from point to point with no seeming transition. Several swayed at the nose of the probe like a crowd of curious ghosts, flattening now in the hard wind pushed ahead of the oncoming shock wave.

It travelled up the cable with relentless speed. A subtle sinuous flexing of the tremendously strong structure, moving inside a silvery envelope of warped air. Little jets of vapour, mostly visible in infrared, spat in every direction as attitude motors on ballonet spars tried to maintain the cable's rigidity. Ori flattened her bot against the cradle and felt a brief moment of bilocation. She was riding her bot, extended into every part of it, splayed flat against the cradle, and she was sitting in her immersion chair, hands cramped inside control gloves, blocks of data floating before her eyes and in the midpoint of the bot's wrap-around vision.

Then, directly below the blunt point of the end cap, sections of track buckled and sheared away from the cable and the Whale hummed with subsonic vibrations as the cable flexed in the collars that held it fast inside the great structure's spine.

Ori's entire attention snapped back inside the bot. She saw a rainbow shimmer of intricate stress patterns race across the cone of the end cap, and then a black fog of superheated atomic carbon, stripped from the cap's cladding of fullerene-diamond polymer, rolled upslope. Ori closed down her external sensors, felt the staging post judder and heave, rattling the probe's flatbed car sideways and up and down against its tracks, rattling her bot against the cradle, twisting it, plucking at it. Everything went white and Ori was back in her body, breathing hard, feeling the floor shudder under her chair, and then the connection rebooted and she was back, and the shaking was still bad but it wasn't as bad as it had been, gentling now, everything suddenly still and quiet.

The hot fog had blinded most of the sensors on the bot's right side, cutting a wide swathe out of its three-hundred-and-sixty-degree vision, but Ori glimpsed movement high above and swivelled and focused as best she could and saw that the magrail above the staging post was disintegrating. Broken sections fell like a shower of spears as the magrail unzipped towards the string of freight cars at the exit of the marshalling yard. The leading car tipped forward and fell away, and the string whipped out above it, snapping apart one by one. The car at the end of the whip dropped straight down, tumbling free in clear air, gone, but the rest struck the Whale's skin as they fell, bouncing off and spinning away in every direction.

One dropped straight towards the staging post. Ori saw it in the brief instant before it slammed end on into the post's outer edge. Its sheath buckled and shattered and its load of carbon nanotubes flew out, a black cloud that completely enveloped the flatbed car and Ori's bot, and then there was a tremendous jolt and everything swung sideways.

The cloud thinned and blew away and Ori discovered that she was hanging upside down with nothing between her and the cloud deck far below. It took her a moment to work out what had happened: part of the staging post's skin and the track attached to it had been ripped open and peeled backwards by the impact of the freight car.

She called to Inas, but comms were out across every channel, internal and external. She knew that she should disengage, leave the bot to its fate and check on damage inside the Whale, but she wanted to see what happened next.

Things large and small were falling past on either side. A hard rain of hoppers and bits of track and machines. Bots twisting in mid-air, limbs whipping this way and that as they tried and failed to snatch at any hold. One slammed into the side of the probe's cradle, close to Ori, and clung there for a moment. And then something struck it and it whirled away. Debris drummed on the upper side of the peeled length of skin, making the flatbed car hanging from its underside shiver and shake. The power to the track was off and only the welds at the bracing posts were holding the flatbed car in place; now they began to fail with sharp little explosions. One side lurched outward, and bots that had been clinging there fell away, dwindling past the end cap, gone.

For a moment, nothing else happened, and then something struck the skin above with tremendous force, and the flatbed car dropped straight down, shedding bots and shards of debris. Ori hung on as sky and cable and cloud deck spun around each other. She had a brief bright picture of the flatbed car smashing into the cable and vanishing in a white-hot flare as the antimatter in the probe's fusion motor let go, and she began to move crabwise up the launch cradle. The tumbling motion pulled her outwards, body-slammed her against the cradle, pulled her outwards again. She crawled over the lip, flattened nine limbs against the skin of the probe, locking them down with millions of nanofibril tubes and claws, and reached out with the tenth. Stretching towards the access point for the separation motor's nervous system, making the connection.

The latches sprang free and the separation motors set around the base of the probe flared and it shot away from the cradle and speared into the streaming white mist of the ammonia clouds. Ori clung on, plugged into the probe's simple nervous system, forcing it to run its stabilisation reflex over and over. By the time its erratic tumbling had been corrected, it had punched through the underside of the ammonia clouds and was falling through clear air again. Another layer of cloud spread far below, tinged dirty yellow. Clouds of ammonium hydro-sulphide, rifted apart in one place to show darker underlayers. A kilometre away from the falling probe, the cable plunged straight down through the cloud deck, dwindling away into unguessable depths.

Ori felt a wild elation that couldn't be contained. She whooped and yelled across every channel, and as if in answer there was a flicker of motion below her and a sprite suddenly stood up on the probe's blunt nose, a cold blue flame that flexed and swayed with the delicate adjustments of a tightrope walker, bending towards Ori's bot, seeming to look straight through the connection, looking straight into the core of her mind.

Something clamped down. Ori lost all sense of motor control and feedback from the bot. Only vision was left, and the wild wail of wind whistling past the falling probe. The sprite was still bent towards her, a blue glow that filled half the bot's field of view, commanding Ori's complete attention. For a moment, she thought that it had climbed inside her head; then fields of data scrolled down and she realised that one of the True supervisors had taken control, and the connection cut out completely and she was back inside her body, cramped and sweating in the immersion chair.

She shut everything down, saw the rest of the crew crowded around her chair. Inas was at her side, helping her stand, saying, 'So how far did you fall?'

Ori peeled off her gloves and straightened her aching back, wanting to fix this moment in her mind for ever. The ghost of the sprite's attention clung to her still; she half-expected to see it burning amongst her crewmates. They were all looking at her, waiting for her to speak.

'I didn't fall,' she said. 'I flew.'

The True supervisor who had shut off Ori's link with her bot stomped into the quarters of crew #87 and found Ori and knocked her down and told her that if she ever did something as dumb as that again she'd be for the long drop. After the True had gone, after Ori had answered her crewmates' questions as best she could, after the communal supper, Ori and Inas retreated to their bunk and Inas told her that she'd talked with the other senior members of the crew and they'd come to a decision. 'You have to make a report. You have to tell the bosses everything.'

'They already know about it. I mean, they took control—' Ori shut up because Inas had leaned forward and touched a finger to her lips.

They were sitting facing each other in the little niche, cross-legged, knees touching knees. Both of them dressed in halters and shorts, tools hung on loops or stuffed in pouches fastened to their intricately engraved belts, both dark-skinned, hairless, and short and squat: tailored for the gas giant's strong gravity. But they had surprisingly delicate faces, with large round eyes and snub noses and small mouths, and their hands were slender, with long, tapered fingers, as if their creators had run out of material after sculpting their muscular bodies and had used leftover scraps for their features and extremities.

Inas said, 'Doing what you did, you made yourself visible to the bosses. You can't pretend it didn't happen any more than you can undo it. You have to explain what you did, and why.'

'I took control,' Ori said. 'I flew that probe away from the cable. I'm not pretending I didn't do it, and I'm glad I did. Because it was the right thing to do.'

But her euphoric bravado was dwindling. She was unsettled by her bunky's serious gaze; was beginning to realise that her little adventure had consequences outside the cosy little nest of the commons of jockey crew #87. And she still had the feeling that the sprite had followed her when the connection with her bot had been cut. Several times during the companionable clatter and hum of supper she'd looked around, half-expecting to see its blue flame standing behind her. Realising at last that it wasn't looking over her shoulder but that it was inside her head, looking out through her eyes. When she'd tried to explain it to Inas, her bunky had been sympathetic but hadn't really understood what she meant, saying that she was bound to feel weird after what she'd put herself through.

Saying now, 'I think what you did was crazy and brave. All of us do. And maybe the bosses will think that too. I hope they do. And I hope they'll think you did it for all the right reasons. Because if they don't . . .'

Ori said, 'I already took a beating.'

'The supervisor didn't hit you to punish you. He hit you because he's frightened of what you did. Of the consequences. He'll have made a report, and sooner or later someone higher up will notice it.'

'Come on, Inas. Nobody upstairs will be interested in my stupid little adventure.'

'Yes, they will. Because you weren't supposed to do what you did. And because it involved a sprite. Especially because it involved a sprite. That's why you have to volunteer your story before they come looking for you. You have to explain what you did, and why. Because if you don't, it will look as if you have something to hide.'

Inas' flat, serious tone chilled Ori's blood. All around their niche was the usual hustle and bustle of the commons. People sitting alone or in pairs in other niches, people mending clothes and gear, a small group working on puppets made from scrap and spare parts, getting them ready for the big competition between the bot crews. Down at the far end of the main drag, Hahana was crouched on all fours, doing a bot-dance, raising up and scuttling sideways on fingers and toes, stopping, flattening, lifting one hand and rotating it to and fro. They could all do the dance, imitating the way their bots moved, but Hahana was uncannily good, raising her head and scuttling backwards now, while crewmates laughed and whistled. Everything was familiar, everything was normal, but it seemed to Ori that everything had changed. As if she was looking at it from the outside, somehow. As if everything was distorted by the opaque, alien presence in her head.

'All right,' she said. 'I'll tell my so-called story. As long as you help me.'

Inas opened a window, told Ori to look straight at it while she made her report. 'Start from the beginning, when the quake hit. And try not to leave anything out.'

Ori did as she was told, getting caught up in the story all over again. 'I was barely hanging on,' she said, at the end. 'Falling at twenty metres per second squared, wind battering me, the air getting thicker and hotter, and the sprite just stood there. And I swear this on my life, it was looking straight at me. Not at the bot. At *me*. As if it could follow the connection all the way back to my chair. As if it knew where I was really at, what I really was. As if it was watching what went on inside my head.'

Inas touched the window and said, 'I don't think you need to tell them about that.'

'It was real,' Ori said. 'As real as you and me talking here and now.'

'I don't doubt that it *felt* real—'

'I know what I know,' Ori said. 'Maybe it will fade. Maybe it's just my imagination. But right now I still feel it. It's still here. Like it left a little part of itself with me. You wanted me to tell them everything. That's part of it, too.'

'All right,' Inas said, and touched the window again.

Ori described how the sprite had seemed to look straight at her, how the feeling of being watched by it had persisted after the connection to her bot had been cut, how it persisted still. A presence at the back of her head. When she was finished, Inas asked her if she wanted to review her report or change anything.

'It is what it is.'

Inas touched the window. It blinked twice, then shrank to a dot. The dot vanished.

'What now?' Ori said.

'Probably nothing.'

'Maybe they'll promote me, when they realise what I did. Why are you looking at me like that?'

'We were made to serve the Trues, and that's what we do,' Inas said. 'And we do it gladly. And because the Trues made us, Ori, they don't think of us as people. We are their tools, with no more rights to independence than any of their machines. They can send any one of us on the crew anywhere, without explanation or warning. And we obey them because that's what we must do. Not because the only alternative is the long drop, but because it is our duty, and nothing else matters. Nothing. Only our duty and our work matters. Everything else, the puppets we make, our dances and our theatre, the murals we paint, the way we decorate our belts and customise our tools and our clothes, your crazy adventure, what *we* have, you and me, Inas and Ori, in the end, none of that means anything to them.'

'It means something to me,' Ori said.

'And to me. And that's why I'm so scared of losing it,' Inas said, and her expression changed as something inside her let go, and she and Ori fell into each others' arms.

Later, the night watch begun and the commons mostly dark and quiet, Ori lay awake in the familiar comfortable niche, her bunky asleep beside her, and wondered why she felt that she was still falling: why she felt that she had a long way yet to fall.

4

In the second summer of the long drought, the Child liked to keep caterpillars in jars. She fed them with leaves of the plants on which she'd found them, watched them spin cocoons, marked the hours and days until a butterfly or moth emerged. She dug grubs out of rotten tree trunks and watched them turn into pupae, watched the shapes of adult beetles appear inside the varnished casings. But mostly she studied fruit flies, which were common, could be easily trapped in bottles baited with morsels of banana, and developed from egg to maggot to pupa to adult in a handful of days.

Her friend Roberto, the son of the hospital director, was disgusted and amused by her new obsession. As far as he was concerned, biology was barely one step up from woo-woo mysticism. Sure, the principles of Darwinian evolution had an elegant and powerful simplicity, but the patchwork compromises generated by the blind reproductive imperative of genes were ugly, needlessly complex, and, worst of all, indeterminate. When the Child showed him sequences from one of her AI teacher's files, demonstrating how the body of a fruit-fly maggot liquefied inside the pupal case as all but a few pockets of cells died in a genetically determined sequence of aptosis, how suites of genes were switched on one after the other, controlling growth and development of the body of the adult, Roberto reacted as if it was the most shameful kind of pornography. Saying that it was a slipshod solution to a problem – how to exchange one suit of armour for another – that shouldn't have existed in the first place.

The Child told him that understanding the ways in which organisms overcame problems of development and survival was the point of biology. It provided a powerful toolkit that gene wizards used to build new kinds of organisms.

Roberto said, 'Is that what you want to be? A gene wizard?'

'Or a green saint,' the Child said, with the unsinkable confidence that only the young and the crazy possess.

Maria Hong-Owen, pleased by her daughter's precocious interest in biology, allowed her to use a corner of the hospital's pathology lab in exchange for help in maintenance of cell cultures. Vidal Francisca, an increasingly unwelcome presence, gave her a microscope for her birthday. The Child was suspicious of the man's motives, but she loved his gift. It could swing in and out and around every detail of the articulated legs and feathery antennae of insects, the flanges and ridges of their armoured bodies, the hooks and saws of their mouthparts. It could make movies of the swarming animalcules in a drop of pond water, track individual rotifers, paramecia and amoebae. It could zoom into the cytoplasm of living cells and show proteins churning and sliding past each other, reveal the herky-jerky motor at the base of a flagellum, the coiling and uncoiling of DNA in replicating chromosomes.

Increasingly, the Child worked alone and unsupervised. Her mother was, as usual, preoccupied by her own work; Roberto was amused by her passion but thought it a waste of time; Ama Paulinho couldn't begin to answer her questions. Only Vidal Francisca pretended to take an interest, but he'd long ago forgotten most of his botanical training, and he was distracted besides by the problems that the drought was causing in São Gabriel da Cachoeira and the surrounding area.

The river was at its lowest level for a century. Summer thunderstorms brought a little relief, but most of the rain ran off the sun-hardened ground, causing flash-floods that quickly evaporated in the pitiless heat. The work of weather wranglers paid by the town's council came to nothing, too. They'd arrived in a massive cargo blimp which they tethered in a sorghum field, and every night they rolled through the town, crowding into bars and lanchonetes, causing all kinds of minor mayhem. Maria Hong-Owen was called out in the middle of the night to attend to one of the weather wranglers' pilots, who'd been stabbed in a brawl with a gang of workers from the tree plantation, and the next evening their captain called at the bungalow with a gift – a bottle of hundred-proof white rum. Dressed in black spidersilk blouson and trousers, a cap with a badge of a fist clutching two lightning bolts and a shiny black bill that shaded her eyes, she looked impossibly romantic to the Child, an avatar that had stepped from one of Ama Paulinho's sagas. Maria did not invite her in, so she stood on the doorstep and in fractured Portuguese thanked the doctor for saving her comrade's life, handed over the bottle of rum, winked at the Child, and marched off, slim, straightbacked, imperiously tall.

Maria warned her daughter to stay away from the wranglers. 'You saw the badge she wore? Those lightning bolts have nothing to do with weather. It's an old fascist symbol. The wranglers are freelance now, but once they were part of the militia that overthrew the democratically elected government of our country. The fight last night started when a group of the captain's "comrades" began to sing one of their battle hymns. They are proud of their past, and the townspeople remember some of it too. Weather was used as a weapon, during the wars after the Overturn. Much of the damage to the forest was caused by natural climate change. But not all of it.'

'But if they use the technology for good—'

'They were bad people then, and they're haven't changed,' Maria said. She was emptying the bottle of rum into the hopper of the kitchen recycler. Her hair was scraped back from her face and there were dark scoops under her eyes. 'They didn't come here to save us. They came here to earn credit. Any good they do is secondary to their main purpose. Can you guess what that is? Think of them as an organism.'

'They want to survive and reproduce.'

'Exactly.'

'But to what purpose? To keep the past alive? There doesn't seem much point in that.'

'They think they will be needed again one day,' Maria said. A light in the recycler's panel turned from red to green; she dropped the empty bottle into the hopper.

Every day for a week, a flock of small, arrowhead-shaped airships crossed the sky from west to east, circling the distant peaks of the Serra da Bela Adormecida mountains and returning westward high above the river. Meshes of green laser light flickered between them as they sailed back and forth, faint in the hot sunlight; thin fingers of cloud spread in their wake. The townspeople gathered each night on the beach at the edge of the river and banged drums and pots and pans, rang bells and set off fireworks, but little rain fell, and the clouds always evaporated before dawn. At last the weather wranglers' blimp lumbered into the air and passed low above the town and dwindled into the hot sky, and the sun shone in solitary triumph day after day after day after day.

33

The R&R Corps and the plantations laid off many workers. Small independent farms failed. The town's population was swollen by people from outlying villages and settlements; food was rationed; there were outbreaks of malaria and typhus; the army imposed martial law because of increased wildsider activity. Someone tried to shoot down an army plane with a smart missile. The town suffered shortages of food and other supplies because of attacks on road and river traffic, and after several bombs exploded in the solar farm and halved its capacity there were irregular blackouts during the day and no electricity at all between six in the evening and eight in the morning.

We were preparing the Child for the war that lay ahead of her. The Fomalhaut system, which by precedence and natural justice should have been her dominion, had been settled by no less than three upstart clades whose ships had overtaken our slow and badly damaged vessel, and now all three were involved in a war in and around Fomalhaut's solitary gas giant, and in the big circumstellar dust ring beyond it. We still had much to learn about the cause of the war and the nature of the clades embroiled in it, but we were certain about one thing: it would be a fatal mistake to become involved.

The Child quickly became used to the hardships and restrictions caused by drought and the conflict with the wildsiders. Because the wildsiders had declared that hospital workers and their families were, like schoolteachers, plantation supervisors, workers in the R&R Corps, and anyone else associated with the government, legitimate targets in the struggle for liberation, she could no longer go to the market with Ama Paulinho, she was forbidden to go on collecting expeditions along the river's edge and into the nearby forest, and her visits to Ama Paulinho's family were curtailed. But she did not much mind. She had her work in the hospital, and she also had her own work: the life of her own mind, growing in strange directions.

After the boy had drowned in plain sight of almost the entire town, she had realised that death could happen to anyone at any time. Even to her. It was not like the change between maggot and fly. It was not really a change at all, but a loss. The body failed and that failure freed the soul – but what was the soul, and where did it go? Ama Paulinho told her that it flew up to Heaven, where it would live for ever in the grace and glory of God. Her mother told her that the soul was immaterial, made not of matter but of spirit, which could not be measured by any

34

scientific instrument, but this was no help because it simply moved the question behind a veil of mystery.

The Child began to wonder if all this talk about the soul leaving the body like a lifeboat leaving a sinking ship was meant to dodge or obscure the stark fact that death was the end. And she began to understand that the stories her ama told her, of spirits that animated the forest and made the trees grow in their appointed places and maintained the intricate balances of every kind of life, were no more than stories. It was not so very different from the sermons of the priests, who also invoked spirits to explain the mysteries of the world. There was God the saviour, who was everywhere in the world, as invisible and impalpable as the sleet of neutrinos shed by the sun. There was his son Jesus Christ, who had died to redeem the sins of every human being, and would one day return to finish his work. There was the Holy Spirit, who gave access to the salvation that was manifest in Jesus. And there was the handmaiden to the Trinity, Gaia, a version or aspect of the Virgin Mary who contained the entirety of the world's intricate cycles and epicycles of climate and ecology. According to the Church, it was the holy duty of the human race to help Gaia heal the scars of the Overturn, but the Child thought she knew better. She knew about ecological niches and ecotypes, non-equilibrium dynamics and resilience, the relationship between diversity and energy flows. She knew about survival of the fittest and the lesson of the intricate diversity of Darwin's tangled hedgerow. She knew about the hard work needed to bring the forest back to life – the plastic tunnels where cloned seedlings were nurtured, the reactors that brewed living soil to replace the alkaline hardpan in dead zones, and so on. The miracle was not that it was a miracle, but that it could be done by ordinary men and women.

There were no miracles, no absolute mysteries, only problems which had not yet been solved. The blooming burgeoning complexity of the world proceeded not from a Word but from the interaction of simple chemicals that in the right conditions could create increasingly complex domains of self-regulating order. Drowned women did not turn into islands; husbands did not run away and become jaguars. There was no bridge between the world of things and the world of spirit because there was only one world. The world in which she lived. The everyday world where death hung like a little dark cloud in a corner of the blue and blameless sky. The trick was not to survive it, but to avoid it.

By now, she had raced ahead of her teacher's biology lessons. She was tinkering with the development of flies, using customised splicing kits. Creating maggots that did not pupate but continued to eat and grow; maggots that pupated but did not undergo aptosis and so were not able to develop further; maggots with metabolic kinks which meant that they processed food inefficiently and grew very slowly, some able to pupate, others not. The giant maggots and developmentally challenged pupae quickly died; only half-starved, slow-growing maggots lived significantly longer than ordinary flies. The Child couldn't tinker with her own genetic make-up because the various tools she needed – tailored viruses and micro-RNAs, splicing protocols, telomere treatments, and so on – were strictly licensed by the government. And gene wizards and green saints jealously guarded their research, especially the secrets which had extended their lives. Although the Child had sent flattering messages to various gene wizards employed by the Peixoto family, only a few had replied, and those with benign vagueness that recognised the Child's interest but did nothing to satisfy her thirst for knowledge. So she set about educating herself, soaking up gigabytes of old, unrestricted literature on human longevity, and when her work on maggots confirmed the work of certain early pioneers, she decided that she could take one positive step towards her goal, and began to cut down her food intake.

It wasn't easy to eat less with her ama clucking over her, but the Child discovered that she could make herself throw up after meals, with a finger down her throat at first, then, when that no longer worked because she'd lost her gag reflex, with soapy water. She didn't do this every day. She had a strict plan, and the will to discipline herself. To take charge of her body and her destiny. She dosed herself with a complex mix of vitamins, mineral supplements and omega-3 oils spun by the hospital's maker. She charted changes in her weight. She studied herself in the mirror every day, felt her ribs and the horns of her pelvis. She worked on her maggots and flies. She tried to devise a plan to trick Vidal Francisca into ordering splicing templates for human genes through the sugar-cane plantation's laboratory, but she couldn't work out how to get past the fearsome government licensing restrictions.

It was her use of the hospital maker that gave her away. One of the technicians discovered the simple programs she'd written, and told her mother; her mother confronted her, and it all came out. The dieting and the ideas about tinkering with her own genome, her plan to remain a child for ever.

Maria Hong-Owen blamed herself. For being too caught up in her work. For failing to spot her daughter's obsession, for failing to realise that her skinniness was something more than a phase in her development. She talked with the Child about her experiments and tried to rationalise away her fears, but the Child was stubborn and refused to listen to reason, refused to accept that she was risking her health to no good purpose. They fought each other to unsatisfactory truces, the Child by turns sulky and shrill, Maria tired and headachy after working long hours in the hospital, where she spent more than half her time arguing with the hospital board about emergency measures, or with remote officials about essential supplies that had never been sent or had been lost somewhere in the supply chain, or had been hijacked by wildsiders or bandits. At last, alarmed by her daughter's flat insistence that she knew better than anyone else about matters that she was far too young to properly understand, Maria said that she would receive some instruction from Father Caetano.

Here is one whose life is not even written in water. One we must create from first principles. A violation of our rules, yes, but necessary if we are to achieve our aims. Besides, there was a church in the little town, and so there must have been a priest or two, and we imagine this one darkly handsome, vigorous and practical, able to navigate the rapids and swift currents of the river and to hike through kilometres of forest and dead zones as he made the rounds of his extended parish.

Like so many priests in the wilderness, Father Stephanos Caetano was a Jesuit, educated in the venerable Colégio Santo Inácio in Rio de Janeiro. His work in São Gabriel da Cachoeira had not given him much opportunity for debating theological niceties, but he tried to do his best by the Child. See them now, sitting in the shaded veranda of his bungalow, talking, sipping iced lemonade made by Father Caetano's wife, a plump homely woman who worked in the hospital's administration, while out in the hot bright little walled garden bees and hummingbirds attend flowering bushes sparingly watered from the dwindling river.

'He pretends to be interested in my experiments,' the Child told Roberto, the next day. 'But even though I explained everything three different ways, he doesn't really understand it.'

'Well, I don't really understand it either.'

'Only because you can't be bothered to.'

Roberto shrugged. A lanky teenager dressed in a one-piece white tracksuit and running shoes, just returned from his daily run. His wiry hair was matted with sweat; his dark skin shone. He'd always run everywhere as a kid, driven by impatience and an excess of energy that the boundaries and routines of the small town couldn't contain, and he still ran now, at least ten kilometres a day. Besides an interest in science, he and the Child shared an ambition to escape the town and make their mark on the wider world. Roberto was already on his way. He'd aced the vestibular for the Institute of Physics at the Federal University of São Paulo, won a scholarship. In a few weeks, at the end of summer, he'd be gone, on a trajectory that the Child longed to follow.

He said, 'Is it so bad, if all you're doing is boring him with biology?'

'He keeps bringing God into it.'

'Priests have a habit of doing that.'

'I told him about spandrels,' she said. 'The old idea that certain properties of organisms are accidental byproducts of function and form, just as the highly decorated spandrels between adjacent arches in cathedrals are accidents of geometry. I told him that our appreciation of beauty in all its forms, our arts, might also be spandrels.'

'You were trying to stir him up.'

'I was bored. I wondered if it was possible that religion was a spandrel. *He* said that all forms of art were ways of praising creation. And therefore, of praising the Creator. So how could I be sure, he said, that they were truly accidental?'

'He isn't stupid,' Roberto said.

'I have to see him again,' the Child said. 'Over and over. Until I'm turned into a good little Christian.'

'That will take some time.'

'And meanwhile you'll be in São Paulo, free as a bird.'

'Ask him about his telescope,' Roberto said.

'He has a telescope?'

'A good one. Twenty-centimetre reflector. Ask him to show you the stars and planets. You'll learn something useful, and it'll keep him off the topic of G-O-D.'

See the Child and the priest, then, sitting on the parched lawn of the bungalow in the hot summer night, leaning over a slate that displayed the telescope's images, directing it this way and that. Gazing at double stars and nebulae, at the Magellanic Clouds and Andromeda, watching for shooting stars, studying the Moon's rugged face.

That summer Jupiter was as close to Earth as it ever got: the brightest star in the sky, rising like a lamp in the east. The telescope easily resolved the Galilean moons and Father Caetano told the Child the story of their discovery by the father of astronomy, Galileo Galilei: how that venerable scientist had realised that their shifting patterns meant they were not distant stars that by chance inhabited the same patch of sky as the planet, but were moons orbiting it. That if moons orbited Jupiter, Earth was not, as the Church asserted, the centre of the cosmos. Galileo, headstrong and unskilled in diplomacy, had angered the Church by publishing his ideas after explicit warnings to abandon them; he'd been forced to recant, but had been vindicated after his death, Father Caetano said, and the Church had long ago accommodated itself to his discovery, and to the discoveries of many other scientists.

This was a point he returned to over and again, one the Child had disputed before. The Church invoked absolute truths encoded in texts which could not be questioned because they proceeded from divine revelation, while all scientific theories were provisional and subject to modification and dispute as more data was gathered: absolute scientific truth was like the speed of light, a value which could be approached but never reached. And so Father Caetano's so-called reconciliation was entirely on the terms of the Church, which cut and adjusted the truth of the world to fit into the frame of its own proclaimed truth.

But the Child was beginning to learn something about diplomacy and strategy, about when it was worth arguing a point and when it was not. So this time she kept her silence, the moment passed, and Father Caetano went on to talk about the properties of the four moons – fiery Io; Europa, with its ocean locked under a thin crust of ice; Ganymede, largest of all the moons in the Solar System, with a smaller ocean beneath a thicker crust of ice and rock; deep-frozen, battered Callisto – and the people who lived on Europa, Ganymede and Callisto, and on the moons of Saturn.

They were Outers, descendants of rich and powerful families who had fled to the Moon to escape the ecological and political disaster of the Overturn. When Earth's three major power blocs had turned their attention towards the Moon, the settlers had moved on, some to Mars, the rest to the moons of Jupiter, and then Saturn. The Martians had been destroyed after they'd declared war on Earth; the Outers living on the moons of Jupiter and Saturn were more peaceable, and quarantined besides by distance. They'd been living there for more than a century. Now, according to Father Caetano, there was talk of reconciliation.

'Not because our leaders want to welcome them back to the rest of the human race, from which they exiled themselves in a selfish act of self-preservation. But because they have developed technologies that would be very useful to us in very many ways, and could make a great deal of money for people who already have too much money.'

Father Caetano talked on, explaining that many of the Outers had lost their belief in God, and thought of themselves as gods ('with a small "g"') because their antecedents had meddled with their genomes.

'They claim to be smarter and kinder than we are. To be more moral. I cannot say if it is true. Certainly, they are vainer than us, to think such things of themselves. Such vanity is always a sin and an affront to God.'

'Even if it's true?'

Father Caetano and the Child were sitting side by side, faces lit by the slate on the table before them, with its faintly restless telescopic image of Jupiter. A bright quarter-moon was cocked above the shadows of the trees at the far end of the garden.

'Especially if it's true,' Father Caetano said. 'If you are clever and kind, you would not boast about it to those not as gifted as you. Because it would not be clever, and it certainly wouldn't be kind. Many people don't like the Outers for exactly that reason.'

'But if they *are* cleverer, they could help us,' the Child said.

'Cleverness isn't everything. Without a proper moral compass, without proper restraint, scientific enquiry can too easily lead to the creation of monsters.'

'Have any of them ever visited Earth?'

It gave the Child a funny feeling to think that people like her were right now walking around on small icy moons in space suits, living in domed cities, tinkering with their biological destiny.

'If you want to meet one, your best chance is to go to Brasília,' Father Caetano said. 'That's where the ambassadorial missions are. They are tall and mostly pale, I hear. And must wear skeletons of metal and carbon fibre, because they grew up in places where the gravity is very weak. So they are weak too. Unable to move around by themselves. If they are gods, they must be very poor gods, I think.'

Father Caetano enjoyed his conversations with the eager young girl. He believed that her challenging mixture of naivety and sharp and original insights helped him to examine and renew his faith, and he also believed that he was doing good, that he was saving her soul from being indelibly marked by the sin of pride. We, who created him and set him in motion, believed it too. He was our agent, after all.

The Child had been so cooperative during her talks with Father Caetano that her mother decided that she should be rewarded. Once a month, Maria and a nurse from the hospital travelled upriver with Father Caetano, to visit those of his parishioners who had refused to move to São Gabriel da Cachoeira when the trouble with the wildsiders had spread from the mountains to the west. The Child could go with them on the next trip. She would help Father Caetano at the service, assist her mother at the field clinic, and be allowed to do a little botanising amongst the ruins.

Picture the Child, then, sitting in the shade of the canvas awning of a skiff making its way upriver. The nurse in front with two soldiers; Maria at the stern with Father Caetano, who was dressed in jeans and a short-sleeved shirt instead of his soutane, his eyes masked with sunglasses, the tiller of the skiff's outboard motor tucked under his arm.

Trees pressed along both sides of the river, standing above sandbanks and stretches of crazed mud and shoals of rocks exposed by the drought. It was seven in the morning, and already hot. The sun had levered itself above the horizon an hour ago and now it glared at eye level. Unblinking, tireless. And it had only just begun its work for the day.

The Child soon grew tired of watching the black water for any sign of the River Folk. A few small birds picking along the water margin. Once a flock of parrots rose up, disturbed by the noise of the motor, flying away through green shadows like a shower of red and gold. Caymans lying on a sandbar like logs clad in armour. Otherwise, only the river and the trees and the hot sky.

At last, the river narrowed and cliffs rose up on either side, casting everything into deep shadow, and the skiff was thrusting up a ladder of muscular currents pouring between big wet rocks. Pausing in pools of water stilled by backwash as if to gather itself, pushing on. The Child held on to her bench as the little craft juddered and bounced and slewed; the nurse, a woman barely twice the Child's age, squeaked and flung her arms around one of the soldiers. At last the skiff breasted the last of the rapids and unzipped a creamy wake along the middle of the river. The cliffs fell back and the skiff rounded a wide bend and the ruins of Santo João do Rio Negro spread across the far shore.

The town had been built two hundred years ago, funded by a Chinese corporation that had planted huge tracts of genetically modified hardwood trees. Felled trees had been rafted downriver to the town's sawmills, and timber had been transported east along a broad highway driven straight through the forest. All that had ended in the great upheaval of the Overturn. The R&R Corps had demolished the sawmills and warehouse sheds along the waterfront, but had left the rest of the town alone. Much of it had long since returned to nature. Avenues and squares and parks choked with scrub and weeds. Apartment blocks and houses empty shells, every window broken, roofs collapsed, concrete crumbling from rusting rebar. Most had fallen into mounds of rubble overgrown by bushes and vines and pioneer trees, lumpy tracts of secondary growth burned by the drought, but a few blocks behind the waterfront had been colonised and partly rebuilt by indigenous people who had never left the area, or who had returned after the Overturn, helped by government initiatives of the past century. Not to repopulate the Amazon basin as before, but to establish small, ecologically sustainable communities that would help the R&R Corps to rewild the ecosystem, turn dead zones into grassland, and grassland into rainforest.

Mass was held in the open air, in a space cleared from scrub. A block of stone shaped and carved by the townspeople served as an altar; the congregation, mostly old men and women, sat on the hard red earth. The Child rang the bell that told the congregation when to stand and when to sit, held the little tray under the chin of each communicant so that not a crumb of the Host would fall on the ground; then, while Father Caetano heard confessions, she helped her mother and the nurse at their clinic.

When the last patient had been dealt with, Maria told her daughter that they had an hour before the skiff left – they could look for specimens in the ruins. The Child knew that this was a ploy to flatter and placate her, but the chance to explore was too good to refuse.

See Maria and the Child walking away from the river, down a path beaten through tall dry grasses towards a cluster of ruined apartment buildings. It was late in the afternoon, and very hot. The sky white with dust. The sun blazing down. The tinny surf of cicadas all around. One of the soldiers followed them, his carbine slung upside down over his shoulder, his camo gear blending with the brittle browns and yellows of the grass.

Vines curtained the ruins; bushes and small trees gripped the tops of walls. Everything dead and dry, seared by the sun. Little lizards flicked away over tumbled blocks of concrete, no different from the lizards in the hospital compound. A perfectly ordinary buzzard circled overhead.

The Child discovered a mosaic mural behind a curtain of withered vines and used a handful of dry grass to brush away dirt, revealing a stylised whale spouting amongst blue waves. Underneath it, picked out in white tesserae, was a date: *Agosto 2032*. More than a century and a half ago. She tried to imagine herself standing on that very same spot in a hundred and fifty years. It wasn't impossible. Many gene wizards and green saints were older than that now. Then she tried to imagine returning in a thousand and a half years . . .

The young soldier cleared his throat, said that it was time to go back. The Child's protests were half-hearted. She would have liked to have reached the line of green trees that ran in a straight line a few blocks away, but she was hot and tired, and felt oppressed by the deep sense of time locked in the ruins, of the dead past all around her. Everything we have comes from the dead. We take so much from them, and never thank them, and they sink into obscurity, nameless, numberless, forgotten. She was beginning to understand that to refuse that fate was no easy task.

'We'll explore some more next time,' her mother said. 'Who knows what else you'll find?'

5

Once upon a time, in the long, golden afternoon of the Quick, the Library of the Homesun had been distributed and mirrored amongst the machines of the cities and settlements of the Archipelago and the minds of the ships that cruised between them. A vast store house open to all. But even then, most of the stuff accumulated in its vast matrices had been as much use as a cup of salt water to a thirsty man. Raw unmediated and uncatalogued spew transmitted from the Homesun to every colony system by an offshoot of an ancient project dedicated to the search for evidence of other intelligent life in the galaxy. Entertainments, sagas, immersions, and all kinds of art works that, stripped of their original context, were bafflingly opaque. News and gossip about people and institutions and movements long dead. Ware and gear that had no obvious practical applications, or required a technological base that the Quick's isolated and decadent civilisation couldn't support. And then there was all the stuff uploaded by the Quick themselves: all kinds of cultural junk; so-called living journals that recorded every transient thought and sense impression of citizens; the results of subjective and introspective investigations procured by processes more like meditation than experimentation, in which acquisition of knowledge was secondary to the emotional and intellectual states achieved during the search. The theosophical quicksand in which so many Quick had disappeared.

The transmissions from the Solar System had fallen silent long before we arrived at Fomalhaut, rescued the Quick from their long decline, and restarted history. We Trues had brought our own databases and archives; the Library of the Homesun had fallen into disuse, haunted only by eccentrics, renegade philosophers and would-be illuminati searching for nuggets of esoteric knowledge amongst the dross. Then the Ghost seedship had arrived, and everything had changed.

It hadn't come from Earth, like our own seedship and the seedship of the Quick, but from a colony at the nearby star of beta Hydri. Our Thing tried to negotiate with the intruders; they pushed back; we struck out at their nascent settlements; agents and avatars which had infiltrated our information networks struck back, the networks fell over, and the highly distributed nodes and matrices of the Library of the Home-sun were poisoned and ripped apart.

After the last of the Ghosts had been destroyed (or so we thought), the leader of our clan, Svern, volunteered to reconstruct and manage what was left of the Library. He believed that the Ghosts had not attacked it on a whim, and was quickly proved right. There was a purpose and a pattern to the damage. The devils, haunts, bogeys, and other monsters which had infiltrated the intricate tapestry of infoscapes had targeted seams and nuggets of scientific, mathematical and philosophical data threaded through yottabytes of antique garbage. But because the Ghosts had lost the first war so quickly and comprehensively, their agents inside the Library hadn't been able to mirror and transmit most of their discoveries. Anyone who followed their trails and managed to defeat them could win back what they'd found.

Svern organised a reconstruction project that gathered up fragments of the Library and knitted them together inside a hyperlinked informational architecture of his own design, which he'd installed in a disused building in Thule's twilight zone. And so my clan became librarians, and because Svern had been forced to borrow credit from the common pool to pay for his visionary project, we had to provide free access to information salvaged from the wreckage or wrestled from the Ghosts' agents. Not just to the other clans, but also to freemartins who won entrance tickets in a public lottery – cowboys and information-leggers armed with attitude and home-brewed agents and gear, obsessives tracking private theories that, according to them, would win the war or make them secret masters of the universe. Although less than twenty per cent of the original Library had been restored, and much of that was junk, with a little luck, considerable judgement and the right analytical gear, there was still plenty of useful information to be gleaned from the ruins, much as mining gliders winnowed precious heavy metals from rainstorms of molten rock on Dis.

45

So it had been for the past three gigaseconds, between the end of the first war with the Ghosts and the beginning of the second, when legions seeded by a few survivors had risen from nests hidden amongst the myriad worldlets of Fomalhaut's dust belt and swept towards Cthuga. A war still ongoing; a war in which, after my fall and disgrace, I'd become a minor foot soldier.

Like every librarian, I had been born in the clan's ectogenetic farm. A selection of genetic information from the clan's files had been randomly crossed according to law and custom, the resulting genome transcribed into DNA, the DNA spun into artificial chromosomes and inserted into a denucleated ovum, the ovum kick-started into mitotic division, and the embryo (me) grown to full-term in an artificial womb, decanted, and raised and schooled on a farm rock in the bosom of a sturdy foster family. I had learned the virtues of hard work and self-reliance, and far too much about vacuum-organism farming, and at the age of eight years by my foster family's antique way of counting time – about two hundred and fifty megaseconds – I had been claimed by my clan.

My foster family had given me a name: Isak. When I took my vows I also took the clan's name, and became Isak Sixsmith, a novice in service of the Library. I expected to live there for the rest of my life, but soon after achieving the rank of navigator I stumbled and fell, and was sent into exile. And now I had been summoned back.

I gave the Horse leave to spend some personal time in the Permanent Floating Market, passed through the checkpoint, with its scanning clouds and data sniffers and guards dressed in scarlet tabards and black hose like mimesists in a mystery, and climbed the broad span that arched above the black water of the moat to the entrance we called the Alexandrian Gate.

It was the first time I had returned to the Library since my disgrace and demotion. The dear, familiar place seemed unchanged yet utterly different, and I realised with a pang of melancholy that it was I who had been changed, by my adventures in the worlds and worldlets of the Archipelago. I was no longer the eager neophyte, with a grand and glorious career ahead of me: I was an itinerant exorcist, bitter and battle-weary, with no home or prospect of advancement, responding with little hope and considerable apprehension to a summons from the only person who could forgive my sins.

A young and shy novice I didn't recognise met me at the entrance and escorted me across the tall space of the Great Court and up a winding stair to the Redactor Miriam's office. It was a long room with black walls and floor and ceiling, lit only by the many windows hung in the air. The Redactor Miriam and her three assistants walked amongst them, monitoring everyone currently using the Library. She seemed not to notice when the novice announced my arrival, and I followed her as she moved from window to window, until at last she asked if I had given any more thought to the offer she had made just before the beginning of my exile.

'I haven't changed my mind, Majistra.'

'Even though the work bores you?'

'I can't say that I enjoy it, but isn't that the point?'

'I've seen your reports. You're growing careless. Cutting corners. Taking pointless risks. Do you think that if a demon kills you it will be an honourable death? That it will redeem you?'

'I hope that I am already doing all I can to redeem myself.'

The Redactor Miriam turned away from the window she had been studying (showing a long open colonnade somewhere in the vicinity of the Hall of Screaming Statues, where the avatar of a data miner was riffling through a raft of longcase files floating in the dusky air) and walked off to a window at the far end of the room. I followed her. When she had finished tweaking the window's parameters, she said, 'We can't let you back into the Library. No matter what Svern promises you, it isn't going to happen. He is our leader still, but his word is no longer final. The consensus is that you should never be allowed to return.'

'Yet he wants to speak to me.'

The Redactor Miriam looked at me for the first time since I had entered her office. She had aged since I had seen her last. The lines at either side of her mouth had deepened and the beak of her nose was more prominent, but her gaze was as sharp and unforgiving as ever.

'A trueborn scion has asked for our help,' she said. 'Such requests are not only inconvenient distractions; they are also dangerous. If you succeed, it will change nothing. You will go back to harrowing hells. But if you fail, there will be a reckoning we cannot afford. And frankly, I have no doubt that you will fail, as you have failed before. Svern chose you and I can do nothing about it. About the only power he has left is to choose who to send to help other clans, and he retains it only because no one has ever before asked for our help. But I can ask you to think of the greater good. If you still love the Library, refuse to help this scion.'

'I cannot disobey him, Majistra.'

47

'We are not excused the tithe, even though we contribute to the war effort by making the Library available to all. You could make a significant contribution by joining the army. The arrangements I made are still in place. You would receive a rank equivalent to full navigator, and you would leave your unfortunate history behind. You might even win some measure of glory.'

'But I could not win back my place here.'

'You would win our gratitude. It's no small thing.'

Like many who have sacrificed everything to an institution or cause, the Redactor drove herself hard and was unable to forgive or forget the errors of those she believed to be less capable or committed than herself. And she also believed that her wishes were entirely congruent with the best interests of the Library. There was no doubt in my mind that I deserved my punishment, but I also believed that it had become a token in the struggle between the Redactor Svern and the Redactor Miriam, who felt that it was unseemly and dangerous that he should continue to have so much influence after his translation. I resented her for that, and hoped to prove that she was wrong. I was, as the Horse so often said, exceedingly stubborn. And I have to admit that it gave me some small satisfaction to see a moment of anger and uncertainty in her gaze when I said, 'I have always valued your advice, Majistra. But now I think I should find out what the Redactor Svern wants of me.'

'Do as you will, then,' she said. 'But don't say I didn't warn you.'

The young novice was waiting for me outside. 'I have to take you to the Redactor Svern,' she said. 'You aren't supposed to wander about on your own.'

'Have you been there before?'

She nodded, solemn and serious as young children are, when burdened with a task they don't fully understand. 'When I first arrived.'

'Then I know you will remember the way. Lead on.'

The translation frame was kept in the Redactor Svern's old office, a square room with a vaulted ceiling down in the basement level. It was otherwise empty, lit only by a horizontal slit of window that gave a view of watery shadows and the silken carpet of silt at the bottom of the moat – the ancient machines that were the heart of the reconstructed Library resided in the basement, and the moat absorbed waste heat generated by their constant activity. The frame stood in the centre of the room, a square window of depthless black that came alive with swarming white glyphs as the novice led me towards it. A moment later I was standing in the courtyard at the entrance to the memory palace inhabited by what was left of the Redactor Svern after his permanent translation.

As always, it was snowing. Snow sifting out of a black square of sky hemmed by high and windowless stone walls, settling on the cobbles on which I stood, defining the edges of the square-cut stones so that the patterns in which they had been laid were as clear and bright as if outlined in neon. Snow capping the heads and shoulders of the stone lions that stood on either side of the arch that framed a view of a gravelled road lined with stark and leafless trees.

When I had first been invited there, a novice no older than the girl who had been my escort, I had turned from that view and found a woman standing behind me. She held a flaming brand that burned potassium red, sizzling and crackling as snow touched it, and wore a blue silk dress that lifted and displayed her breasts, pinched her waist, and fell in elaborate flounces and folds to her feet. The silvery pelt of a small animal was wrapped around her shoulders, its narrow head resting above the deep cleft between her breasts, the tip of its short, black-furred tail caught between its sharp teeth. Her face was white with powder, the shape of her eyes was exaggerated with black pigment, and her lips were dyed black. The effect was both disturbing and arousing. She answered my stare with a smile and turned – the back of her dress was cut to the beginning of the swell of her buttocks – and stepped to the narrow iron door set in the stone wall, which slid aside with a soft rumble. I followed her across the threshold, and through the rooms beyond. She walked like a dancer, never once looking back to see if I was following, the pale and lovely column of her bare back glimmering in the red flicker of her torch.

I knew very well that she was only an eidolon, an illusion created by the same machines that maintained the illusion of the memory palace, but I fell in love with her all the same. I never again saw her, but every time I was summoned to talk with the Redactor Svern, I always hoped that I would turn from the stone arch and find her waiting for me. I turned now, and found myself alone in the snowy dark. Alone, I crossed the courtyard, touched the iron door and passed through, and followed the familiar route through the chambers of the memory palace.

The first was crowded with statues carved from a translucent white stone that reminded me of the complexion of the eidolon (on my second visit I had paused to examine each of them, but although several were a little like her, she was not there). The walls of the next were pierced with arched windows that showed views of other worlds and other times. There was a chamber cluttered with machines: a pile of black cubes set with thousands of red, blinking lights; an ordinary tractor of the type used by my family to travel around the vacuum organism farms; an ancient spacecraft, its white upper half pouched and angled like the head of a monstrous insect, its lower half partly wrapped in golden foil, the whole perched on four silver, spidery legs. A chamber with rough rock walls hung with flags and banners, and every kind of armour ranked beneath them, some pieces twice as tall as me, some less than half my height, with helmets shaped like the heads of animals or globes with gold or silver visors. Most stood motionless, but several turned to watch as I went past. A chamber whose walls were inset with dioramas of animals and birds in various habitats. A chamber crowded with the skeletons of enormous animals, the largest shaped like a spacecraft streamlined for atmospheric entry, and hung from the ceiling. A chamber filled with big glass models of viruses. An empty chamber whose floor was paved with polished limestone flags, each containing the dark, foetal form of a fossil. A chamber of ranked cases that each displayed a single handweapon. A chamber whose walls were crowded with portraits of people in strange and antique dress.

And so on, and so on. A string of marvels, with other strings leading off left and right from crossways and apses. But I walked straight on, as always, until at last I reached the chamber that usually contained orreries modelling settled systems, their clockwork mechanisms swinging brass and silver and ivory globes and swarms of asteroids and planetoids around golden suns.

And found instead that it was dark, and filled edge to edge with an immersive simulation of the Fomalhaut system. The vast outer belt of comets and dust clouds, rocks and planetoids and dwarf planets circled the outer edge of the square chamber, and the flaring point of Fomalhaut floated in the centre, so bright, so intensely white, that I had to look away from it. I didn't see the Redactor Svern coming towards me until he eclipsed its baleful light. As always, he manifested as a small man scarcely taller than a Quick, with a wise, wrinkled face and a bald pate fringed by wisps of straw-coloured hair; as always, he was dressed in a long black duster whose hem hissed over the floor. He stopped at the inner edge of the dust belt, his deep-set eyes two smudges of shadow as he looked at me across a plane of floating motes.

'Let me show you something,' he said, and turned and walked clock-wise around the belt to a point some sixty degrees away. He made a quick gesture, and a web of blue threads suddenly ran through the glowing motes, some stretching out and vanishing, others braiding one into the other.

The Redactor Svern pointed to a small curdle of blue light where all the threads converged. 'Here is the Archipelago, first settled by the Quick a millennium and a half ago. The threads are the trade routes we established since our arrival, linking our mining and farm worldlets,' he said, and gestured again.

Lines of red shot out from several points along the outer edge of the dust belt, close to where I stood, branching and rebranching, bending towards a bright point that flared at the inner edge of the belt, where red and blue threads met and mingled.

'This is a real-time feed,' the Redactor Svern said. 'Mirrored from Our Thing's archives. You can see that the Ghosts are further advanced than most people know. One hundred and ninety megaseconds ago, they pushed forward some fifty million kilometres and overtook a cluster of farm worldlets. From there, they are beginning to mount attacks on Cthuga itself.'

I knew just how badly the war was going because dealing with hells meant that I spent far too much time talking to the military, but out of respect to my old master I didn't say anything. I also knew that he would get around to what he wanted to tell me in his own good time, and in his own way.

He walked forward and touched with a forefinger the little speck on which the blue and red threads converged. It inflated into a large, banded globe as big as his head, circled by a ring system many times its diameter; he spun it with the offhand ease of a juggler in the Permanent Floating Market.

'The Quick discovered all manner of strange quantum effects in the core of Cthuga. Some of our philosophers believe that they might yield weapons that can win the war. Others believe that they are manifesta-tions of some form of computational system. A Mind. Some say that this Mind was created when the Quick dropped their seedship into the heart of the planet. Some believe it may be a truly alien mind. The Ghosts believe that it has not yet been created, and is reaching back into the past to make sure that it is born at the proper time. That they can use it to reach into their own past, and fulfil the ancient prophesies of their founder . . .' He looked at me and said, 'Have we talked about this before?'

'About the Mind in Cthuga? A little, Majister.'

'I talk too much, to too many people, but it's the only way now that I can influence the world of things. And you are too polite to complain, Isak. You indulge me.'

'I always learn something new, Majister.'

'There's little new here, I'm afraid. The Ghosts advance on Cthuga, and its orbit carries it towards their territory, and away from ours. They are already probing its defences. It will not be long before they mount a full-scale attack. We do not know if they can do what they want to do, but we must do our best to stop them.'

'That we can talk about this, Majister, suggests that they will not be successful. We would not be here if they had changed the past to suit themselves.'

'In this particular universe, at this particular point in space-time, it may be true. But philosophers claim that there are many other universes entangled with this one, and if those universes in which the Ghosts are successful outnumber those in which they are not, then ours will become a remote and isolated island with no influence on the main currents of the future. That is what we are fighting for. To preserve the past, which we Trues hold so dear in any case, so that we will be free to determine our own future.'

Majister Svern spun the globe again. Underlit by Cthuga's sere light, his face seemed more like a mask than usual, animated by something other than mere human intelligence. 'When you first came in, I noticed that you flinched from the image of Fomalhaut. Do all bright lights affect you in the same way?'

'Everything that reminds me of my disgrace affects me, Majister.'

'Do you feel it with you still? As if something is following you, or watching you?'

He had asked this question before. I gave him the same answer now as then.

'I have dreams about it,' I said.

'One of our philosophers claims that the Mind in Cthuga has been growing more active. That it has been contacting various Quick workers. I find it interesting that haunts and demons in the Library have also been growing more active. It may be a coincidence. Or it may be that the Mind is reaching out to the Ghosts, and the increased activity of demons and haunts is part of the Ghosts' plans for the final stages of the war. Perhaps you are a casualty of war, rather than the victim of an unfortunate accident.'

'Arden and Van were victims,' I said. 'As were their kholops. And they died because I was derelict in my duty. Because I ran away.'

The confession was still painful. Like a rough-edged stone stuck in my throat.

The Redactor Svern didn't seem to hear me. He spun the ringed globe once again, then shrank it down and set it back in place.

'The elder clans despise our clan because they believe that we are too close to the Quick, and have contaminated ourselves with their decadent philosophies,' he said. 'They say that our best hope of winning the war is to keep ourselves pure. Purity is strength. That is how we gained ascendancy over the Quick. That is how, according to them, we will defeat the Ghosts and destroy every trace of them in the Fomalhaut system. And after that, well, perhaps we will find a way of crossing the great gulf between Fomalhaut and beta Hydri, and we will destroy the Ghosts in their home system, too. It's a pretty fantasy, founded on ideology rather than fact. As for its usefulness, well, I have shown you how badly the war is going. Anyone who discovers a weakness in the enemy that can be exploited, or a weapon that can be used against them, will be feted as a true hero.'

He fell silent. When it seemed that he would not speak again, I said, 'Does this scion think that the Library contains something that can stop the Ghosts reaching Cthuga?'

'No doubt you are wondering what this has to do with you. Why I brought you back, after . . . all this time.'

'The Redactor Miriam told me that a trueborn scion needs our help. No more than that.'

'I suppose that she also told you that you'd be a fool to volunteer, because you'll almost certainly fail.'

'I hope I will not.'

'And that if you succeed, you will have no reward.'

'I deserve none.'

'And then she asked you to refuse the obligation I'm about to put to you.'

'She asked me to quit the Library at once and join the army, so that I would not have to meet you in the first place.'

'Yet here you are.'

53

'Yes, Majister.'

'The scion's name is Lathi Singleton. She is one of the last of an old family in the oldest of all our clans. Although her position in it is greatly diminished, she is still powerful and dangerous. She contacted me directly, and by custom I cannot refuse her request.

'I didn't choose you because I pity you or feel that you have been treated unfairly, Isak. And I'm not using you to score petty political points against the Redactor Miriam. I am beyond all that. I chose you because of all of us you are best fitted to succeed. And if you succeed, I promise you that your punishment and exile will be ended. Not because it is in my gift, but because it will change everything. Let me explain what Lathi Singleton wants of us, and you'll understand.'

As I quit the Library through the Alexandrian Gate, I sent a message to the Horse, telling him to find me at once, and wandered off towards the Permanent Floating Market, thinking about the strange meeting with the Redactor Svern and feeling a bitter-sweet nostalgia for the carefree times of lost innocence when I had once sported in the teeming aisles with fellow novices.

When I'd descended the sweeping span of the bridge that crossed the Library's moat, the outer tip of the plate had been touched by a last gleam of light, but down in the market it was, as always, midnight. The overlapping leaves of the iron sky pressed overhead; the stalls, geos and tented arenas glowed in a thousand different pastel hues, like so many sea anemones at the bottom of a deep pool. As I stood at one of the stalls, eating noodles, the faces of the people passing its shell of soft pink light seemed to open like flowers. The strange beautiful faces of Quicks. The faces of Trues, hard and closed as fists. And there was the Horse, smiling his crooked smile, his hair a disordered flame, sauntering up to the stall and leaning next to me, his head scarcely higher than my shoulder, his upper lip wrinkling back as he watched me spoon more hot sauce on my noodles.

'It's hard to tell if you're celebrating or trying to kill yourself,' he said.

'It's the only way to give this stuff any kind of taste. Where have you been?'

'Here and there. Round and about.' The Horse ordered a bowl of tea from the young Quick behind the counter, a pale yellow fragrant infusion that made the stuff I'd been served seem like unrecycled drain water. 'So,' he said. 'Am I still working for you, or is this a fond farewell before you take up arms against the enemy?'

Many of you – even in these enlightened times – will be shocked by his easy familiarity. But we had trained together, he'd stood by me after the desperate incident that had killed two other navigators and their kholops and left me disgraced and demoted, and we'd survived many scrapes and adventures since. Although we could never be friends, after my disgrace he was the nearest thing to a friend that I possessed. His given name, the name allocated by a bureaucratic subroutine of the tank farm where he'd been quickened and brought to term and decanted, derived from the genetic templates which had been crossed to create him, was Faia op (8,9 cis 15) Laepe-Nulit; the Horse was the name he'd chosen for himself after he'd been bought by the Library, the name that other Quicks knew him by, the name I had begun to use after my disgrace. An ancient beast of burden that had possessed, according to him, many noble virtues. He'd been raised and trained to be a navigator's assistant, had taught me as much about the craft and traditions of my profession as any of my tutors, and possessed the unassailable belief that one day he would make his mark and win his freedom. He liked to tell me stories about Quicks who'd done just that. He liked to tell me all kinds of stories. There was nothing he liked better, it seemed to me, than to talk, to spin fanciful dreams out of thin air. Whenever I called him on his endless chatter, he'd smile and shrug and say that his sharp wit and quick tongue were all the advantage he had, so it was necessary to exercise them as much as possible. He used that same wit to flatter me, of course; because he was good at his work and because of his undimmed faith in me, I put up with his teasing banter and his endless prattling about his futile ambitions, his fantasy that we were true friends. Blood brothers.

I added another spoonful of hot sauce to the last of my noodles. It was good stuff: I was sweating like a pacer at the finish line.

'A scion of the Singleton clan has disappeared,' I said. 'His mother thinks I can help her find him.'

'That's different, at least. How will we do that?'

'She wants us to harrow a hell that he uncovered before he disappeared,' I said, and told the Horse what the Redactor Svern had told me.

Yakob Singleton was the only surviving child of Lathi Singleton. He had been something of a rebel in his youth, but had settled down and distinguished himself working for the Office of Public Safety. During one of his investigations, he had uncovered information about an active hell. He'd hired a data miner to help him explore it, and that was the last anyone knew of him.

'His mother believes that he is still alive,' I said. 'She wants me to search the hell and find whatever it was that made him walk away from his work and his family. Also, find anything that points to where he has gone.'

'Since he's almost certainly dead, that won't take long,' the Horse said. 'What about the data miner? Did he vanish too, or is he locked up somewhere?'

'She killed herself.'

'You mean, the demon that got inside her head made her kill herself. Probably after it did the same thing to her client. I can see why we have been given this job,' the Horse said. 'It's dirty work, and it isn't going to end happily. At least, not for Lathi Singleton.'

'I'm not sure it will do me any good, either,' I said. 'The Redactor Miriam took the trouble to make it clear that nothing can absolve me.'

'Do you want absolution?'

'She told me I'd fail. I want to prove her wrong.'

A flower floated in the Horse's bowl of tea. He plucked it out between finger and thumb and nibbled at it, saying, 'Did it occur to you that she might have told you you'd fail to goad you into volunteering us for a task that would most likely lead to further disgrace?'

'I lack your twisted logic.'

'Also my common sense. If you fail, the Redactor Svern's influence will be diminished, and you will still be damned. If you succeed, it will benefit the Library, and the Redactor Miriam will do everything she can to make sure that you are not rewarded. She believes that she will win however this plays out.'

'The Redactor Svern thinks that Yakob Singleton found something important. Something that could change the course of the war. And win me absolution, too.'

The Horse smiled. There was a petal caught between his teeth. 'But he would not or could not tell you what it is, or how he knows it is so important.'

'He also thinks that there may be a link between the Mind in Cthuga and the demon that killed our friends and comrades. And he wonders if there's a link between that demon and the hell that Yakob Singleton discovered.'

'And that's why he chose you. You're caught between his obsession and the Redactor Miriam's politicking.'

Anyone else would have beaten him for that. I gave him a hard look and said, 'As far as we're concerned, all that matters is the hell. After I've spoken to Yakob Singleton's mother, we'll crack it open, deal with whatever's inside, and move on from there.'

'I'd better unpack and test every one of our algorithms, then. It's been a while since we've used the full array.'

'I'll take care of the gear. I want you to do what you do best – talk to your friends and acquaintances, and anyone who might know anything useful about Yakob Singleton.'

'So you do have doubts about what your old master told you.'

'No. I have doubts about what Yakob Singleton's mother told him.'

6

They came for Ori two days after the quake. She was working with her crew out on the skin of the Whale, repairing damage to the marshalling yards, when the connection to her bot shut down and she found two Quick in the scarlet halters and black shorts of the public service crew standing either side of her immersion chair.

'You're wanted for interview,' one said.

'Upstairs,' the other said. 'Right now.'

Ori stood. There was no point asking why she was wanted. She knew. She'd been expecting it. All around in the dimly lit room her crewmates reclined in chairs, hands and feet cased in feedback mittens, luminescent strings and streamers flowing over their faces, their attention projected elsewhere. As she followed her escorts out of the room Ori glanced over at Inas, felt a cold needle of regret pierce her heart, looked away. No point asking if she could say goodbye, either.

They rode an express elevator a long way, two kilometres to the decks where Quick administrators and Trues lived. The two PSCs standing behind Ori, saying nothing. At the end of the ride, she was taken down a service corridor and left alone in a cold, brightly lit room. Standing because she had not been told that she could sit. Trying not to shiver. Trying not to think. Trying to ignore the faint but insistent pressure of the presence at the back of her head.

At last a Quick came in, a drab clerk not much older than Ori. She opened a window that displayed a montage of images and video clips culled from the viewpoints of Ori's bot and the bots of her crew during the confusion and wreckage after the quake had struck, stopped the flow of the montage when the flatbed rail car and probe dropped away, with Ori's bot riding it.

'You have to explain everything that happened,' she told Ori. 'Starting with why you were on the flatbed rail car.'

'I already filed a report.'

'It isn't my idea,' the clerk said.

'Right.'

The clerk listened to Ori's story about the long fall, letting her tell it in her own words without comment or question, and closed the window.

'What now?' Ori said.

'I hope it works out for you,' the clerk said, without meeting Ori's gaze, and left.

Ori waited even longer, this time. She was squatting with her back against one of the walls when a True came in. A man in army uniform, caged in an exoskeleton. A fat pistol holstered at his hip, a captain's silver starburst on his left breast. He told Ori to stand in the centre of the room and circled around and around her, the little motors in his exoskeleton ticking and whining.

'We think you may be a wrecker,' he said at last. 'We know you used the confusion of the accident to destroy that probe.'

'No, sir.'

Ori's head was pounding and adrenalin was pumping through her body.

'"No, sir." That's all you have to say?'

'The probe this one and her crew were working on broke free, sir,' Ori said. The True had stopped in front of her, but she didn't dare look at him. 'This one and her crewmates did everything they could to lock it down—'

'Your crewmates did everything they could to lock it down. And when it broke free you just happened to be riding it. Why? For fun? Because you wanted a cheap thrill?'

'No, sir.'

'You had a reason. Tell me.'

Ori told the truth, feeling a cold flush of shame. 'Just before the quake hit, this one climbed on to the flatbed rail car. It would have been better to fasten the bot to the platform, as the others did. But this one wanted to see what happened. Out of ego. Out of wrongfulness. The truck was struck by debris from a chain of freight cars higher up. It fell. This one fell with it.'

'Why did you launch the probe?'

59

'This one believed it might strike the cable and cause serious damage if its payload was breached.'

Ori spoke as humbly as she could. She knew that she had done the right thing, and also knew that she should not expect praise or reward. She had done it without first asking permission. She had acted on her own. She had behaved as if she was a True. She had been crazy.

'You claim to have had some kind of close encounter.'

'There was a sprite,' Ori said reluctantly.

'And you claim it did something to you.'

'This one feels it left something of itself behind.'

The True studied her, then opened two windows. One showing the beginning of the montage of stills and clips that the clerk had played, the other a section through someone's skull that exposed the lobes of the brain, with little puddles of green and yellow and blue caught in a web of red threads.

Ori felt the presence at the back of her head stir and move forward. The sprite, or a fragment of it. Her passenger. Inas still refused to believe that it was real. And for most of the time, as far as Ori was concerned, it was little more than an itch inside her skull, a hum like the faint but continuous mingled roar of the Whale, a word unuttered, a thought or memory she couldn't quite grasp. But then it would come to stand behind her eyes, and she knew. She knew that it was real. That it really was inside her head, a bundle of unknown and unguessable thoughts and intentions, separate from her own thoughts, her own intentions.

When she'd been very small, one of her first jobs had been to load cartridges of goo into a sleeve pump attached to one of the tanks that collected the floor-washings of the machine shops. The pump injected the goo into the big tank with a percussive thump, and for a moment a long finger of white goo stood inside the dirty water. And then it began to disperse as the nanobots suspended in it chased down precious flecks and atoms of metal. Whenever the passenger moved forward, Ori thought of that finger of goo. Was frightened that the passenger would disperse inside her brain, chase down and consume every scrap of thought and memory . . .

The True was talking, telling her that she was going to tell him the whole story all over again. He told her that the window showed her brain activity, pointed out the areas that would light up when she lied. 'When they do, you're mine,' he said.

Ori had been through struggle sessions before, confessing faults to her crewmates and accepting their criticisms, but this was something else. The True was cool and precise, asking the same questions over and over, taking her story apart sentence by sentence, jumping on every contradiction and uncertainty, asking her to explain and justify every move she'd made.

She answered as truthfully as she could. Humble and submissive. Hunched into herself, flinching away from the True's gaze, trying not to look at the flickering patterns of her own brain activity. She felt as if she was being crowded into a smaller and smaller space, caught between fear of the True's cold disdain and fear of the presence inside her head. Towards the end, she was so worn down that she was about ready to confess to anything and everything, yet an irreducible sliver of stubbornness remained; she continued to insist as politely as possible that the sprite had appeared in front of her and she had felt its intimate scrutiny, and felt some part of it still.

'You showed initiative,' the True said. 'Taking command of the probe like that. A lot of people think that's dangerous. They don't like the idea of Quicks thinking for themselves.'

Ori hung her head, waiting for her punishment.

'Why you're not going to take the long drop right now, someone is interested in you. Because of your close encounter. You're going to be tested. If you fail, you fall. And even if you pass, you'll probably fall anyway. Because the man who thinks he has a use for you, he's crazy,' the True said, and walked out, stiff as a pair of scissors in the embrace of his exoskeleton.

The light went out as the door shut on his back and Ori was left alone in the dark. An hour. Two hours. Her bladder ached and sent a hot wire to her groin, and she was exhausted and still horribly afraid, and tired of being afraid. Convinced that she was going to die here because she'd done the wrong thing while trying to do the right thing. But she wasn't alone. Something was standing at her back. When she twisted around to look at it there wasn't anything there, of course. Only darkness. But she could feel it.

At last the light came back on, sudden and stark in the white room, and the door slid back and the two PSCs stepped in and told Ori to come with them.

They rode down in a big, slow elevator, the kind used to move machines around. Ori wondered if she was being taken to the end cap.

Wondered if the True had lied to her; wondered if she was going to be given the long drop. The elevator stopped and the doors opened to reveal a hangar space and a small crowd of Quicks inside a rectangle marked with yellow paint on the floor. The PSCs marched Ori across the space, shoved her across the yellow line, told her to find a spot and wait her turn.

All of the Quicks waiting there had been touched by sprites during the quake. Ori told her story, heard the stories of others. One had been riding a bot that had fallen from the Whale's skin during the quake – had fallen a long, long way with a sprite wrapped around it. Two others had been confronted by sprites while riding machines in a garage. Two more had been visited while they rode bots hunkered down in a vacuum-organism farm. And so on, and so on. All retained to some degree or other the impression that the sprites they'd encountered were with them still. All were haunted by ghosts in their heads.

One by one they were taken away for medical examination. Most returned; a few didn't. It wasn't clear if those who had returned had passed or failed the tests. It took a long time to process everyone. PSC guards tossed food packs and water bottles into the rectangle every six hours. Everyone had to share two portable shitteries. There was nowhere to sit or sleep but the floor. Not one dared to step across the yellow lines that enclosed them. It was unthinkable to leave without permission.

At last, Ori was called forward and escorted to the examination area, a space at the far end behind portable screens. She was told to take off her clothes and she was prodded and scanned from scalp to toes by a small team of medics, passed from one to the next like a piece of meat. When the last was finished with her, she was allowed to dress, and escorted back to the rectangle.

She was one of the last to be examined. The medics packed up and left; the lights dimmed, and most of the Quicks inside the rectangle tried to get some sleep. Ori sat cross-legged, eyes closed, trying to communicate with the presence inside her head. Asking it what it was, what it wanted. Trying to move the centre of her attention to the warm dark at the back of her head where it lived. She jerked awake when the lights in the hangar snapped on. The guards were shouting, telling everyone to wake up.

'Stand up and get into formation! Five lines, right now!'

'Face forward, backs straight!'

'Get ready to meet the commissar!'

'Commissar Doctor Pentangel on deck!'

Ori stood amongst the others, standing in the middle of the second rank, her heart beating quickly and lightly. The guards snapped to attention as troopers moved across the open space ahead of the tallest True that Ori had ever seen. Very tall and very pale, with a shock of black hair and a beard like an inverted triangle. He wore a long white coat that hung open at the front, showing glimpses of the girdle and arm- and leg-clamps of his exoskeleton as he tick-tocked towards the Quicks standing in orderly rows inside the yellow rectangle painted on the floor.

He looked at them for a long time, his sharp gaze sweeping back and forth. Smiling at last, saying, 'My children.'

7

The Child lay on her bed, staring up at but not seeing the stars that floated above her in the darkness, listening to the voices of her mother and Vidal Francisca rise and fall in the living room of the bungalow. It was after midnight. They thought she was asleep, but she was not. She was trying to train herself to do without sleep.

'I would never put her in danger,' Maria said.

'You know that I did not mean it like that,' Vidal Francisca said. 'But there *is* a risk, given the current situation. As you know very well.'

'She helped Stephano at Mass, she helped me in the clinic,' Maria said. 'It was good for her in all kinds of ways. Especially, it was good for her to get out of town. You know how much she loves nature.'

'There is nature here. An unfortunate abundance of nature,' Vidal Francisca said.

The Child felt a squirm of disgust. She loathed the way the man used jokes to try to trivialise any argument he was losing. She loathed his unctuous manner and his wide smile, so white, so false. His habit of never passing a mirror without looking into it. The slick of black hair brushed back in an attempt to disguise the island of naked scalp on top of his head, and the little pigtail he liked to stroke and twirl. His air of effortless superiority. His unassailable assumptions about the way the world worked.

Her mother said, 'I appreciate your concern, Vidal. I do. But I think I know what's best for my daughter.'

'My concern is as much for you as your daughter,' Vidal Francesca said. 'Also for Father Caetano.'

'Stephano would not allow me to go if he thought there was a risk.'

'Those people should come here. At least until the current situation is resolved.'

'The forest is their home.'

'They don't live in the forest.'

'They go to and fro. It's where they get their food. It's where they do everything that's important to them.'

'You realise that some of them could be wildsiders,' Vidal Francisca said. 'And if wildsiders think you are useful to them . . . I know I don't have to explain it.'

'Now I understand. This isn't about my daughter. It's about me.'

The Child recognised the tone in her mother's voice and knew that she was angry and was trying to hide it. And felt a little gleeful thrill, wondering if her mother had finally seen through the man.

'I care for you both.'

'The clinics are an important part of my work, Vidal.'

'The hospital board might take a different view.'

'Is that a warning?'

Vidal Francisca started to say that he was only trying to explain what others on the board were thinking, but Maria cut him off, saying that he could tell his friends that if they had any concerns about her work they should speak to her directly, saying that she had three operations tomorrow, she needed to review her notes.

In her dark bedroom, the Child felt a sudden surge of happiness. So solid she could hug it to herself. At last Vidal Francisca had overreached himself. Her mother had taken charge of the course of her life after the death of her husband, and Vidal Francisca had been very careful to respect that freedom. But now he'd shown that he was no better than all the other men who presumed that they knew what was good for women, who believed that women needed the protection of men because women were weak and essentially childish.

So the Child hoped that this little spat might be the beginning of the end of Vidal Francisca's patient siege of her mother's honour. It had begun after he'd been appointed to the hospital board. Soon afterwards, he'd begun to drop by the bungalow to discuss matters related to the running of the hospital and gossip about the affairs and petty rivalries of the town's prominent citizens. Maria had started to look forward to these visits, tidying the bungalow, dispatching the Child to the care of Ama Paulinho. Soon enough she and her daughter were visiting Vidal's house, as guests at parties or other social gatherings, or dining in splendid isolation on the terrace that overlooked the sloping garden and the fields of the sugar-cane plantation beyond.

At first, the Child liked these visits. Vidal expressed what seemed to be genuine fascination with her experiments with fruit flies, and talked about his studies for his degree in agronomy at the University of Manaus. She liked the microscope he gave her for her birthday. She liked the way the rooms of his house swung out from its core and moved to follow the light, and folded at night like the petals of a flower, and she liked its garden, kept green and alive during the drought by an irrigation system that in the evening sprayed water in sweeping arcs that tick-tocked back and forth over flower beds and lawns and stands of trees. She liked wandering there in the warm dusk while Vidal and her mother talked on the terrace. She watched the leathery jostle of the bats that came to feed on the fruit trees. She studied the fireflies dancing over the lawn, identifying three different species by the frequency of their blinking. She checked her beetle traps, picked choice specimens from the weird and monstrous alien life that flocked and clung to the sheet of luminous cloth she'd stretched between two trees.

She liked Vidal's horses, too; loved riding the smallest, a chestnut gelding that belonged to Vidal's daughter, along the riverside path, or through the dry forest, or along trails that crossed the vast monotony of the sugar-cane fields. She learned about the various genetic tweaks engineered into the hybrid cane, the insect pests that attacked it, its fungal, viral and bacterial pathogens. She watched the machine that planted billets in raw red earth, learned that the stands which grew from each billet could be harvested up to ten times before decreasing yields justified new planting. She watched the chopper harvesters at work, ungainly machines exactly as wide as a row of cane, cutting the stalks at their bases and stripping leaves from them: the stalks went into one transporter and the leaves went into another. She was given a tour of the sugar-cane mill by the foreman, who had the biggest and whitest moustache she'd ever seen, and a scar that transected the puckered and empty socket of his right eye. He explained that cane had to be transported to the mill as quickly as possible because its sugar content began to decline as soon as it was cut, showed her how each batch was tested for trash percentage and its brix value – the fraction of sugar in aqueous solution. He showed her how the processing line of the mill washed the stalks and chopped and shredded them with revolving

66

knives, and mixed the pulverised material with water and crushed it between a series of rollers to extract the sucrose-rich juices. The residue went to generators that burned it to generate the electricity that ran the plant; the juices went to bioreactors where the sucrose was broken down to glucose, the glucose was turned into ethanol by a simple fermentation process, and the ethanol was dehydrated and turned into biofuel. The leaves were processed separately, to harvest organic precursors used in another set of bioreactors to produce plastics.

The mill and the bioreactors and refinery plant were impressive, but very low-tech, using principles that predated the Overturn. And although sugar cane exhibited one of the highest natural photosynthetic efficiencies, and the hybrid strains grown on the plantation had been tweaked, a little less than twelve per cent of the many kilowatts of sunlight energy that fell on the plantation's fields was captured and turned into biomass. Even the cheap biogel that people painted on their roofs was twice as efficient at converting the sunlight that fell on them to electrical power.

The Child was becoming very interested in photosynthesis. When Roberto had come back from his first semester at the Federal University of São Paulo, he'd shown her how the logic of quantum mechanics integrated with messy biochemistry at the point where light-harvesting centres transferred solar energy to the reaction centres that transformed it to biological energy. Struck by photons, the light-harvesting and reaction centres oscillated with wave-like behaviour, allowing the electrons that transferred energy between them to select the most efficient of all possible paths and minimise energy loss. And these wave-like properties also entangled centres that were not strongly coupled by oscillation, so that everything beat to the same pulse: the heartbeat of the sun. You could think of a field or a forest as a quantum computer, Roberto had said. Able to run every solution to a problem at once, and select the best – the fastest, the simplest – from a myriad entangled possibilities. The molecular couplings at the heart of artificial photosynthetic systems evoked the same kind of quantum entanglement, but were not yet as efficient as those in plants, algae, and photosynthetic bacteria.

The Child wondered if the solar farm's photosynthetic system could be coupled with some kind of artificial metabolism that fixed carbon dioxide into glucose and other organic molecules, and discovered work done on nanotech vacuum organisms developed by colonists of the moons of Jupiter and Saturn: an early contact with the work of the gene wizard Avernus, her great rival in years to come.

All of this was very stimulating, but it led to her first real confrontation with Vidal Francisca. When she tried to explain her ideas about creating artificial organisms that could synthesise from scratch everything his mill and his bioreactors and his refinery currently produced, he was frankly patronising, refusing to look at the spreadsheets she had prepared, telling her that the plantation was supported by government grants that encouraged use of traditional technology in rewilded areas. And besides, he said, no one would underwrite any kind of research based on Outer technology. The Outers were dangerous anarchists who had quit Earth during the Overturn like rats deserting a sinking ship; later, they had mounted a cowardly sneak attack on their former home by diverting the orbit of an asteroid. Earth had saved herself by a vast collective effort that was not yet ended, and it should not be endangered by introducing technology that could undo all that good work. When she was a little older, he said, the Child would understand the historical reasons why stability was so important.

By stability, the Child thought, he meant the status quo that benefited him and men like him. For it was men who ran the world. The president of Greater Brazil was a woman, yes, but she was only president because her first husband had been president before her, and had died young. But for the most part men ran the world, and far too many women collaborated with them. Women like Vidal Francisca's daughter, a brainless creature more interested in finding a husband than in learning useful skills that she could use as a foundation for a career.

The Child had never liked Vidal Francisca, but now she had an ideological justification for her visceral animosity. Now she could rationalise and develop her contempt, and dare to express it openly.

'He's stupid and vain,' she told her mother. 'Those clothes he wears. That horrible furniture in his house. And the way he looks at you. The same way he looks at those horses of his.'

'I thought you liked his horses. And anyway, he doesn't look at me that way.'

'He *does*,' the Child said. 'You don't see it because he only does it when you aren't looking at him.'

'A woman knows how a man looks at him,' her mother said. 'You'll learn that when you're old enough.'

'I'm never going to grow up. And I'm never going to marry.'

'Neither am I.'

'*He* has other ideas,' the Child said, full of cold contempt at her mother's stupidity.

And so she was inordinately pleased when Vidal and her mother fell out. It was a crack in the man's smooth mask; a way to expose his true nature. The next day, she told Ama Paulinho all about the row, and her ama agreed that he had been very foolish.

'Your mother is always slow to forgive. And in matters like this, when her professional honour has been slighted . . . No, she will find it very hard to forgive him, and I do not blame her.'

Ama Paulinho's broad smile showed the Child, for a moment, the handsome young woman that she had once been.

'No more Vidal Francisca,' the Child said, and clapped in delight. 'He can go to hell.'

Ama Paulinho chastised her, but it was half-hearted; she had been watching the developing romance with increasing dread, worried that she would lose her job if Maria Hong-Owen married, and she shared the Child's happiness about this setback. They convinced each other that this was the beginning of the end of Maria's unfortunate relationship, so the Child was horribly shocked when, a few days later, her mother told her that Vidal would be coming with them on their next trip to Santo João do Rio Negro.

'He will see for himself that it is perfectly safe,' Maria said. 'And then he will tell his friends on the hospital board.'

'Is that what he told you?' the Child said. 'That he wants to help you?'

'I know you don't like him. But try to imagine that his motives aren't always bad.'

But the Child wouldn't be appeased. 'It's another way of trying to take control. You'll see.'

8

Nowhere else in the Archipelago is privilege and status so nakedly displayed as in Thule, the thistledown city, the city of tiers. It was built by swarms of machines long before the first generation of Quicks was created from their seedship's genetic templates. The machines dropped a superstring of entangled gravitons into the centre of an icy planetesimal to deepen its vestigial gravity (one of the many technologies we have lost or failed to master), blew a roof shell from its surface and spun a forest of fullerene and diamond spines to support it, cooked off an atmosphere and a hydrological cycle, extended platforms from the spines at different levels and landscaped their surfaces. Platforms near the bases of the spines, just above the elaborate interlacing of the buttress roots that clutch the silica rock core, and in the permanent shadow of platforms higher up, support Quick kennels and tank farms, and congeries of machines and makers that recycle waste water and waste material, regulate partial pressure of the various components of the atmosphere and perform other essential maintenance tasks, and spin all kinds of goods, from styluses to skycars. The platform which bears the Permanent Floating Market and the Library of the Homesun is down there too. Above this twilight zone are platforms where freemartin True live and work in dense urban arcologies, and above those are the platforms owned by great clans, where trueborn scions live in sculpted parklands and estates.

That was where I went to meet Lathi Singleton, travelling alone in a flitter that rose straight up from the park at the tip of the Library's platform, rising past platform after platform until there was only the roof of the sky above, then angling across empty air towards a parkland platform. I glimpsed a river running through parched grassland and clumps of red rocks, and then the flitter was settling towards a walled courtyard behind a square tower built of black stone and cantilevered out above empty air like the prow of a sea-going ship in one of the primordial sagas.

I was met by a squad of flunkeys and scanned by a cloud of tiny machines that briefly fluttered around me like so many butterflies before one of the flunkeys stepped forward, dismissed the others, and led me across the courtyard and through an arched gate. I followed her down steps of white stone to a long, broad lawn flanked by black cypress trees and statues of men and women in antique dress. It was a simple, beautiful scene: the lawn a dense uniform green, the cypresses all exactly the same height and trained and clipped into the likeness of twisted flames, the statues carved from clean white stone that seemed to glow with inner light, so skilfully made that it would not have seemed unlikely if they had stepped down from their plinths and taken up their lives.

The flunkey told me that she had left this part of the platform unchanged, a memorial tribute to her mother and father, and I realised with a shock that my escort was no steward or factor but the woman I had come to meet, Lathi Singleton. She was tall and slender, wore a long green tunic cinched tight at her waist by a broad leather belt, and walked with a long confident stride. I had trouble keeping up with her as she led me towards a fountain set against a backdrop of cypresses at the far end of the lawn.

'My mother loved formal gardens,' she said. 'The whole platform was once like this. Staged, manicured . . . We'll walk a little, while we talk. You'll see how my tastes differ from hers.'

Embarrassed by my error, I stammered out some formula about being honoured. I supposed then that she had assumed that I would know who she was, which was why we had not been introduced, but I think now that she wanted to catch me off guard so that she would have the advantage over me, even though her status and privilege gave her all the advantage she would ever need.

'I was told that your library was once a monastery,' she said. 'In the decadent era before we arrived, and saved the Quick from themselves.'

'It was empty for many years before my clan found a use for it, Majistra. But before that, it's true, it was once a refuge for followers of the Two-Fold path.'

'It explains why you look the very picture of a monk. Your shaven head and bare feet. Your plain black clothes. We too often unconsciously ape the memes of the past. Our own past, and the past of the Quick, their so-called Golden Age . . . I suppose you librarians might be especially susceptible, working as you do with their knowledge bases.'

'Some believe so, Majistra. But we are trained to be aware of the hazards of our trade.'

The Singletons, first amongst the elder clans, were fierce and implacable defenders of the status quo. As far as they were concerned, Quicks deserved slavery because they had turned themselves into subhuman sybarites; slavery was a mercy, in fact, for the only alternative was extinction. That was why I hadn't brought the Horse with me. Not only would his presence at the meeting have been an insult, implying a status he could never deserve, but Singletons had been known to casually dispatch other people's servants, attendants and kholops at the slightest provocation. And even on his best behaviour, the Horse was never far from a provocative remark.

Lathi Singleton studied me. Her dark eyes were narrowly shaped and set close together, like the eyeholes of a duelling mask. Her hair like a silvery helmet. She said, 'Did you bring the tools of your trade?'

'I carry them with me always, Majistra.'

'They link you to the Library.'

'They contain a copy of a small part of it. A simulation used for training purposes, and to demonstrate our work to clients like you, Majistra. It's perfectly safe.'

'I understand that the Library itself is not. That even librarians may be harmed, despite their training.'

It was plainly a reference to my downfall and disgrace. The impulse to ask her what she knew about it suddenly gripped me with a physical force that took me a moment to master.

I had spent most of the previous evening with Master Navigator Bo, who in his bluff straightforward manner had schooled me in the courtesies and conventions appropriate to someone of Lathi Singleton's rank. I must never ask her a direct question, he had told me, and I must answer all of her questions as truthfully as possible while imparting the minimum of information. He'd taught me various elliptical formulae and phrases, and tested me until he was satisfied that I'd got them off by heart and knew how to use them.

'Never forget that this is much more than a simple test of your skills,' he'd said. 'We must provide whatever help she requires, but she will almost certainly want more than the help we must give her by covenant and custom. She will try to find out our strengths and weaknesses. She will try to enlist your sympathy. She will try to get inside your head. And she will have been given her task because of her talent, not her rank or looks, so do not make the mistake of underestimating her. Remember always that she is far more dangerous than anything you'll find in the Library.

'So then. Be polite, be deferential, say as little as possible, and apologise for your ignorance if she presses too closely on our secrets. Above all, don't try and be clever. That's your main weakness, Isak. You talk too much, and you like to have the last word. But if you let her do most of the talking you'll be fine. You might even learn something useful. Try to be clever, though, and it'll be all over for you.'

Remembering Master Bo's advice, I answered Lathi Singleton's gibe with as much humility as I could muster, saying, 'My clan has worked hard to make the Library safe, but we are few and it is very large, and we still have much to do.'

We had reached the stone bowl of the fountain. It was considerably larger than the plunge pool in the Library's communal baths, although much shallower. In its centre, a muscular pulse of water shot high into the air, higher than the tops of the cypresses, splashing into the unquiet pool cupped beneath. The air smelled of iron and electricity. Lathi Singleton dipped a hand in the water lapping at the edge of the bowl and raised it dripping and sipped from her palm. I wondered if I was supposed to do the same, but she was already walking away, and I followed.

A steady spout of water poured from a notch in the fountain's bowl, feeding a stream that ran off along a channel cut in the lawn, rippling clear as glass over a bed of white and gold quartz pebbles. We followed it through a rank of cypresses and emerged at the edge of a short steep slope of loose rock and clumps of dry grass. The parkland I had glimpsed from the flitter stretched away beyond, a mosaic of dusty browns and reds enlivened here and there by vivid green stands of trees. The sky had taken on the dusky rose of sunset, and clumps of stones glowed like heated iron in the low and level light. Rounded hills rising on either side hid the margins of the platform: the parkland seemed to stretch away for ever, like the landscapes of sagas set on old Earth.

73

Lathi Singleton dismissed my praise of the illusion, saying that it was simple stagecraft. 'My interest is in the biome itself. The plants and animals, and the patterns and balances they make. This one is modelled on Africa. You have heard of Africa?'

'It's where we first became what we are, Majistra.'

'I once kept a species of early hominin in this biome. *Australopithecus afarensis*. The reconstructed genome is contained in the seedship library; it was easy to merge it with Quick templates. And of course we hunted the usual Quick variants as well. But those happy days are long gone,' Lathi Singleton said, and walked off down the slope, stepping quickly and lightly beside the stream, which dropped down the slope in a ladder of little rills and waterfalls and pools, its course lined with red and black mosses and delicate ferns as perfect as jewels.

It grew warmer as we descended, and by the time I caught up with Lathi Singleton, at the bottom of the slope, I was out of breath and sweating. The stream emptied into a wide pool of muddy water whose margins had been trampled by many kinds of feet. Scaly logs lay half in and half out of the water on the far side. When one yawned, its mouth two hinged spars longer than a man's arm and fringed with sharp teeth, I realised that they were a species of animal.

'They won't hurt you because they can't see you,' Lathi Singleton said. It was the first time I had seen her smile. 'None of the fauna can see or smell anyone unless I want them too. Come along. I've arranged a little picnic. We'll eat, and I'll tell you what I need you to do, and why.'

We skirted the pool and followed a narrow path through tall dry grass to a pile of red rocks crowned by a slab where cushions had been set around a low table. Beyond a large flat-topped tree, animals a little like the totemic animal of the Horse, striped black and white, grazed on dry grasses. Lathi Singleton told me to sit, and began to unpack plates of sour miso, rice cakes, and dewy slices of fruit from a cooler. 'You are allowed to eat, I hope.'

'Yes, Majistra.'

'And can you drink? We have beer and wine. Also – this is a favourite of mine – a brandy made from wormwood,' she said, setting up a small city of bottles in the centre of the table. Her hands were large and square; her fingernails were ragged and crested with red dirt.

'Water would be good, Majistra.'

'Is it part of your discipline, that you can't drink alcohol?'

'I never acquired the habit.'

74

'If you want water, you'll have to trek back to the water hole. Ah, but we have white tea. Will that do?'

I thanked her and accepted a bowl of jellied cubes, and she settled into a pile of cushions opposite. She said, 'You harrow hells for a living.'

'It is my duty, Majistra.'

'And you fight demons.'

'When I have to.'

'Tell me about the one that almost killed you, in your Library.'

I felt a freezing shock.

Lathi Singleton smiled again. A bright flash, there and gone. 'Did you think I wouldn't do some research into the person the Library sent to help me? Did you think I'd just accept you, without finding out all I could? Tell me all about your little accident, or I'll send you back straight away.'

I had told the story many times before, of course. To the Redactor Svern. To those senior members of our clan who had judged and sentenced me, and in formal confession to my peers. I had thought about every moment, every detail, over and over; there was not a day since when I had not thought about it. Even so, I did not find it easy to tell it to Lathi Singleton, but I did my best to lay it out as truthfully as I could. I had no other choice.

It had started out as a routine task in an obscure sector of the Library known as the Forum. My clan has been restoring what is left of the Library for a long time, but large areas are still unexplored. Most contain little of interest and nothing of any especial danger, but some hide voids where information processing halts, or leechpits that steal processing power, and others are infested with demons, haunts, and various other malignancies. All of these are fixed within particular niches and locations: free-roaming demons had been exorcised long ago. At least, that was what we believed. And because the Forum was well inside the boundary between the known and unknown, we had not been expecting to encounter anything dangerous when we set out to investigate unusual activity encountered by a data miner.

There were six of us, Arden and Van and myself, and our kholops. We were engaged in the basic, repetitive task known as 'running the runes': using a set of simple algorithms to peg down any anomalies in the sector. It contained little of interest. Streets of small blockhouses converging on a large drum-shaped building faced with columns and statues standing in niches. Yottabytes of data encoding narrative art forms many gigaseconds old, much corrupted, the rest of no use to anyone now living except for a few specialist historians and memorialists.

We worked slowly and steadily, defining blockhouse after blockhouse of discrete yet very similar units of data, and at last reached the small square in front of the large building which gave the sector its name. It stood more than twice as high as the slovenly blockhouses crowding around it. It was always sunset, in the Library, the light red and horizontal, the shadows long and deep. The Forum was silhouetted by the sun, which was half-eaten by the horizon. So big that if you looked at one edge you couldn't see the other, granulated with the black freckles of sun spots, and fringed on its western side by the fiery arch of a prominence.

Arden was the first to notice the fine detail of the Forum's statues, columns, pediments, and other decorations: a clear warning that something was wrong, that something operating at a very high processing level had forced this part of the sector to jump to a higher resolution. The Horse flung me an audit and I shouted a warning, and at the same instant the demon burst out of the Forum's square entrance.

When you enter an unoccupied room and the lights come on, you may be momentarily blinded by what seems an intolerable brightness. The demon was far brighter than that. It was as if a new star had been kindled in front of us, burning an intolerably brilliant hole in reality.

In one instant it stood before us. The next, before we could recover from the shock, it was on us. We tried to establish a perimeter, and we failed. Loops of raw processing power flicked out all around; flagstones exploded to dust everywhere they grounded, and the dust whirled in complex reiterated figures. We barely managed to counter the first attack; the second overwhelmed us. Van went first, and his kholop tried to run and was caught too. Both of them frozen shadows in swirls of burning dust, blinking out as their links to the translation frames were cut, but too late, too late. The Horse and I looked at each other, and knew that there was no time to throw up any kind of shield. The demon was too quick, too powerful. We ran, and Arden and her kholop chased after us and were caught by dust and consumed. In that brief interval, the Horse and I were able to break into a blockhouse and safely disconnect while the demon raved beyond the slabs of dumb and stubbornly inert data.

All this in a little less than a millisecond.

Van and his kholop died almost at once. The demon had traced the links back to their translation frames, punching through firewalls, overwhelming counterstrikes, getting inside their skulls and overloading the electrical activity of their brains. They suffered a series of massive seizures before they could be extracted from the translation frames, and although they were placed on life-support their brain activity was permanently flatlined. Arden and her kholop lived a little longer, driven insane by malignant subroutines. The Horse and I were quarantined, and, after the alienists were satisfied that we had not been infected, I was interviewed by the Redactor Miriam and then brought up before the full council of the Library and tried and sentenced.

I was sweating hard when I had finished telling Lathi Singleton all this, yet felt cold to the marrow of my bones. She pressed a small glass into my hand and told me to drink, and I obediently swallowed the measure of white liquid. Bitter fire hollowed my mouth and its warmth bloomed in my chest, and gradually I stopped shivering, and was able to answer Lathi Singleton's questions about my work as an itinerant exorcist. I told her about the last hell that the Horse and I had harrowed, just as I've told you, and she said that she was pleased by my honesty and the courage.

'Let me match your candour with my own,' she said. 'First, I'll tell you something of my family history. It's a sorry story, mostly involving untimely deaths. My father and mother are dead, both of them killed in the war. My mother was a warlord, my father a senior member of her staff. Their ship was crippled when the Ghosts pushed forward unexpectedly, and my mother blew it up rather than be captured. Two of my father's brothers and one of his sisters were likewise killed in battle. My mother's eldest brother died after his ship lost power, approaching Dis. One of her sisters died in a hunting accident; the other died of an autoimmune disease. A good number of their children died, too – I won't bore you with the list. And my partner died, in the war, and so did our daughter. She insisted on volunteering against all my advice, and she was killed on some nameless rock when a horde of child-things infiltrated the forward supply station she commanded.

'In short,' Lathi Singleton said, looking directly at me with no particular expression on her face, 'I am one of the few survivors of a tragic chapter in our clan's history. All I have is this little square of dirt, and my son, Yakob. What were you told about him?'

'That he was working for the Office of Public Safety, Majistra. And that he found a hell and afterwards disappeared, while the data miner who helped him killed herself.'

'An accurate but cruelly abrupt summary,' Lathi Singleton said. 'Let me tell you about my son. I want you to know what he was like because I believe it may help you to find out why he disappeared. And I want you to see him as a person, too.

'I believed that he could play a large part in restoring the honour and esteem of my family, and for that reason I wanted him to enter politics. For several years he worked as assistant for one of my cousins, an ancient and distinguished representative in Our Thing. But he rebelled against this apprenticeship and in spite of my express wishes and commands he joined the Office of Public Safety – and not as an officer, but an ordinary trooper. I was not happy about this, as you may imagine. The Office of Public Safety protects us from outlaws, criminals, and wreckers, but it is in no way a route to political influence. The only consolation was that Yakob had been something of a dissolute in my cousin's service, but during his training he buckled down and aced every test, and on graduation started out walking a beat like any ordinary trooper. And this wasn't some comfortable assignment in a calm and comfortable neighbourhood reserved for cadres and entrepreneurs. No, it was in one of the industrial worldlets, a trashed wasteland littered with manufactories dedicated to organosynthesis, element refining and heavy fabrication, inhabited by convicts, former convicts, and internal exiles.

'Yakob soon distinguished himself by his quick and fearless action in disturbances large and small, by securing the arrest of a gang of corrupt officials, by his patient work in tracking down the criminals who had made and distributed a batch of jeniver that left more than a hundred people blind and brain-damaged, and his help in arresting a serial killer who sold on the black market the meat of Quicks he had murdered and dismembered. His success almost reconciled me to his rebellion. The arrest and execution of the serial killer led to promotion and a move to Thule, where Yakob quickly uncovered a minor case of preferment in an obscure office of the Ministry of Defence that led to the reopening of an old unsolved homicide case and eventually brought down one of Our Thing's senior advisers. After that, he was involved in a string of less spectacular but equally knotty cases, and won promotion again. And then he discovered the hell, and he disappeared.'

Lathi Singleton had told me her son's story very calmly, but her strong hands were twisted together in her lap.

'My clan is powerful, but I have lost almost everything,' she said. 'This platform was once a happy hunting ground for my immediate family. Now I rent most of it out as a place of execution, where wreckers and other traitors are hazed by their peers or put to death by wild animals. I have no influence amongst those who could help, and they have no inclination to help me. If his colleagues know anything, they have not shared it with me. That is why I have turned to your clan for help. In the small hope that something in the hell will give a clue as to his intentions.

'He found it on T. The war worldlet at the outer edge of the archipelago. I know little more than that. Neither his colleagues nor the authorities on T have been helpful. But I do know one thing. It's the reason why I contacted your clan. Before she killed herself, the data miner who helped Yakob explore the hell said that it contained a back door. One that led to your Library.'

'With respect, Majistra, I don't think that is likely. We have not completely mapped the Library, but we do know that the fragments from which it was built did not contain any back doors or other connections.'

'I am only telling you what I know. Whether or not it is the truth I cannot say. I was told that Jakob found a back door to some part of your Library, and there he found something he believed to be valuable. I don't know what it was. He hired a data miner to help him, and she is dead. She killed herself. The Quick who told him about the hell is also dead, or has been disappeared. His colleagues are as vague on that point as on all others. All I know is that after Yakob explored the hell he'd found, he went off to search for something, and he has not returned. Perhaps he is somewhere in the Archipelago or on one of the colony worldlets, exploring some lost habitat of the Quick. He could even be here in Thule, going amongst her citizens in deep disguise. More likely he has ventured beyond the known worldlets, out into the vastness of the dust belt. I want to find out where he went, and what happened to him, and the first and best clue lies in that hell. And that is why you are here.'

'I have been sent to help you, Majistra. And I will do my best.'

'Your clan will benefit by acquiring a new fragment of the Library, or by closing a back door you knew nothing about. And I will know what

79

happened to my son. I do not expect loyalty to me, little monk, but I expect your clan to honour custom and contract.'

'As they have, by sending me here.'

'They have sent someone who has been disgraced and sent into exile. Not the best of their kind, but the least. Why should I not feel insulted?'

I found it hard to meet her cold, searching gaze. I was in her power. She could kill me by her own hand, or have me killed by one of the animals she had recreated. Few in my clan would mourn me; no one of any importance would question my disappearance.

'I failed once,' I said. 'But I have never failed since.'

'And I will make sure that you do not fail me. Look there,' Lathi Singleton said, and pointed to the dry grassland beyond the slab of rock where we sat. It had grown darker, but a sliver of light lingered at the far end of the platform, casting long shadows across the reddened landscape. After a few moments, I saw something moving past the solitary flat-topped tree that stood in the middle distance. Someone was jogging towards us out of the dusk's bloodlight, moving at the apex of a long shadow.

'There are few people I can trust,' Lathi Singleton said. 'My younger brother's daughter, Prem, is one of them. She and my son were close, as children, and she has sworn to find him alive, or avenge his death. She'll go with you. Or rather, you will go with her.'

She came scrambling up the rocks, Prem Singleton, stepping from one to the next with a flowing grace, vaulting to the lip of the slab where Lathi Singleton and I stood. She was young and slender, barefoot and bare-legged, dressed in a simple white shirt that fell to her thighs, her bob of glossy black hair highlighted with silvery threads and cut straight across her forehead, just above her eyes. In repose her face would have been merely pretty, but the restless and mischievous intelligence that animated it lent her a striking beauty that reminded me of the eidolon that had led me through the Memory Palace when I had first met Majister Svern. The resemblance wasn't especially close, but it was enough to undo the laces of my heart.

She stood there, hands on hips, and looked straight at me. Her eyes were large and dark brown, and I could feel her gaze move over my face.

Lathi Singleton introduced us, although I scarcely heard what she said.

'Well, then,' Prem Singleton said to me. 'Why don't you show me this famous Library?'

9

Commissar Doctor Wilm Pentangel told his new recruits that they had not been selected by him, but by the Mind at the heart of the world.

'You were all visited by so-called sprites during the recent event, and the experience has imprinted all of you with an indelible signature. As others have been touched in the past, so you have been touched now. The Mind is trying to communicate with us. We do not yet fully understand what it wants, but you will all help advance that understanding.

'We are at a tipping point in history. The Ghosts were driven back from Cthuga at the beginning of the war, and now they are reaching out towards Cthuga again. It is clear that they came to Fomalhaut because they wish to communicate with the Mind. We do not know if it wishes to communicate with them, but we do know that it wishes to communicate with us. I have been working long and hard to make full contact. That so many of you stand here today proves that the day when I achieve my aims is close at hand. All of you have been touched. All of you have been selected. Every one of you possesses some quality that attracted the Mind, and now a small part of it resides in your consciousness. Every one of you has the potential to change the war, and so change the course of history. Remember that always.'

The commissar paused, standing tall inside his long white coat and his exoskeleton. His sharp glittering gaze passing over the ranks of Quick. Ori tried not to flinch when he looked at her for a second, and lowered her own gaze and did not look up until he started to speak again.

Saying that they had much work to do and only a little time to do it. 'You will all be thoroughly tested, and you will all be thoroughly trained.

I must remake all of you in a handful of days. Some will fail me. It is inevitable. The rest will have the honour of knowing that they will have contributed to denying the enemy what it desires and ending the war. Now my assistants and kholops will organise you into groups, and tell you what needs to be done. To work!'

They were divided into five groups, and used standard kits to build five commons around the edge of the hangar space. They assembled partitions, divided the central space into training and testing areas, and set up and tested immersion chairs and the other equipment. When the philosopher-soldiers of the commissar's crew were satisfied that everything was in order, the punishing routines began. Neurological tests of every kind; taking turns in immersion chairs, where they learned how to handle drones in virtual simulations; indoctrination sessions; housekeeping tasks – cleaning and polishing decks and partitions, preparing and serving meals, and routine maintenance of the hangar's recycling systems – and six hours sleep.

It was intense and exhausting. Ori and the other recruits were forbidden to talk to one another, but it was possible to have brief, whispered conversations while doing scut work, swap stories about their encounters with sprites, speculate about what would happen to them after they finished training.

Everyone agreed that even by True standards the commissar was crazy. He was the scion of an obscure clan who had been pursuing a line of research into the origin and behaviour of sprites that had been considered marginal and mostly worthless. His theory that Cthuga had its origins outside the Fomalhaut system, that it was a wanderer captured by the young star, and that it contained an ancient alien intelligence, was widely derided. And then the quake had struck, and the commissar had seen a pattern and seized the opportunity to promote himself and his work. He had correlated and mined records and reports, determined that almost two hundred Quick had been affected by close encounters with sprites, and won the resources to turn as many as possible into living probes.

Even those amongst the Quick recruits who believed that there was a Mind inhabiting Cthuga's core – and not everyone believed there was – thought him crazy. They claimed that the Mind was derived from the mind of the Quick seedship, which had achieved true self-awareness and flung itself into Cthuga and vastened itself long before the Trues had arrived at Fomalhaut. Some claimed that it was preparing to liberate them from the tyrannies of the True, and they had been touched by the Mind and had received living parts of it as a first step in that liberation. They were holy vessels. They were carrying a holy fire. Others believed that the Mind had grown so vast and strange in its new environment that it had no interest in them apart from a small residual curiosity about its origins; that if it had been intending to free them, it would surely have done so by now, and since it had not, it never would. And others thought that there was no evidence that the sprites had anything to do with the Mind, and were not even evidence of its existence.

Ori was amongst the agnostics. She didn't believe in the Mind, but she didn't disbelieve in it, either. All she knew was that something had touched her, had become a part of her. Still, some of the stuff in the indoctrination sessions was entertaining. She learned, for instance, that the sprites were created by fluctuations in Cthuga's magnetic field so powerful that their induced electrical fields affected the link between bots and drones and their operators, and made neurons fire in the retinas of the operators' eyes and in their visual cortices. Operators did not 'see' sprites through the cameras and other sensors of their bots and drones (which did not record the presence of the sprites) but in their mind's eye. The cold violet flame that Ori had seen had been an hallucination caused by interaction between her bot's uplink, the sprite's intense magnetic field, and her own brain. But there was no explanation as to why the brains of some operators were permanently changed by these encounters while others were not. And if the True philosophers had any ideas about the long-term effects of the changes, they kept them from the recruits.

Ori knew only one of the other recruits in her group, a sour little person named Hira. They'd worked in the machine shops before Ori had been promoted to jockey crew #87. Back then she and Hira had been in neighbouring crews; Ori had played handball and rush and high-low castle against her, and once had comprehensively trumped her in a shadow play. Hira had got into trouble after Ori had moved on to ride bots, and had been demoted to one of the crews that rode the big, dumb machines that patched and healed cancerous and necrotic lesions in the Whale's halflife skin. She had been working out on the skin when the quake hit, a sprite had sprung up around her like a cold flame and had messed with her head, and here she was, philosopher fodder.

'You're nothing special,' she told Ori at the end of their second day, as they cleaned one of the bathrooms. 'You might think you're a hero because of what you did with that probe, but you aren't any better than me, or anyone else here. We're experimental animals fooled into thinking we're being trained to do important work, when really we're going to end up as bait. Live meat on a hook hung out to attract monsters.'

'Monsters?'

'There's more and more activity around the Whale, and all around Cthuga, too,' Hira said. 'I heard it's because the enemy is coming. The Mind is getting excited about that. It's reaching out. It wants to make contact. And when it does, when it touches the enemy and learns what they have to offer, it'll turn on us.'

'Where did you hear that?'

'You know how Trues are. They talk to each other as if we're not there. And I've been talking to people who heard them talk. Why we're here, we were in the wrong place at the wrong time. The commissar claims he will use us to make contact with the Mind. His bosses think they can use us to get some insight into how the Mind might attack us, and how they can defend themselves against it. They say they're training us, but this is really the first of a series of experiments that will test us to destruction.'

Ori remembered now that Hira had got into trouble for spreading gossip about the senior member of another crew. She was insecure because her ambition exceeded her talent; she liked to pretend that she knew more than she did to make herself seem more important, to make herself the centre of attention. Ori made the mistake of teasing Hira, questioning the logic of her assertions, asking why, if the Mind was planning to attack Trues, it hadn't ever latched on to one of them. Hira was in the middle of recounting a wildly improbable story about Trues who, having been driven insane by contact with the Mind, had been exiled to a secret pelagic station, when one of the supervisors discovered them. They were promptly scourged, assigned to extra shifts of cleaning work, and warned that if they broke regulations again they'd be given the long drop.

Ori tried to keep away from Hira after that. The woman was trouble. Her talk about infection and the malignant intent of the Mind might be silly fantasies, but they skirted close to sedition. The best way to get through this was to ignore all speculations, and buckle down. She didn't mind the scut work, which was no different to scut work back in the jockeys' commons, and she tried not to mind the invasive and unpleasant tests, the way the philosopher-soldiers handled her like a piece of meat. Paralysing her with nerve blocks. Inflicting casual pain. Talking about her as if she couldn't understand them.

Once, they did something that intensified the vague and ghostly presence of the sprite. For a moment it seemed to be standing in front of her as she lay spread-eagled and helpless, and everything around her flared bright and sharp. Then it was gone, and a cold front of endorphin shock rolled across her. The world went completely flat and lifeless and she was sinking away from it into darkness and she didn't much care. 'We're losing her,' one of the Trues said, and one of the machines around her raised a spidery articulated arm and shot her full of something that slammed her back inside her aching skull, back to the world.

She couldn't ask the Trues what they had done, but she would have done anything to experience that feeling again. She would even have given up the chance to fly for it.

That was the good part. The flying. It was only in virtuality to begin with, and the drones were stubby and slow, nothing like the swift sleek raptors that Ori had coveted for so long, but it was flying all the same, and she was determined to master every aspect of it as quickly as possible.

The supervisor of Ori's group, Teo, was a tough, practical, hard-headed old bird who'd been working for the commissar ever since he'd arrived on Cthuga.

'You have to forget everything,' Teo told her charges. 'Everything about your former life. It no longer exists. What you once were no longer matters. All that matters now is the change you're undergoing, and what you're going to become when it's finished. There was no before. There's only this. This is the world. Our world, sole and entire. And the commissar is our god, like in the old, old stories. He made the world and he made us too. Yes, he did. Everything you think you remember, about a life before this? He made those memories too. And he made the Mind, to give us a purpose. And that purpose is to fly straight and well, and to attract as many sprites as we can. Either you learn how to do that, or you'll take the long drop. Not for wasting my time, but for wasting the commissar's.'

To begin with, Ori had to unlearn everything she knew about riding bots. She'd been in daily and intimate contact with her bot for more than three hundred days, a symbiotic relationship that had left deep imprints in her body and the motor centres of her brain. Now she had only a short time to shake off every reflex and habit, and learn how to ride a new and very different body, one that locked her legs together and turned her belly into the maw of a ramjet, and her arms into vanes, binding them to her sides and locking her wrists to her hips; the only freedom of movement that she had was in her hugely enlarged thumbs and fingers. She learned how to think in three dimensions at all times, how to use the drone's visual, acoustic and radar sensorium to continually sweep out a spherical volume kilometres across. She learned how to tilt and feather the vanes to adjust attitude, how to avoid stalling, and how to surrender to the drone's autopilot if she did stall, how to activate hover mode.

Truthfully, it wasn't much more than a point-and-click operation. She could choose the flight path and make gross manoeuvres, but the drone's autopilot made most of the fine adjustments, gave warnings about rough or choppy air and other dangers, and would take over from her if she ignored those warnings. She was bait – Hira had been right about that, at least. She was riding the machine because her presence in the downlink might attract the attention of sprites, and the drone gave off all kinds of complex, pulsing electromagnetic signals and visual displays designed to attract them, too. But she was also doing what she'd always dreamed of doing. She was flying.

At the end of every session in the immersion chair, Ori had to endure more medical tests, or do hours of housekeeping work before she could climb into her sleeping niche. She had little time to reflect on her new situation, or to miss the familiar, comfortable commons of jockey crew #87, or to wonder what Inas was doing. Her dreams were always about flying, and always ended in the same way: a long tumbling fall, fighting battering winds as she tried and failed to restart her motor, falling and falling into hot crushing darkness from which she woke in a panic, chest heaving as she tried to grab air, heart thumping so loudly that it seemed to echo off the sides of the cramped sleeping niche. She'd reach for Inas' hot, muscular body and find only air. She'd open her eyes and see light burning at the margins of the niche's curtain, hear the hum of pumps and the small noises of someone tinkering with a rig, one of the philosopher-soldiers talking, and someone else laughing. She'd remember where she was, and calm down and fall asleep again, and wake when her supervisor ripped back the curtain and told her to move her sorry ass, it was the start of a brand new shift and it was time to get to work.

Teo bullied and cajoled Ori and everyone else in the group; Ori's own pride and stubbornness made her repeat every action until she got it right, and then repeat it again, over and over, until it was a reflex.

At last, everyone was assembled before Commissar Doctor Pentangel, who told them that their testing was almost over. They would rest tonight, and tomorrow they would complete a final test before they received their assignments.

Ori stood in the last rank this time and was able to count those standing in front of her and to either side. There were at least fifty people missing. Two had failed in her group; many more in others. The official line was that those who'd failed had been returned to their ordinary duties, but everyone knew that they had been given the long drop. Disappeared like a piece of malfunctioning machinery that wasn't worth repairing, like toxic trash. It could still happen to her.

There were no housekeeping duties afterwards and the recruits were allowed to associate freely as they cooked and served and ate their evening meal. They speculated about where they would go, whether to the train or to one of the pelagic stations. Hira, at the centre of a small group of acolytes, seemed as usual to know more than most. She said that the train was for the best recruits because it faced the most dangers.

'The further down you go, the more sprites you find,' she said. 'Sprites, and other things. Things that can eat you whole, from the inside out.'

'We used to frighten each other with stories like that when we were little,' Ori said. 'Ghouls and ghosts and other horrors.'

'Just because they were stories told by children doesn't mean that they aren't true. Every story must grow from something, after all.'

Hira seemed unreasonably cheerful about the prospect of meeting monsters. She claimed that she had aced her tests, and said that it didn't matter how well they flew, fast or slow. They only flew to attract sprites. They were all bait.

'That's what this last test is about, I bet. Not just about flying, but about what we attract. And if you don't attract anything . . .' She held out her hand palm down, thumb up, then slowly turned it down.

10

Vidal Francisca sat in the stern of the skiff with the Child's mother and Father Caetano, chatting casually, utterly at ease. As if he was the master and commander of the little vessel as it powered upriver. Dressed in a camo blouson and trousers and polished boots laced up to his knees, a pistol holstered at his hip, an aluminium case at his feet.

The Child watched him from the shade of the awning, reviewing her plan. She was surprised at how calm she felt and thought it a good sign. Vidal Francisca wanted to show that he could protect her and her mother. Wanted to prove that they needed him. That they couldn't do without him. All right, then: she would call him on it. Challenge his arrogant assumption and show him up for the fool that he was. She looked off at the trees crowded above crazed and cracked humpback mudbanks along the edge of the river, hugging her knees, doing her best to hide her glee.

After helping Father Caetano at Mass, the Child went straight to her mother, who was already seeing the first of her patients in the tent of the field clinic while a queue of women with babies cradled in their arms and small children clinging to their skirts waited outside in the hot sunlight. The Child said that Vidal Francisca wanted to explore the ruins, asked if she could go with him.

'I want to show him the mural we discovered.'

'As long as you don't go any further. And wear your hat,' her mother said – but the Child was already running off to find Vidal.

He was at the edge of the old dock where the skiff was tied up, watching one of the drones he'd unpacked from his aluminium case skim out across channels of water that ran between sandbars. He'd bought the drones to supplement his house's security, and had once allowed the Child to fly one. It was shaped like a flying saucer, light and quick as a hummingbird, driven by a pair of bladeless fans. She'd quickly mastered the simple controls, sending it swooping noiselessly over the darkening lawn, now high, now low, now looping around the big pepper tree, darting in and out of the branches, until Vidal had grown nervous, and told her she had done very well but it wasn't a toy, she should please bring it back. And she had, flying it straight at him, watching his face grow bigger on the little screen of the control tablet, laughing as he swore and ducked when the drone flashed past, a fast curve that ended in a crash stop above the illuminated amoeba of the swimming pool. He'd snatched the tablet from her, a moment of anger getting the better of his self-control, and had sworn again when he'd mishandled the controls and nearly dropped the drone in the water.

Now the Child was on her best behaviour, telling Vidal that her mother had given her permission to botanise along the edge of the ruins: would he like to come with her? Saying, when he expressed doubt, that she and her mother had walked there last time, she was sure it was perfectly safe.

'My mother said that I should ask one of the soldiers to go with me,' she said. 'But I would rather you did.'

It was as easy as that.

See the man and the Child walking through the long grass beyond the square. A little drone drifting along about a dozen metres overhead, almost invisible against the hot white sky. Vidal Francisca cupping the control tablet in one hand, flicking back and forth between views from the drone above his head and the drones stationed above the square and the field clinic, at the jetty down by the river. His eyes masked with mirrored sunglasses, a bush hat shading his face, his stupid little ponytail sticking out behind.

The Child walked beside him, keeping up a stream of chatter. When they reached the margin of the ruins, Vidal stopped and looked all around; the drone rose up, turning on its axis, surveying the overgrown apartment blocks and the mounds of rubble beyond. It was very hot, very quiet. The air glassy with heat, rippling above solitary stretches of wall standing here and there, scrub wasteland humped with overgrown heaps of rubble settling into earth. The Child pointed to a vivid slash of green in the middle distance, told Vidal that was where she and her mother had gone last time.

The man took off his sunglasses and mopped sweat from his face with one end of the red handkerchief knotted around his neck, and put his sunglasses on again. 'It looks a long way,' he said.

'It's really not far. And it's shady there. Full of flowers and butter-flies.'

The Child, after studying satellite images of the ruins of Santo João do Rio Negro and comparing them with old maps, had determined that the green line was a deep channel that had once been part of the town's flood-control system. When they reached the edge of its steep slope, Vidal made a show of surveying the trees and bushes that grew along its floor amongst tangles of broken concrete and splintered tree trunks, and declared that it would be too dangerous to explore further.

'We'll take a break before we head back. You can look around up here, but keep in sight.'

He sat down and took off his hat and fanned himself, unbuckled his water bottle and offered it to the Child, who refused with a shake of her head. The drone's white disc hung above the trees, glinting as it turned this way and that. Nothing else moved around them. In the mid-distance, a tree growing in the channel was in flower, a blaze of ardent red amongst variegated greens.

Vidal said, 'You are like one of the Indians. You walk like them, quick and quiet. And you see everything around you.'

The Child shrugged off this compliment. She'd become interested in intelligence-boosting drugs recently, and after extensive research and experimentation had managed to manufacture small amounts of a neural booster by methylation of a proprietary pain killer. She'd taken fifty milligrams of this home-brewed stimulant before they'd set off, and it was kicking in nicely now. Everything around her stood out with pin-sharp particularity. She could feel every drop of sweat that crawled down the back of her neck as she showed Vidal the little collecting bottles in her satchel and said that she was going to look for beetles – she was certain she would find some new and interesting species of beetle under the stones.

'Be careful. There will be snakes, I'm sure. Also scorpions and centipedes. The big ones that sting.'

The Child nodded dutifully, and made a show of using a stick to tip up stones one by one. Taking her time, moving away from Vidal and the solitary star of the drone. When she was certain that he had lost interest in her, she took out the phone she'd hacked, checked once again that it had locked on to the drone's signal, and touched the icon shimmering above its screen, a triangle with a stylised eye in it. The icon flashed from red to green, and the Child ran straight down the slope of tilted cracked concrete slabs that lined the wall of channel, into the deep shadows under the trees. Dancing and leaping and twisting over sprawling roots and stubs of broken concrete, ducking under loops of vine and coming out of the far side of the trees into the avalanche of hot sunlight, slick with sweat, her heart going like anything.

Off in the distance, a plaintive voice called her name.

The Child felt a surge of glee and excitement. Her plan had been very simple, like all the best plans, and it had worked perfectly. She'd downloaded the hack from a site on one of the darknets that Roberto had once showed her. It was an old design that cut into the feeds of security cameras and transmitted the visual equivalent of white noise. She had tested it on the security system of the hospital, used it to lock on to the feeds from Vidal Francesca's drones during the open-air Mass.

Now they were down, and she was free. All she had to do was stay hidden for a couple of hours, then walk back to the dock and claim she'd been kidnapped by wildsiders but had managed to escape. After that, after he'd put her in danger and failed to do anything useful, Vidal Francisca would be blamed and disgraced. Her mother would never talk to him again.

The Child pressed on through the strip of forest, moving away from the sound of Vidal's voice. She'd check out the flowering tree, she thought. See what kinds of insects it attracted, pass the time there until everyone was absolutely frantic with worry, and then she'd stroll back and tell her little story.

She was about halfway there when she saw a shadow detach from the trunk of a big thorn tree, thought for a horrible moment that Vidal had caught up with her. But the figure was too small, a boy about her age, a slim bare-chested boy in ragged cotton trousers stepping towards her, a rifle slung at his shoulder.

He was wearing a mask, the Child thought. But then he smiled at her, a smile that was so very wide it seemed to split his face in half, showing his pink tongue lolling amongst a narrow barricade of white fangs. And she realised with a thrilled shock that his mask was not a mask. He was a boy with the small sleek head of a jaguar.

For a long moment the Child and the boy stared at each other. The Child's skin was suddenly cold all over. Her mouth was dry. She started to ask the boy what he was, who had made him, and he shook his head and put a finger to his narrow mouth. An incongruously human gesture that made him seen even stranger, even more alien and frightening.

In the distance, beyond the trees, Vidal Francisca called the Child's name. The boy cocked his head, the shells of his mobile upright ears flicking forward; then in a swift smooth motion he raised the rifle to his shoulder and fired off two shots at a scrap of sky caught amongst leafy branches. The Child clapped her hands over her ears in shock as small green birds exploded from a nearby tree, whistling each to each as they fled. The boy stared straight at the Child for a moment. Something soft in his lambent gaze. Something like pity, or like love. And then he stepped backwards and by degrees melted away into the shadows under the trees.

Vidal Francisca called again, close now. She could hear him smashing through the undergrowth, coming towards her. And she had nowhere to run.

11

Watched narrowly by Lathi Singleton, I scanned Prem Singleton and showed her how to put on and adjust the gear. I told her that the training programme was just like a saga or any other viron, explained that the gear paralysed voluntary control of her musculature and channelled it to an avatar, that it managed the transition from one reality to another, and so on, and so forth.

Prem Singleton endured my instruction with a kind of dutiful impatience. 'I've fought all kinds of monsters in my time,' she said, when I'd finished. 'But I never thought I'd be fighting dream demons. Bring it on, Isak. Do your worst.'

'I'm going to show you what the Library of the Homesun looks like, Majistra, and demonstrate a few common traps. As for fighting demons, that takes a certain amount of instruction and practice. It isn't possible to replicate that experience in the little time we have.'

I had no intention of allowing her to follow the Horse and me into the hell that Yakob Singleton had discovered, of course, and was already thinking of various strategies I could use to make sure she didn't.

Prem laughed and said, 'Is that a fancy way of saying that you don't want to share your secrets, demon-slayer?'

'Forget about heroics and do as he asks,' Lathi Singleton said. 'This is a serious business.'

Prem said to me, 'Is it going to be anything like this so-called hell?'

'If the hell is modelled on the Library, yes. But hells take many forms.'

'Remind me how many you've harrowed,' Prem said.

'Thirteen, Majistra.'

'Does that include the demon you ran away from?'

'It was exorcised by others more experienced than me.'

'I've made you angry. I apologise. I didn't mean to question your qualifications.'

She didn't seem apologetic; she seemed pleased and amused. And I was angry, yes, but I was also exhilarated. She wanted to challenge me, and I wanted to meet and best her challenge.

'If you two are going to spar,' Lathi Singleton said, 'it might be more useful if you did it in this training programme.'

We went through together, Prem Singleton and I, into the garden so familiar to me from countless training sessions and exercises. As always, it was winter. Snow dusted the flagstone paths and the clipped box that edged the formal flower beds, where brown sticks stuck up from frosted earth. Long shadows stretched everywhere. The square stone tower at the far end of the garden reared against a sky bloodied by perpetual sunset.

Prem touched her face, then stamped a foot, raising a brief muffled echo. 'I thought I'd feel different.'

'The nervous impulses that reach your brain on the other side are mirrored here.'

She looked all around, alive and eager. 'This doesn't look like much,' she said. 'Where are these traps you talked about?'

I took her up through the tower, engaging various traps and minor entities. At first, Prem was amused by the exercises required to negotiate the lower levels, but she quickly grew bored and didn't bother to hide it.

'We dress up certain rooms in our hold every Candlemass,' she told me. 'The windows are darkened and the rooms draped with tall black cloths that form a maze. You can walk through some parts; in others you have to crawl through low tunnels, as if you are being reborn. Which is part of the reason why we celebrate Candlemass, of course. It marks the death of your childhood, and your rebirth as an adult, with adult rights and responsibilities.'

'It sounds like a charming custom.'

Prem looked at me with a mix of scorn and pity. 'It's a test of fitness. Some of the children who enter the maze don't reappear. Not many, these days. But always one or two. When people say they are scared to death, they're really talking about moments when they're most alive. And that's what it's like. There are flickering lights and odd breezes, projections that give glimpses of strange and terrible creatures. Draperies of

94

cobwebs. Blood dripping from one part of a ceiling. Bodies mutilated in horrible ways. Screams from a place always in front of you, or behind you. Whispered threats and lewd invitations that come from the air next to your ear. There are actors, too, and Quicks modified in various monstrous ways. They jump out at you, or stage mock fights. You could be one of the actors, Isak. In that costume of yours, you would fit right in with the other players.'

'The horrors you've seen here might seem tame and tawdry, but we are at a low level in the suites. If we go higher, you'll get a better idea of the real horrors you might encounter out in the Library.'

'Can we get to where we're going as quickly as possible? Or do you take some kind of twisted pleasure in boring me to death?'

'Come this way,' I said.

We had paused in a colonnaded passage between two scenarios. A neutral space, although there was a trap at the far end, a slow sink into which most novices stumbled. I'd managed to avoid it more by luck than judgement when I'd first been tested, spotting the dust motes that hung unmoving in a beam of red sunlight slanted in front of the archway that led to the next scenario. As long as you kept out of the light by edging along the wall in which hundreds of memorial tablets were set, you could pass safely, but just one touch of the light froze the processing space that supported your avatar and released a minor demon from a trap in the ceiling.

Prem followed me around one of the stone pillars and said, when I opened a door that until I touched it looked no different from the rest of the pillar, 'Is this another silly trial?'

'You asked me to get to our destination as quickly as possible. It's this way.'

Like other navigators, I had tutored apprentices after I had gained my full set of algorithms, and knew how to move quickly from one part to another through jumps, short cuts, and back doors. I took Prem through one of the back doors now, a metal stair that wound in a tight corkscrew up a stone chimney that pierced three floors and emerged on a broad balcony high above the dead garden where we had entered the training suite. Prem walked to the waist-high balustrade and leaned out, taking in the view of crooked roofs and spires and towers stretching away to the horizon.

As I stepped beside her, she grinned at me, and said, 'It's so big! I didn't realise!'

'Even in its current debased state, the Library contains worlds.'

'And it looks so very old.'

'Much of its architecture is based on an ancient city on the home world. The City of a Hundred Spires, otherwise known as the Golden City.'

'Is it your design?'

'It is the design of the Quicks, who first made the Library. We are rebuilding it in the image of what it once was.'

'You cleave to the past instead of making something new.'

Prem's knowing smile made me feel that I'd said too much, or said the wrong thing. I said, 'The destruction of the Library at the beginning of the first war was a major setback. We must first return to where we were before we can move forward.'

'Only if you want to keep moving in the same direction,' Prem said. 'Can we get there from here? Is there another secret door?'

'That is only a representation of one small part of the Library. To reach the real thing, we would have to pass through one of its translation frames. And I am afraid that you would not find the real thing half as pretty. We've been working here for four generations, but most of the Library is still ruined or warped. If we'd continued on the tour, you would have seen something of that, in the upper levels.'

'I hope to see the real thing next time,' Prem said. She leaned out and looked straight down at the winter garden, with its conifers and white paths. 'What if I jumped? Would I die?'

'It would end this session.'

'Some of those demons would kill me, but the fall wouldn't?'

'Your avatar would fall because it is affected by the physics of the Library, which are modelled on the physics of the real world. Demons and the other haunts can harm you because they can infect your mind via the link with the avatar.'

'Would it hurt?'

'You would find yourself going mad. Thinking thoughts that you knew were not your own. Or you would lose control of your senses, or of your body.'

'I mean if I jumped.'

'I have never tried,' I said, and saw what she was going to do, but reached for her a moment too late.

She vaulted on to the flat top of the balustrade with such ease that I knew then that this wasn't the first time she had controlled an avatar.

Standing at the very edge, she looked straight down, then glanced over her shoulder at me. Saying, 'We could try it together.'

'We could walk back through the suites. There's something you should see, before you go.'

I was in an agony of indecision. I wanted to stop her doing something stupid, not least because it would reflect badly on me, but because of her status I didn't dare reach out and lay a hand on her.

'I've seen enough of your silly little frights,' she said. Poised at the very brink of the vertiginous drop, she looked more desirable than ever. Reckless and bold.

'I can assure you that what happens in the Library or a hell can have consequences in the real world,' I said.

'Let's see,' Prem said, and stepped off into the void and dropped straight down, feet together and arms by her side, like a diver entering deep water from a height. I looked away, but the flat final sound of the impact echoed up from the walled garden.

Even using short cuts, it took a good ten minutes to reach the garden and return to the slab of rock in Lathi Singleton's biome. It was fully night, now. The landscape sketched in shades of black beyond the hearth-glow of small faint lights that spun over the remains of the picnic. The two women, Prem and Lathi Singleton, sat side by side, watching as I stripped off my gear.

'Is he competent?' Lathi Singleton said.

Somewhere out in the dark, something howled on a long mournful note that raised the hair on the back of my neck.

'Oh, I think we're going to have a lot of fun together,' Prem said.

97

12

Ori woke from a dream of falling and heard the voices of the supervisors outside her sleeping niche, ordering everyone to get up and fall
in. It seemed that the recruits had been divided into ten teams that
would take turns to ride a little way down the cable and fly real drones,
out in the real air. Ori was assigned to the tenth team, the last to
descend, and although she told herself that going last was good, a sign
of trust, she was dismayed to see Hira marching off to the train at the
head of the first team. She hadn't realised until then how much she
disliked the woman.

After a long, long wait, Ori's team was led out of the hangar, through
an airlock and a long connecting tunnel to an adjoining hangar, this one
very much larger. The team was led past stacked goods of every description, through sectors for sorting and storage where lifters and other
machines trundled back and forth, past low rectangular bunkers, some
with windows, some without, to a curving inner wall of thick, transparent
diamond. It was the sheath that held the cable inside the Whale, and the
cable could be dimly seen inside it, black and grooved and latticed. Ori
and the others were marched into a big airlock set in the wall of the
sheath, crossed a short tunnel beyond, and were processed two by two
through a smaller airlock. Ori was one of the last to pass through, into a
narrow crescent of a room with a mesh floor. She followed the others
up a ladder that rose through a long tube, passing floor after floor, the
ladder beginning to vibrate under her fingers and toes as she climbed,
until they emerged in a small, low-ceilinged disc of a room in which
immersion chairs were arranged like spokes in a wheel. Ori realised then
that they were aboard a train, and the deep hum and the vibrations she
could feel in the soles of her feet meant that it was under way.

It did not travel far. By the time Ori and the rest of the team had checked out and activated the immersion chairs they'd been assigned, it had halted. Teo told her to take it easy and follow the instructions, but Ori hardly heard her. The drone was coming online and she was extending into it, and when the mask clamped down and the sensory feed kicked in she was *there*, clamped in a launch cradle that everted from the hangar pod and swung out and up into daylight.

She was hanging prone, head down, the hangar carriage beneath her belly, a drone sitting in a cradle on her left. Just like the beginning of every simulation, except that the simulations had always been set in infinite volumes of clear and empty air, and now she was looking straight down at a deck of pale white cloud that sheeted the sky for as far as she could see, sculpted into mountains and valleys and great continents. Flotillas of smaller clouds hung here and there above the cloud deck, more or less at the level she hung. The small clouds cast perfectly defined shadows on the cloud deck, and a sharp narrow line haloed with rainbows of refracted sunlight cut through them, running off towards the flat horizon: the shadow of the cable on which the train rode.

Ori switched to the drone's rear sensors (it was a little like turning her neck) and saw the cable rising above, dwindling into a narrow thread, crossing the great filmy shadow of the ring-arch and vanishing into the zenith of the blue-green sky. Somewhere up there, its vast bulk lost in vast perspectives and sunlight dazzle, was the Whale and everything she had known in her life. The tank farm and the nursery where she'd spent her brief childhood. The machine shop where she'd worked first, the air-conditioning plant, the commons of jockey crew #87 and the marshalling yard spread across the flank of the Whale. Where Inas and the rest of the crew were probably working right now, prepping drones for the long drop. Ori felt a swell of hopeless longing pass through her, and then, with a kind of jolt, the rest of the drone's systems came online. Its internal checksum showed that its power, guidance, and navigation packages were all working. A clock started up, running back from thirty to zero; off in the distance, a red dot appeared, a virtual marker floating above the cloud deck five klicks away.

'There and back,' Teo's voice advised her. 'Try not to screw up.'

The counter reached zero and started to flash; the drone beside Ori flared away from its cradle, its blunt triangles dwindling into frigid sunlit air. Ori followed more cautiously, puttering along at a shade under a hundred kilometres per hour in a dead straight course as the other drone dwindled away towards the red dot. Cross-currents buffeted her when she left the shadow of the cable, juddering in little vortices along the control surfaces of her vanes, introducing a significant vibration into the drone's stubby wings. The autopilot flashed a warning, but she kicked up her speed a little and was able to stay in control, driving straight on at a steady pace. The other drone flashed past, travelling in the opposite direction, as she neared the red blotch of the way point. She swung around it and headed back, towards the vertical pillar of the cable. The train looked toy-like against the cable's bulk, clinging to a track that was no more than a faint vertical line. As the cable began to fill Ori's forward vision and the sun went behind it, the autopilot locked her out and the drone pitched up in a sharp J-turn, balancing on its thrust as it fell with clean machine precision towards the cradle of its pod and the link cut off and Ori was back in the immersion chair, her first and last practice flight over.

Teo told Ori and the rest of the team that they had all done well. That they wouldn't return to the Whale, but would ride down on the train to the place where they would start work at once.

Ori felt a little flare of triumph. She'd been right: the Trues had saved the best until last. The rest of the team were happy too. They fetched bowls of tea from the cramped kitchen niche and sat on the floor around the immersion chairs and joked about the flocks of sprites they'd attract, the wonders they'd see.

The train descended a long way, stopping several times in refuge loops to allow trains carrying raw materials to the tip of the cable to pass before moving on again. Ori experienced a dropping sensation like riding an elevator, mixed up with her relief and happiness. Felt as if she was floating, leaving behind her old life, yes, but beginning a new and glorious chapter.

The air grew warm and humid, despite the roaring fans of the air-conditioning system. There were creaks and groans in the walls and bulkheads, sudden alarming cracks and snaps, as atmospheric pressure gloved the train ever tighter.

At last, the train stopped and Teo selected one of the recruits and sent her down the companionway, told the others to sit quiet and wait their turn. Ori wondered if everyone else was pretending that they weren't afraid of what lay ahead. A few minutes later, the train started up again, descending, slowing, stopping, and the next recruit was dispatched. So it went until it was Ori's turn. She followed a floating arrow down to the service level above the drone hangars, where two philosopher-soldiers, dressed in yellow coverall uniforms under their exoskeletons, were waiting by the open door of an airlock.

Ori felt a sense of stolid resignation clamp over her – the survival mechanism for her people, who had no say in their fate, who could at any moment be uprooted from their niche at the whim of any True. Despite Teo's assurances, it was possible that she had failed after all. Perhaps she was about to be expelled into the frigid and poisonous air, and the long fall to the sea of hydrogen that wrapped the core. Although she'd burn up long before she reached it, her body mashed by pressure and charred and fragmented and blown to ashes and the vast world's four quarters. She did not struggle. There was no point in trying to struggle. She straightened her back and did as she was told and marched into the airlock, and at once the halves of the outer door parted, exhaling a gust of cold stale air, revealing a small, dimly lit chamber.

'You'll serve here for ten days. The station's AI will tell you what to do. Try not to kill yourself. The commissar hates it when that happens,' one of the philosopher-soldiers said, and shoved her hard in the small of her back.

Ori tumbled over the lip of the open door and behind her the two halves of the door slammed shut.

PART TWO
TERMINATION SHOCK BOUNDARY

1

The Child did not tell anyone about her encounter in the ruins of Santo João do Rio Negro. She was too shocked, to begin with; she did not want to believe what she had seen. Because if a boy could have the head of a jaguar, the model of the world she had chosen – unified, explicable, utterly transparent to reason – must be shadowed by the world she had rejected. The world conjured by her ama's fairy tales. A world animated by the breath of pure spirit, where good and evil were as real as quarks and gluons. A world where a drowned boy was not dead but awaiting transformation and rebirth, where miracles could be conjured by nothing more than belief, and truths were not resolved by equations that balanced the fundamental forces and properties of the universe but were veiled in mystery and proceeded from an inexplicable aleph.

We made sure that she did not need to tell her mother or to anyone else about the boy with the jaguar head. Vidal Francisca had his own version of what he called their little adventure. The girl had wandered off into the strip of forest in the old flood channel, he told Maria Hong-Owen, and she'd been spotted by a party of wildsiders. Three of them at least, he said, with who knew how many more lurking in the forest and the ruins all around. Luckily, he'd realised that something was up because they'd jammed his security drone, and after a brief exchange of fire he'd managed to chase them off.

'God must be praised for two reasons,' he said. 'First, they shot at me instead of the poor girl. And second, they missed.'

He was already turning it into a story. Trimming inconvenient facts, smoothing the rest into a more shapely form, making himself the centre of the escapade. Within a few days he had entertained most of his friends with his account of the attempted abduction of the girl, and his daring rescue. The danger a mere inconvenience. The wildsiders – by now a small band, desperate and ragged and starving – a joke. Oh, they'd managed to neutralise his security measures, but probably more by luck than judgement, and they'd completely failed to follow through. He'd seen them crash away through the trees, he said. He'd taken shots at them, might even have winged one of them. And so on, and so on.

The Child dreamed of the jaguar boy that night. Dreamed that he was standing in the shadows at the foot of her bed, his eyes blank luminous discs. She stared back, paralysed with terror, trying to scream, unable to breathe. And then he came around the side of the bed, stepping daintily, leaning over her, and she lashed out and woke up, tangled in a sheet, heart racing, and cried out because a tall shadow moved in the doorway. But it was only her mother, coming into the bedroom and sitting on the bed, taking her daughter into her arms, smoothing her hair and telling her that it was all right, she'd had an adventure but it was over now. She was home. She was safe. And the Child started to cry, the first time she'd cried since her so-called rescue. Because she knew that her plan to make Vidal Francisca appear foolish and unreliable had completely backfired. Because she knew that it would be even harder to get rid of him now.

The jaguar boy came to her every night after that, but none of her dreams were as bad or as vivid as the first. Mostly, she was walking in the forest and he was walking with her, either somewhere ahead, half-glimpsed through trees and slanting beams of sunlight, or no more than a presence at her back. She still had not told anybody about him. He was her own private mystery, a problem to which she applied her naive but rigorous logic. She would drive back the shadows of the other world by the light of reason.

She had seen someone in the overgrown flood channel. That was a plain hard fact. She had seen a boy; he had been armed with a rifle; he had fired two shots; the shots had brought Vidal Francisca running. The boy had been real, all right, but had he really had the head of a jaguar? Perhaps he'd been wearing a mask after all. Or perhaps he'd been afflicted with some kind of tetralogical deformity that had reduced the size of his head. He'd painted his face with pigment as camouflage or because of some kind of private ritual, and shock and imagination, coupled perhaps with a side-effect of her home-made drug, had done the rest.

After spending a little time researching wildsiders but finding little to satisfy her curiosity amongst government propaganda and echo chambers of rumour and unsupported assertions, the Child paid a visit to Ama Paulinho's father, Josua Gonzagão. The old man's house was crowded with the families of relatives who had fled the drought-stricken countryside, and most of the old garden had been given over to a clapboard dormitory, but Josua was unchanged, gaunt and leathery, bald as a turtle, dressed as always in a white linen shirt and white drawstring trousers, enthroned on the couch in his back room with the big screen pumping out news from every corner of the whole wide world.

He wanted to know all about the Child's adventure, and she told him what she'd told everyone else. How she'd been searching for beetles when she'd come across the boy, how he'd fired two shots, perhaps to signal to his friends, and how he'd melted away into the shadows under the trees when Vidal Francisca had come running instead. She didn't tell Josua that the boy had the head of a jaguar, because it would certainly get back to her mother, and then all the other lies and evasions would come out – her plan to make Vidal Francisca look like a fool, baking military-grade amphetamines, hacking his silly little drone. Instead, she asked the old man if the boy could really have been a wildsider. After all, he hadn't been any older than she was.

'Some wildsiders are people who lost their land when it was rewilded, but most are bandits and criminals,' Josua said. 'But whatever they are, many have families, as we do. They have children, and their children are taught from an early age to fight. Also, they kidnap children, and force them to fight. They indoctrinate them, and give them drugs to make them brave and crazy. They are often very cruel, the children. Two of my friends were taken prisoner, and later we found them . . .'

The man's hands, dark and crooked as tree roots, were knotted together and he was looking past the Child, at something from the long-ago.

'Soldiers searched all around the ruins in Santo João do Rio Negro. But they didn't find anything. It was as if,' the Child said, choosing her words with care, 'the boy I saw really had melted away. Like a dream.'

'Well, of course. Wildsiders do not live in one place. They live everywhere, and nowhere. You don't find wildsiders. They find you. That's what we always said, on the front line, and it was true. They would appear, and attack, and disappear. Sometimes we would find a place where they had camped, in the forest. Marks on the trees where they had slung their hammocks. Branches cut away. A trampled place by a stream. Nothing else.'

The old man fell silent, looking at the past again, and the Child, scared and excited, raised the question she'd come to ask. She was wondering, she said as casually as she could, if wildsiders ever wore masks, or if they changed their appearance to look like animals.

'Some of the wildsiders have totem animals,' Josua said. 'They believe it gives them strength and courage when they fight. They wear some part of it in a little bag. A claw or a tooth. A hair or a feather. It is a very old magic. Before men were men, such things were believed. There are pictures of animals on certain rocks in the mountains, made by the old ones.'

'Like jaguars?'

'Why not?'

'I read they sometimes make themselves look like their totem animal.'

The old man thought about that. At last, he said, 'You hear all kinds of stories about wildsiders. Many of them fantastic, although I suppose some of them might be true. I once saw a little girl . . . But perhaps I should not tell you this.'

'Oh, *I'm* not a little girl any more.'

'Of course. But when you are as old as I am, when you are half as old, you'll wish you were.'

'What kind of animal did she look like, this little girl?'

'She looked like a little girl. Just four or five years old. Comrades of mine found her in the badlands. This was hundreds of kilometres to the south. It was all naked rock there. The forest had died and big storms had blown away most of the soil and hard rain had washed away the rest. My comrades were driving in convoy, and when they stopped for the night she tried to sneak inside their perimeter. I suppose she was looking for food or water – there was no water there, you see. Just sand and rock. Nothing growing.'

'How had she got there?'

'That is a good question. She was ragged and starving, poor thing. I suppose she had lost her family, or they had lost her. So my comrades brought her back to their camp, just behind the front line. I saw her myself when I passed through. She had been with them for five weeks by then, and she was healthy enough. A friendly little thing, too. Quite intelligent. The only thing was, she had tusks,' the old man said, and crooked his forefingers at the corners of his mouth. 'Like the tusks of a wild pig. Yellow and curved up towards her cheeks.'

'Real ones?'

'If you lose a tooth, they implant a bud that grows into a new one. You understand? All of my teeth have been regrown that way,' the old man said. 'I suppose someone had taken out several of her teeth and implanted buds. But not the buds for human teeth.'

'Or tweaked her genome,' the Child said.

The old man shrugged. 'My comrades collected credits amongst themselves, to pay for the surgery to remove them. It was no easy operation. Their roots had grown through the upper jaw, into the cheek bones.'

The Child nodded, thinking about the kind of surgery required to make someone look like a jaguar.

Josua said, 'Apart from the tusks, she was completely normal. They named her Mamoré, after the dead river where she had been found. Little Mamoré . . . I wonder where she is now.'

'Did she have the operation?'

The old man jerked out of his reverie. 'Oh no. No. A few weeks after I visited their camp, my comrades were attacked one night. Two of their trucks were blown up, their generator was knocked out, two huts were hit with rockets. Wildsiders rode in out of the dark and killed six men and women and wounded many more. And they took the little girl. Mamoré. I suppose it was her family, come for her. I suppose they tracked the convoy back to the camp.'

'I suppose,' the Child said, although she thought it was quite likely that Mamoré had used the camp's comms to ask for help. It was her experience that adults always underestimated the capability of children.

She talked about wildsiders with Roberto, too, in their private little corner of a darknet, and he was helpful and reassuring. Telling her that many wildsiders wore masks, while others made themselves look fiercer with tattoos, plastic surgery, and tweaks. And they often doused themselves with psychoactive pheromones, he said.

'They are immune, of course. But anyone who is in close contact with them is immediately overwhelmed.'

'Francisca is going around saying he saw a whole party of wildsiders,' the Child said.

'There you are. It's quite possible to change someone's reality by changing their perception of it.'

'He says he fired at them. That he rescued me from their clutches. But he didn't. He grabbed my arm and dragged me through the trees, out of the channel. *Then* he fired, but he was only firing at foliage and shadows. And then we both ran. I think he was more scared than I was, but somehow he has turned himself into a hero. As far as my stupid mother is concerned, he can't do anything wrong.'

They talked about that for a little while, the Child rehearsing her old grievances until Roberto said he had to go. 'I have a class. Take care. And don't worry about Vidal Francisca. Sooner or later he'll show his true colours.'

The Child didn't believe that it was as simple as that. Vidal Francisca was a vain and foolish man in many ways, but he knew people, knew how to flatter and amuse them, how to stroke their egos and make them feel good. Watching him smooch and flirt with her mother was disgusting, but the Child knew that she lacked the skills to play him at his own game, knew that she'd have to find another way of showing him up for what he was. Still, at least she had a satisfactory solution to the puzzle of the boy with the jaguar head. He had not been some kind of supernatural apparition, or a monster escaped from the twisted dreams of the past. No, he had been a wildsider with some kind of minor cosmetic modification that her imagination and fear had monstrously magnified. It was no more fantastic than that. She was relieved, and a little disappointed. Part of her, the part of her that wanted to be the first person to live for ever, still believed the stories of her ama. For if there were creatures in the world as fantastic as River Folk or talking ground sloths, then it would not be impossible to cheat death.

We also knew that the boy with the jaguar head was no supernatural creature. That he was as real as the Child, or her mother, or anyone else in the quotidian world – the world of her lost past, the world we had recreated to the best of our ability. But he should not have been there because we had not invented him. He had appeared from nowhere, without our permission or knowledge.

You may think that we should have been able to control everything in the Child's world because we had created it. To erase what was not wanted, or to run events backwards to a critical point and force them into a safer and more predictable course. Indeed, those powers, and many others, were in our gift, and we did in fact freeze the world for a short while (you may have thought it was a figure of speech, in the story we are telling of the Child's story), while we debated whether or not to intervene. But although we had set the story in motion, it was a very difficult and perilous undertaking to attempt to micromanage events. Everything was interlinked. Everything affected everything else, and not always in predictable ways.

No, the Child's world was too rich and strange for linear control. It proceeded with its own logic. We could intervene with what would appear to be miracles, and we could manipulate or possess various characters, but we could not directly interfere with the Child's consciousness or override her free will. Not only because of the risk of serious damage to the cloud of agents that were the constituent parts of her personality, but also because we had not created the story to take charge of the Child. We had done so out of love and duty. The Child was our mother, born again. And we wanted a true resurrection. We did not want to force her to make the right choice once we reached our destination, because we would have to change her personality, make her more docile, strip her of much of the vital complexity that defined and informed her genius. We could guide her, yes, and instruct her as best we could. But she had to take that final step on her own, or else it would be worthless.

We were not the mistresses of our mother's story. We were its servants.

The heart may beat more quickly when it responds to a hormonal flood, but what does it know about the confusion of love? Does the small intestine understand the significance of the ritual wafer as it breaks down the wafer's complex carbohydrates to glucose? Those of us cut to find persistent patterns in human lives and human history recall the stories of the long-ago and ask how much the horse of the humble parfait knight understands of its master's quest. It knows the road but not the reason it carries its master down that road. It knows the weight of its master and his armour. It knows that each day it sets out on another of an unending series of long and exhausting journeys through strange and new places. It knows the heat of the sun, and the cold whip of winter wind and rain. It knows a plodding routine punctuated by bright and bloody moments of combat or intervals of respite when it shares the stables of some strange castle with others of its kind. And at the end of its master's quest, when he enters the ancient chapel in the heart of the forest and kneels before the Grail, his horse stands outside, waiting patiently as always. Perhaps the grass it rips from the flower-starred turf is sweeter than mundane grass. Perhaps it feels dim and unknown emotions stir inside it when the pure and holy light of the Grail floods through the open door of the chapel. But does it understand how close it stands to the ineffable? Has it any conception of infinite mercy and wisdom? Is it changed?

We were as a flea in the mane of that horse. As a worm in its gut.

We do not seek to excuse ourselves. There were checks imposed on what we were allowed to know and do, and what we were allowed to think, limitations built into our original design, but that is no excuse either, for we were created to protect our mother and in the end we failed. And even now, in the wreckage of that failure, we do not know if it was a glorious failure or a cruel defeat. There is so much we do not know. We do not even know the limits of what we do not know. This story about our mother's story is not an excuse or an attempt to exculpate ourselves. It is an attempt to impose a metrical frame on the abyssal depths of our incomprehension.

We do know that by the time the jaguar-headed boy appeared we were irrevocably committed to our plan. Five centuries had passed since the accident in which the original of our mother was lost, but much of that time had been spent repairing and reconstructing the ship and its systems, and shaping it for its final purpose. When at last we quickened the Child's story, Fomalhaut was the brightest star in our sky, and we were passing through the inner edge of its cloud of long-period comets. When she kept watch over the drowned boy, and first vowed to never die, we were approaching the bow shock, where the scant gases and rare dusts of the interstellar medium, at an average density of a single atom in every cubic centimetre, were stirred and churned by the turbulent front of Fomalhaut's heliopause. The drought was two years old and the Child had just begun instruction with Father Caetano when we passed through the heliopause itself, the boundary between interstellar space and the bubble of Fomalhaut's solar wind; when she met the jaguar-headed boy, we had just crossed the termination shock boundary, the point where the average velocity of particles blown outward by Fomalhaut's solar winds dropped to subsonic speeds as they began to interact with the local interstellar medium.

And now, at last, we were falling through the heliosphere proper, towards the outer edge of Fomalhaut's great dust belt and the insignificant rock that was our final destination. The rock where we hoped our mother would choose to hide while the war between the clades which had reached Fomalhaut ahead of us played out. Where she would acquire knowledge of her new home before deciding what to do.

That was our plan. We had studied the war as best we could, and had concluded that any attempt to interfere in it without proper preparation would be fatal. Nor could we make an alliance with either of the two sides. One was an old enemy, the Ghosts; they had been comprehensively defeated by our mother before she left the Solar System, and it was their nature to never forget or forgive. The other, the so-called True People, was a crude, cruel, backwards-looking and completely untrustworthy clade which had enslaved descendants of the peaceful posthuman clade which had first settled Fomalhaut. We were certain that if we made ourselves known to them, they would either make our mother their slave, or strip her of every particle of useful knowledge before killing her.

And so we had decided that the best course of action would be to hide, and bide our time. It was a conservative plan, yes, and required stealth and great patience rather than the usual bold, swift strokes by which our mother had so often defeated her enemies. We would have to work hard to teach the Child the qualities required to carry it out, for they were utterly foreign to her nature, but we believed that it was the only way she could survive contact with those who had usurped what was rightfully hers.

So we could not end the Child's story when it began to deviate from its chosen path because we did not have enough time or resources to start over. We worried that the appearance of the jaguar boy was a spy for one of the warring factions, or that we had failed to completely purge our rebel sisters and all their works from the ship's systems, and that he was a precusor of a resurgence of the insurrection that we had defeated centuries ago. But although we searched long and hard we could find no trace of him, and in the end we decided that he was no more than a glitch in the matrix that generated the Child's story, and allowed it to flow on.

For a while, it seemed that it was continuing to move in the right direction. Maria Hong-Owen grew closer to Vidal Francisca after he saved her daughter's life. Soon enough, they would make the decision that would send the Child to the school in Manaus, where she would be taught everything that would prepare her for her marriage.

We made plans to make sure that it would happen as soon as

possible. There was only a little time left. It was time to push the Child towards the right direction.

It was a mistake. But we did not know it then.

There was so much that we did not know.

2

We travelled to T, Prem Singleton, the Horse, and I, on one of the ancient Quick ships: a fragile-looking cluster of bubbles elaborated around the central axis of a motor pod. None of the bubbles were especially large and most were occupied by young scions of the Singleton clan on their way to T for officer training before heading out to the front, making a lot of noise as they celebrated their last hours of civilian life. The Horse and I found a quiet spot in one of the bubbles in the innermost layer, where the scions' baggage and other cargo was stored, and the squad of Quicks who controlled the ship's flock of defensive drones were quartered. We tethered ourselves as best we could amongst a clutter of weapon cases, travelling wardrobes and trunks, and linked our securities. It was very likely that we were being watched, and while we couldn't guarantee that our link was completely unbreakable, it made us feel safe enough to exchange confidences. I gave the Horse a quick precis of my interview with Lathi Singleton; he told me what he'd discovered about her son.

'It's not exactly a straight story, but I'll try my best. To begin at the beginning, I did exactly as you asked. I hired someone to act as my proxy and ever so discreetly and carefully search the net. But he didn't turn up anything beyond the usual gossip and rumour that's attached to scions of the first families. Trivial feuds and adolescent dalliances, scandals over nothing very much in particular. Most of it put out by so-called rivals and self-styled enemies, inflating the ordinary stuff of life into cosmic drama. I can tell you who Yakob Singleton is supposed to have slept with first, who he may or may not have been sleeping with when he disappeared, who likes him and who only pretends to like him . . .' The Horse smiled his lopsided smile. 'But I wouldn't dare to test your patience.'

'You're already testing its outer edge. Keep to the point. Prem Singleton already suspects we are colluding behind her back.'

'She's having too good a time carousing with her doomed cousins to bother with her kholops. Which is what we are, even though you won't admit it.'

'I know very well what I am, but you seem to have forgotten who *you* are. Perhaps you can start by explaining where you got those clothes.'

The Horse had turned up at the ship just a few minutes before it left Thule's hub, dressed in a yellow tunic of soft buttery leather that fell to his knees, with a high collar and many pockets, all different sizes and colours, and scarlet hose and matching scarlet slippers. Looking clownishly ridiculous and unsettlingly exotic at the same time, and irritatingly pleased with himself.

Prem had been unaccountably amused by the Horse's costume, greeting him with genuine courtesy, telling him that he was a valued member of our small crew. She did not possess a kholop or any other kind of servant.

'There are many of us in the army who have fought side by side with Quicks, and have grown to like and respect them,' she told me, and asked if I found that shocking.

I told her that my clan was often accused of being too friendly with Quicks, and said that as a result our kholops had an independence others found disgraceful. 'The Horse is, unfortunately, an extreme example of that independence. Let me know if he ever oversteps the line.'

'Oh, I find his eccentricity charming,' Prem said.

Now the Horse told me that there was a very simple explanation for his new clothes. 'The credit you gave me wasn't enough to pay for the information you wanted, so I wagered it on a sure thing in one of the fighting pits and more than trebled it. Enough to sprinkle around as required, with a little over to buy something better fitted to the circles I had to move in than our usual gear.'

'I'm failing to imagine any corner of civilisation where your costume could be considered acceptable.'

'Of course you are. You have led a sheltered life. And you are wise enough to know that, and to send me to deal with matters outside the narrow confines of your upbringing and training. To cut a long and interesting story short, a simple search turned up nothing useful. I had to look elsewhere, which led me to the criminal edges of the city of tiers. And there I learned that although Yakob Singleton worked for the Office of Public Safety, he was no ordinary trooper or investigator. He had been assigned to the Department for Repression of Wreckers, which fabricates conspiracies to draw in Trues it suspects of harbouring wrecker tendencies. When they are deeply enmeshed, it arrests and disappears them.'

I said that I found it hard to believe that people could be disappeared for doing something they hadn't done.

The Horse cocked his head in the bird-like way of Quicks. His eyes gleaming like twin stars in the shadows of the cargo that crammed the bubble. 'Yakob Singleton and his colleagues were purveyors of fantasy. They fashioned stories for a special kind of audience. Plots involving sabotage and assassination, conspiracy theories . . . All conjured from whole cloth, pieces of fully furnished theatre. The people targeted and ensnared by the department are not selected at random, of course. They are selected because they have wrecker tendencies. That is why they willingly enter into conspiracies instead of walking away from them, as any sensible and honest person would. And so their criminal tendencies are safely channelled into areas that are wholly controlled by the department, and when they are arrested they are guilty of real crimes, and are punished accordingly. After, of course, they have been thoroughly interrogated and have given up the names of everyone they know who might also harbour the same tendencies which drew them into the net in the first place.

'There's a rumour that all the acts of successful sabotage and assassination carried out by wreckers were hatched by the department, but I'm sure that can't be true,' the Horse said. 'After all, it would mean that there aren't really any wreckers, and that the department isn't engaged in protecting public safety but in threatening it so that the public will agree to any and all measures to protect them from harm – even if it means giving up some of the very rights and liberties those measures are supposed to protect. And besides, according to my informant, Yakob Singleton and his colleagues stumbled over a genuine conspiracy just before he disappeared. A mystery cult that believes that one day a ship will appear and free us from the burden of your rule.'

'I've heard of such things. They're harmless fantasies.'

'Most are. But this was an old cult – perhaps one of the oldest. And it wasn't hoping for a new ship, but a very old one.'

The Quick seedship had arrived at Fomalhaut first, the Horse said, but not because it had been the first to leave the Solar System. The True seedship had left long before, but it was slower and less sophisticated, and the Quick seedship had overtaken it. But there was also a third ship, launched long before even the True seedship, and because it was even slower than the other two, both had overtaken it.

'I've heard of that, too,' I said. 'But it should have arrived long ago, at about the same time as our seedship.'

'Four gigaseconds afterwards,' the Horse said. 'More or less.'

'But it didn't, because it had some kind of accident, and was lost. It exploded and the debris hasn't yet reached Fomalhaut. Or it failed to stop accelerating and fell past us. Hardly surprising. It was incredibly ancient. One of the first seedships to leave the Solar System.'

'It began its journey some three and a half teraseconds ago,' the Horse said. 'And some people believe that it is still on its way.'

'Your people. These mystery cultists. Did they find it? Is that the conspiracy Yakob uncovered?'

'I don't know. I know they were looking for it. Watching the window of sky it must pass through if it ever approached Fomalhaut.'

'If it is so old, what use is it?'

'Spoken like a true True.'

'I'm trying to think like Yakob Singleton. He broke his contract with the Office of Public Safety. He must have had a better reason than some incredibly historic but intrinsically worthless relic.'

'I think I have the answer to that,' the Horse said. 'The thing about this ship is that it wasn't a seedship. It's so old that it actually carried a passenger.'

He opened a window between us: a gas-giant planet banded in autumn colours and gorgeously ringed. Unlike the gigantic rings of Cthuga, these shone with diamond splendour. They were divided by a large gap into a narrow inner circle and a broader outer circle, and those two circles were in turn divided by gaps of various sizes, the whole as intricate and beautiful as a toy.

'Saturn. A sister planet of Earth,' the Horse said.

'That's where the ship came from?'

'From one of the moons.'

He reached in and the view expanded towards a portion of the outer edge of those rings. Detail resolved – narrow lanes divided by hair-thin gaps laced together within the broad lanes of luminous material, spokes of darker stuff thin as smoke radiating out across the lanes – and the diffuse edge of the rings slid past and the view centred on a speck that expanded as the viewpoint fell towards it. A rough, battered worldlet, its sunward side stamped with two large craters that sat side by side like eye sockets, giving it the appearance of a lopsided skull. A sharper crater below its sockets like an off-centre mouth open in a gape of surprise. Its forehead rising to a gently lobed crest. Everywhere pocked with smaller craters, spills of black shadow caught inside their rims. Nothing special. Nothing that would look out of place amongst the icy worldlets of the Archipelago.

The Horse explained that it was a co-orbital moon, sharing a very similar orbit with another moon of a similar size. The moon in the lower orbit travelled faster than the one in the higher orbit, and when the first caught up with the second they swapped positions: the second moon drew away from the first, travelling along its new, lower and faster orbit until it caught up with the first moon and they swapped again. This moon, Janus, was where the ship came from. In fact, the ship had been part of Janus, at one point. A chunk that had been carved out of it and grew mass-driver motors and separated and slowly accelerated away and kept accelerating, until it had climbed out of the gravity well of its parent planet and then the gravity well of the Homesun.

'At a point just beyond the outer edge of the Homesun's Kuiper Belt it dropped laser stations it had fabricated, and grew sails that the lasers pushed against,' the Horse said. 'Perhaps the stations failed at some point; perhaps the sails were damaged or fell into disrepair. For whatever reason, its journey took far longer than it should have.'

'And its passenger? This gene wizard?'

'That's where it gets very interesting. She was an enemy of the Ghosts. She helped to drive them from the Solar System long ago, in the second pan-system war.'

'Even if she were still alive, it does not mean that she would be a friend to us.'

'Or to the Quicks. But they hoped she would be. The people watching for her ship.'

'They hoped she'd save them from the enemy, and from us.'

'They hoped she would save you from yourselves.'

'So they were wreckers of a kind,' I said.

'I prefer to think of them as dreamers,' the Horse said.

'And Yakob Singleton took them down. And no doubt tortured the location of this hell from one or all of them.'

'It's stranger than that. Yakob Singleton and his people had been watching them, hoping some bigger fish would swim into their shoal. A Quick dedicated to violent overthrow of the tyranny of the True, that kind of thing. Several of the cult were in their pay, and Yakob was the one controlling them. And one day all the cultists were killed. They met together and died together.'

'Who killed them? A rival group?'

'They attacked each other with broken furniture and their hands and feet and teeth. It was a bloody massacre, famous in certain circles. There was a cover-up, of course. The massacre was blamed on a rival group, everyone supposedly in that rival group was disappeared, and that was that.'

'They found something. A hell. And a demon got out.'

'Probably more than one, given how the cultists died.'

'The same hell that Yakob Singleton opened up, just before he vanished. The one we're going to harrow.'

'It's good, solid information,' the Horse said. 'Well worth the price of these fine clothes. Not that you paid for them, of course.'

'And how can you be sure you weren't fed an elaborate piece of fiction?'

I knew very well that the Quicks who performed or drudged in the Permanent Floating Market were bent and twisted by their work. They wanted to be like Trues and they hated us and wanted us gone from their city and their worldlets with equal and opposite force. They lived fast and high: drinking and drugging when not working; dancing to wild music played by musicians who came straight from performing degraded versions of 'traditional' Quick music to entertain Trues; betting on free-form wrestling matches and duels with all kinds of bladed weapons. Trues flocked to the fair to sample this kind of colour and raw authenticity, but it was in truth a poor and twisted reflection of our own appetites, our own corruptibility. It was a commonplace that you could buy anything you wanted in the Permanent Floating Market if you had the credit, but you could never guarantee that you would get what you hoped for.

But although I wasn't entirely convinced about the Horse's story, it was no surprise to learn that there was more to Yakob Singleton's work than I'd been told. It was all of a piece with his mother's desire to manipulate and control me. She'd caught me off guard by pretending to be one of her own flunkeys; she'd asked me to tell the story about the demon when she already knew all about it, and had matched the sunset of the biome where we'd met to the sunset of the Library in an obvious piece of psychological manipulation. And, of course, she'd sent her niece to keep watch over me.

The Horse pretended to be insulted, saying that he might have lost his edge while working out in the boonies and rough edges of the Archipelago, but he was no easy mark for peddlers of grey information.

'You do have experience in that area,' I said.

'And you're protected and sheltered by the Library, and by the narrow focus of your work. The only people you meet are officials worried that they will be held accountable for an intrusion by enemy forces, and soldiers half-scared to death that they'll be turned by demons. They might not be pleased to see us, but they need our skills. And we use them to fight in simple conflicts. Good versus evil. Light versus dark. Us versus demons. But Yakob Singleton was involved in something far more ambiguous. Anyway, whether or not you believe it, I've told you all I learned, which is all my informant could be persuaded to tell me. If it doesn't satisfy you, I understand completely, because it doesn't satisfy me. But there it is.'

I thought about it. 'Yakob Singleton found evidence that this ancient ship is still functioning, still travelling towards Fomalhaut. Something the mystery cult discovered. Something in this hell we've been sent to harrow. He quit his job because he did not want to give it up to this mysterious department, or to the Office of Public Safety. He wanted it for himself. Or for his poor downtrodden family . . .'

The Horse said, 'It's a nice story. Why don't you tell it to your new friend, and ask her if any of it is true?'

'She may not know any more than me.'

'Oh, I doubt that. She's family. You aren't.'

'That's another reason why I don't want to ask her. Because this is caught up with Yakob Singleton's family history. His mother made that quite plain. This isn't just about finding an errant son. She thinks that he found something valuable, too – something that could give his family some advantage, and help it to win back its place in the clan hierarchy. We can't allow ourselves to be involved in that, because it would seem that my clan is taking sides in the affairs of another.'

'There's so little difference between all of you,' the Horse said. 'Yet you make so much of it.'

'Yes, why can't we all just get along, like the Quick? How is that working out for you, by the way?'

'I can see why we've been chosen for this. We have the experience, but we are also expendable.'

'We're here to do a job. We'll do that. No more, no less. If we find something that might explain where Yakob Singleton has gone, then it will be a bonus. But his mother can deal with it.'

The Horse smiled. 'Get in, get out, move on.'

'It's worked for us so far. I appreciate the effort you put in to finding out about Yakob Singleton. It maps out problems and complications we must avoid. But in the end this is just another job.'

'There's another complication we haven't considered yet,' the Horse said. 'Lathi Singleton sent us to harrow the hell that her son found, but the Office of Public Safety may have a claim on it too.'

Prem Singleton found me after the ship had completed deceleration and was beginning its final approach to T. I was in an empty bubble in the outer layer. Its external surface was completely transparent. T was a lumpy speck revolving in a stately circle off to starboard, and because it was high above the plane of the ecliptic as well as at the leading edge of the Archipelago, there was nothing but stars beyond. I'd killed the bubble's lights and it seemed that I floated amongst a sea of stars: bright stars and stars dim as dust, stars of all colours. I was so absorbed in them, and scions were making so much noise close by, that I didn't see or hear Prem Singleton enter until she eclipsed a segment of the starry sky, asking me if I was ready for work.

I said that I was, and hoped that she was too.

'What we're doing here, that doesn't count as work. My real work is at Cthuga,' Prem said.

'The demons that my clan and I face come from the Ghosts,' I said. 'We fight the enemy just as your clan does.'

'You fight for the past. We fight for the future.' Although she had been partying with her fellow scions ever since the ship had departed from Thule, she did not seem drunk or stoned at all. She spoke lightly, but with a determination I hadn't heard before. As if she was at last talking about something she felt strongly about. 'I should be going out there with my cousins. Going back to the war. They don't know what they're getting into, and I do. They're so young . . . I mean, some of them are a lot older than me, but they don't know anything really. How old are you? Eighteen, nineteen?'

I translated my age into the obsolete measurement that the Singletons and the other founder clans still used. 'A little over twenty years,' I said.

'I suppose you'd say six hundred and thirty megaseconds. Why do you use that metric, by the way?'

'The work we do is clocked at speeds best measured in seconds and fragments of seconds, Majistra.'

'We're almost the same age, however you measure it. Could practically be twins. Chronologically, I mean. But in every other way I'm so much older than you, and my cousins. I feel as if I aged a million years, out there. And now it's their turn to go naked into that good night. Which is why our army is in such poor shape. Officers gain experience in the field, but they aren't allowed to practise it if they survive. No, we have to make way for a new wave of volunteers, with no continuity of experience and operational knowledge. It means that each new generation of officers can vigorously apply innovative tactics and techniques, but it also means that we never learn from our mistakes, and our tactics are driven by short-term thinking. And too often by whatever sentiments are current in the dominant clans, rather than by strategic needs. And meanwhile the enemy never rests, is always driving forward.'

This was so perilously close to wrecker talk that I thought it best to say nothing.

'You know what's funny?' Prem said. 'There is continuation, of a kind, in the Quicks on the front line. Most new recruits die almost at once, but those who survive get to serve directly as adjuncts for officers. Who if they have any sense, if *they* want to survive, listen very closely to their seasoned adjuncts. Stage one, when you've just arrived, you tell them what needs to be done, ask for their suggestions, then order them to do it that way. That way you might last long enough to get to stage two, when you tell them what has to be done and how to do it, and if they suggest a different way of doing things, then that's how you roll instead.' She turned to look at me, her profile a charcoal sketch against the starlight. 'How do *you* roll, by the way?'

I had to ask her what she meant.

'How do you and your kholop decide what to do?'

123

'I suppose I might be at a version of your stage two. I tell him what to do, and if he suggests an alternative I think about it and decide whether we do it my way or his.'

'That's what you were doing earlier, down in the hole.'

'We were wondering how to deal with you,' I said.

Prem laughed. 'I bet you were, too. Does that come with the package? Your pathological honesty?'

'We try to tell our clients the truth. Sometimes that involves telling them something they don't want to hear.'

'Mmm. You know, I can't tell if you're a noble man for whom truth is paramount, or a fool who doesn't know how to tell a lie when necessary.'

'Perhaps there's little difference between the two.'

'Help me decide. Tell me what you think I don't want to hear. No, don't bother. Because I know. You're worried that I will interfere with your exorcism or harrowing of Yakob's hell. That I might do something that will put you in danger. Or even worse, stop you fulfilling the contract you made with Lathi. Well, no need to worry. Lathi may not trust you, but I do. Why? Because you have an ideal of honour so old-fashioned that it might have been handed down on a tablet of stone by the very hand of the One God.'

'I'll take that as a compliment.'

'Why not? Maybe that's what it's meant to be. And besides all that, I have other things to do, and you'll have other things to worry about. Worse things than me getting in the way of your spells and incantations.'

It wasn't until we arrived at T that I realised what she meant.

3

The small blister of the observation post was divided into two levels and each level was divided into several compartments. Judging by the number of sleeping niches, it had been meant to house a crew of at least two Trues and sixteen Quick, but Ori had it all to herself. She'd been born and raised in a crowded nursery in the Whale, and when she was five she'd started work in the Whale's busy upper levels. And even working out on the skin of the Whale, she'd always been surrounded by other bots and immersed in the background chatter of the crew. Now, apart from the post's AI and the passenger in her head, which had withdrawn into the unseeable darkness at the back of her skull, there was no living person, True or Quick, within twenty kilometres of her, and she was a very long way down the length of the cable, at about the furthest reach of the train. Far below the stratosphere where the Whale floated, far beyond Inas and everyone she had ever known, in the upper region of a searing calm of hydrogen and helium gas that was some two thousand kilometres deep, growing hotter and more and more compressed as it reached down to the zone where helium began to rain out, and beyond that the zone where hydrogen gradually changed from liquid to gas. A vast featureless layer stratified only by temperature and pressure.

It was utterly dark in every direction, interrupted only by the running lights of the construction trains that went past with monotonous regularity, rising out of the darkness below or falling out of the darkness above. A machine activity that required no intervention and could continue for decades or centuries after human tenants quit the Whale. Ori soon learned to ignore it. She had her own work to do.

It was exactly like the work she had practised over and over in virtuality, and in truth the AI did most of it, scanning a broad volume around the observation post and monitoring the white noise of the planet's electrical and magnetic fields for anomalous signals, sorting and cataloguing them, sending anything of interest up the pipe to the train. Ori was little more than a spark of organic intelligence dangling in the hot compressed darkness for the delectation of whatever might come cruising by. Meat on a hook. She dropped sondes and other one-shot probes manufactured in great quantity by the post's makers, and she launched hot-hydrogen ballonets that were tethered to the post by monofilament lines kilometres long and went floating off on impalpable currents, lights pulsing and flashing in what Commissar Doctor Pentangel and his crew of philosopher-soldiers believed to be mathematically intriguing patterns. She used the station's laser arrays, too, cutting the dark with calibrated beams, or lighting up the flank of the cable with vast pulsing displays. And every day she fired up one of the drones and took it out into the dark.

The station's AI instructed her in the use and deployment of all this equipment, admonished her if she did too little, rewarded her with sweet or tangy treats when she matched the parameters set for each activity. It wasn't much company, the AI. Exhibiting zero affect, responding only when it was absolutely necessary. Its voice at once halting and monotonous, a mechanical parody of human speech. Ori had met more personable floor cleaners. And there was no direct line to the Whale. All communication went through the AI, and it would not relay any kind of personal message.

She did her best to stay alert and disciplined, and established a routine on which she could peg passing time, but that routine soon began to drift. She spent a considerable part of her downtime trying to communicate with her passenger. Talking to it, trying to centre herself inside her own head, trying to draw it out. It was there, she could feel it, but it was silent and still. A watcher in the dark, just like her.

Once, she grew so frustrated by its mocking silence that she began to scream at it. Pacing up and down, smacking her head with her fists, shouting. Daring it to come out. Threatening to harm herself if it didn't. When she began to bang her head against a bulkhead the station's AI puffed tranquilliser into the air, and Ori woke several hours later with a parched mouth and a bad headache and a vile sense of shame.

She lost herself in reveries about the life she'd left behind. Inas. Falling asleep in each other's arms. Waking beside her. Her touch and

her smell. Her rough laugh, her tender gaze. Their conversations about
the small change of life in the commons, over a meal, over a pipe. The
way her bot moved, out on the skin of the Whale. The way they worked
together and the way they lived together. Inas had told Ori to forget all
that, but she couldn't.

And at all times she could feel the hot dark pressing in on the
diamond-fullerene blister of the dome: a stifling claustrophobia that
came in slow, heavy waves. There was little relief to be had from riding
the drone. The cable was the only point of reference, a vertical line
studded with little lights that gleamed starkly against the absolute
darkness, dwindling away above and below. Beyond it, despite the
drone's navigation package, which conjured a grid precise to the nearest
centimetre from the planet's magnetic field, the darkness had no
dimension. A void without form or meaning. An ocean of night that
could at any moment pinch shut her little bubble of air and light.

On her first excursion, she circled the cable and moved up and down
it, discovering that the observation post was set to one side of a larger
structure, one of the garage depots used by the machines that had first
extended the cable into the upper edge of the gas giant's hydrogen
sea. A rack of low half-cylinders clamped to the flank of the cable,
several of them extending horizontal platforms and spars. Everything
was still, empty, quiet. Abandoned in place. One of the cylinders was
still pressurised and its heat pumps were still working, maintaining
its interior at a comfortable twenty degrees centigrade. Ori liked to
check it on her way out and on her way back in, scan for motion inside.
Without conscious thought she elaborated a fantasy that it was inhabited by a hermit of fabulous age who had elected to exile herself
there, as hermits did in the glory days before the True had arrived.

There was a hatchway in the floor of one of the compartments of the
post. It was sealed, and the AI refused to explain its purpose. Ori began
to wonder if it opened on to a passage that ran through the interior of
the cable to the garage depot. Sometimes, at night, she woke convinced
that she could hear a faint scratching under the floor, or felt that
someone had been standing over her. She'd flood the dome with light,
her heart hammering, her skin clammy, and look everywhere for the
intruder. The AI was no help, claiming that it did not monitor the
interior of the post.

'That is not my function.'

'Can you do it?'

'That is not my function.'

'But can you do it if I asked you to do it?'

'I am not able to act on your request.'

Sometimes Ori would lie across the hatch, with her ear pressed to it. Hearing nothing but the whisper of blood cells jostling through the capillaries of her inner ear. She stuck hairs across the fine, almost invisible joint between floor and hatch. Wondered if she could somehow bring a sonde through the airlock and have it watch her while she slept.

She knew that these fantasies were dangerous. An expression of her deep desire for escape. And she knew that she was being watched. That if she deviated from expected behaviour patterns or failed to carry out her assigned tasks she would face the long drop. But she couldn't help going through the routine of checking the hatch every morning, of swinging past the abandoned depot on her way out and on her way back, and by and by began to fabricate another fantasy: that the sprite which had ridden with her would find her again. They had a connection, after all, that was why she had been recruited. Perhaps this connection, impalpable yet unbreakable, would draw the sprite to her, and its manifestation would redeem her weakness. She would prove that she was unique, a lightning rod for the ineffable. The sprite would come to her, and she would bind it. She wasn't sure how, but first she had to make sure that it could find her. She had to call to it. Pierce the veil of the unforgiving dark.

Now that she had a purpose, she worked with vigour. Drawing up tables and schedules of activity, making sure that random patterns were truly random, and thinking up patterns that were obviously patterns by basing them on sequences of prime numbers. She tried to imagine what sprites wanted. Why they were drawn to Quicks. Why that one particular sprite had been drawn to her.

Like all her sisters, Ori could call up memories and examine them as a True might examine a picture. She fell inside herself many times, conjuring the chain of stark bright instants that had begun when the probe had pitched away from the launch cradle. Turning everything over and around. Looking at the way the bot had been splayed on the probe, at the moves she'd made, and the moves she hadn't made. She went out and duplicated that dying fall, letting the drone drop as far as she dared, until at around a hundred and fifty kilometres below the obervation post the limits of the little machine's tolerances were reached and she had to pull up before it was crushed and incinerated by increasing temperature and pressure.

She did this over and again. Falling close to the cable and at varying distances from it. Falling silently. Falling while broadcasting patterns. But still she saw nothing, and if the AI sifted anything unusual from the planet's radio noise, the rest of the electromagnetic spectrum, subtle shifts in atmospheric circulation around the cable, and all the other parameters it was monitoring, it did not tell her. It would not even tell her if anyone else had ever seen a sprite here. Ori supposed that they must have done, for although sprites were uncommon, they were not rare. And she also began to think that her failure to spot any manifestation or detect any other evidence of unusual activity was in itself significant. That the absence of any activity was useful evidence was her only hope of passing this test.

She took the drone out and tried again.

And again.

And again.

One night she dreamed a dream of floating outside the observation post. She was not riding a drone, but she was somehow present. A viewpoint without form or dimension hung a little way from the vertical stroke of the cable. She could see the cable perfectly well, and the rack of the garage's half-cylinders, and the blister of the post, which was crowned with flickering light. Sprites, circling like dancers joined hand to hand. There were too many to count, but Ori felt that there was only one, stitched through brief intervals of time, joining hands with itself. Flickering in and out. She tried to move towards it and could not, and woke on the hard pad of her sleeping niche, dim light brightening as she sat up. She called up a window that showed an external view of the observation post and clicked from camera to camera but saw nothing unusual. Curves and angles ghostly in infrared against grainy dark. Frames of still life. She ran them backwards, and saw nothing. Knowing that she was being stupid, knowing that it had been a dream, and even if it had been real the cameras wouldn't show anything. She called up other records, found no nodes of magnetic activity or electromagnetic spikes. A hump in background noise as a train went by, nothing else.

She was fully awake now. The hypnogogic state where anything seemed possible had dwindled away. Everything was no more than itself. The clean bare walls, the stalk of a stool by the kitchen shelf and the square black box of the maker, her hands, the passenger inside her skull, in the dark behind her eyes, behind the place where she lived.

'What do you want?' she said, startling herself, and the AI asked her what she meant.

'I want to check something.'

She sent a drone out. The lights of the cable rising above, dwindling away below. The dark all around, and the thing she hadn't noticed before, shifting cells of different shades of darkness, all sizes, swarming around each other like the patterns she saw when she closed her eyes. She watched them for a long time. She tried and failed to crossmatch and correlate them with the drone's instrumentation.

The darkness was alive, and only she could see it.

'All right,' she said to her passenger. 'All right. Now show me something else.'

4

Vidal Francisca's steady and indefatigable campaign to woo Maria
Hong-Owen had been strengthened by his having saved her daughter
from an unimaginably gruesome fate at the hands of wildsiders, but
he still had much to do. He was a vain man, but he was not stupid, and
knew that Maria could not be won over by trivial favours and gifts.
Instead, he persuaded her to join his committee of concerned citizens,
which had got up a militia that patrolled the streets of the town at night,
liaised with the army and the R&R Corps, and doled out shelters,
cooking implements, sleeping bags and other essentials to refugees. The
committee also supplied extra medical supplies to the hospital, which
was now working at full stretch to cope with the additional problems
caused by the influx of refugees. There had been an outbreak of a
vomiting sickness: dozens of young children were being brought to the
hospital with high fevers and dangerous levels of dehydration. Many
of the refugees had serious endemic health problems, too. Parasites,
genetic problems that needed therapies the hospital couldn't provide,
syndromes associated with old age that were likewise untreatable . . .
Maria said that it was as if they were back in the twentieth century,
before modern medicine had been developed.

Rumours and counter-rumours about the campaign against the
wildsiders swept through the little town. Every fresh arrival brought
new horror stories. Wildsiders had set up an ambush on the Trans-
Amazonian highway and destroyed thirty road trains, setting fire to
them and shooting anyone who tried to escape. They strung the ears of
their victims in grisly necklaces. They honoured those of their comrades
killed in combat by eating part of them, and before going into battle
drank blood taken from captives kept especially for the purpose. Their

women were worse than their men, and tortured and humiliated soldiers with degrading sexual rites. They were savages, soul-drinkers, spirits of the forest come to take revenge on despoilers. And so on, and so on.

Ancient propaganda ripped from the matrices of the ship's files, redeployed against the intruder into the Child's dream of her becoming.

The R&R Corps had stopped all work and dismantled its front-line camps in the forest; only a skeleton crew remained in its depot. The army set up forward positions along the main highway, flitters and drones flew regular patrols above the renewed forest to the north, patrols scouted the hills and the lower slopes of the mountains, and plastic scout boats voyaged up and down the river, all to little purpose. The enemy was mostly unseen, setting traps and ambushes, engaging in brief fierce firefights and abruptly slipping away. It was like fighting ghosts. The army sustained casualties on a daily basis, but although it was certain that the enemy had been hit hard on several occasions no bodies were ever found.

Vidal Francisca hired a crew of mercenaries to protect the sugar-cane plantation. They were from the north, some with skin no different in colour from the browns and blacks of ordinary people, some pale as ghosts. One, a young woman, had red hair and bright blue eyes and freckled skin. Something that the Child had never before seen. It was interesting how very small variations in people's genetic make-up could have such a pronounced effect on their appearance, and on other people's attitude towards them.

Most of the mercenaries spoke little or no Portuguese, but they were quiet, efficient, and unfailingly polite. They patrolled the perimeter of the plantation and checked its buildings, escorted Vidal Francisca wherever he went, the man riding in his electric car in his white suit and straw hat like some minor potentate, and they escorted the Child and her mother whenever they travelled the short distance from the hospital to Vidal Francisca's house. They wore tunics and many-pocketed trousers that were pale green in default mode and when activated bent light around the wearer, turning them into human-shaped distortions like the mirages that shivered above the roads in the bright hot afternoons. Mostly, they sat around the utility barn where they bunked down and had set up an immersion tank that showed a panoptic view of the plantation and the surrounding area, patched from drones which whispered high above.

The mercenaries tolerated the Child's questions, let her play with the tank. The red-haired woman, Sara, showed her how to strip down her pistol and put it back together. It had two fat short barrels side by side and fired what Sara called SARs – slow autonomous rounds. They were the size of honey bees, possessed a propulsion system based on two chemicals that generated volumes of hot gases when mixed together, sprouted fins that could alter their trajectory, and were different colours according to the load they carried. One kind burst in sticky nets; another delivered powerful electric shocks; a third carried a mix of fluorescent dye and a chemical that according to Sara smelled like a corpse that had been kept in a trash can in the full sun for a week.

'The dye and the stink are hard to wash off, so we can track and identify the bad guys if they get away,' Sara told the Child. 'If they're stupid, they run back to their friends. And so by letting one fish go we catch many more.'

The mercenaries had weapons that fired deadly rounds, too, and the plantation's perimeter was sown with smart pop-up mines and patrolled by armed drones. But it was better, Sara explained, to take down any intruders with non-lethal weapons. 'We need to know what their disposition is. How they travel, how many of them there are, what kind of weapons they have, how many days of food and water they have, what their morale is like. All that stuff.'

'But you haven't found any yet.'

'They know we're here. And they know that we have better weapons than the army. So they keep away from us. Which tells us what?'

'They're smart.'

'Also that they have good intel. From people embedded in the town, most likely.'

Sara spoke fair Portuguese, and was patient and good-humoured. She pretended to be interested when the Child talked about her small menagerie and the cell cultures she looked after, and she answered as best she could the Child's questions about the north, and the mercenary life.

One day, the army mounted a big counterattack in the hills on the other side of the Rio Negro. Many of the townspeople climbed to the top of the Fortaleza hill to watch. They made an event of it. Picnics and barbecues, a small maracatú band. The Child went up there with Ama

Paulinho and her family. People ate and drank and watched as, beyond the small grid of the town laid out across the promontory, beyond the bend of the river and the low slopes of forest, army flitters manoeuvred above hilltops and poured down streams of tracer-laced rounds or shot off drones that flew in long and controlled arcs towards unseen targets, terminating in satisfying eruptions of red flame and smoke. The Child used a pair of field glasses that she had liberated from Vidal Francisca's house. At maximum magnification, their infrared feature showed tiny white shapes moving up the dry hills – soldiers, sweeping for any of the enemy who might have survived the aerial bombardment.

Gradually, a pall of smoke from explosions and fires set in the dry forest spread out and obscured the lower slopes of the hills. As the setting sun glowered through layers of smoke, cruise missiles began to slam into the tops of the hills and the folded valleys between, a chain of explosions that sent columns of black smoke rising high into the hot still air. And then fighters from the base in Barcelos screamed in from the east, flying between the hills and the mountains and flashing in the sun's red light as they tore through columns and veils of smoke. Six, eight, twelve of them. Raptors, according to one of Ama Paulinho's cousins. As the thin shriek of their engines reached the watchers on the Fortaleza hill, fire erupted in their wake, a long curtain of orange flame boiling through the folded landscape, falling back before flaring up again with renewed strength.

'That's that for the poor bastards,' the cousin said, and along the brow of the Fortaleza hill people clapped and cheered, and the maracatú band struck up a military polka.

The fires on the hills across the river burned all night, and a filthy snow of carbon flakes fell on São Gabriel da Cachoeira. The next day, army patrols combed the blackened hills across the river, and found not a single corpse. And so we continued our war against the intruder.

Meanwhile, the Child was preoccupied with her own private war. It was clear that Vidal Francisca was conducting his campaign of seduction on several fronts. Even Ama Paulinho was being seduced. Vidal Francisca had persuaded her father to join his committee of concerned citizens, and several of her cousins patrolled with the militia.

The Child, having learned hard lessons about power and the psychology of seduction, the uses of flattery and engaging self-interest, of indirectly buying your way into someone's trust, of giving to receive, tried to make herself useful. She devised plans to test the river water for parasites and pathogens, drew up schemes to plant out gardens in what had been the futbol field to augment the refugees' diet, and created a virtual prototype of a simple culture system for a tweaked strain of chlorella algae rich in vitamins and essential amino acids. She knew that these schemes would work, they were timely, they could save lives, but nothing came of them because she was a child, and no one took her seriously. Not even her mother, who praised her for her hard work, and said that she should focus all that energy on her education. Even worse, her mother showed the plans to Vidal Francisca, who showered the Child with unwelcome and patronising flattery about her intelligence and vivid imagination.

At last, the Child finally mustered the necessary amount of courage to put the question she absolutely needed to ask. One pleasantly warm sunny morning at breakfast, she asked her mother if she was going to marry Vidal Francisca.

Her mother's reaction was completely unexpected. She laughed.

The Child persisted. Now she was set on the path, she would see it through to the end. Saying, 'It's as if you are already married.'

Her mother looked at her with sober appraisal. 'Because he acts as if he owns me, you mean.'

'Because you spend so much time with him.'

It was as close as she could come to asking about whether or not her mother and Vidal Francisca were sleeping together. The idea sat inside her like a cold stone.

Her mother said, using a soft and reasonable tone of voice that the Child hadn't heard for some time, 'Do you know what emancipation means?'

'It's what happened to the slaves. They were freed from bondage. From the power of others.'

'As were women. Once upon a time, women were the equals of men. Not only by law, although that was important, and the result of many hard-fought and difficult battles. But also by culture and by custom. Men came to accept that women should have the same rights of self-determination that they enjoyed. But then there was the Overturn, and the great crisis caused by sudden and catastrophic climate change. Famines, resource wars and plain ordinary wars. The collapse of the global economy and shifts in power.'

'People went up to the Moon.'

'The rich, yes.'

'They fled to places like New Zealand at first,' the Child said. She wanted to show that she knew all about history. 'Places that weren't badly affected by the Overturn. But there were too many refugees, so they went to the Moon. And then to Mars and to the moons of Jupiter and Saturn. We had a war with Mars.'

'Yes, we did. And on Earth there was a war between men and women. And women lost. You won't see it in the history texts, but it is true all the same. As true and real as any war fought over boundaries or oil or water,' the Child's mother said. 'Women were free, and then they were not free.'

'We're free now, aren't we? And the president, she's a woman. She rules over everyone, man and woman.'

'She was the wife of the president before her,' the Child's mother said. 'When he died, it was useful to her family and his family that she took his place and continued to rule as he had. Continued to make sure that his policies and political positions were upheld. Also, she is very intelligent, and as cruel and ruthless as any man. She removed enemies who opposed her, and she married again so that she would seem to be under the nominal control of a man. Although her second husband is, like her first, much weaker than her. An exceptional woman in every way, yes. But hardly typical.

'In times of crisis, the strong always take control of the weak. They are no longer constrained by law or by custom. They claim that they are protecting the weak, but they are in truth exploiting them. Using them. That's what happened during the Overturn. The rich went to the Moon and abandoned the poor, here on Earth. And in Greater Brazil and elsewhere, democracy was overthrown. Gangsters took over, with the help of the military. Foreign interests. Although by then, the difference between the two was hard to distinguish. And that was the end of democracy, and two centuries of enlightenment and emancipation. Women were no longer partners of men. They became the property of men. Keepers of the houses of men. Incubators of the children of men. With no rights to property of their own, or to the children they gave birth to.'

'Why? Why did they let it happen?'

'They didn't. Men took control by force. As men do, when unrestrained by what we like to call civilisation. Not all men, but a majority. Because they are stronger. Because they are unencumbered by

136

pregnancy and maternal instinct. Because they are fundamentally irrational, by the standards of civilisation. Biological imperative makes them so, as biological imperative makes us irrational, in a different way. But we are smarter than men. Do you know why?'

'Men don't need to be smart if they are strong.'

'It's true. We must live by our wits. As the dispossessed must always do.' Then the Child's mother did something she rarely did, these days. Leaned across the table and took the Child's hands in hers and looked into the Child's face. Saying, 'Always remember that. Whatever happens. Remember that we are smarter.'

There.

That's done, at last.

The lesson the Child never forgot. The golden thread that ran through the warp and weft of her life. Inextricably bonded with her mother's anxious gaze and her tight dry grip, the sunlight slanting through the window and falling on the table's breakfast clutter.

The Child had talked about these things with her mother before, of course. She had been brought up in what was then called the old liberal tradition to believe that she was as good as anyone else, to believe that rank did not confer any especial intellectual or moral privilege, to believe that everything should be questioned, and nothing accepted until it had been throughly examined. But later in her life, whenever she thought of her mother and the things her mother had taught her, she always recalled that moment. It was the archetype of many such moments. So lives are shaped backwards, by what we choose to re-member.

Maria let go of the Child's hands now, leaning back, saying, 'War changes everything. It shifts the balance from intelligence to strength and the willingness to solve problems by violence. That's how it is here, you see. War makes it so, always.'

The Child thought about it, and said, 'Daddy wasn't like that.'

'He was enlightened. It was coming back, enlightenment among men. And I was lucky to meet one who was more enlightened than most.'

'Vidal Francisca isn't like Daddy.'

Her mother looked at her for a long moment, then said, 'He thinks he is. He thinks that what he is doing is for the best. The best for me, and for you.'

'So you won't marry him,' the Child said, completing her chain of logic.

'I'm protected,' her mother said. 'Because I'm a widow. If I was not, things might be different. As it is, Vidal must respect the memory of your father. Why? Because in a way I am still the property of your father, as far as Vidal is concerned. He can never completely own me because in his view I am already claimed.'

This didn't entirely satisfy the Child. She wanted to believe her mother, but her suspicion and fear ran too deep. She believed that her mother had betrayed her own principles, had sought the help of Vidal Francisca because, despite all she'd said, she couldn't protect herself. She was happier, yes, and the Child was happy that her mother was happy. But around Vidal Francisca her mother wasn't her usual self. She too often talked about silly and trivial things, and listened to the man talk with respect he didn't deserve. She seemed younger, some-how. She paid more attention to her appearance. Vidal Francisca bought her clothes and jewellery and perfume, and although she told him she couldn't wear perfume because of her work – some of the sick couldn't tolerate it – she wore the clothes and jewellery at dinner parties and other social events. Ama Paulinho commented on these changes with approval, but the Child disliked and feared them. Feared the loss of her mother's proud stubborn independence, and the loss of her own freedom.

The Child vowed again that she would never marry. That she would never allow herself to be encumbered by children. That she would prove herself better than any man. She would protect herself. She would need no one but herself; she would never bind herself to any man. And for a long time she had kept to that vow, until she'd quickened an illegal clone in her own womb and raised him to become a useful ally and accomplice in her dealings with the world. Soon afterwards, out of political expediency, she'd seduced a scion of the Peixoto family and had allowed herself to fall pregnant by natural means. But before they could formalise their relationship her lover had been killed in a silly little action against bandits, and their son had been a grievous disappointment, undisciplined, rebellious, dissipated. She'd had many other children after that, but all were flesh of her flesh and radically tweaked and cut. Cohorts of servants helping her work towards goals they could not understand. We are no more than the latest iteration of her strange and wonderful family, as willing and unworthy as all the rest.

The mercenary, Sara, more or less agreed with the Child's mother, saying that while it was true that women fought in the army and worked in manufactories and the R&R Corps alongside men, that did not mean that they were equal.

'When there's something worth having, men make sure they take most or all of it. They don't stop to think about it. As far as they're concerned it's their God-given right.'

'But you are like a man. You fight like a man. You work with them. Don't they see you as a fighter first, and a woman second?'

'I fight as a woman,' Sara said. 'Not as a woman pretending to be a man. You see the difference?'

The Child nodded. She liked that Sara didn't care what other people thought of her. That she stood up for herself against men as well as women.

Sara said, 'In the north, if you are poor and landless, you do what you have to, to survive. Doesn't matter if you're a man or a woman, everyone is in the same shit, with only a few ways out.'

'Men don't try to stop you joining the army?'

'There are more wildsiders in the north. More bandits. And there's trouble in the cities, too. Too many poor people, too much discontent. And the bosses can't get enough of the right kind of men. A lot of women can't hack it, it's true. The job is tough and men are stronger, mostly. Mostly, but not always,' Sara said.

As usual, when she wasn't on patrol, she'd shucked her camo gear and was dressed in shorts and a vest with pockets and pouches that left her arms bare. She flexed her right arm, showing the definition of her muscles, making the snake tattoo that coiled from shoulder to wrist jump.

'Most of the time it's the same old same old. The men pretend to think we're equal, the ones who aren't assholes, but in their heart of hearts, deep down? They know we're not. Because everything around them feeds that unconscious assumption, and they're blind to their own faults. The only time it doesn't matter what equipment you're packing between your legs is when you're in the shit. All that matters then is that you can do what needs to be done, and that your buddies are watching your back, just like you're watching theirs.' Sara paused, then said, 'Your mother mind, you hanging with us rough tough soldiers? Listening to us talk dirty like this?'

'She doesn't care what I do,' the Child said, and felt a sudden pang of sorrow because she realised that she believed it.

＊

On the nights that her mother visited Vidal Francisca straight after finishing her work at the hospital, the Child stayed behind with Ama Paulinho. Her ama went to bed early and slept soundly, and the Child often climbed on to the roof of the bungalow and looked up at the stars or watched the lights of the town flicker amongst the trees. Dreaming of escape. One night, a week or so after her talk with her mother, she was sitting cross-legged in the warm dark when she felt a presence behind her and turned. A figure stood on the edge of the roof. He was slight and bare-chested, dressed in ragged trousers tied at his waist with a rope, and he had the head of a jaguar.

The Child felt her heart catch. Felt a cool electric tide rise inside her. Felt the hairs on the back of her neck and the soft down on her forearms stand up. She got to her feet, moving slowly and carefully, as if he was an animal that might take fright. Tried to speak and found her mouth was dry. Swallowed, tried again.

'Who are you? What do you want?'

The boy raised his hands to the height of his chest, held them out on either side, palms up. As if cupping invisible weights.

The Child said, 'Can you understand what I'm saying?'

The boy moved his strange sleek head up and down.

The Child glanced at the little screen on her wrist. She had by then hacked into the hospital's security. She could see herself in infrared but could see no trace of the boy at all. But there he was.

'Are you a wildsider?'

The boy moved his head from side to side.

'Did they make you? Did you escape from them? Where did you come from?'

The boy shook his head again, and stepped up on to something unseen and climbed into the sky on invisible corkscrew steps, turning faster and faster until he was a tiny pale blur shooting away into the zenith of the starry sky to a place where we could not follow him.

The next morning, waking in her bed, the Child wondered if she'd dreamed the encounter, but she had the distinct memory of sitting up on the roof for a long time afterwards, watching the rigid span of stars that glittered and twinkled overhead, and the swift points of satellites and ships moving from west to east. She'd stayed there until she heard the noise of a vehicle outside the hospital compound wall, realised that her mother had returned from Vidal Francisca's house, and quickly climbed down into her bedroom. And then, yes, fell asleep: but only then.

She used the back door she'd inserted into the hospital's security and reviewed the footage. Saw herself, sitting on the roof, standing, talking. Played the segment again, zooming in on her face. She was awake. Her eyes were open. Blinking. She looked scared, more scared than she remembered feeling. Looking up, as if following something as it rose. Yes. Exactly as she remembered, except there was no trace of the boy.

We could find no trace of him, either. He had appeared before the Child, and then he had vanished through a back door – and that had vanished, too. We had conjured up a small action against wildsiders to make sure that the Child could not leave the town, and thrown up strong defences around her, and he had bypassed everything.

The Child's story was beginning to deviate significantly from what was known, and we knew now that the jaguar boy was no glitch but an intruder whose origin and powers and purpose were unknown, but we were in too deep to turn back. The outer edge of the dust belt spanned the sky from horizon to horizon, with Fomalhaut's bright spark caught in its centre. There was not enough time to start over. We had to press on. And so, early one evening in the garden of Vidal Francisca's house, the Child was coming back from her light trap, carrying several choice specimens in cages she'd woven out of dry grass (a skill her ama had taught her), when she heard her mother and Vidal Francisca talking on the terrace. The Child had been walking straight towards the soft glow of the terrace along a path edged with a luminous rope; now she slipped sideways into darkness and moved stealthily across the dark lawn.

She was still buzzing from a dose of her home-brewed stimulant, which had helped her to vanish inside the flickering school of her thoughts for most of the long and boring dinner and the two adults' conversation about things and people the Child had no interest in. Everything around her seemed sharp and slightly separate. The flow of warm air on her skin, blades of grass yielding under her sandals, the heavy flutter of a hand-sized lunar moth in one of the cages at her hip, the scratching of a beetle in another, the whisper of a drone somewhere above the house. A chain of suspended moments like stepping stones across a stream, one yielding to the next as she wove between the trimmed shapes of the bushes planted below the terrace. She pressed the length of her body against warm stone and listened to her mother and Vidal Francisca talking about their plans to visit Manaus, and what to tell the Child, who knew that it was coming, the worst thing, unstoppable.

Soon, everything would change. We would reach our refuge, everything wrong would be made right, and our mother would be made safe until she could rise, renewed. It was our last best contrivance, and we had to engineer it carefully and make sure that every part of it was consistent with the story we had spun round the Child. Meanwhile, we could only hope that the jaguar boy would not come again until we were ready to deal with him.

5

T was the main arsenal for the war effort, the centre of the Archipelago's defences, and a singular body besides: a rocky asteroid that, after it had been ejected from the wreckage of Fomalhaut's inner system, had been captured by the 2:3 orbital resonance with Cthuga shared by the planetoids and worldlets of the Archipelago. It had been smashed apart at least once, and most of the fragments had fallen back together under their own gravity into the shape of a lumpy peanut. The larger of its two lobes was slashed with a long and irregular rift that meandered from pole to equator, its surface was heavily cratered, and the edges of the craters were still raw and sharp.

The Quicks and their machines hadn't touched T, but we had settled on it at the beginning of the first war with the Ghosts, and our mining machines had cut an intricate network of tunnels through its regolith, searching out seams of silicates and traces of metals, and these tunnels were now threaded with adamantine fullerene cables that reinforced the asteroid's structural integrity. Its minor lobe was covered in a sprawling carpet of barracks and manufactories, refineries and graving yards and docks; its major lobe was patched with training grounds of every description, where troops practised infiltration and combat methods in mocked-up habitats and farms. And its deep rift had been roofed over and pressurised and landscaped, creating a habitat where the cadres in charge of T and their families made their homes, and officers and veteran troops, specialists and philosophers, could enjoy their leaves in a variety of sanctioned playgrounds.

All of this had been built by True machines, using True technology. It was the very symbol of our strength, and we were stupidly proud that it had never been attacked.

Our ship made its final approach to T through layers of drones, smart rocks, one-shot gamma and X-ray lasers, kinetic cannon, particle-beam throwers, plasma mines, and strange attractors. As soon as it achieved a parking orbit at the edge of a small cloud of ships large and small, old and new, Prem Singleton and her cousins departed in a small flock of flitters for a barracks and processing centre under the bulging dome that capped T's minor lobe; the Horse and I dropped to the deep rift in the major lobe, where we were met by a crew of troopers and prefects. As was customary, I had informed the authorities that I was coming to T, but when I told the official in command of our reception committee that I would like to get to work as soon as possible, she said that her boss wanted to talk to me, and escorted the Horse and me to a flitter that dropped into the rift. We fell beside a sheer wall of pyroclastic basalts clad in gossamer sheaths of construction diamond, and docked at a skinny building of some twenty storeys that clung to the wall some way above a broad, forested terrace. The Horse was led off by the troopers; I was taken to the office of Marshal Panchaanan, the chief of T's internal security service.

It was a spherical room at the base of the building, with a porthole window that looked out across the gulf of the rift towards the folds and bulges of the far wall. We sat in a nest of cushions in front of that window, the marshal and I, and he served me tea himself and then explained that my services weren't required because the hell had already been harrowed and made safe.

After I'd taken a moment to get past my surprise, I told him that the Library had no record of this. And since only my clan, by custom and contract, could harrow hells, it put both of us in a difficult position.

'That is why your visit piqued our interest,' the marshal said. He was quiet-spoken but his gaze was searching and seriously intelligent. Neat and straightbacked in scarlet uniform tunic and trousers, his black hair swept in a high wave. 'We'd very much like to discuss it with you.'

'I'd very much like to know who you employed to harrow your hell.'

'Bree Sixsmith did the work and reported back to the Library. Don't you wonder why your people didn't tell you? Why they sent you here on a fool's errand?'

'They didn't know the hell had been harrowed because Bree Sixsmith didn't tell them. She couldn't, because she's dead.'

She had committed suicide following an encounter with a demon shelled in a doppelgänger: when she destroyed the doppelgänger, the real demon had been freed and had penetrated her defences and lodged in her mind. This was immediately after my disgrace and for some time many in the Library had believed the demon that had killed Bree was linked to the demon that had killed Arden and Van. Nothing had ever been proved, but it had deepened and darkened the cloud of infamy that clung to me.

After I had explained this, the marshal threw a packet at my security and said, 'Is this her?'

I studied the images, and said that it certainly looked like Bree Sixsmith. There was biometric data too, but I couldn't verify that without checking against records held in the Library, and said so.

'She arrived after we sent the usual notification to the Library,' the marshal said. 'We had no reason not to believe she was other than what she seemed to be.'

'Did you talk directly to someone in the Library, or post the request in the usual fashion? It could have been intercepted. Or it wasn't sent at all. After she harrowed the hell, did you send anyone inside to inspect her work?'

After the slightest pause, the marshal said, 'She provided a full record of her work. She had searched every part of the hell, found nothing of any significance, and sealed it.'

'How do you know that it is not the record from some other harrowing, rather than the record of what she did here? My clan entered into a contract with Lathi Singleton in good faith, Marshal. It was not a task we relished, believing it would cause trouble for us, but we must see it through to completion. I suggest that you contact the Library directly, and do it quickly. Whoever this person is, she was not acting for us, and she might not have done what she claimed to have done. She might have released any demons inside the hell rather than binding them, just to begin with. Talk to the Redactor Svern. If you do not want me to enter this hell, ask him to send someone else. But do it quickly.'

Fortunately, the marshal was neither stupid nor vindictive. He told me that the Horse and I would be allowed access to the hell so long as we provided a full real-time feed, a concession I was happy to make. I would inspect it and do anything necessary to make it safe, and then the marshal would decide how to proceed from there.

'There is one condition. Before you report to Lathi Singleton, you will report to me,' the marshal said.

'You'll see everything we do.'

'But we might not understand all of it. You'll enlighten us afterwards with a full and frank account.'

A posse of troopers and prefects escorted the Horse and me to a busy interchange at the edge of the rift's roof, and a capsule took us at great speed through a rapid-transit tube that cut a long chord beneath T's surface. I told the Horse about my interview with the marshal, and we reviewed the records that one of the prefects gave us and worked up a strategy and prepared our gear. Providing the feed that the marshal had requested was simple enough, but we were still demonstrating it to the prefects when the capsule slowed and drifted into the terminus of the line where, with a thump and a jerk, the airlock at its nose mated with the airlock of the station.

The station was attached to a habitat that was cut into the sheer cliff of the inner face of a crater rim wall and overlooked a level dusty plain that fell away under the naked black sky. Lights raised on tall poles were strung along the roads that criss-crossed the plain, and set around ships that sat in cradles or under domes. It was a junkyard, a cemetery for ships that had been badly damaged in engagements with the enemy, retrieved, and returned to T for inspection and analysis. We passed the wreck of a big corsair, its hull riddled with holes of every size, swung around its stern and the torches of its fusion motors, twisted and warped like mutant flowers by some imaginable flux of energy, and ground on towards another dome.

An ancient Quick pinnace sat inside, an asymmetrical cluster of bubbles scarcely larger than our tractor. One of the prefects told us that it had been part of the first assault on the resurgent Ghosts, a comprehensive disaster that had grievously underestimated the enemy's strength. Every ship had been killed; this one, like many others, had been brought back to T and had sat in the graveyard ever since, until Yakob Singleton and a data miner had boarded it and discovered the hell cached in its mind.

After the Office for Public Safety had discovered what Yakob Single-ton had done, the ship had been isolated, and the hell had been harrowed – or so they thought. Because we had no idea what the person who called herself Bree Sixsmith had actually done, the Horse and I treated it like any other newly discovered hell. We set up a perimeter and sent in probes, and discovered nothing more than a small, low-bit-rate viron barely able to maintain the integrity of the simplest aspects of our avatars. It had not merely been harrowed; it had been collapsed.

'Well, that's that,' the Horse said.

'We'll check everything,' I said.

There was little chance that anything of any significance survived in there, but we tailored our avatars to the viron and went in anyway, emerging at the base of a rectangular block of a building sketched in wire-frame that broke up into blocky pixels when I attempted to increase resolution. All around, similar towers soared up to a sky the colour of a headache, fading away on every side into illimitable mist. Inside the building, the Horse and I climbed a long winding staircase and soon found that it contained a Möbius warp, a twist that between one step and the next returned us to the base of the building. A simple trap of the kind I had demonstrated to Prem Singleton in the training suite, except this one didn't contain a nasty surprise. We climbed back up the staircase and dropped through the twist and started to climb again.

'I'm insulted,' the Horse said.

'That's why we must remain alert. There may be other, more dangerous traps.'

'There isn't enough bit rate to support a child's conjuring trick. This wasn't much to begin with and it's less than nothing now.'

'Lathi Singleton said there was a back door to the Library.'

'If there was, it isn't here any more. We'd see the leakage. How many times are we going to climb this thing?' the Horse said.

We had reached the point at the staircase where the metrical frame of the hell was warped.

'Until I'm satisfied that there's nothing hidden beyond it, and that it doesn't go anywhere else,' I said.

'You won't admit that this has been thoroughly harrowed, will you? That whoever did this was better than you.'

'Better than you, too.'

'All right, let's go around again.'

Eventually, by dumb persistence, the Horse and I discovered an entry point that took us somewhere else: a seemingly limitless level stretching away under a low ceiling supported by squat pillars set at random intervals, where a trace of processing activity yet remained. It wasn't much. A faint irregularity in the low-resolution fabric of the floor, but as significant as a bootprint in the dust of an uninhabited rock.

There had been a doorway here, once. It had been sealed and reduced, there was no way of reconstructing it or finding out where it had led to, but it had been there.

We pulled our avatars out of the hell, collapsed it to the smallest amount of information required to describe it, and archived the kernel inside a secure file. I worked up my report on the return journey to the rift; there was little to it other than the fact that the hell had been made safe, and once had been linked to at least one other viron. The prefects went off to talk to the marshal; the troopers took the Horse and me to the forest that covered a setback terrace halfway down the side of the rift, about two kilometres above the thready ribbon of lights and neon of the rest-and-recreation complex.

The trees grew very tall in T's shallow gravity, their soaring trunks bursting into fluffy clouds of leaves at the very top. They were linked by walkways and ziplines, and shell-like cabins and lodges occupied platforms slung between them or built around their trunks, to house officers and other senior personnel on leave.

The Horse and I were lodged in a cabin little bigger than one of the bubbles of the Quick ship that had brought us to T, high up in the canopy of one of the trees. It was comfortable enough, but it was a jail all the same: because the marshal couldn't prevent me reporting to Lathi Singleton once I left T, he had decided to keep me there until he had discovered who 'Bree Sixsmith' really was, and who she was working for.

The troopers were stationed below the cabin and a small flock of drones and a sentinel net monitored us, but I determined at once that it was easy enough to fool their security, just as my fellow novitiates and I had often fooled the security net of the Permanent Floating Market using gear designed to crack and unriddle the knottier and far more dangerous encryptions of hells and broken networks. Within a few hundred seconds, I had set up illusions of both the Horse and myself, and rendered us invisible to the gaze of the machines – they saw us, but did not register us. We inhabited a floating blind spot.

'That's all very well, but we're still stuck on top of a tree,' the Horse said. 'We can't climb down because troopers occupy the platform below ours, and we can't jump because the fall would be fatal even in gravity as shallow as this. Or do you have wings hidden on your person?'

'I did think about gliding, using fabric ripped from the screens,' I said. 'Then I realised that if we can't climb down this tree, we can climb down another. Or at least, you can. The canopy of this tree meshes with its neighbours.'

'You're closer to a monkey than I am,' the Horse said. 'And even if we escape this tree, we're still on T.'

'So is Prem Singleton. And as luck would have it, I forgot to tell the marshal about her.'

There was a moment when I thought my plan wouldn't work. The Horse clambered along a branch that jutted towards a neighbouring tree, but it grew so thin at its extremity that his meagre weight caused it to bow down through almost ninety degrees. Clinging to it by hands and feet, the Horse looked down and around, glanced up at me and winked, and then threw himself across the gulf, and disappeared in a flurry of foliage.

I sat down and waited, reviewing what we had found in the remnants of the hell, thinking about the implications. A thousand seconds passed, and another thousand, and another. I was pacing to and fro in the confined space of the cabin, looking out in every direction across the treetops, when I saw a flitter racing towards me. For a moment, I thought the marshal's prefects had come to take me away for interrogation; then I realised that it was as invisible to the security net as I was. It came to a crash stop and slid sideways until it rested in the air a pace or so from the entrance to the cabin. Its canopy slid back and the Horse said, 'Where do you want to go?'

6

Ori wrote up her dream and the patterns she'd seen in the darkness as part of her daily report. She told herself not to expect a response, but couldn't help thinking that it would interest the philosopher-soldiers. Perhaps even come to the attention of Commissar Doctor Pentangel. The train would return and take her off-station and return her to the Whale, where she'd be welcomed and rewarded . . .

But it was a feeble little fantasy. The dream had been no more than a dream. The patterns no more than some kind of hallucination. The growing sense of the passenger inside her skull no more than a desire for companionship. None of it verifiable by the AI or by the surveillance system or by any other external test. But the fantasy kept creeping back. Because wasn't subjectivity the point? Wasn't that why she was down here? An observer. An instrument, like any other. It wasn't what she saw. It was about what she thought she saw.

She was used to dealing with practical problems. Fixing things. Real work that had an immediate and obvious effect on the real world. She was good at it, and it was satisfying. Either something worked or it didn't, and if it didn't you thought about it and tried something else and kept at it until it did. But the dream and the change in her perceptions couldn't be unriddled by the rough and ready empirical logic that broke down problems in the world of things into easily understood steps. She'd had the dream, and then she'd found that she could see that the darkness had form. The two things were connected: had to be, because one followed straight after the other. But what was the connection? Was the dream a symptom of the change inside her, or a premonition, or was it some kind of signal? Had her passenger, her secret sharer, sent her a symbolic message while she was asleep because that was the only way it could communicate with her?

Maybe there had been some kind of change in her brain function, but she lacked the apparatus to detect or measure it. In the end, she decided that there was no point worrying about it. If you didn't have the tools to do the job, you could only do what you could with what you had.

Still, she couldn't help wondering whether the others in the other observation stations had been changed in the same way. If they had dreamed the same dream, and found that they could see things in the dark that they hadn't been able to see before.

Three days later, she had another dream. She was walking through the rooms of the observation post, looking for something she needed. She couldn't quite remember what it was, or why finding it was so urgent, but as she searched and searched for it a sense of failure, frustration, and impending doom grew inside her. As if she'd swallowed something smooth and hard and indigestible. It seemed that she searched for a long time, in the dream, and at last found a door she hadn't seen before, its circle outlined by a sliver of violet light. She opened it and saw a white room with a sprite burning in the centre, tall and unwavering and pure and true. Her sprite. It spoke to her, and then she woke up, in the dimness of the observation post, the hum of pumps in the air, on the cool hard floor underneath her.

Somehow she was in a room in the upper level. Lying there, trying to remember what the sprite had told her, the sense of it already gone and the flavour of it fading too, leaving only a feeling of loss. Immense desolation. As if she had glimpsed another, better world, and knew she would never find it again. She told herself to pull herself together. Talking to herself as if she were Inas, telling herself to get up and check every room, find out why she had woken there on the cold hard floor.

She checked every room, and every room was empty. There had been no electromagnetic disturbances inside the observation post, or outside it. It had not been a visitation. It had been a dream. Even though she'd expected it, her sense of loss and loneliness increased another notch. She asked the AI for surveillance records of the last six hours and it opened a window and she fast-forwarded through images of herself asleep until she saw herself stir and sit up. The surveillance showed her clambering from her sleeping niche and wandering from room to room. Moving slowly and uncertainly, as if in a place that was utterly unfamiliar. Her eyes open, searching.

She wrote up a report. She rode a bot outside. The patterns were still there, liminal, shifting, pulsing. Lovely and mysterious and scary and compelling.

Perhaps she was becoming something else. Her mind changing, the way people's bodies changed when they became ill, either from a flaw in themselves, some gene or suite of genes mangled when they'd been quickened, or from a change induced by a random confluence of radiation particle and DNA. They became ill and they couldn't work, and they were culled. It could happen to her. She fell back on her routines, the comfort of work. If she stopped working the AI would cull her. She knew it. Her body would be recycled or it would be given the long drop, and the observation post would receive a new tenant. But as long as she could work she'd be all right.

She dropped sondes. She dropped probes. She launched ballonets and pulsed the dark with laser arrays and flew drones in patterns all around the cable and further out. She did what she'd been told she'd been chosen to do. But she couldn't shake the idea that the real reason she'd been sent to the observation post wasn't anything to do with attracting sprites. No, she'd been locked away down here because she was infected. Because Commissar Doctor Pentangel knew that she would change in dangerous and unpredictable ways, and wanted to study those changes.

One day she woke to find two philosopher-soldiers standing over her. The same pair who'd ejected her from the train, dressed in the same orange tunics under the black straps and joints of their exoskeletons. For a moment she thought she was dreaming, but then she realised that she could smell their sweat, and the warm silicone lubricants of their exoskeletons' little motors.

The train had returned. Her exile was over. It had lasted just twenty-nine days. She had thought it much longer.

As the train ascended towards the Whale, the pair of philosopher-soldiers subjected Ori to an elaborate round of tests, treating her as usual with callous indifference. She endured it, answered their questions as best she could, and at last they told her to get dressed and report upstairs for debriefing.

'This one is unsure about who she should report to,' she said.

'Just go all the way to the top.'

A capsule elevator took her up the spine of the train, past the machinery that recycled air and water, past tanks of spirulina and yeast, to a small crowded garden, lush and green under a glowing ceiling, where Commissar Doctor Wilm Pentangel was waiting for her. He instructed her to tell him everything she could remember about her dreams and not to leave out any detail, no matter how trivial. While she talked, he pottered amongst the plants, tick-tocking stiffly in his exoskeleton, stroking leaves, touching flowers, misting a tangle of roots with a sprayer, nipping off leaves that had browned and shrivelled. His pale face intent under his shock of black hair. The hot dark pressed on the dome above, making the lights inside seem brighter than they were and unreal, as if emphasising the unnaturalness of this garden here, deep inside the furnace heat and pressure of the gas giant's interior, where the train and everyone and everything aboard was alien and out of place.

When Ori finished, there was a long silence. She stood as still as she could, her skin flushed and prickling, feeling uncomfortable and out of place while on the other side of a thin screen of dangling stringy plants the commissar bent like a hinge and scrutinised a small animal that scrambled over white protuberances shaped a little like rocket vents. It was about the size of Ori's thumb, sturdy and armoured, with a fat swollen abdomen furred in yellow and white, three pairs of legs articulated like the commissar's exoskelton, and a pair of small, glassy wings.

Ori watched it too, slowly became aware that the commissar was watching her. Meeting his bright blue gaze for a moment, flinching away. The busy little animal backed away from a creamy vent-thing and the commissar extended his forefinger and the animal clung to it, its furry plump abdomen pumping in and out. The commissar raised it to the level of his eyes and studied it.

'I don't suppose you've ever seen a bee before,' he said. 'Some live collectively in congregations that are almost all of them infertile female workers. A little like you and your friends, yes? And a little like the Ghosts, who live in hive communes in which the needs of the individual are secondary to the needs of the group. But many species of bee are solitary. Like this one. She makes a nest of flower petals and lays eggs there, and collects pollen and nectar from flowers to feed her young until they metamorphose and leave the nest. Ah, but do you know about flowers?'

'This one knows little about plants.'

'These are orchids, only lightly tweaked to grow as vines. The flowers are their sexual organs. Here.'

The commissar plucked one of the white protuberances and picked it to pieces, naming each part and describing their function. Petals and sepals, stigma, pistil and ovary. He plucked another and held it to Ori's nose and told her to smell it.

She breathed in obediently: a prickling sweetness made her sneeze.

The commissar snorted with amusement, reached out and touched Ori's face. His cold fingertips trailing down her cheek. She kept absolutely still, her pulses beating in her throat and wrists and ankles. He tucked the flower behind her ear and studied her with a solemn amusement.

'You Quick made yourselves into unnatural things, so my ancestors had no compunction about tweaking you so that you would serve us, and tweaking some of you over again, strengthening your musculature and skeletal structure and your circulatory systems so that you could live and work in Cthuga's steep gravity. That was my grandmother's work, mostly. Did you know that? I suppose not.'

He spoke slowly, as if recalling a story he'd half heard, long ago. His gaze fixed on her, but somehow unfocused. Like Inas, when she and Ori got serious together, but Ori didn't want to think of that. His hands moved over her face as if endowed with independent life, cupping it, stroking it, moving downwards across her torso. She stayed absolutely still, frozen with fright, convinced that he was going to kill her because she had failed him.

'Your ancestors called themselves posthumans, believing that they were the new improved next best thing,' he said. 'A new species, more intelligent, more compassionate. Free of the glitches in thought and instinct that burden humans like me. True human beings, the original species, more or less. And yet we triumphed. The changes your ancestors made to themselves turned out to be of no benefit when it comes to fitness, because intelligence is not by itself a survival trait. And so we merely human Trues easily conquered them, and turned them into a servant race. And then the Ghosts came, and perhaps they'll conquer us, as we conquered you. The ancestors of the Ghosts were the first of the so-called posthumans, and they retain many of the so-called flaws that make us stronger than you. You might say that they contain the best of the Quick and the best of the True. That is why they are such a formidable enemy.'

His cold hands were underneath her loose coveralls now, prying and prodding and poking. Ori endured it as she had endured the examination by the pair of philosopher-soldiers. Tried to uncouple her mind from what was happening to her, as if her body was a bot and she was riding it . . .

The commissar pushed her backwards into a bower of ferns, forced her down on to the nest of cushions there and knelt and straddled her, his exoskeleton stiffly clicking. He was murmuring in her ear, telling her that she was such a strange thing, not quite human, not quite animal, so strong, so sturdy, so obedient, so pliant.

'Tell me you'll do anything I want.'

'This one has done her best to obey instructions.'

'Tell me straight. Don't use that damned indirect slave speech. Look at me,' the commissar said, and cupped Ori's face with one hand, thumb and fingers digging into her cheeks, forcing her to meet his gaze.

'This . . . I will do what you want.'

'That's better. That's good. You're the best of them. The best of my little helpers . . .'

She could feel his hips grinding against hers, his thighs against her thighs, the straps and rods of his exoskeleton digging into her. He was holding her face with one hand, forcing her to look at him while his other hand was busy between her legs. Then he was moving against her, and the pain was inside her but it was bearable, she could bear it, it wasn't as bad as the awful intimacy of being forced to look at his face, of breathing in his sour breath. He was breathing hard and his face was congested with blood. And then he shuddered and it was over. He lay still for a moment, his weight pressing full length on Ori. She closed her eyes, waiting for the bullet, the killing shock, the icy tree of poison in her blood, and then he rolled off her and she felt air on her bare skin, felt something seeping out of her.

When she dared to open her eyes, the commissar had pushed to his feet and wandered off around the garden's spiral path, poking at plants, touching them, stroking them. Ori pulled her coveralls together and sat up. Sore and bruised and still frightened. The flower slipped from behind her ear and fell to the cushions.

'It isn't possible to verify your reports,' the commissar said, after a while. 'Not that I don't believe your accounts of the dreams and the rest. I do. All of the Quick sent down to the observation posts reported similar experiences. They did not see any sprites, but they dreamed about them. And several, like you, saw patterns in the darkness. It is possible that those dreams were no more than hallucinations caused by the failure of your minds to understand and integrate a wholly alien experience. But I think not. I think that they were attempts at communication, or symptoms of some radical, ongoing change in your states of consciousness.

'The quake, the way so many of you were changed by your encounters with sprites – it means something. Something is happening. A change is coming . . . Do you know how many years I have spent, searching for hard evidence that the Mind exists, and is aware of us?'

Ori didn't say anything. It was the kind of question Trues asked when they already knew the answer. Usually when they were looking for someone to blame for something.

'Far too long,' the commissar said. 'Far too long. Some in my clan consider me a fool and an eccentric. As do many outside of it. I am despised. I am a laughing stock. I am a madman who has squandered his time chasing after a chimera, an illusion. And yet I am right. There is a planetary consciousness. The sprites are its agents. Fractal twists of strong self-generating magnetic fields. Emergent epiphenomena. Manifestations of more complex processes that we have not yet been able to locate, let alone measure. I don't know what it is or what it wants, but I do know it exists. And I also know it is the reason why the Ghosts are coming here. We beat them back when they first arrived at Fomalhaut, but we failed to extinguish them completely. They hid away and grew, and now they believe that they are strong enough to capture Cthuga. And why do they want to do that? Not because they want to conduct physics experiments. We've been doing that for fifty years and have found nothing useful. No, they want to contact the Mind at the heart of the world. And if they do that, all will be lost.

'I know this. There is no doubt in my own mind. It is the tipping point of the war, and it is nearly upon us. And you,' the commissar said, turning to look at Ori, 'you and all the other Quick who experienced close encounters with sprites, you're the key to the mystery. Only I knew what it meant, when reports of those close encounters started to come in. I tracked all of you down and I trained you and devised an intensive programme of research. And now, just when the solution is within my grasp, it has been snatched from me.'

He breathed in with a violent shudder and turned away and walked around the path to the bower of ferns. Ori stayed absolutely still, averting her gaze as he loomed over her.

'You are the key to the war,' the commissar said. 'You and the others. It is no coincidence that the quake happened when it did. The Mind knows. It knows that the Ghosts are coming. And it wants to speak. To us. To them. Your dreams are significant. I am sure of it. But there is nothing to be done. Nothing. You are needed elsewhere. All of you are needed. I fought hard and long against fools who fail to see the entire picture. I tried to make them understand what the enemy wants and why we must make contact first, and now I have been betrayed.

'You are going to be redeployed. All of you, all of my children, will be scattered across the face of this planet. But you will work for me still. If you see any sprites, you will tell me. If you dream about any sprites, you will tell me. Is that clear?'

'This one wants to do her best.'

'Of course you do. And you will. I know it. I chose well, and if there had been enough time . . . Well, there is still time. Go now. The technicians will give you a way of communicating with me. A simple implant that can piggyback on the common net. But know this. It can kill you, too. And it will, if I'm displeased in any way with you. If you do not report to me regularly, I will reach out, and it will all be over,' the commissar said, and reached out now and set his forefinger in the middle of Ori's forehead. Then he laughed, and stepped back. 'But I know it won't come to that. You are mine, now and always. Go now. When we meet again, it will be to celebrate my triumph.'

7

A comet was prominent in the sky above São Gabriel da Cachoeira. A fuzzy green star with a long faint tail from which it hung for an hour each evening before following the sun down into the west. A bad portent for the war, many said, and at every Mass Father Caetano and the other priests said special prayers for the safety of the town and everyone in it.

The Child told him that some of the refugees had sacrificed a goat to ward off the comet's bad influence.

'The old religion runs deep in the people. I respect it even if I don't believe in it. You should respect it too.'

'It's hard to respect mumbo-jumbo.'

'It's hard to respect arrogance, too.'

They were sitting in the warm dark of Father Caetano's garden. The feed from his telescope glowed between them, showing details of the coma thrown off by the comet's nucleus: shells of gases larger in diameter than Jupiter, expanding away from the nucleus as the Sun heated it and drove off gases that were ionised by the ultraviolet component of sunlight and driven backwards by the magnetic field associated with the solar wind, creating a tail a hundred thousand kilometres long. The ions glowed because electrons boosted to unstable orbits shed photons as they collapsed back to their original state, and because the comet's gases were rich in cyanogens and diatomic carbon its glow was dominated by their blue-green emissions.

All of this was wholly explicable, firmly grounded on basic scientific principles. And yet it was eerie and beautiful, too, completely outside of ordinary human experience, and the Child couldn't help wondering if the comet really was a portent.

Her mother and Vidal Francisca had gone to Manaus together. Vidal Francisca to do some business; her mother to have the first holiday she'd enjoyed since taking up her position in the hospital. They'd flown there that morning, in a small plane hired by Vidal Francisca, and would return in three days. The Child dreaded what would happen then; feared the worst.

Later, after Father Caetano had walked her back to the hospital compound and she had climbed on to the roof of the bungalow, the Child watched shooting stars streak across the starry sky. Radiating out from a central point a little to the east of zenith. The comet had set, but the pale smoke of its tail still streamed up from the west, and the sliver of the new moon was entangled in it like a corpse caught in waving river weed. A star fell. And another. Streaks of light flaring and winking out. The Child made wish after wish, until at last she fell asleep and the last of the comet's tail fled west, and our little ship, riding backwards on a tail of plasma, fell towards the great belt of dust and icy rocks that circled the star Fomalhaut.

Neither wishes nor prayers did any good. The Child's mother and Vidal Francisca came back from Manaus and announced their engagement.

Maria Hong-Owen told the Child before she told anyone else, talking quietly and seriously, saying that she knew that it meant a big change, but it was a good change and she wanted the Child to be happy about it. The Child tried her best. She knew that her mother was in love. She knew that she should be happy that her mother was happy. She knew that she couldn't stop the marriage, and shouldn't even if she could; knew that she should concentrate on the positive aspects. But she felt only a hot black knot of anger and fear that kept her apart from the fuss and excitement, exhibited at best a cool indifference that too often was broken by eruptions of defiance and irrational anger. She was always ashamed afterwards, but she couldn't stop it. It was as if she was possessed, ridden by one of the little gods invoked by the Indians in their hectic ceremonies.

And then she discovered that there was something worse than the impending marriage. Two weeks later, her mother and Vidal Francisca told the Child that they had arranged for her to take up a place in a school in Manaus. The same school that Vidal Francisca's daughter had attended. A Catholic academy with an excellent record of dealing with gifted children, well-equipped science laboratories, and a full programme of extracurricular activities.

And so the Child was trapped by a knight move. Betrayed by everyone around her. With a bleak and empty feeling, she saw the rest of her life laid out in front of her. No more experiments of her own devising. No more freedom. Instead, a rigid timetable, enforced worship of God and Gaia, and at best some dull job in the civil service until she became the possession of a man.

Up to this point, we had not intervened in any gross way with our mother's story. Sometimes, we had made some small adjustments (if there ever was a real Father Caetano, it is vanishingly improbable that he would have had such a convenient interest in astronomy), but otherwise the story of her life had been as close as we could make it to the story of her original. But now we changed it. Nudged it towards a predestined point. For although the Child's mother did marry the supervisor of a sugar-cane plantation, it was not until after the Child had left home. And the Child did not leave home because she was sent to a parochial school in a provincial capital. No, she left at age fourteen because she had won a posting in an obscure agricultural facility owned by the Peixoto family: her way out, the beginning of her brilliant career.

Athough we were trying to prepare our mother for a life of study and quiet contemplation, to prepare her for long years in which she would hide from the intruders in what was rightfully her domain, and slowly grow in strength and power, it was in the end still her choice to make, of her own free will. We could not make that choice for her, and neither could we force her to make the right choice. We could only urge her towards it, gently, and with all of our love. But we did not have as much time as we would have liked. And besides, her story, and ours, had already been changed in ways beyond our control or comprehension.

And then it changed again.

8

The Horse and I met my contact in a teahouse at the western end of Glitter Gulch. It was a dark little bubble, the teahouse, kitted out in a style popular during the first flush of our conquest of the Fomalhaut system. Couches and giant cushions slowly rotated through stands of luminous flowers. At the hub, an orchestra thing played a tinkling serial music. The ceiling was a simulation of T's black sky.

Sprawled on a low couch, picking at a bowl of jellied cubes of red tea, I could see the running lights of ships in parking orbits, and the sharp bright stars of several worldlets against the faint, frosty arch of the Belt. It looked so beautifully peaceful, out there. The mine fields, drones, watch stations and hedgehog emplacements that defended T and the rest of the Archipelago were, like the battles and smaller actions as the enemy advanced on several fronts through the Belt, rendered invisible and irrelevant by sheer distance.

The person I had summoned was late, and I was anxious and sweating inside the casing of my stolen clothes. I was costumed as a myrmidon; when he'd borrowed the flitter, the Horse had also appropriated several uniforms, and this one fit better than the others. The Horse, sitting at my feet, was dressed in the neat grey coveralls and peaked cap of a military bodyservant.

Only stubborn pride stopped me from leaving; I had nowhere else to go except to return to the tender mercy of the marshal. I ordered another bowl of tea from one of the servitors, and resurveyed for the sixth or seventh time my neighbours as the platforms slowly waltzed around each other. Wondering if any were spies or plants. There weren't many customers, which was why, no doubt, my contact had chosen this place as a rendezvous. An ill-matched couple, a man about my age and a much older woman, lay on facing couches, talking in low and confidential tones. A ship's captain in navy silver sucked on the mouthpiece of a waterpipe as she stared up at the virtual rendering of the sky, as if surveying the barbican of an enemy. Two old women were playing some kind of board game, considering each move as if the fate of the universe hinged on them.

At last, a large gold-skinned woman dressed all in red appeared in the entrance beyond the orchestra thing. Tisin Nemo, queen of T's data miners. She'd made a fortune after discovering a lode of exotic physics in the Library, had squandered all of it, and then had built up another fortune dealing in black-market information and scraps of enemy gear brought back by front-line officers. I'd worked with her soon after my disgrace, when I'd been brought in to decontaminate a handgun looted from an abandoned Ghost forward position. My clan had an informal arrangement with her. We certified that the gear she dealt in was safe, and made safe any that wasn't; she kept us informed about hells and other fragments of the original Library discovered by other data miners.

Our securities met and duelled as she threaded her way through the slow orbits of the platforms towards us. Authentication protocols were exchanged like hostages; attempts to probe deeper on either side were repelled.

'I'm intrigued by your costume,' she said as she settled, majestically and carefully as a caravel docking, on the end of my couch. 'Have you finally taken the Redactor Miriam's advice?'

I ignored her feint, knowing that she wanted me to ask how she knew about the Library's internal business, and said, 'This is a trivial matter, but you are obliged to settle it in full, and to my satisfaction.'

'There's no need to remind me of my obligations, Isak. I was working for your clan while you were still uncombined codes in the gene bank. Is this "trivial matter" the Library's business, or something personal?'

'An investigator in the Office of Public Safety, Yakob Singleton, found a hell here. He employed a data miner to get inside it. Afterwards, Singleton disappeared, and the data miner killed herself. I want to know everything about her. How she died. Whether she talked to anyone about her work for Singleton before she died. The names of her friends, and of her enemies. The names of everyone she owed money to, and of everyone who owed money to her.'

Tisin Nemo picked a cube from my bowl and popped it between her blue-black lips. 'I heard that you were allowed to inspect the hell.'

'It had been collapsed to a minimum-energy level. There was nothing of use left. If there had been, I wouldn't be here.'

'I also heard that it contained a back door to the Library.'

'So the data miner did talk.'

Tisin Nemo popped another cube into her mouth. 'This red tea is rather more-ish, isn't it?'

Her playful evasiveness was trying my temper. 'I have nothing to give you. Either you'll abide by the agreement or you won't.'

For a moment Tisin Nemo vanished behind the barrier of her security: a wall of burning obsidian topped with a prickling barricade of offensive protocols. Then the wall dissolved and she laughed. 'I didn't come here to fight you, Isak. I came to help you. Let me do it in my own way.'

'How did you know about the back door?'

'It's common knowledge. You aren't the only person who wants to know what Yakob Singleton found, and where he went to afterwards. The Office of Public Safety has been asking around, in their clumsy fashion.'

'What did you tell them?'

'Who says they talked to me?'

'Like me, they would have come to you first.'

She ignored the attempted compliment. 'Did you really find nothing at all in that hell?'

'I found a trace that suggested it had once contained a link. But I could not reconstruct it.'

'Whoever collapsed it knew what they were doing, then. Obviously it wasn't the data miner hired by Yakob Singleton. She lacked both the skill and the gear. I did hear a rumour that someone from the Library had harrowed the hell, but I discounted it. After all, Bree Sixsmith is dead. Or am I mistaken?'

'It is possible that the person who harrowed the hell is an imposter.'

'It is also possible that Bree Sixsmith is a traitor who faked her own death.'

'You have no reason to call her a traitor!'

On the platform moving past ours, the captain broke off her reverie and stared straight at me.

Tisin Nemo said, 'Are you angry because of the slur on your cousin's name, or is it the thought that she might have faked her death and betrayed you that really hurts?'

'Someone like you has no right to accuse someone like her.'

Tisin Nemo calmly took another cube of red tea. 'You want me to help you. But if I am to be of any use, I need to know everything you know.'

'I know that Bree Sixsmith is dead. She was contaminated by a demon and walked out of an airlock. My clan received her body, and it was incinerated and the ashes were moulded into a lifemask, and placed in our hall of honour.'

'Someone certainly died,' Tisin Nemo said. 'You received a body disfigured by exposure to vacuum and low temperatures. I doubt that anyone troubled to verify that it was Bree Sixsmith's body because no one expected it to be anything other than hers.'

'I would have to check,' I said.

'I wouldn't bother, because I know I am right. When did this all happen, by the way?'

'Some forty megaseconds ago.'

'About a year,' Tisin Nemo said. 'If Bree Sixsmith faked her death and defected a year ago, this trivial little matter of yours goes deeper than Yakob Singleton's discovery and disappearance, doesn't it?'

'If you know anything about it, you should tell me. The Library will reward you for any useful information.'

'I'll give you my best guess, for free. Yakob Singleton found something. His discovery was a threat to someone else. So much so that they had to take a big risk, and moved in and shut it down. You found a back door. Do you have any idea as to where it might lead?'

'It was only a trace. I couldn't reactivate it. And now that I've told you all I know, tell me about the data miner. Tell me what you didn't tell the Office of Public Safety.'

'She had a bad gambling habit. She was in debt. It's possible that Yakob Singleton had her silenced, but from what I can tell it isn't his style. But it's also possible that she sold information about the hell to her creditors, and they silenced her so that she could not tell anyone else. If you want to know more, you'll need to pay a visit to the Billion Blossoms.' Tisin Nemo flashed a little package of information to me. 'They'll want something in return, of course. I suggest you clone and coarsen the amusing little protocol that induces blindsight in surveillance systems.'

I told her that I would give her advice some thought.

'How is Svern these days?'

'Much the same.'

'That's one of the problems with being permanently translated,' Tisin Nemo said, rising in a rustle of scarlet fabric. 'You don't ever change. Good luck, Isak. I hope we meet again in happier circumstances.'

'We could be walking into a trap,' the Horse said. 'If the Billion Blossoms killed the data miner, they could as easily kill us. And for the same reason. To keep the secret of that hell safe.'

'Tisin Nemo is not exactly a friend of the clan,' I told him, 'but she has no good reason to betray us and send us to our deaths. To begin with, it would be bad for business.'

'Your cousin must have believed she had a good reason to betray the Library,' the Horse said.

I stopped and turned on him and said, 'You will not speak of the dead like that.'

The Horse looked up at me, his eyes blinking independently, and said, with the fake humility he employed when he was upset, 'This one might have been mistaken about sharing his thoughts on the subject.'

'If you have something worth sharing, share it. But remember that we have no evidence that Bree faked her death. Most likely, someone impersonated her. And if Tisin Nemo is right, the Billion Blossoms know what she found in that hell. They know where the back door leads. And when we go there, we'll be one step closer to finding out what happened to Yakob Singleton.'

'Maybe the Billion Blossoms killed him *and* the data miner,' the Horse said.

We were moving towards the eastern end of Glitter Gulch, taking a long and complicated route through narrow streets and courtyards off the main drag. Past gambling joints, past tattoo parlours and chop-houses, past saloons and bars where soldiers knocked back shots of ethyl alcohol chilled with drops of liquid nitrogen and enlivened with benzene, liquid camphor, formaldehyde, and a variety of esters and psychotropics, past sex parlours and free-fall emporiums, the blooming, buzzing confusion of their virtual frontages jostling together without plan or pattern, filling the air with vivid hallucinations that offered vices catering to every conceivable human appetite. Reward and encourage-ment for the part of the brain where primitive emotions and appetites writhe like alligators in a pit, the part that is the seat of every destructive impulse.

165

We Trues are proud that our brains are as unmodified as every other part of us. The war was a direct result of that aboriginal wiring. And Glitter Gulch was a naked expression of its basest impulses.

There was a saying that had a quarter of the energy and aggression expended in Glitter Gulch and other places like it been harnessed for the war effort, we would have been celebrating victory six hundred megaseconds ago. I could see now that there was some truth to this commonplace observation, although it was hard to know how things could be arranged otherwise. We Trues prize individualism and independence above all things, and so Glitter Gulch was a necessary vent for those qualities in those who would soon be regimented and dragooned into fighting in disciplined order.

Officially, its raw licentiousness was sanctioned because it boosted camaraderie and reduced attempts to mutiny, desert, commit suicide, or go rogue – to turn your weapons on your officers and fellow soldiers. Unofficially, it was a loose collective run by gangs of scions who fought amongst themselves to extract every credit from the accounts of soldiers and sailors, and the men and women who designed and made the ships, machines, weapons, or maintained supply lines. It was a place rife with crime and violence. The habitat of pimps and whores, gamblers and grifters, thieves and trimmers and knockout artists found nowhere else. Throwbacks to a more primitive era.

The Billion Blossoms was one of those gangs, a loose alliance of several minor clans that in the real world had even less power than mine, but down in Glitter Gulch was as powerful as any of the senior clans. Tisin Nemo had given me an introduction to someone in the gang who was willing to help me. The help would not be given freely, of course. I would have to do something in return – I hoped it would be no more than exorcising some minor hell that had fallen into their hands, or verifying that booty liberated from some Ghost rathole wasn't contaminated.

The Horse and I hurried to our rendezvous still cloaked in our anonymity, but took random turns in the maze until I was as certain as I could be that we were not being followed by the Office of Public Safety, one of Tisin Nemo's people, or anyone else. All around us civilians and soldiers and sailors bounded along in groups, or ambled arm in arm or stumbled in solo trajectories towards oblivion. Feral tribes of children in uniform roared along one block where smoke-houses and bars sold milk laced with psychotropics. I saw a trio of rangers, women permanently arrested in the middle of pregnancy. I saw men and women tweaked in trivial and serious ways. I saw a man riding a Quick modified as a beast of burden, with stout legs and a humped and crooked back fitted with a saddle.

Most people ignored us, but as we crossed a crowded plaza one soldier who was too stupid or too stoned to get out of our way challenged me. I was tall but the man overtopped me by a head or more and his bare arms were as thick as my waist and he had tusks in the corners of his mouth that he exposed in a snarl, asking me what my problem was.

My security threw a nightmare at him, lodging it in the implanted interfaces that allowed him to control his weapons and vacuum suit. He screamed and thrashed, wrestling with horrors only he could see and feel, and bumped into a woman almost as large as he was, with a shaven head and black plastic pegs sticking from her forehead. She laid him out with a blow to his jaw. His companions roared and charged at her, her companions charged at them, the entire plaza dissolved into a battleground, and the Horse and I took to our heels.

Reeling with laughter, we dodged through an archway into a small square courtyard with a dead tree standing in the centre, bare trunk and branches stripped of bark and the smooth wood glowing white as a ghost. Circles of light dropped from floating sparklights overlapped on a floor of scuffed plastic with luminous green spirals sunk in its translucent depths. The walls were tiled with mirrors and chromos of pornography and battle scenes. On one side of the dead tree was a scattering of tables where a few Quick sat; on the other a stage where a Quick guitarist sat on a stool, bent over his woman-shaped instrument and playing trilling riffs to a beat set by his stamping foot, and a Quick singer stepped up beside him and pressed his fists to his throat and began to sing a song of heartbreaking beauty and sorrow.

It was the place that Tisin Nemo had aimed us at. My security had guided me there during our headlong flight.

A man in a quilted ankle-length surcoat ambled over and spoke my name and said that he had been sent to bring us to the meeting place. He smiled when I said that this courtyard was surely the meeting place.

'You have met me, so in one sense it is,' he said. 'But it is not the kind of place where confidences can be exchanged. And in any case, the man you want to talk to never leaves his room these days, and we don't care to trust people like your friend Tisin Nemo with his whereabouts. In fact, no one outside of his circle knows it. Hence this halfway house. Hence me. I'm nothing in the order of things. Less than even your servant. I'm to guide you if you want the meeting, or to take your regrets to my master if you don't. It's all the same to me.'

He wasn't much taller than the Horse, and had a small head with blond hair sleeked back, the ends curling on the collar of his surcoat. His manner was at once servile and arrogant, as if he was discharging a duty he didn't much care about. He was also completely transparent to my security. I do not mean that I could see everything he carried. I mean that my security was unable to register more than a sketchy presence; it couldn't even detect the gross activity of his brain or the clockwork of his heart and lungs. It was as if he was an eidolon, and yet he stood four-square and solid before me.

I told him that Tisin Nemo would alert the Office of Public Safety if we did not return within the next ten thousand seconds. It was a lie, of course, but I felt I needed some kind of safety net.

'I heard the Office of Public Safety is already looking for you. They aren't having any luck, as you've cloaked yourself, but it is another reason why I was sent. In case you were the bait for some kind of trap. As I said, I'm of no consequence. If I got snapped up,' he said, with a fine bitterness, 'no one would care.'

The Horse was sending me tremors of agitation through his security, making it plain that he wasn't happy. I ignored him.

'We're working outside the jurisdiction and without the permission of the Office of Public Safety,' I said. 'But when we are done, we'll have to return to the marshal who interviewed me when I arrived here. We have no other way of leaving T. And if we aren't finished by the deadline, my friend will tell them where we went.'

'Ten thousand seconds – that's three hours? You'll have much less time than that to make your deal. The man you want to talk to is very busy, and this is a small matter to him. An inconvenience, really, but he is fond of your friend and is willing to grant her this small favour.'

I laughed at this disingenuous attempt to make it seem that I was the supplicant to some important scion. 'He needs something from me, or he would not have agreed to see me. And I need something from him. I'm sure we can come to a mutual arrangement.'

'Then why are we still talking when we could be walking?' the man said, and led us across the courtyard to a passage on the far side that plunged between two high walls and was so narrow that we had to go single file. The Horse pinged me again, telling me that it might be better to return to the marshal and seek his help in winkling out the criminal who had the information we needed.

Our guide said, 'I can't stop you talking amongst yourselves, but I hope we trust each other enough that we can all speak openly.'

'You are cloaked,' I said. 'That's hardly open.'

'We are all cloaked, my friend. You make surveillance avert its gaze, which works as long as no one notices the hole you make in the world. I, on the other hand, make it believe I'm someone else. If you're wondering why my security is so much better than yours, the answer is simple. T is the centre of the war, everything passes through it at some point, and we fish its waters and sometimes make a useful catch. The once proud and mighty race of which your servant is a downgraded descendant forgot more than we'll ever know.'

'It isn't Ghost technology, then.'

'We have a little of everything,' the guide said, and led us out of the passage and across a wide boulevard, threading through the crowd with a deftness that made it hard to keep up with him, dodging into another passage, telling us that it wasn't far now, deflecting my questions about his master with skilful vagueness.

'He's a unique man, as you'll see soon enough,' he said. 'I'm not surprised you're eager to meet him, but you'll have to contain your curiosity. It doesn't do to speak of him here.'

'Then he can't be as powerful as I thought.'

'We're on his turf now. That's why we don't speak of him. Any more than we speak of the air we breathe.'

We crossed a string of small courtyards, emerged at the upper level of a fighting arena, and followed a broad ramp that spiralled down, past levels where small, lightly tweaked animals – rats and cats, bantams and dinopterids – scuffled in little combat pits, to darker levels where heavily armed animals fought each other, animals fought Quicks, and Quicks tweaked in various disgusting ways fought each other. The place had once been tricked out with all kinds of lux, but it was shabby and faded now. Stretches of the ramp's illuminated floor were dim or flickering, or even dead; the rails around the combat pits were greasy and scratched; the walls of the pits were scabbed with old blood, and the patter of the pitmen was tired and jaded.

We paused at the rail of a pit where a man-sized dinopterid was kicking at the belly of another, its hooked spurs slashing and slashing, harrying its hapless opponent backwards until it reeled into the wall and collapsed. The languid applause of the sparse audience distracted the victorious dinopterid for a moment. It looked all around, panting, beak agape and its scarlet throat pulsing, then it shook itself from crest to tail, and stooped over its dying opponent and pecked out its eyes.

Our guide licked his lips and told me that I could have plenty of fun here after my meeting, and I could have no better guide than him.

'I am here on business,' I said.

'And this is *my* business. Officers and armigers like to think they know all about form and bet accordingly, but I have inside information. I can give you infallible tips, and only take a small cut of your winnings.'

'Some other time,' I said, shooting a glance at the Horse when he started to speak.

We went down and down, passing other pits, passing cabanas and platform bars, emerging above a pair of big pits at the bottom of the spiral, their rims ringed with platforms and walkways. Both were lighted but only one was in use, and people crowded around it. Crossing spotlights shone on the two mechas that stood at either end. They were roughly man-shaped, standing about ten metres tall and possessing two pairs of arms equipped with buzzsaws and all kinds of cutting-edge weapons, and on the right-hand shoulder of each a Quick jockey sat in a crash cage. A woman strolled around the base of the pit, extolling the combat virtues of the two machines while they brandished their weaponry and shot sizzling lightning at their feet. Then white vapour billowed up and the two mechas, controlled by their jockeys, stamped towards each other and engaged five-metre-long chainsaws like swords, clashing in ponderous close-quarter strike and counterstrike that sent gouts of sparks fountaining to either side. The first bot stepped back and swept its chainsaw in a low arc and slashed chunks from one of its rival's legs, and then we descended past the rim of the pit and saw no more.

Our guide touched a blank wall and a camouflaged door shimmered into existence and we entered a warm and humid service sub-basement. A maze of corridors and chambers where food and drink and drugs were synthesised in compact manufactories, sewage was processed, and all kinds of machines were repaired and maintained. We saw only a little of this; our guide ushered us into a compartment of a low, jointed vehicle equipped with a dozen pairs of stumpy legs, its canopy closed over us, opaque to visible light and the additional senses of my security, and it set off in a kind of lurching run that buffeted us from side to side in the padded compartment, turning right and left at what seemed like random intervals, skittering down long slopes and climbing steep grades.

The Horse touched my security with his, told me that he was memorising every twist and turn of this silly diversionary tactic, in case we needed to track down our guide's master at a later date.

'I have no intention of coming here again,' I said.

'You might have to, if he turns out to be untrustworthy. And I'd say the chance of that is about even.'

At last the vehicle slowed from a mad gallop to a lurching trot. Our guide hunched around and told us to prepare ourselves to meet his master. 'Let him ask questions. Don't ask any yourself. And answer truthfully – he'll know if you don't.'

'I seek only the truth,' I said.

'Don't we all,' the guide said, and with a quick, complicated gesture dismissed the canopy of the vehicle.

And yelped as a burly figure seemingly made out of shimmering glass plucked him from his seat and dumped him on the floor of the low and dark chamber where we had stopped. Another figure shimmered through the near dark, and stepped close and revealed her face. It was Prem Singleton, peeking out of her camo shell as if leaning through a window hung in the air.

'You're late,' she said.

9

As soon as Ori and the rest of the recruits had boarded the freshly spawned pelagic station *The Eye of the Righteous*, they were assembled on the hangar deck and addressed by the station's commander, Barba Tenkiller, who told them that from this moment forward they would dedicate their lives to the one true task: hunting for every kind of enemy intrusion.

'Every day, the world's orbit carries it a little closer to enemy territory. Every day, the enemy gets bolder. They've been testing the security net and dropping probes into the atmosphere for more than twenty years now. The probes keep falling, they won't stop falling, and they're going to be falling faster and faster. It's our job to deal with them, and anything else the enemy sends against us. There aren't many stations and the world is very large, so we have our work cut out. But we will do our very best. I will make sure of it. If you show any sign of slacking or doubt, you will be swiftly and surely punished. If you fail a second time, you'll get the long drop.'

Commander Tenkiller was the oldest True that Ori had ever seen. She wasn't much taller than a Quick, with broad shoulders and wide hips and a plain, frank, deeply lined face. Her white hair was thready and sparse, showing a scalp freckled with the scars of carcinomas killed by viral treatment. She wore a starburst on the breast of her black tunic and unlike the other Trues she was neither armed nor caged in an exoskeleton. Later, Ori would learn that she'd served ten years on picket duty in Cthuga's oceans of air, working her way up from trooper to commander. Her heart had given out while slogging against the pull of the gas giant's gravity, and had been replaced with a synthetic one. Most of her arteries had been replaced too, and her bones had been reinforced with fullerene scaffolding spun *in situ* by tweaked bacteria. But despite the toll on her health she had re-upped for three straight tours of duty, and at last she had been rewarded with her own command.

She said now that she was a member of a cult who believed in the one true God, Who had created the universe and quickened human beings and given them the ability to choose between good and evil.

'I know you Quicks don't believe in anything much, except perhaps that the so-called Mind that hides away in the heart of the world will one day rise up and save you from your well-deserved servitude. Let me tell you that my God is far stronger. He created the universe and everything in it, including your petty little Mind. He is everywhere at once, and sees everything, and He's on the side of the righteous. Get right with Him, and you won't have to fear that you won't defeat the enemy. They think they've made themselves into a god, and maybe they have, but my God shits on them just like He shits on the Mind. We're going to pray to Him now. We'll pray together twice a day. It will strengthen your gestalt and it will give a few moments of quiet reflection. Use it to build your belief that you are on the side of everything that's right.'

Commander Tenkiller clasped her hands against her breast and closed her eyes and intoned a prayer to her God, invoking His swift and merciless justice, asking Him to smite his enemies and strengthen his soldiers. The True troopers, officers and pilots and the Quick flight technicians and Ori and the other recruits imitated her. Hands clasped, eyes closed, Ori felt her passenger move forward, felt it recoil when she opened her eyes at the end of the prayer.

The commander told the recruits to strip down, it was time they were inducted. The troopers stood by while pilots and technicians shaved off the recruits' hair and dusted their naked scalps with white powder. Then Commander Tenkiller moved amongst them, using a pigment stick to mark the forehead of each of them with a red circle with a dot in its centre.

'Now you're marked with the eye, and you're one with each other and with the station,' Commander Tenkiller said, when she had finished. 'Get to your quarters, and get to work.'

That was their first day aboard their new home, after days riding inside the spartan hold of an argosy out from the Whale, a long voyage that spanned a quarter of Cthuga's fat globe, all the way to the mother station that had spawned *The Eye of the Righteous*. The mother station rode the permanent gales above the tops of the clouds where high pressure and temperature drove complex carbon-sulphur cycles of synthesis and dissolution. It was a vast irregular raft hung beneath a tall cluster of hot-hydrogen balloons; boom arms radiated in every direction from its edges, like a snowflake or a squashed spider, and from the boom arms vast trawl nets ten kilometres wide were shot down into the clouds. The nets – called dew catchers for some obscure reason – were spun and maintained by tiny machines, and the threads of their fine but diamond-tough mesh were coated with tags which reacted with and bound to specific compounds. When enough tags were saturated, the nets were reeled in and fed through the try works along the edges of the station's raft, where the bound organic compounds were stripped and sorted and processed and dispatched to batteries of makers that spun and assembled new stations which were launched into Cthuga's unceasing rivers of air.

The Eye of the Righteous was the newest of more than six hundred pelagic stations responsible for patrolling the entirety of the outer atmospheric layer of the gas giant, some eighty billion square kilometres. It carried a pod of predators, and three pods of combat drones that acted as both scouts and lures for enemy activity. An elite cadre of Trues piloted the predators; Ori and the other new recruits were tasked with flying drones, and performing every kind of routine maintenance work besides.

Ori didn't mind the induction ceremony. She'd had worse hazings when she'd transferred from one part of the Whale to the other, and her humiliation was shared by the other recruits. It was far less troubling than what had happened between her and Commissar Doctor Wilm Pentangel in the garden at the top of his train. She'd heard of such things, but she'd always discounted them as fables. The kind of stories Quicks liked to tell each other, delighting in visceral horrors that made their own situation seem almost homely. Ritual murders. Consumption of the flesh of Quicks. A ceremony involving a table with a hole in its centre, large enough to accommodate the top of the head of the Quick victim, which was surgically opened so Trues could dine on her living brain. Ori's possession by Commissar Doctor Pentangel was less horrific but more sordid than these fairy stories. The awful desperate grappling and the penetration of her body. The corruption of the act of love. She knew that she was property, like all Quicks. An asset rather than a person. A working unit without rights. But no other True had ever used her with such brutal intimacy. It was as if he had stained her soul. She had been the victim, and yet it was she who felt ashamed.

Worst of all, she couldn't escape him. He'd forced her to become a spy, making daily reports that the device implanted by his philosopher-soldiers encrypted and sent via the military net. She hated this duty and was permanently scared of being discovered, but she had no choice. She had been warned that if she failed to make a report by the appointed time, the device would induce crippling headaches that, according to the philosopher-soldiers, would grow increasingly worse until they killed her.

Anger about the way he'd used her, was still using her, fuelled lurid fantasies of revenge. Ori was scared that the device would detect and report them, and was angry with herself for being scared. A vicious cycle. Work was her only comfort. She discovered that she'd missed the comfortable routines of work, and the comforts of companionship, the noisy squabbles and laughter of the commons, the familiar games and jokes. It was a sharp reminder of what she'd lost, of Inas and her friends and companions in jockey crew #87, especially as most of the recruits quickly paired up, but she discovered that she didn't mind being alone in the crowd.

She didn't even mind much that one of the new recruits was sour little Hira. Who'd told Ori as soon as she could, after they'd been loaded on to the argosy, that she would have had her turn down in the hot black dark if the war hadn't grown worse, and she would have succeeded where everyone else had failed. And told everyone else that Ori thought that she was special because she'd been selected to spend time in a tank down in the depths, talking to sprites. Ori tried her best to shrug it off, although she worried that Hira would somehow find out about what had happened between her and Commissar Doctor Pentangel, or even that she *had* found out and had told everyone. That everyone knew. That every glance and conversation was tinged with speculation and pity.

Fortunately, Hira soon found another target for her petty jibes. Another recruit, Hereata, who'd also spent time in one of Commissar Doctor Pentangel's observation posts, and had supposedly suffered some kind of mystical union or vision. Hereata wouldn't be drawn on this rumour. She possessed a weird gentle serenity, seemed to scarcely notice Hira's increasingly aggressive goading or the mocking of other

Quicks, and was given to sudden piercing insights. Once, she told Hira that she was angry because she was too scared to open herself up to the sprite which had bonded with her; Hira scoffed loudly at this, but Ori noticed that she was uncharacteristically quiet and thoughtful for a day afterwards.

Ori couldn't help wondering if Hereata had also been abused by the commissar, if she'd also been recruited to spy for him, but was too ashamed to ask. That shame also stopped her from talking to Hereata about their common experience of serving in the observation posts. In the end it was Hereata who brought it up, one day down in the chill bright drone hangar. Saying, as they checked the systems of the launch cradles, 'You were touched too.'

For a horrible moment, Ori thought that Hereata was talking about the commissar, and she blushed hotly and turned away. But Hereata followed her and said, 'It was in a dream, wasn't it? A dream about looking for a sprite and finding it in a room. A room in the post that didn't exist.'

'You had that dream too?'

'I had all kinds of dreams. Although they weren't really dreams.'

'What were they, then?'

'Messages at first. And then conversations.' Hereata spoke in a matter-of-fact manner, as if discussing the weather.

'You talked to the sprites?'

'The sprites were the messages. Or rather, they were both messenger and message. Their simple presence tells us that the Mind exists. And that it wants to talk to us.' Hereata smiled her sweet and simple smile.

'Did you tell them?'

'Trues want to understand. But I don't think they can, not really. Their minds aren't like our minds.'

'You mean they're too stupid?'

'They're too complicated. Our ancestors stripped away some of the agents of consciousness when we became what we are. Removed the dangerous ones. The Trues still have everything. They are unchanged. Like our common ancestors, who walked out of the dry plains of Africa into the rest of the world, and then walked beyond the sky. They have all kinds of voices in their heads. We have one.'

'Not any more.'

Hereata smiled. 'What do you hear? What does it say to you?'

'I looked for it,' Ori said. 'In my dream. And I didn't find it. Maybe if

176

I'd found it, it would have explained itself to me. All I know is that it's there.'

'Yes,' Hereata said. 'That's the message.'

Ori wanted so much to tell this strange, calm, kind person about what had happened to her. What had been done to her, by the commissar. It was like a physical pressure.

Hereata said, 'Did you look for the room, after you woke up?'

Ori nodded. 'I think I was a little crazy. Or scared. And it was only a dream, but it seemed so real at the time that when I woke up I thought the room was real, too.'

'It's real,' Hereata said, and reached out and placed her cool palm on Ori's forehead. 'Here. It's here.'

'In my head?'

'In your mind,' Hereata said, and that was when their conversation was broken up by Hira and her friends, and Hira loudly denounced them for wrecker activity.

It was a ludicrous charge, but Ori and Hereata were subjected to a self-confession session with the rest of the recruits who shared their shift – an informal court run by Quicks that dealt with every kind of minor infraction amongst the Quick crew. Hira accused Ori and Hereata of plotting and conspiracy, saying that they both believed themselves superior to the rest of the Quick crew. She couldn't explain what they'd been conspiring to do, and her accusation was a ridiculous self-righteous rant that most of the Quicks didn't take seriously, but in only a few days Hira had acquired several acolytes who were almost as vindictive and small-minded as she was, and besides, everyone was anxious to show that they were loyal to their new commander. In the end, it was decided that Ori and Hereata should be tasked with additional cleaning work, to give them time to reflect on their crime of selfish and superfluous thought, and Hereata was transferred to the second shift to minimise any further contact between the two of them.

Ori had to report this humiliation to Commissar Doctor Pentangel, and did her best to keep out of Hira's way after that. Whenever she saw Hereata, they exchanged looks, and once they passed in a companion-way and Hereata told her to remember that her dream hadn't been a dream. That she would understand if she looked inside herself.

'If I tried to talk to the thing in my head, you mean?'

'You have to go deeper,' Hereata said, and might have said more, but Ori heard someone coming and moved on.

Hereata couldn't seem to help answering questions and accusations as truthfully and honestly as she could, and Hira and her acolytes went out of their way to ask her leading questions, mocking her answers, inflicting all kinds of petty humiliations on her. Soon, almost everyone agreed that Hereata was both dangerous and pathetic. A holy fool who could get them all into trouble by claiming that Quicks were somehow superior to Trues. Sooner or later, she would do something to anger the Trues, and that would be it, she'd be for the long drop.

Ori hated this group thinking. The idea that ideas were dangerous. But she didn't speak up for Hereata because she'd already been accused of conspiracy and couldn't risk being accused again. More shame; more guilt; a deepening feeling of loneliness worse than anything she'd experienced in the observation station.

Yet she was not entirely unhappy. There were the comforting routines, maintenance and scut work, the twice-daily prayer sessions led by Commander Tenkiller. And there was the flying.

Ori and the others flew fast, long-range drones equipped with lures designed to attract enemy activity, and sensors designed to detect it. Ori had to fly her drone in strict formation, and keep in contact with the other jockeys, and of course she never left the station because she flew it by wire from an immersion chair, but for six hours every other day she escaped into the endless sky. It almost made up for everything else.

10

One night, a few hours after she had gone to bed, the Child was shocked awake by a distant explosion. It rattled the pebbles and skulls and specimen jars on her shelves, and several luminous star-shaped stars in the constellations glued to the ceiling fluttered down to the sheet that covered her. She swung out of bed and padded to the window and swiped it clear. Beyond the dark line of the compound's boundary wall, a huge orange glow shifted and flickered in the sky.

The door opened behind her and her mother said, 'Come away from there. It isn't safe.'

'Something blew up,' the Child said. 'Was it wildsiders?'

'Clearly,' her mother said, and with a quick gesture blanked the window. There was enough light in the room from the open door to sketch their reflections in the dark glass. They looked very alike, the Child realised. Her mother's hair was light brown and cut short and her skin was several shades darker, but they had the same narrow face, the same small mouth and high cheekbones, the same pinch at the inner corners of their eyes.

'Listen,' her mother said. 'I have to go over to the hospital. In case they bring in casualties. You'll have to come with me, so get dressed.'

Whenever there was trouble, Maria Hong-Owen took charge of the emergency room. And tonight Ama Paulinho was at her father's house; the old man had suffered a small stroke several days ago.

The orange light was lower in the sky when they crossed the courtyard. A siren wailed far off. Maria took the Child's hand in a firm grip and they walked quickly, shadows wheeling around them. Two nurses were waiting in the bleak emergency room, with its green walls and three short benches, tiled floor with the drain in the centre, curtained treatment alcoves. The Child helped one of the nurses lay out sterile bandages and dressings and instruments on a trolley while Maria woke various scanners. One of the junior doctors came in, dressed in a ratty T-shirt and grey jogging pants; he spoke briefly with Maria and went out again. After that, nothing happened for a long time. One of the nurses sat at the desk, his slate tuned to the town's emergency channel. Spurts of voices, long silences.

The Child was half-asleep when two young men helped in a much older man, followed by a trio of anxious women. The Child recognised the older man: he worked in the hardware store, a kindly fellow with a bushy white moustache who always expressed interest in the Child's special orders. He was looking around as if bewildered to find himself there; then Maria and one of the nurses took charge, guiding him into an alcove, drawing the curtain. The Child watched the old man's relatives huddled in a knot, talking in low anxious voices with the second nurse, breaking apart when Maria pulled open the curtain and told them that she would keep their father overnight for observation but he would be fine.

The nurses and the Child and Maria shared tea from a flask. Maria told the Child, 'It wasn't anything. A panic attack that exacerbated existing angina pectoralis. I gave him aspirin to thin his blood. Why?'

'In case he has a heart attack.'

'To make it less likely, yes.' The Child's mother smoothed the skin under her eyes. 'That's all the excitement we're likely to get. No civilian casualties – we can be grateful for that.'

Later, after Maria had gone upstairs to check the surgical ward, the nurse told the Child that the old man lived with his family on the side of the town close to the army base.

'A drone came down the street. It saw something it didn't like and exploded, and shrapnel smashed the window of the old man's bed-room.'

'It was chasing wildsiders?'

'Shadows, most likely,' the nurse said. 'Or a stray dog or some other animal. The wildsiders were probably long gone when the ammunition dump blew up.'

He let the Child listen to the emergency channel until Maria returned and said they could go back to bed. An hour later, the Child was just beginning to doze off when she heard voices. Her mother and Ama Paulinho talking elsewhere in the bungalow, both speaking quietly but with some force. Ama Paulinho saying that he was only a child. No more than a child. Her mother saying that of course she would come but first she needed to know. She must know. She had the right. A pause, and then a choked sound. After a moment the Child realised that her ama was crying, and felt a strange kink in her chest. She swung out of bed and in bare feet padded to the door of her bedroom and cracked it open. Stood there listening, her mother saying again that she had the right to know.

'I would never put you in danger. I swear that.'

'They should bring him here.'

'I told them. They say he is too badly injured to move. So bad, so bad. And so young . . .'

There was a long silence. The Child, listening at the door, scarcely dared to breathe. She could feel her heart thumping in her chest.

At last her mother said, with the cold snap in her voice that meant she had come to a decision and didn't like it, 'I'll go. But I'll take one of the nurses.'

'They said to come alone.'

'That's the deal. Tell them that.'

'They will not like it.'

'They can take it or leave it.'

Another pause. Then Ama Paulinho said, 'I will ask them.'

Ama Paulhino talked to someone on her phone in the choppy patois that she used around her family. The Child understood most of it, a one-sided argument about whether or not the doctor – the Child's mother – should or should not come alone. Ama Paulinho pleaded with the person at the other end of the phone, swore on the life of her father that it was not a trick or trap, and at last told the Child's mother, 'They agree.'

'All right. How do I get there?'

'They wait for you, outside. It is all right. Really. They trust you. They will not do anything foolish.'

'Nothing more than they have already done. You will stay here. Look after my daughter.'

'Of course.'

'If anything happens to me—'

'It will not. I swear.'

'There will be a note on the hospital system. I will erase it when I come back. But if I don't . . . then it will explain everything.'

'It won't be necessary. But I understand.'

'I hope you do.'

The two women speaking formally, not as friends.

'I have to talk to my daughter,' Maria Hong-Owen said, and the Child barely had time to fly back to bed before her mother slipped inside the room. She sat on the side of the bed, telling the Child that she knew she was awake, saying, 'I have to go out. Someone is badly hurt. His friends can't or won't bring him here, so I have to go to him. To do what I can. I'll be back soon. Try to sleep. Paulinho will be here if you need anything.'

The scent of her mother, as she bent over her. The brush of her mother's hair on her cheek, the quick dry touch of her mother's lips. The Child lay still, feigning sleep. Her mother saying softly, 'I love you, and I will be back before you know it.' Her weight leaving the bed, the light from the door going out as it closed.

The Child waited a full two minutes before she got out of bed. Cracked the door and slipped through, tiptoed down the short hallway, peeked out. Ama Paulinho was sitting on the couch and rocking to and fro, eyes closed, hands twisted together in front of her face, a rosary caught between her blunt fingers. The Child tiptoed back to her room. She slept in a long T-shirt; all she had to do was pull on jeans, tie her sneakers together by the laces and hang them around her neck, and she was ready to go. Shivering with tension. Opening the window, stopping, coming back to the bed, arranging pillows under the sheet, one of her old dolls. It didn't look much like someone asleep, but it would have to do.

She'd slipped out at night so many times that it was by now second nature. Climbing on to the sill of the open window, clutching the frame with one hand while reaching up with the other, finding the end of the knotted rope. Pulling it down and swarming up it, hauling herself on to the roof, which was still warm from the unrelenting sun of the day just past. She drew up the rope and put on her sneakers, looking all around.

The orange glow still lit the sky to the east. The Child drew warm night air through her nostrils, breathing deep, all the way to the bottom of her lungs. A faint sweet charred odour. She stepped quietly to the far edge of the roof and knelt there, watching the main hospital building, every window dark except for one in the top right-hand corner, the high-dependency ward, and the two windows of the emergency room on the ground floor.

She felt alive in her skin, every sense operating at full capacity. Suppose her mother had already left . . . But there she was, hurrying out of the hospital door with a man, one of the nurses, Raul, following right behind. The Child flattened herself against the roof like a cat. Watching as her mother and Raul opened the gate and went through, then pushing up and jumping from the roof, a sudden rush and a thump, landing on hands and knees on hard-packed dirt.

After that, it was easy. She'd long ago cloned a security dongle; now she used it to open the gate, slipped outside. There was a stand of ornamental bushes close to the gate and the Child crouched amongst their big leathery leaves, looking right and left, seeing a flicker of shadows under the big flame tree that stood in front of the house of the hospital director. Figures moving away, slipping into shadows beyond the house and the tree.

The Child followed. Glancing up at the window of Roberto's bedroom out of habit, crossing the dark garden behind the house, easing through the little gate in the tall hedge, catching a glimpse of her mother and Raul following a slim figure into the shadows that drowned the service alley. It was easy to track them, even in the near-dark. Once, the Child heard something overhead and froze, remembering what the nurse had said about drones – but it was only a bat, attracted by the rank scent of a night-flowering yucca. She moved on, padding quickly and quietly. Stopping at the mouth of an alley when the trio waited at the far end as a jeep went past. Once she even got ahead of them, and crouched under a jacaranda bush as they went past, shadows on shadows. The Child caught a glimpse of the guide: a slight figure bulked out in a long, hooded garment that blurred its own outlines, but when the guide turned to beckon on the Child's mother and the nurse, the Child saw the face framed by the hood. A young woman's face. The Child was disappointed – she'd had the foolish notion that the guide might have been the jaguar boy.

They had cut across the western side of the little town, and were now making a wide loop around the rear of the docks towards the river. Past a shuttered manufactory, past low warehouse sheds, a fenced yard where old vehicles rusted amongst dry weeds. The Child watched the three figures cross the river-front road. Two of the street lamps were out, probably not by accident. The trio passed through the middle of this penumbra and vanished into darkness under the trees on the far side.

The Child knew that the strip of trees bordered a drop to a strand of pebbles and rocks exposed by the drought-shrunken river. If the guide was going to take her mother and Raul on to the river she had no chance of following them; she could turn back now, be back in her bed in less than fifteen minutes. But her ama had said that the boy had been too badly injured to be moved far, and this was more or less the closest point on the river to the army base. She imagined people carrying the wounded boy here, hoping to make a rendezvous that somehow failed, realising that his only chance lay with bringing a doctor to treat him on the spot because it was too difficult and dangerous to carry him through the town to the hospital . . .

She sprinted across the road, jumped the dry ditch on the far side, felt her way from tree to tree in the absolute darkness beneath them. Taking small steps, hands held out like a tightrope walker. She was scared of stepping on a snake, and when one of her hands brushed a heavy hanging loop she almost cried out. But it was only a vine. She moved on, step by step, towards the liquid sound of the running river. A murmur of low voices. A faint light for a moment defining the edge of the drop to the little beach. The Child heard her mother say that the boy was going to die whether he stayed here or was moved. Someone else started to say something, and her mother interrupted.

'All I can do is make him comfortable.'

A woman said, 'The boat will come.'

A man said, 'The boat will never come now. The boat is lost. We must give up the idea of the boat.'

The woman said, 'We can't wait here long. They're widening their search perimeter all the time.'

The Child's mother said, 'You can leave him with me. I will make him as comfortable as I can.'

'It is not seemly to abandon him while he is alive,' the man said. 'But if his suffering is ended—'

'I will not do that for you,' the Child's mother said.

'Show us how to do it properly,' the woman said. 'So he does not suffer. If you are certain it is hopeless, it will be a mercy, yes?'

The Child had been edging closer all this time, and now she could see light below and off to her left, a faint red glow that illuminated her mother's intent face as she knelt beside someone prone on the ground, the shadows of three other figures crouching beside her. They were under an overhang of roots and dirt, at the top of the slope of pebbles and boulders that dropped towards the wide black river.

The Child's mother was talking quietly and urgently, saying she would be no part of a mercy killing, saying she would do her best to make the boy comfortable, and the man said he would make him comfortable himself and there was the sharp crack of a gunshot, winging out across the river. The Child cried out, scared that her mother had been hurt. Shadows moved under the overhang and a figure stood up, a man looking this way and that before starting towards her hiding place. She edged backwards and lost her footing and fell, rolling down a short slope into a breadth of empty air, landing with a shock. The man caught her by the scruff of her neck and hauled her to her knees, ripping her T-shirt. A light flashed in her face for an instant, and her mother said, 'Wait! Wait. It's all right. It's my daughter.'

And things dropped down from the black sky and narrow lances of blue light shot out from them, probing the steep bank, lighting up naked rock and the rooted boles of trees, lighting up stretches of pebbly ground and the people under the overhang. The Child saw her mother's face, saw the nurse, Raul, beside her, saw a young woman stand up, her arm coming up with a knot at the end of it, a pistol, and the woman was suddenly at the intersection of three overlapping circles of blue light and there was a snapping noise and she twitched and shuddered and fell down.

The man let go of the Child and she fell to her knees and there was another snapping noise and the man pitched backwards. Lights flashed in the trees above the shore; men shouted to each other. The Child dared to push to her feet, ready to run, and something swooped in front of her, a fat disc the size of a dinner plate that shone a pencil of blue light straight in her eyes, four fan motors humming and stirring the air.

Her mother called to her, told her not to move, and then the blue light went out and the drone dropped to the Child's feet and we lost control of the story.

No, we had already lost control. But now it became absolutely clear that we were no longer in charge.

The lights dancing through the trees were growing closer and brighter. A shadow stepped in front of their leaping glow. A slight figure with a small sleek head. The jaguar boy.

185

He held out a hand towards the Child and said, 'Come with me if you want to be free.'

Maria Hong-Owen called and called to her daughter, but the Child was already running, chasing after the jaguar boy along the shoreline, into the darkness.

11

As we followed Prem through the big, dimly lit chamber, she explained that she and her friends had taken control of this pirates' lair for the moment, but couldn't hold it for long. I had a hundred questions to ask, but the one at the forefront of my mind was how she had found out about the connection with the Billion Blossoms.

'That's easy,' Prem said. 'They found me. Or rather, they contacted Lathi.'

'I don't think I understand,' I said.

'I do,' the Horse told Prem. 'The Billion Blossoms offered to sell Lathi Singleton information about her son. But the price was too high, and so she sent you and your friends to steal it.'

'It wasn't that the price was too high,' Prem said. She did not seem to mind or notice his impudence. 'It was a matter of pride.'

I said, 'Am I to understand that I was not hired to uncover useful information, but to act as a diversion for you and your cousins?'

'They were up for a bit of fun. And it *was* fun, as far as they were concerned.'

'There will be repercussions. You have hit the Billion Blossoms. They will hit back.'

'My cousins are shipping out soon. They won't come back here, those of them that survive. And the Billion Blossoms has no real leverage or power outside Glitter Gulch. That's why they made a big mistake when they chose to tangle with my clan,' Prem said.

'I believe I understand how they must feel.'

'Oh, don't feel sorry for yourself. I admit that I needed you to keep the Office of Public Safety busy—'

'They were holding me prisoner.'

'And you saved me the trouble of freeing you by getting free yourself. You're more resourceful than I thought, Isak. And I'm glad. Because we have much to do together, you and I.'

I stopped walking, drew myself up, and said as solemnly as I could, 'You must understand that I am no longer bound by contract and convention, Majistra. The basis of that arrangement has proven to be false. And your actions here have put the honour of my clan at hazard.'

Prem Singleton studied me. I felt utterly transparent to her gaze. It was one of those moments when possibilities open on a variety of futures. I knew that the direction my life would take depended on what she did next, and I could see that the Horse knew it too. He was watching us with a sly and knowing look, as if we were actors in a saga he had devised.

After a moment, Prem said, 'Any arrangements your clan made were with my aunt, not me. If I were you, I'd take it up with her.'

'As I said, that arrangement is over. But I would like to suggest a new one.'

Prem smiled. 'With me?'

'Why not?'

'And if I don't?'

'The Billion Blossoms has the records of the data miner your cousin hired. Perhaps some freelance exorcist or data miner can unriddle them. Although I doubt it, for otherwise the Billion Blossoms would have done it already.'

'How did you know about the records?'

'I persuaded the Office of Public Safety to allow me to examine the hell that your cousin found. It has been collapsed. Any information it contained has gone. But data miners always record their every action when they explore the Library. The one your cousin hired would be no different. After she examined that hell, she sold her records to the Billion Blossoms to cancel a gambling debt, and they killed her to make sure they had the only copy. You want me to riddle it for clues about what your cousin found, and why he disappeared.'

Prem stepped forward and seized me in a hug and kissed me hard on the lips and stepped back. For a moment, I felt that gravity had flattened out completely. The hood of her camo gear was thrown back, and she had a fierce and eager expression that made her look lovelier than ever. I confess that I was excited too. Primed, perhaps, by the trip through the gaudy temptations of Glitter Gulch, and the descent through the bloody offerings of the fighting arena. Triggered by the hard kiss that still tingled on my lips and fizzed in my blood.

The Horse was having a hard time hiding his glee. He knew that if he so much as smiled, I would have to beat it out of him, for form's sake, and after a moment, he turned away and pretended to examine the shadowy vaults overhead.

Prem said, 'You have your gear and your experience. I have luck, wit, and the help of some good friends. Anything we find helps your clan and the cause of my family equally. Do we have a deal?'

'We do.'

'Then let's move on. We have business here, and little time.'

'One more thing. Now that we are equal partners, you may remove the tracking device you secreted on my person. That's how you knew I was coming here, isn't it?'

'Oh, that,' Prem said. 'You swallowed it during the picnic with my aunt. Your body will get rid of it in the natural way soon enough. Meanwhile, you have to admit it's been useful.'

'You'll forgive me if I don't express my gratitude.'

'Don't be so sniffy, Isak! We're having fun, aren't we? I bet even your kholop is enjoying himself, in his way.'

'This one would not have missed this for anything,' the Horse said.

A round doorway set in the high, wide wall at the end of the chamber gave on to a lighted room beyond, with glass panels on either side fronting cabinets in which armoured suits the size of Quicks stood. Another door stood open at the far end, leading to a walkway that stretched out across a huge cylindrical pod fitfully illuminated by lamps that floated here and there in the darkness like dim and wandering stars. Shapes shrouded in silvery cloth were stacked and racked in the open space beneath and a ceiling curved overhead: I realised that we had just passed through an airlock into the cargo space of a ship buried in the floor of Glitter Gulch.

Prem Singleton bounded along the walkway; the Horse and I followed with more care, looking all around. Below us, a string of flat-roofed cabins was set in the centre of the maze of shrouded shapes; Prem led us down a steep stair to a platform in front of the entrance to the first cabin, where ten men and women lay prone with their wrists and ankles bound by the kind of smart cord that contracts every time you make a movement. All of them were young, hardly more than children. Two man-sized shapes shimmered towards us. One exchanged a packet with Prem, who told the Horse and me that there'd been several attempts to probe the perimeter, and although her cousins had taken care of them, we should get down to business straight away.

'The man you were going to meet?' she said. 'He's through here.'

'And the records of the data miner?' I said.

'They're in the same place.'

Inside the first cabin, an old woman lay dead on a pale carpet amongst antique plastic furniture. Prem barely glanced at her as she stalked past, pushing aside a hanging at the far end and stepping through into the second cabin. Two dead men sprawled close together, one no older than me, the other an old man with halflife flowers braided into his long white hair. Ancient tapestries shrouded the walls, flickering with scenes of the great and glorious long-ago, when Trues had briefly ruled half of Earth. A patch of the white fur that covered the floor had been scorched by the discharge of an energy weapon and a man-sized vase standing in a corner had a fused hole punched through it and the cabin reeked of ozone and char.

I pointed to the old man. 'Is that him?'

'His son,' Prem Singleton said, and led the Horse and me into the next cabin.

It was a long room where creepers and fan palms grew on either side of a tiled pool. At the far end a large shadow floated in the cold blue light of a bubbling aquarium tank. As Prem led us down one side of the pool I saw it was a man: an incredibly ancient man, all leathery skin and prominent bones, netted in wires and tubing. Something crunched under my foot. The shell of a little camera drone. Others lay scattered on the floor.

Prem rapped on the tank's thick glass, close by the head of the mummy-thing. 'I told you I'd be back,' she said. 'And I've brought the man who can unlock your little secret.'

I felt as if I had stepped through what I'd thought was an ordinary door, and found myself in a saga. 'That's the leader of the Billion Blossoms?'

'Another of your race's great achievements,' the Horse said. 'An eternal living death.'

'Oh, he isn't dead,' Prem Singleton said.

'Kill me now,' a voice said out of the air. It was as flat and flavourless as distilled water and seemed to speak directly in my ear. I looked around as anyone would, but of course there was no one behind me.

Prem Singleton's camo shimmered and faded. She was dressed in a one-piece form-fitting black garment with armoured plates over her back and breasts, black boots, black fingerless gloves. She studied the mummy-thing, and said, 'Give it up easily, and I'll consider your request.'

'You killed my children. Go to the Ghosts.'

'They fought and died honourably. Honour their memory.'

The mummy-thing looked so absolutely dead, lips wrinkled back from yellow teeth, eyes blank as stones, that I felt a physical shock when its head turned amongst wires and streaming bubbles, jerking from side to side as if seeking Prem Singleton's face. I suppose it had watched and acted on the world outside its tank through the drones, but they were gone now, and it was blind and helpless.

'Swear you will release me,' it said.

Prem Singleton pressed her right hand against the tank's glass and said, 'I swear I'll do my duty by you if you give me what I want.'

'Your friend is from the Library of the Homesun.'

'Yes.'

'Tell him I will let him in.'

'Thank you,' Prem Singleton said, and looked over her shoulder at me and told me to do my worst.

'I don't understand,' I said. 'Where are the data miner's records?'

Prem Singleton tapped her fingernails on the tank. They were black, and shaped to sharp points. 'In his head,' she said.

Breaking into the mind of the leader of the Billion Blossoms turned out to be no harder than harrowing a minor hell. A neural net had taken over most of his brain's functions, as a vine in a jungle worldlet will take over the form and function of the dying tree it enfolds. He might not have been alive at all, in the strict sense: the agents of his personality and consciousness appeared to have migrated or to have been copied into the net. He was a simulacrum. A ghost inhabiting the ruined mansion of its own brain.

Access was straightforward, then, but the experience was far stranger than any exorcism. It was as if the Horse and I had been plunged into a cloud of ghosts. They pressed in all around us, needy unravelling constructs of cobwebs and fog hung in an empty null space. Everything flat and insipid and so desperately sad. A few briefly parasitised my sensorium and triggered emotions and memories that were not my own;

although I managed to dismiss them, the encounters struck at the very core of my sense of self.

It got to the Horse, too. When we disengaged, after mirroring and studying the package of information that our algorithms had assembled from tagged fragments scattered throughout the ghostly cloud, he looked even paler than before. Saying with affected carelessness, 'I always wondered what went on inside those unreconstructed brains of yours. Now I know, and I wish I didn't.'

'He really does want to die,' I told Prem Singleton. 'He's been like that for a very long time. The old woman and the old man weren't his daughter and son. They were his great-great-grandchildren. He founded the Billion Blossoms and his family would not let him die.'

'You have what we came for.'

'Oh yes. He kept to his side of the bargain.'

'And?'

'And it's worse than I thought. A major breach in the Library's integrity.'

'Show me.'

I showed her. It was a map of the hell that Yakob Singleton had discovered, before it had been collapsed: a low-resolution copy of a part of the Library known as the Brutal Quarter. I was discomfited that I'd failed to recognise it, but told myself that the resolution was extremely degraded, and I had not been expecting to find anything resembling any part of the Library because no part of the Library had ever been mirrored in any hell that my clan had ever explored and exorcised. Yet there it was: a citadel of towers clad in mirror-glass that reflected a blue sky in which argosies of fluffy white clouds endlessly sailed from nowhere to nowhere. The towers soared above plazas with formal beds of withered shrubs, dry fountains, and sculptures like metal sails or gigantic replicas of internal organs. Everything on an inhuman scale. No sign of life apart from a solitary bird-thing that endlessly circled the top of the tallest tower.

Viewed from that height, the inhabitants of the original of the Brutal Quarter must have seemed like ants as they had scurried about their business. And like ants they had once been part of a super-organism, an ancient corporation knitted from interlinked machines and people that had survived for some fifty gigaseconds on Earth, growing and changing and adapting. In the end, the only true business of the corporation had been its own survival, and at last it had grown so cumbersome that various parts of it had gone to war against each other, and it had fragmented and fallen apart. Yet part of it survived in the Library: exabytes of ancient records of transactions and commercial skirmishes, accountancy systems and contracts, all of little historical interest and no extrinsic worth, and a simulacrum of its ancient, primal core.

I took Prem Singleton to the location of the gateway whose trace I'd discovered in the collapsed hell, showed her that it led to the original of the Brutal Quarter in the Library, told her that Yakob had gone through alone, and had not told the data miner what he had found there.

Prem said, 'Can we go through?'

'Unfortunately not. This is only a copy,' I said, and displaced our avatars to the edge of the flat roof of the tallest building. There, looking out past the citadel of towers to repetitive grids of information-poor suburbs stretched under a gunmetal sky, I tried to explain the significance of what I'd found. That a back door into the Library of the Homesun was unique in the experience and lore of my clan. And if there was one undiscovered back door, it followed that there must be others hidden in the ruins of Quick machines scattered across the Archipelago. Unregulated and uncontrolled access points through which anything might intrude.

'Your treasury is open to any data miner who happens to stumble across one,' Prem said, after I had explained this. 'No wonder you're upset.'

'Worse than that, they could be used by Ghosts and demons,' I said.

I was thinking of the demon I had encountered, of course. The demon that had destroyed Arden and Van. The demon that had been the direct cause of my disgrace and downfall.

Prem said, 'If Yakob found one back door, he would have gone on to look for others. Perhaps he found something on the other side of the gateway that pointed towards them.'

'I don't know what he found, but I do know that he left a message,' I said, and pointed to the bird-thing that all this while had been circling high above us.

'It's written on the bird?'

'On a minute package of information lodged like a flea in the generic construct of the bird-thing. All it contains is the name of a worldlet. The worldlet, no doubt, where another back door is located.'

'Which one is it? We'll go there at once.'

'There's something else. The packet was addressed to you.'

'To me? Really?'

'Were you and Yakob working together?'

'If we were working together, why would I need your help to find him?'

'You needed someone to open this the copy of the hell. And you knew where it was hidden.'

'I knew that because the Billion Blossoms tried to blackmail my clan. I'm Yakob's cousin, Isak. And his friend. He would have guessed that Lathi would ask me to look for him if something went wrong.'

It made sense, but it seemed too pat. As if she'd had the explanation prepared long before I'd asked the question.

She said, 'Either we share everything, or we can't be partners.'

'Avalon,' I said. 'That's where your cousin went. It's a small and insignificant worldlet under military control.'

'Then it shouldn't be hard to find out what he did there.'

'I agree,' I said, and shut down the gate.

As Prem and I stepped from the translation frame, the mummy-thing's voice creaked in the air around us.

'Kill me now.'

Prem looked at me, a hard look that meant she had not finished talking about the clue her cousin had left. Then she turned to the tank and told the mummy-thing, 'I said I'd do my duty by you and I will. Families are important. They're what stop us descending into anarchy. I am here to help someone in my family; someone you tried to blackmail. And now I've had my satisfaction, I can't allow you to renege on your responsibilities. I will let you live, and take charge of what's left of your family.'

The voice screamed, a thin harrowing sound on one note, growing steadily in volume. I clapped my hands over my ears; Prem Singleton studied the front of the tank and waved her hand in front of one of the lights at its base and the scream cut out.

I said, 'He didn't try to blackmail your family. His great-grandchildren did. He was their prisoner.'

'Are you always this sentimental, Isak, or do you sympathise with that thing's plight because you went inside his head? I'm not punishing *him*; I'm punishing his family. I'm sure that he contains all kinds of information that his family want kept secret, and soon he'll be in the hands of the Office of Public Safety. Talking of which, they're beginning to notice the edges of our little action. We have to go.'

194

She stepped forwards and kissed me, then pushed me away and darted out of the chamber. I chased after her. I believed then that I had no other choice. I also believed that by withholding the exact location of the second back door, which had been lodged in that little packet addressed to Prem, I had a small but crucial advantage. I was wrong, of course.

12

The shifts of the Quick drone jockeys didn't match Cthuga's swift diurnal cycle. Sometimes Ori flew over the white plain of the cloud deck, beneath the cold bright spark of the sun and the vast and narrow shadow arch of the rings, which at this equatorial latitude cut the sky more or less in half. And sometimes she flew at night, the cloud deck faintly luminous under a black star-strewn sky.

Best of all were the dawn flights. As the bright point of the sun levered itself above the distant horizon, every insubstantial tower and ridge in the cloudscape threw immense shadows westward, rainbows conjured from feathery spindrifts of ammonium-ice crystals suddenly bridged neighbouring towers, and everything seemed to gain solidity in the hard pinkish light, until the sun rose further and the shadows shrank and the clouds became clouds again.

Ori and the others in her crew flew their drones a long way out from the pelagic station: a thousand kilometres wasn't out of the ordinary. They flew a lot of practice runs, and did a lot of work in simulations, too. Their combat drones were much faster and less forgiving than the drones of the observation station, and the flying was trickier than in the searing black calm of the depths. Everything was travelling east in a river of frigid poisonous air at about three hundred kilometres per hour, but there were subtly clashing currents and vortices that dragged and plucked at Ori's drone, sometimes flinging it hundreds of metres above its course, sometimes carving out pockets of lower pressure that dropped the drone a kilometre or more, into the streaming vapours of the cloud deck.

Predators flew even further. They were an ancient design, fast and quick, flying right on the edge of stability. If it wasn't for the AIs that constantly trimmed and adjusted the angle of attack along the edges of their wings and micromanaged the profile properties of their skins, controlling the laminar flow over their entire surface, they would fall out of the sky at cruising speed even in clear air. They only came into their own in combat mode, during the brief powerful surges when they flew at multiples of the speed of sound.

So far, there'd been no contact with the enemy. Ori knew about combat only from simulations. The enemy dropped probes at random intervals in random places; no patterns had been deduced from the plethora of contacts. Their ships approached Cthuga at high relative velocities to minimise contact with the defensive pickets scattered ahead of and behind the gas giant as well as in orbit around it, and performed braking manoeuvres that cut through the outer edge of the atmosphere several times before they had shed enough delta vee to enter safely without burning up. Orbital drones attempted to intercept enemy ships as they skipped in and out of Cthuga's atmosphere, the security net predicted likely entry points, and the closest of the pelagic stations dispatched their predators in hot pursuit while their drones simulated the electronic and radar signals of large structures to tempt enemy probes into traps.

Some of the enemy probes dropped straight down, deploying chutes to control their fall: these were the hardest to take out because the window for interception was usually less than an hour between the time the probe entered the atmosphere and the time it fell beyond the reach of the predators and their missiles and drones. Others flew extended missions, shedding secondary probes or attacking picket ships or aerostat stations. A few, not many, made sorties against the Whale, which had its own defences. Everyone knew that the enemy didn't want to destroy the Whale because they wanted to use it. If the enemy ever overwhelmed the defensive network, the Whale would be destroyed in place, to deny the enemy its prize. And if that happened, Commander Tenkiller told her crew, everyone on every pelagic station would be stained indelibly with shame, and even dying in battle would be no redemption.

One day, *The Eye of the Righteous* began to alter its configuration. Its lower half flattened and spread out, turning the station from a fat, inverted teardrop to a stout and somewhat ungainly triangular wedge, and the four clusters of thrusters at its waist migrated towards the stern.

Inside, clusters of hot-hydrogen ballonets and pods and hangars disconnected from each other and swung through ninety degrees and reeled inward, moving out of the way as structural spars lengthened or contracted like muscles. The blisters of the lifesystem migrated to the midsection of the dorsal side, which was now a blunt prow, and the drone and predator hangars shifted forward, coming to rest at either side of the central spine. By now, the station had lost headway and was drifting with the wind. It was beginning to rise, too. And it was no longer a station. It was a ship.

Inside the lifesystem, the alarming thumps, gratings, pops and twangs of the reconstruction ceased. The abrupt bouts of tilting and sliding stopped too; there was only a slow and steady rocking as the ship ascended. Ori and the other drone jockeys had been busy for most of the day, packing away everything loose in the living quarters and mopping up spills. Now the transformation was complete, they were able to take in the view.

The Eye of the Righteous was rising high above the cloud deck. The sky was darkening to a hard indigo; the great ring-arch that divided it in two glistened like grapheme. The sharp white stars of two orbital forts were rising in the east, one above the other, and the southern border of the equatorial band, a stormy ribbon of vortices and fretted curves generated by friction with the neighbouring band, which rotated around the gas giant in the opposite direction, was coming into view dead ahead, a range of low dark plateaus and mesas floating out at the edge of the world.

Presently, the main engines ignited. The ship had reached cruising altitude and was beginning to move south.

Every crew member, True and Quick, was animated and electrified. The transformation could mean only one thing: action was coming. After evening prayers, Commander Tenkiller explained that a pod of enemy ships had been detected three hundred thousand kilometres out from the planet. They would arrive in ninety-eight hours and their most probable point of entry was somewhere in the boundary layers of the south equatorial band. This was a recent tactic, Commander Tenkiller said. Although most of the enemy probes were lost when they hit the permanent storms and vortices of the boundary layers between two counter-rotating bands, predators and drones couldn't chase down the survivors until they reached calmer regions, and by that time they would be scattered all around the planet.

'The enemy don't care about their losses,' she said. 'They only care about ours. Remember that always.'

The Eye of the Righteous reached a way point shortly after midnight. Ori woke to an alarming absence, realised that the motors had cut off and the ship was rocking, gently rocking. Drifting on the great current of air again. She couldn't get back to sleep, and at last levered herself out of her niche and rode the elevator down and clambered along the companionway to the drone hangar, now more than twice as long as it had been before the ship had reconfigured itself.

She was checking her drone's motor when one of the old hands, Lato, found her.

'Fighting fever, we call it,' Lato said. 'People can't sleep, thinking about what lies ahead. And because they haven't slept, they can't fight properly when the time comes to fight.'

'I'll be all right,' Ori said.

'And you want to *do* right, because you've the taint of being different.'

Lato was slightly built for a Quick, which meant that she was a little taller than she was broad. Her shaven scalp was covered in glistening tattoos, interlocking patterns of geometric figures. She rarely smiled, but she did now.

'Don't worry,' she said. 'I didn't come down here to spy on you or accuse you. I'm not worried about what people think. I only worry about how they do, and you do all right. No, I want to share something, and as you're the only one in our shift awake . . .'

She threw a packet at Ori, and they were no longer in the hangar but hung somewhere above the ship. Looking up at a black sky full of stars, with the shadow of the ring-arch slung from east to west.

Ori was by now used to these abrupt transitions from reality to a battle scenario or, as here, a view patched from the ship's external eyes. She lowered herself carefully to the hard rubber floor of the catwalk and asked what she should be looking for.

'Follow the ring-arch up from the western horizon,' Lato said. Her voice seemed to come out of nowhere, close to Ori's left ear. 'There's a bright star about three-quarters of the way up. Sirius. See it?'

'I see it.'

'Do you see a faint line crossing the sky just below it, like a shadow or reflection of the ring-arch?'

'Like a thin haze of cloud?'

'That's the belt. All the dust and other junk that orbits further out than Cthuga. Now, think about this: Cthuga and the belt both orbit the sun, and the rings orbit Cthuga's equator, but why are the ring-arch and the belt in different places in the sky?'

'It's summer, in this hemisphere. So the axis of Cthuga is tipped at an angle to the sun.'

'That's part of it. What else?'

Ori tried to think of an answer, said at last that she didn't know.

'Most don't. We aren't told about it, and we aren't curious, most of us. We aren't bred to be. But this is important – maybe you can work out why when I tell you the answer,' Lato said. 'What it is, the belt and everything else apart from Cthuga orbits the sun in the same plane. But Cthuga's orbit is tilted with respect to that plane. You follow?'

Ori was good at visualising spatial relationships. She imagined the globe of the world sunk to its waist in the flat disc of its rings, tilted at a slight angle towards the spark of the sun, so that it was also tilted with respect to the big disc of dust and debris of the belt behind it. Then she imagined that tilted world trundling in an arc that took it above the plane of the belt . . .

She said, 'I think I see it.'

Lato said, 'And do you see how it affects the way the enemy attacks us?'

'The enemy live in the belt,' Ori said. 'At night we're tipped one way against the belt. And by day we're tipped in the opposite direction. So if the enemy comes straight at us along the plane of the ecliptic, where they hit will depend on the time of day.'

'Basically,' Lato said. 'Although it's more complicated than that, of course. Nothing travels in a straight line over long distances in any kind of gravity well . . . There. You see?'

It was a faint point of light, a new star suddenly flaring slightly above the faint band of the Belt, to the west of the star Sirius. It must have been moving fast, because it drew a streak across the darkness before it guttered out. Ori started to ask what it was, but then more stars appeared, streaking out in every direction from a central point, fading one by one even as more were born.

The display lasted for about ten minutes. A few of the stars were very bright, drawing streaks of pure white light across the sky that faded out to oranges and reds. Gradually, fewer and fewer stars appeared, stragglers flaring one by one at longer and longer intervals until at last the sky was quiet and dark again.

'The enemy,' Ori said.

'Some of them.'

'But they aren't supposed to arrive for ninety hours.'

'Nor will they. Those were outriders. Suicide probes discovering the limits of our defences. And those defences are a long way out, far beyond the orbits of Cthuga's outermost moons. It always happens the same way,' Lato said. 'The enemy sends probes straight at our defences, and the defences destroy them. And then the second wave comes, trying to push through holes identified by the first wave. What we try to do is make deliberate holes in our defences, so that the enemy will punch through in places of our choosing. Places where we can be ready for them.'

'They always do it the same way?'

'So far. Maybe they're not very smart. Or maybe they just don't care about their losses, like the commander says. Maybe they figure that sooner or later they'll overwhelm us.'

The night sky vanished. Ori pushed to her feet, thanked the veteran for showing her the battle.

'That? It wasn't anything,' Lato said, and handed Ori a strip of patches. 'Slap one on your arm, you'll sleep nice and deep and wake up ready for anything. You'll need it. They'll be here soon.'

A day and a night passed. The entire crew was kept busy with preparations for combat. The drone jockeys spent most of their time in their immersion chairs, running simulations in which they lured a variety of enemy probes and other craft into killing zones where the predators could pick them off. Ori and the rest of the new recruits kept getting knocked out before they spotted probes, and the True predator pilots ragged them about it. New recruits were also bad luck, according to the pilots. They were strange attractors that generated all kinds of chaos that was best kept way out front, away from everyone else.

'Some of you can fly a little, but none of you can fly well enough.'

'You're only here because there wasn't time to raise new batches of real drone jockeys.'

'Let's hope the enemy has a sense of humour. Maybe they'll die laughing when they see how badly you handle your machines.'

The taunts coming rapid-fire. To begin with, it seemed flattering.

After all, it was the first time that most of the pilots had paid real attention to the recruits. But then the taunts sharpened to threats.

Always remember, the pilots said, that we're the ones risking our lives out there. If we fuck up, we're gone. That's why, if you do something to fuck one of us up, or do anything that puts our lives at risk, the rest of us will come back and exact a price. We'll flog all of you around the ship, and then we'll select the guilty party for the long drop, and a couple of others at random. And they'll get to wear p-suits, so they can experience every moment of it, all the way down until heat cooks them and pressure turns them into a pancake.

And that wasn't even the worst that could happen – becoming a fried pancake. No, the pilots said, the worst that could happen was being captured by the enemy. They'd flay you down to your nervous system and extract every bit of information from you, just to begin with. And then they'd take your brain and stick it in one of their halflife monsters. You'd still be you, and you'd also be a monster, obeying their orders, knowing you were a traitor, racked with horrible pain, unable ever to escape. And the only thing that stands between you and that, the pilots said, is us. You do right by us, and we'll keep you and the ship safe. You fuck up, and we will fuck you up twice as hard and twice as long.

There was a last meal before the mission, a last prayer session. Ori was trying to come to terms with the hard reality of what was coming, could tell by the way everyone stood stiff and quiet around her that they were as nervous as she was. Captain Tenkiller told them that numbers of the enemy had been revised. This was a big attack. One of the biggest for some time. She wished them all good luck and good hunting. Everyone was subdued after that, even the veterans.

Ori began to feel a little better when she made the final prep. Attending to her drone, following routines that had become as familiar and commonplace as breathing, calmed and centred her. At last, she zipped herself into her immersion chair and everted into Cthuga's night. And fell with the other drones, taking her assigned place at the rear of one of two lines that formed an arrowhead formation. The air here, high above the cells and spikes of the cloud deck, was cold and thin and calm. It took only a little attention to maintain trim and altitude, and proper distance from the drone ahead and the drone behind. Ori had plenty of time to look all around.

The ship was already falling behind, a chip, a speck, a mote lost in the vastness of the black sky. Running silent and dark. Cloaked.

Transparent to the drone's radar and microwave and the rest of its sensors. The cloudscape unrolled far below. It was no longer a calm and level plain. Here, near the edge of boundary layers dragging past each other in opposite directions, it was an intricate scrollwork of cells and eddies and long streamers, faintly luminous, lit here and there by the restless red strobings of lightning storms bigger than worldlets, generated by friction between the two bands.

Above, the black sky and stars and the rigid span of the ring-arch. The AI of Ori's drone bracketed an area twenty degrees north of its heading, low above the curve of the horizon, where the enemy force was expected to enter the atmosphere. Her passenger was quiet, far back in the dark behind her eyes.

The drones flew east at a steady six hundred kph, twenty-six of them, each separated from each by five kilometres. At last the supervisor spoke, said that the predators had left the ship. And soon afterwards the drones were on station, above the pale eye of a semi-permanent storm embedded in laminar flows and intricate swirls. Ori began to fly doglegs from point to point, a small part of a pattern woven across ten thousand square kilometres of sky, and broke out the signal package and began to broadcast. Electronic noise, false radar images, chatter. All low-level and fragmented, as if leaking past corrupt shielding, a honey-pot simulation designed to lure in enemy probes. Bait.

An hour passed, and another hour. The predators were on station now, moving in wide and random circles beyond the drones' honeypot. The supervisor spoke at intervals, telling the jockeys to stay frosty, chiding one or another of them if they exceeded error parameters.

And, in the south, a star fell.

It fell in a long curve, arcing in above the cloudscape. It was small and faint and white, suddenly flaring blood-red and winking out.

For several seconds nothing else happened. Then new stars appeared amongst the fixed stars. Two sets of them, moving quickly towards each other in short brief arcs, radiating out from opposing central points, passing in opposite directions, flaring, vanishing. All in perfect silence and without registering on any of the drone's senses. Whatever it was, it was happening beyond the planet's atmosphere: Ori used a simple triangulation method to determine that it was slightly over fifteen thousand kilometres away.

And more of these patterns were appearing all over the black sky in the south and east, tiny and bright and sharp and distinct. Ori, still flying her drone point to point with mindless regularity because she hadn't been told to do anything else, imagined opposing fleets of ships firing at each other as they passed. A hundred of them, two hundred. Going out one by one until the sky was quiet again. Then something flared dead ahead, a little way above the area where the enemy was expected to enter. It brightened and spread, a kind of gauzy grid of faint electric-blue lines defining a loose net that was growing across the sky, dividing it into cells hundreds of kilometres across. It was the defence net, generated by forts orbiting at the inner edge of the rings.

Soon, tiny lights began to swarm inside the net's grid, swirling and darting here and there with quick and seemingly aimless agitation. Lights in a particular patch of black sky would turn towards each other and suddenly swarm together and there'd be a terrific flare and when it faded the net in that part of the sky would be dimmer. And while this was happening, stars began to fall. Some fell straight down. Others corkscrewed violently. Some flared and expanded into pale blotches that dropped ragged clusters of tiny tumbling contrails and went out; others vanished below the horizon. Little bursts of radio noise, hardly distinguishable from the fraying crackle of lightning storms. Blips of high-energy particles. X-rays and gamma rays, intense fluxes of neutrons.

'Here we go,' the supervisor said. 'Stay on station. Whatever happens, do not deviate.'

The enemy had arrived.

Ori continued to fly dogleg patterns under the net that wrapped the sky. It was beginning to unravel now, the net. Threads were breaking apart, disintegrating. Fewer and fewer stars fell, and almost all of them exploded into tumbling debris fields as they were struck by the energy and impact weapons of Cthuga's inner defences, and then there were no more falling stars.

For a little while, it seemed as if the attack had been met and defeated. But then there were blinks of lights in the sky around Ori's drone, ballooning and fading. She took immediate evasive action, just before the supervisor told her to go go go. She pulled hard left and spiralled down in a random pattern, strewing little clouds of drones and chaff to either side.

The drone was feeding her all kinds of information and its flight AI was chattering wildly because she'd exceeded every kind of tolerance. It was plunging towards the outer edge of the eye of the storm, falling more or less nose down, velocity building fast, and she began to pull out because if she didn't do it now the drone would break up. There was a tremendous judder and the drone pitched wildly as it levelled out, threatening to go into a spin, but then she had it under control and the AI stopped screaming at her and began to adjust trim and drag characteristics.

She was alone in the clear air, less than a hundred kilometres above the storm. She began to veer left and right at what she hoped were unpredictable intervals, looking for survivors, trying to assimilate what had happened to the predators and the other drones. Ionisation trails stood up from the cloud deck, tall pale threads beginning to bend and fray as they were caught by the westerly air current.

The supervisor told her to keep circling – they needed data.

'This one would like to ask how many drones survived.'

'Yours and one other.'

'And the predators?'

'Cut the chatter. Keep circling.'

The woman sounded worried and frightened, and Ori felt frightened too. The enemy had reached down from high orbit and casually swatted the predators and most of the drones from the sky, and they hadn't been able to defend themselves.

The trails matched those of a known kinetic weapon, according to the drone's AI: a multiple warhead that punched projectiles – nuggets of pure iron flashed to plasma and bound by hyper-Tesla fields – through the atmosphere at a significant percentage of the speed of light. No way to avoid them. Only pure chance that her drone hadn't been hit.

She wondered about the other drone that had survived, but didn't dare ask the supervisor and kept flying circles. The remnants of the sky net were still dying back, its grid disintegrating, expanding into a general haze. And there was something badly wrong with one of the orbital forts. It had grown brighter and fuzzier. Enhanced views showed that its cratered surface was fracturing at one of its poles and the fractures were spewing fountains of ice particles and water vapour, feeding a kind of shawl of ejected material. Cthuga was full of portents too. The usual slow wash of its radio signal was perturbed by squawks and rumbles and staccato hisses, and across the spectrum signals pulsed at different speeds like so many heartbeats. To the north, curtains of green and yellow hung in a long array, folded and pleated in intricate patterns.

At last, the eastern horizon grew a slim lens of light that flared against the base of the ring-arch. Day was coming. As the bright spark of the sun leaped up, the supervisor came on line and shouldered Ori out of the way, cutting her off from control of her own drone. It began to reset itself, preparing for a suicide dive, and then she was cut out of the loop completely, and her immersion chair began to unfold and tip up to vertical.

The chairs in the big dimly lit chamber were open and empty, apart from one other. Hereata sitting up in it, looking at Ori with dazed confusion.

The battle was over. The war for Cthuga had begun.

PART THREE
THE DUST BELT

1

If the boy with the head of a jaguar had a name, he could not or would not tell the Child what it was. Shrugging when she asked him, hands held out in a gesture of negation.

'Then I'll call you Jaguar Boy,' she said.

Again he shrugged.

He could speak, and his speech was not as malformed as it might have been, given his animal mouth and his animal tongue and palate. But he did not say very much, conveying meaning more by eloquent gesture and looks than by words, and he didn't respond to any of the Child's questions – where did he come from, were there others like him, where were they going.

At first, she wondered if he was in some way mentally handicapped. Certainly his brain, constricted by his sleek narrow skull, must be smaller than hers. And how much of it was animal, and how much human? He seemed to understand only a little of what she said to him, and ignored the rest or dismissed it. Yet he was lively and alert, and his movements were purposeful and poised.

He was handsome, too, she decided. He wasn't a monster, or a clumsy chimera stitched from parts, but was as elegant and fully formed as any product of natural selection. The black commas and dashes on the dusky golden-brown fur of his head faded into dappled patterns on his neck and shoulders; white fur on his throat thinned into a soft stubble where the cords of his neck defined a hollow at the top of his naked chest. His slim, narrow-shouldered build meant that his head did not look disproportionately small, and it was beautiful, his head. Shapely, proud, with alert, pricked ears, dark fur on the broad snout between his round yellow eyes, the stiff fans of whiskers either side of his muzzle. He held his head high, swinging it to the left and right as he walked, the rifle slung on a bare shoulder, his bare feet interrogating and gripping the ground. Taking possession of it with each step. Mapping it into reality.

They walked a long way the first night, past the edge of the solar farm to the north of the little town and on across dry cracked earth and scrub into the forest, following a narrow animal track that wound through scant drought-killed undergrowth and around and between the buttress roots of tall trees. Jaguar Boy had given the Child a pair of night-vision glasses that showed everything in grainy shades of white. A ghost forest through which they walked and walked, the Child excited and not at all sleepy, and not at all afraid, either. Feeling instead a heady defiance. She had made her choice and she was determined to stick to it.

Near dawn, they found shelter in a kind of cave under the roots of a fallen tree that rested at a slant in the arms of its neighbours. They shared Jaguar Boy's water bottle and the Child dug a hollow in the dirt to fit her body while Jaguar Boy perched on a stout root above her, silhouetted against light that slowly filled the clearing made by the fallen tree. She was exhausted by their trek but slept fitfully, waking after a couple of hours as a troop of capuchin monkeys descended a neighbouring tree, each carrying a macambillo fruit. One by one, they dropped them in front of the Child and when the last had made its offering they all fled as one, screeching as they chased each other up a tree and went crashing off through the canopy.

The Child asked Jaguar Boy if they were friends of his. He shrugged and picked up one of the orange fruits and split it with his thumb and ate with delicate nipping motions of his stout incisors. The Child broke open a macambillo too, ate the sweet pulp, cracked the seeds between her teeth. It was so good that she ate another at once, then told Jaguar Boy she had to go pee. He shrugged again.

When she came back, he was still sitting on his root, watching a pair of butterflies tumble above the tall grass in the clearing. The hot air was heavy as velvet. She asked him where they were going, and he surprised her by pointing east; she'd thought they would be heading north-west, towards the hills where the wildsiders had their strongholds. When she asked him about this, he pointed east again, saying, 'People live there. People you need to meet.'

'Wildsiders?'

Jaguar Boy shrugged and yawned – an unsettlingly wide and deep yawn that would have dislocated a human jaw.

The Child said, 'Are we going there now?'

'After dark. Rest now.'

The Child dozed fitfully, waking once to hear a helicopter whomping somewhere in the middle distance. She sat up and looked for it, but the trees closed everywhere overhead apart from a narrow patch of sky directly above the clearing. The pulse of the helicopter grew nearer, then slowly faded away into the rapturous silence of the forest. She supposed that the army was searching for her, and she felt a pang of sorrow and guilt, wondering how her mother felt. But her mother had betrayed her, and the pang quickly passed.

In the brief blue evening they ate more fruit and went on. The Child was still unafraid. The night-time forest was a spooky place, but she was confident that she could navigate it. She knew which trees and bushes bore edible fruit or berries and which had bark that yielded strong fibres which could be woven into twine and nets. She knew about hollow vines that yielded a mouthful of water when cut, moss that could be used to make antiseptic poultices, how to find a river by following the slope of the ground, and much more. She found a handful of berries on a skeletal bush, dry but still sweet. And she spotted a heavy cluster of pupunha fruit and shared them with Jaguar Boy, who cracked the husks with his strong jaws.

'I thought you'd eat raw meat,' she told him. 'But I suppose your digestive system is just like mine.'

Jaguar Boy smiled his wide smile. In the false light of the Child's glasses, his markings looked like the tattoos of the initiate of some un-named increate god.

They walked on, and at last reached a road, with wide margins of dry scrub on either side and the dark wall of the forest rearing up against the night sky on the far side.

Stars were shooting across the sky.

The Child unhooked her glasses, saw that the sky's black dome was gridded with a faint net of blue cords that met at knots or nodes of brighter blue. Each square of the luminous mesh subtended a full two degrees of sky, far larger than the moon when it was full, knitting a pattern that stretched from horizon to horizon. Beneath this sky net, falling stars drew long bright streaks that radiated from opposing focal points in the sky, meeting more or less overhead, passing each other and terminating in little flowers of red or green or white. Forming a great figure that reminded the Child of a mitotic spindle in a dividing cell at anaphase, when the two sets of replicated chromosomes draw away from each other. She knew that many meteors were fragments of spent comet nuclei captured by the sun's gravity well; regular showers like the Leonids or the Caprids appeared year after year at the same time and in the same part of the sky when Earth crossed their orbits. She also knew that there were no such showers at this time of year, and yet there it was, not one but two great displays flinging themselves at each other, burning across the sky and dying in extravagant bouquets of fiery light.

Jaguar Boy pointed east. Two large stars were rising, one after the other. The Child knew that certain ancients had called comets hairy stars: these stars were hairy indeed, one burning sullen red, the other a dirty green-white, each radiating spikes and fine featherings of fire like a child's drawing of the sun. Their light was bright enough to cast shadows, the Child's and Jaguar Boy's mingling with the spidery shadows of the dead bushes and clumps of dry grass and visibly shrinking as the two stars raced up the sky with startling swiftness, moving faster than any satellite or power station.

They moved, it seemed, beneath the faint blue net, which was beginning to fall apart. A node would flare brightly and stars would fall, some streaking straight down, others tumbling eccentrically. The Child followed one as it tumbled, saw it gutter and almost go out, saw it flare brightly again and shatter in a shower of meteors that fell and faded in graceful arcs. There were great holes in the net now, and still stars fell, or streaked across the sky from the nodes to the west and the east and exploded like fireworks.

The Child, full of wonder and awe, not at all frightened, asked Jaguar Boy what was happening, and he spoke one word.

'War.'

'War? Like the war between China and Russia before the Overturn?'

But Jaguar Boy was already walking away, and wouldn't answer any of her questions as they crossed the road, which still retained the day's baking heat, and moved through the dry and gullied scrub towards the forest.

When they reached the trees, the two hairy stars were sinking towards the east. The great net in the sky was grievously holed; stars were still streaking across the sky. The Child put on her glasses again as she followed Jaguar Boy into the forest, and when they came out into open ground at the margin of a river some hours later the sky was black and quiet and the stars were fixed in their eternal patterns.

Jaguar Boy led the Child along the bank of the river, moving upstream, high above banks of mud that sloped to the shrunken water-course. A tall berm or dam of logs spread across their path, vanishing into the trees on either side. Lights burned here and there on its flat top. The Child asked who lived there, thinking that they had come at last to an encampment of wildsiders.

'This is the home of the River Folk,' Jaguar Boy said. 'They are expecting you.'

2

While Prem was engaged with arranging our ride from T to Avalon, the
Horse and I managed to merge our securities and have a quick, private
conversation. He asked me if I was going to attempt to contact the
Library; I told him that it wouldn't be a good idea.

'We know there is at least one traitor in the Library. There may be
others. So any contact at this point may endanger our mission.'

'I confess to being confused as to what our mission is, now that we
are working for someone who is no longer the Library's client,' the
Horse said.

'I am not working for Prem. My interests happen to coincide with
hers.'

'If only we could be certain of her interests.'

'We both need to find this hell. That's enough for now.'

'If it exists.'

'You saw what I saw.'

'I saw a dream inside the skull of a dead man,' the Horse said, with a
whole-body shiver. He seemed to have shrunken inside his borrowed
coveralls. Somewhere in our brief adventure he'd lost his cap.

'We'll find this hell and locate and define its back doors,' I said. 'And
then we'll return to the Library and tell all.'

'I hope this redeems you. I really do. But it is a heavy hope to hang on
such a frail thread.'

'If I fail, it is my failure, not yours. But I will not fail,' I said.

I was confident that I could find and harrow the hell, but I was not
sure what I would find in it, and I had serious doubts about my alliance
with Prem Singleton. Despite her denial, it was obvious that she had
her own agenda, that she had not agreed to help Lathi Singleton find

her son out of friendship or familial loyalty, but because she'd been involved from the beginning in his search for data about the ancient starship. And now he was dead or in bad trouble, or perhaps he had betrayed her and disappeared with the knowledge they'd been searching for. In any case, she had her own reasons for wanting to find him.

She definitely had traction in the right places and knew how to use it, securing passage for us on a freighter that would make a diversion to Avalon, but my plan to question her during the trip was quickly thwarted. We'd barely kicked off from T's port when Our Thing announced that the enemy had breached Cthuga's defences, entered its atmosphere in force, and established a beachhead. Every kind of fighting was still going on, from drones battling drones with kinetic and high-energy weapons to desperate hand-to-hand combat in pelagic stations, but Our Thing claimed that we had won a great victory: the Ghosts had thrown a large percentage of their resources at us, and had been defeated and repulsed.

Prem announced that she had to consult with her clan and suited up and went outside, leaving me to discuss the news with the captain of the freighter, a cynical veteran who believed that although the action at Cthuga was a major battle, a big push and a big push back, it wasn't decisive. We'd been fighting for so long, the captain said, that it was inconceivable that a single event would end the war one way or another. As far I was concerned, the battle for Cthuga was a remote and distant scuffle, hardly unprecedented and of unknown significance to my quest to locate and characterise the back doors into the Library. Still, I remembered the Redactor Svern's little lecture, back in his memory palace, and wondered if he was pleased to have been proven right.

Prem spent most of the rest of the trip outside. I listened inattentively to the war stories of the freighter's captain while watching her in a discrete window, perched in her p-suit at the end of one of the load booms that radiated like a spiky necklace from the midpoint of the long trunnion spar that coupled the tiny lifesystem to the motor pod. But I had no way of knowing who she was talking to, or what she was talking about.

At last, Avalon swam into view. As it expanded from a faint star to a fuzzy disc the ship's crew – half a dozen Quicks who, wedded to symbiotic p-suits, their arms and legs replaced by tentacular implants, spent their brief lives in raw vacuum – readied a transit pod. The Horse and I suited up and climbed inside. Prem joined us, still cloaked in her security, still talking to her clan, and the pod shot out along the boom and fell towards Avalon while the freighter accelerated away towards its final destination.

It's an icy worldlet, Avalon. An irregular ovoid sphere clad in lightly cratered plains of water-ice fractured with pressure ridges. A tug intercepted our pod and carried us halfway around Avalon's waist in an arc that terminated at the port that sprawled across the flat floor of an impact crater. As soon as we debarked, we were surrounded by an escort of troopers in full armour. The Horse was marched off in one direction, and Prem and I were marched off in another. I told Prem that I was impressed by the reception but it was hardly necessary; she said that it was nothing to do with her. She was quiet and reserved; preoccupied, perhaps, with the implications of the attack on Cthuga. It was left to me to tell the captain in charge of the troopers that I needed my kholop if I was to perform my work properly.

'There's nothing for you to do here,' the captain said. 'Everything is under control.'

'What is under control? What happened here?'

'The prefect will explain everything.'

'If Yakob Singleton opened up a hell here, I very much doubt it.'

'The prefect will explain everything,' the captain said again.

I was still arguing with him when we entered a capsule that immediately and at great speed dropped two kilometres down a vertical shaft. Vicious deceleration brought me to my knees and two troopers moved in on either side and lifted me up and carried me by main force to the flat slab of a cargo sled. Once everyone was aboard, it glided away down the centre of a broad serviceway cut through the upper part of a small sea that Quick machines had melted in the adamantine water-ice of Avalon's crust with shaped antimatter bomblets, and was kept liquid by heat pumps connected by superconducting cables to the worldlet's silicate core, which still retained heat from the decay of aluminium isotopes.

The serviceway's tunnel dwindled away for kilometres ahead. The air was freezing and the walls of the serviceway were transparent diamond and water pressing all around glimmered ghostly blue in the bright lights floating overhead. The sled was the only moving thing visible. No Quick workers, no bots. Just the transparent walls and floating lights flashing past. At last we halted at the centre of a workpod that encircled the serviceway. Security bots hung in the air, weapons everted. Several scanned me; my security hardened as they tried to get inside my armoury and for a moment I was deaf and blind. When the spasm passed, the captain of the troopers was in my face, wanting to know what weapons I was carrying.

'They are not weapons. They are the tools of my trade,' I said.

'Security says they are weapons. Hand them over.'

'I can't do that. They are particular to my clan. And I may need to use them.'

The captain repeated his demand. The pair of troopers held me fast and a security bot hovered behind him, the muzzle of a glaser aimed at me as it pulsed my security every thirty milliseconds, trying to find a way inside.

Prem stepped up and said that she needed my skills. 'Your prefect will need them too.'

'Everything is under control,' the captain said.

'You don't know that. I don't know that. Only this man can know for sure.'

Prem looked slim and vulnerable amongst the armoured troopers, but she showed no fear and carried herself with forthright authority.

I sensed traffic as the captain consulted someone. He said, 'On your responsibility, Majistra.'

'All of it is my responsibility.'

The troopers picked me up again and carried me down a passage to a platform that overlooked a long, red-lit chamber, where I was unceremoniously dumped on the floor in front of a heavyset man in scarlet and yellow: Dyal Cardinale, the prefect of Avalon, according to my security. He looked at me, then at Prem, affecting nonchalance.

'I appreciate your offer of help,' he said. 'But as you can see, everything is under control.'

'Where is my cousin?' Prem said.

'He came here and did his work, and left.'

'Where did he go?'

'I regret that I did not enquire,' the prefect said.

'I'll want traffic records,' Prem said.

'I'll show you everything,' the prefect said.

Prem turned to me and said, 'What do you see, Isak?'

I got to my feet, moving slowly, aware of the troopers and the drones watching me. Below the platform, troopers stood over a small crew of Quick workers who lay face down on the floor, hands clasped on the backs of their necks. Beyond were ranks of cradles, each brimful of water, each containing the small sleek form of a newborn Quick adapted for aquatic life. The newborns chirped and trilled and splashed, agitated no doubt by the sudden change in their routines. Everywhere else was still and quiet, and I told Prem so.

'This isn't the locus of the infection,' the prefect said. 'We have dealt with that. No, this is the locus of an insurrection. And as you can see, we have dealt with that, too.'

'My cousin came here to look for something,' Prem said.

'And he found it, and dealt with it,' the prefect said.

'A hell,' Prem said.

'What else?'

'It is in the mind of one of the heat pumps installed by the Quick construction machines,' I said, and recited the coordinates that I'd pulled from the brain of the undead leader of the Billion Blossoms.

Prem gave me a sharp look, then told the prefect that we needed to go there at once.

'There is no need.'

'With respect, you don't know what you are dealing with.'

'With respect, I believe that we do,' the prefect said, with wintry politeness. 'After the pump's mind had been purged by your cousin and his assistant, I discovered that several workers had died. It seems as if they had fought each other to the death, using fists and teeth and nails. Very messy. I also discovered a clandestine comm line to the heat pump. It was obvious that they were wreckers, and that they had been controlled by demons in the hell hidden in the pump's mind. So I took appropriate precautions.'

Prem said, 'My cousin had an assistant? He came here with some-one?'

The prefect said, 'He had specialist help. Just like you.'

'Did she claim to be working for the Library of the Homesun?'

'Was her name Bree Sixsmith?'

Prem and I had spoken at the same time.

The prefect looked at me, then at Prem.

Prem said, 'No doubt you have confirmed my authority.'

'Yes, Majistra.'

'Then you will help me understand what they did here.'

The prefect threw a packet of information at me, and told Prem, 'I have just given your servant a copy of their report. Their authority was confirmed at the highest level of security. I had no reason to doubt that they were acting in anything other than an official capacity.'

He wore rings on every finger. Some were the kind that augments memory and other mental facilities; others were the kind that command machines. He was twisting one, a plain black band on his right forefinger, back and forth. I was certain that it was some kind of weapon.

'She turned him,' Prem said to me. 'She caught up with Yakob and she turned him.'

'I think so too,' I said. 'I'm sorry.'

'Do you have any idea what they found?'

'According to their report, they harrowed and erased a hell,' I said.

'After they used the gateway inside it,' Prem said.

'The hell they claim to have erased was nothing like the one in the ship,' I said. 'It wasn't a copy of part of the Library, but appears to have been a genuine hell, inhabited by a clutch of minor demons. But even on a first reading, it seems very thin. Generic. As if patched together from records of other hells.'

The prefect said, 'It was a real hell, with real demons. They infected my workers.'

'I would like to inspect the heat pump,' I said. 'No doubt every trace of the hell has been erased, but I think it likely that something was left behind. A trap.'

Prem understood. 'Those workers were cultists.'

'I think so. They used the gateway to access data stored in the Library. After your cousin and Bree Sixsmith left, they wanted to find out what had been done to their archive. They looked inside the heat pump's mind. And they found a demon.'

'And it made them kill each other,' Prem said. 'How elegant.'

'They worked here,' the prefect said. 'The Quick infected by the demon. They worked in this place. These prisoners also worked here, and may have useful information about the conspiracy. You are welcome to question them in any way you see fit. I have held them in isolation. I have put the entire sector in isolation. Nothing in or out until you arrived. The situation is completely contained.'

'There is no situation,' Prem said. 'Not any more. The Quick who died weren't wreckers. They were . . . guardians. They kept safe something which has been stolen from under your nose.'

'And that was?' the prefect said.

'There's no way of knowing now,' Prem said, with perfectly calibrated bitterness.

I knew she was lying, but the prefect did not. He gestured at the Quick prisoners sprawled below us. 'They might know.'

'They are alive. Therefore they are innocent,' I said. 'Everyone who had anything to do with this conspiracy, so-called, was caught in the trap, and infected by the demon.'

'Let them go,' Prem told the prefect.

The prefect shook his head. 'I will deal with them as I see fit.'

His smile was colder than ever. I felt sick. I knew that he knew that he possessed the authority to kill the Quick, and he was determined to exert it. To redeem his status. To prove to Prem that her authority was not absolute.

'If you won't let them go, then release them into my custody,' Prem said 'I will take them with me for further investigation.'

'They are quarantined,' the prefect said.

'There is no need for the quarantine.'

'I believe there is. You can question them here, of course. And then I will deal with them.'

'I give you my word that they are innocent. Harmless.'

'They worked with wreckers. They are tainted, whether or not they know it. I cannot take the risk that the taint will spread.'

'The workers who died were not wreckers,' Prem said.

'If you have evidence to back up that assertion, I will of course examine it,' the prefect said.

'Do we have proof, Isak? Can you show this man that Yakob's report is faked?'

'Bree Sixsmith may have patched up the characteristics of the hell she and your cousin supposedly harrowed from reports of other harrowings. But I would have to check the records of the Library to determine that.'

'What about the heat pump's mind?' Prem said.

'I don't think I can allow you to examine it,' the prefect said.

'I don't think you can stop us,' Prem said.

'Your servant claims that it may contain some kind of trap,' the prefect said. 'If that's true, it must remain in quarantine until it can be destroyed in place.'

Prem held the prefect's gaze. Her face was still and calm, but she was poised as if to spring at his throat. He raised his right hand and aimed the plain black band on his forefinger at her; I prepared to hurl a nightmare, aware that the troopers around us had shifted their stances in readiness for action.

At last, without looking away from the prefect, Prem said, 'Let's go, Isak.'

'I should like to look inside the mind of that heat pump,' I said.

'I don't think you can.'

'Before you leave, I want you to witness the last part of the containment strategy,' the prefect said, and flicked a packet at his troopers.

Those down on the floor of the hatchery stepped back as drones swung in over the prone prisoners and in a rapid tattoo fired infrared lasers that cooked their brains to boiling soup. The prisoners shuddered as their skulls popped and cracked. Troopers moved past them to the ranks of cradles, scooping out newborns and dropping them on to the floor to drown in air.

Prem caught my arm. 'Come on,' she said. 'There's nothing left for us here.'

Her face was still set with glacial calm, but red light swam and glittered in her eyes and sparkled in the tears that slid one after the other down her cheeks.

3

Ori and the rest of the crew of *The Eye of the Righteous*, awake for more than forty-eight hours, running on kaf and meth, were still trying to come to terms with the enormity of their situation. All the pilots were dead and all the predators were lost; more than half of the elite crew which had maintained the predators and served the pilots had committed suicide. Most of the drones were gone. The planetary net was down, every link broken. Radio yielded only the crackle of a distant storm and the slow, deep heartbeat of the planet's magnetic field. There was no way of contacting anyone else. They were entirely alone, cast adrift in the vast and empty sky.

One good thing: the fall of the net meant that Ori didn't have to send any more reports to Commissar Doctor Pentangel. And despite the warnings of his philosopher-soldiers, the device they'd implanted hadn't punished her when she'd missed the last deadline. Perhaps those warnings had been empty threats, or perhaps the device was intelligent enough to know that it wasn't her fault she couldn't send reports: Ori didn't care. She wondered how Inas was, what she was doing, whether the Whale had been attacked, but otherwise had no time for regrets, no time for the past. She was living from moment to moment, experiencing everything with a pure and lucid intensity.

'We're in a tight spot, but we're not helpless,' Commander Tenkiller told her crew. 'We will make more drones and turn them into flying bombs. We will convert the launch cannon into kinetic weapons, and we will search the library of maker templates for useful weaponry, or for tools that can be turned into weapons. We have suffered a grave setback, but we are not out of the fight. When we confront the enemy, we will have a few surprises in store. We will give back more than we get. This I promise.'

Some of the crew were given the task of prepping the small number of spare drones and assembling various kinds of explosive loads from components spun by the ship's makers. The rest, including Ori, set to work converting the launch cannon. Buttoned up inside their chairs, they each woke a maintenance bot and walked them out of the hutches and across the upper deck of the ship in bright clear early morning light. The sky empty except for a feathering of cumulonimbus clouds, the great span of the ring-arch, and the baleful spark of one of the orbital forts burning low in the west.

The launch cannon were guide rails ringed with a series of super-conducting hoops that ran the full length of the upper surface of the ship. Drones attached to sleds that ran along the rail were accelerated by magnetic fields generated by the hoops, each kicking it faster and faster until the sled crashed into the retaining buffer at the far end of the gun and the drone shot off; once it had cleared the ship, the initial acceleration imparted by the cannon was boosted by solid-fuel rockets to a velocity that would sustain air-breathing flight. Simple machines, the launch cannon, dumb as a bag of spanners and with no moving parts except for the sled and the load grab, but the circuits that coordinated the priming and discharge of the hoops were delicate and frangible, there were safety devices that had to be stripped out or circumvented, and the hoops themselves were constructed from an intricate knit of superconducting plastics. It took Ori and the rest of the crew all day to break down one cannon and use the modular components to make four smaller units, and then plug in reprogrammed control circuits and check everything for integrity.

Towards the end of the day, Ori found herself working alongside Hereata, fixing the bolts that held the terminal unit and retaining buffer of the railgun in precise alignment. Each bolt possessed a spark of intelligence that sensed its position relative to the others and could minutely alter the angle at which it was fixed, to allow for small flexings in the ship's superstructure. They cheeped anxiously when they were removed, and continued to cheep in the bots' catch nets; no one had worked out how to switch them off.

After a little while, Hereata said, 'Hira has an interesting idea. She claims that the Mind called down the enemy. She says that's why the

223

defences failed. Not because the enemy overwhelmed them, but because the Mind reached out to them.'

'It sounds like another of her fantasies,' Ori said. 'Nothing you should take seriously.'

'We know the defences failed. We do not yet know why.'

Ori selected a bolt from the net slung between her bot's forward manipulators and inserted it in the chair that held the rail to the sector plate. 'That doesn't mean we should accept the first silly explanation that someone cooks up. Especially someone like Hira.'

Hereata said, 'Hira also says that our drones survived because we're linked to the Mind. And because the Mind is allied to the enemy, we're a danger to the ship.'

'She told you that?'

The bolt's cheeping slowed as Ori tightened it, stopped when it was properly seated.

'Her bunky did. Lani.'

'I told you how Hira was, back on the Whale,' Ori said. 'She hasn't changed. When something bad happens, she looks for someone to blame. But if you're worried about what she's been saying, we could call her out. Confront her. After all, she has a piece of a sprite in her head, just like us. She served time on an observation station, just like we did. If we're linked to the Mind, so is she.'

'But her drone was destroyed,' Hereata said, 'and ours survived.'

Ori laughed.

'I know. It's ridiculous,' Hereata said. 'But if we confront her, she'll say that we're doing it because we really do have something to hide. And people are scared, Ori. They might listen to her.'

'Lani got to you, didn't she?'

'I don't like her. She is a violent person.'

'Don't worry about her. I'm on your side. And Hira can hardly tell Tenkiller or any of the other Trues about this stupid fantasy of hers, so it won't come to anything. It's just talk.'

'Unlike Hira, I don't claim any special insight about what the Mind may or may not want,' Hereata said. 'But I have been thinking about it. It seems to me that it is constrained by the logic of its situation. And logic gives it just four choices. It can side with us. The Trues and the Quicks. It can side with the enemy. It could choose to fight both us and the enemy, and drive us off its world or destroy us. Or it can remain aloof, either because it does not choose to fight, or because it does not even notice that we are fighting each other. Even though we are fighting over who should make contact with it.'

'I like the idea that it stays aloof,' Ori said. 'Things are bad enough as it is, worrying about what the enemy is planning to do.'

'But it hasn't stayed aloof,' Hereata said. 'It touched me. It touched you. And all the others. Even Hira.'

Ori said, 'What's yours doing, right now?'

It was a little like talking about sex, she thought. Embarrassing and illicitly thrilling.

'My sprite? It has been very quiet.'

'Mine too.'

'I wonder what that means.'

'It means they aren't interested in what we're doing,' Ori said. 'It means they're staying aloof.'

They worked on in silence and were finishing off the final checks on the terminal section of the truncated railgun when stars began to fall from the sky. Stars radiating out from a point a few degrees west of the burning moon, falling in long fiery streaks that passed above the ship. Ori tried to focus on the bright point at the head of one streak, but couldn't make out much more than a fuzzy white speck a few pixels across.

Hereata flashed a pict of the speck's absorption spectrum: carbon doped with titanium and wolfram.

'Fullerenes,' Ori said.

'My best guess also. No doubt a heat shield.'

Ori watched a falling star drop behind the horizon, followed by another, and another. 'There are so many of them.'

The stars continued to fall. Brighter now. Leaving distinct contrails. Then one exploded directly overhead and both Ori and Hereata flinched, clamping to the surface of the ship with all of their bots' limbs. Ori replayed the explosion in slow motion, saw a triangular shape break apart into several sections that tumbled away, burning. Chalices full of flame . . .

The ship juddered as its main motor fired up. A moment later Commander Tenkiller's voice cut through the background chatter of the other Quicks, ordering them to assemble on the general deck.

The commander was in formal dress, black jacket, trews slashed with scarlet, and a gold skullcap, flanked by the two surviving Trues in their exoskeletons and yellow and green uniforms, their breasts splashed with

225

merit and valour bars. She'd dispatched flocks of autonomous micro-drones on a scouting expedition, she said. Enemy activity had been detected some eight hundred klicks upwind and they were going forward to engage. She did not yet know what they would encounter, but they would meet the enemy with glad hearts and minds, and strain every sinew and neuron to win a victory.

'I cannot promise you more than that. We have no safe haven now. We can only fight. And even if we do not win, we will make such a mark against the enemy that it won't be forgotten any time soon. We are already under way and will be within striking distance inside ten hours. There is still much to do, and we will all of us work together to make sure that we are ready when we need to be ready. On a personal note, I want to say that I am honoured by the presence of each and every one of you under my command. I know that you will not fail me, or fail your comrades-in-arms. Now, let us pray.'

She led prayers to the One God for deliverance from the enemy and a great victory, and her second-in-command stepped up and gave the new orders of the day, and everyone went back to work. Ori saw Hira moving off amongst her acolytes, saw one of them, Hira's bunky, Lani, turn and give her a frank and hostile stare. Ori stared back, and felt a small satisfaction when Lani looked away and turned and hurried to catch up with her friends.

Work was good. Work helped Ori forget everything else. She rode her bot and helped to move explosive loads and to check out the systems of the reconstructed railguns. There was a round of dry firing, supervised by Commander Tenkiller herself. Five of the guns worked and three failed in various ways, and the crews set to tracing faults and fixing them.

As they worked on, a few more falling stars streaked overhead, dropping past different parts of the horizon. And then there were no more.

After the failed railguns had been retested and passed fit for duty, Ori and the others were rotated off shift and given a four-hour break. She snagged a tube of water and a tube of vegetable paste, returned to her chair and lay down and slept. And jolted awake a little over two hours later to the soft ululation of the general-quarters alarm. She activated her chair and woke her bot.

It was early in the morning. Fomalhaut's tiny disc glaring a handspan above the horizon in the east; a few stars still showing in the west. And stars were falling high above, leaving thin white scratches as they ripped across the sky's dark blue dome. Ten, twenty, fifty. Tracking algorithms showed that the stars were falling to the south and east of the platform, burning down the sky, punching through the cloud deck about seventy klicks away. Too far away for the bot's cameras to grab any detail, but Ori imagined the stars breaking apart inside the cloud deck to hatch enemy predators, the new-born flock turning, hunting, looking for targets, locking on to them . . .

Commander Tenkiller came on line, issuing crisp calm orders to prep the railguns for immediate firing. As Ori and the rest of the crew began to move towards their stations, more stars fell. Some shot straight overhead; others fell on either side. Ori saw one plunge past the port side, less than twenty klicks out. A finned shape falling straight down, vanishing into the cloud deck, where sporadic glows were appearing, burning foggily inside the thick veils.

The Eye of the Righteous was beginning to turn. Ori saw a trio of bright shapes flash past, shockingly close, trailing long cords of shock-heated soot. She didn't see the one that hit the ship.

It struck somewhere forward of her position. There was a terrific slam and a flash and debris flew up and the curved upper decking of the ship rippled. Ori's bot was flung backwards in a long arc and slammed into a winch. She grabbed hold of the winch's housing as the deck yawed. Damage reports popped up and there was something wrong with the feed: she couldn't see anything clearly and fine motor control was fading in and out. Then everything failed completely. For a moment, she was in her chair, hearing panicky voices shouting at each other, and then a secondary link kicked in and she was riding her bot again.

It had started up its autorepair sequences in the few moments she'd been gone. Rerouting control of its fine manipulators, clearing dead patches in its three-hundred-and-sixty-degree vision. But its sonar and deep radar were still down, and joints on two of its limbs had lost lubricant; it walked with a distinct limp as Ori steered it towards the point of impact at the bow of the ship.

At least half the bots that had been working outside were gone: knocked off the ship by the impact. Some of those left were working on the railguns; one signalled to Ori.

'There may be more of them. Help us, damn you.'

'The ship is damaged,' Ori said. 'Internal comms are down. We need to know our situation before we can work out what to do.'

The curve of the upper surface had acquired a distinct lean, tilting forward and to the right, and a hole some ten metres across had been punched into the plates close to the prow. Ori crabbed her bot over buckled plates. The edge of the hole exposed layers of insulation and fibrous fascias of pressure tanking, all of it distorted, as if a bubbling, dripping, roiling slough of liquid had been instantly frozen. Infrared and ultraviolet overlays revealed patches of activity. Hot spots. Intricate feathery streaks and veins that pulsed and shifted, extending fine threads into hull plating around the gash like some kind of horrible rot of the inanimate.

Ori extended an arm equipped with a set of probes and micro-manipulators. Zoomed in on one of the invasive threads and saw that it was composed of rod-shaped microscopic units, each attached to its neighbours by hairlike pilli. Even as she watched, rods pinched in half at their waists and the two halves pulled apart and promptly began to grow. Nanomachines, each with intricate internal architecture, extending and dividing in rhythmic pulses of activity.

Three other bots crabbed towards her. One was ridden by Hereata, the others by two drone jockeys, Aata and Ulua. Hereata said that she had seen the impact, and threw a pict at Ori: a deeply foreshortened view of a dark fleck falling beyond the truncated curve of a contrail that was bent into a sinusoidal shape by winds moving at different speeds at different heights in the sky. The fleck slipping sideways in the sky, seeming to skip towards the viewpoint in a series of skidding lunges, growing larger with shocking speed, jerking in and out of frame as the optical system of Hereata's bot tried to track it, slamming straight through the prow of the ship in a flash of flame.

'It steered straight at the ship,' Ori said.

'It took out the Trues' lifepod,' Ulua said. 'No one knows where the commander and her officers are.'

'This stuff is growing,' Aata said, stepping back from the edge.

'I know,' Ori said. 'We have to do something about it right away.'

'We have to find someone in charge,' Ulua said.

'I think we may be in charge now,' Ori said.

She seemed to be at the centre of a ringing calm, the way she'd felt riding the probe down through the cloud deck after the quake. Except this was real. She wasn't safely lodged inside the Whale's comforting bulk. This was happening to her. She felt a jolt of excitement, and also felt, for the first time in days, her passenger stir behind her eyes.

'Leto and Tche were down there,' Aata said. 'They were preparing the last of the drones . . .'

'They might still be down there,' Ulua said. 'Trapped between bulkhead doors. We should go down and look for them.'

'I have a better idea,' Ori said, and launched a fly-by-wire probe, spinning it out and down. The impact had punched through the hull plates and pressure tanking, smashed structural spars. The Trues' lifepod had been sheared away, two ballonets had ruptured and collapsed across the wreckage of broken spars, and the hangar that had housed the predators was torn open. It was pitch black inside, but the probe detected shifting pulses of infrared around the edges of the rupture. Radar imaging of the hangar itself showed that walkways had collapsed or detached, a jumble of wreckage caught amongst the launch cradles – and then the connection dropped. Something had cut into it, was trying to pump information into the drone's nervous system. Ori shut off the link and had the bot run a self-check, then picted images and analysis of the damage and the infection to the others.

'We have to cut this away before it spreads,' she said.

'It is already spreading,' Hereata said, pointing to a distinct fan of fine black thread that had pushed out from the narrow rim of rot at the border of the gash.

They sent down more probes to map the damage, and were comparing the wreckage with schematics, trying to work out where they could begin cutting away the damaged and infected parts without compromising the structural integrity of the ship, when without warning the connection to Ori's drone was cut. She was back in her body, back in the chair, looking up at someone – Lani – who was straddling her chest and holding a cutter to her throat.

Ori could feel the point of the cutter pricking the soft flesh under her jaw. She lay very still, moving only her eyes, seeing Hereata and the other two jockeys pinned down by other members of Hira's circle, seeing Hira herself facing off Quicks crowded at the hatch, hearing her say that everything was under control now.

She had a grim but triumphant look, saying loudly that Ori and her crew had been planning sabotage but they'd been stopped just in time.

A few people began to protest. Hira stood firm, arms folded, staring them down. Saying, 'These people are wreckers. Their drones survived the first attack because they are in league with the enemy. Now they have brought the enemy to us. We found them gloating over the damage and planning to make it worse. They would have killed all of you, but I have stopped them.'

'We're trying to save you,' Ori said, and winced when Lani pressed down with the point of the cutter. Skin parted with a flare of pain; blood wormed down the side of her neck.

'Let them speak,' someone said.

Ori locked gazes with Lani. She had a hot and wild glint in her eyes that Ori didn't like at all, and she was sweating and there was a faint tremor in the hand that held the cutter. Ori said as calmly as she could, 'Will you let me up?' Feeling the point move against the wound in her neck with every word.

'Be quiet or I'll hurt you bad,' Lani said, her voice thick.

'We don't do this to each other,' Ori said. 'We aren't Trues.'

Several people repeated this. Hira looked all around, then clapped her hands. 'Listen to me. Listen. We have only one chance of survival. We must remove these wreckers before they call down the enemy again. Are you with me, or are you with them? Think carefully. Choose the wrong side, and you choose the enemy.'

Ori looked at Lani and said, 'I'm going to sit up so that I can talk to Hira. I won't do anything silly, and you won't either.'

'You can't tell me what to do,' Lani said, and slashed Ori's cheek, scoring so deep that the point of the cutter went through skin and muscle and Ori felt it grate on a tooth. She yelled to let out the shocking pain, and suddenly people were crowding in. Lani lashed out at them, but someone caught her arm and wrenched the cutter from her grip, and someone else caught her from behind and pulled her to the floor.

Ori swung out of the chair and planted her feet on the floor and stood. She was trembling all over and was holding her cut cheek. It was beginning to burn, and she could feel blood slick and wet under her palm and blood pooling under her tongue. She spat a mouthful of blood on the floor, wiped her lips with the back of her hand.

Hira said in the sudden silence, 'Let her talk. It won't change anything.'

Ori looked all around. Hereata and Aata and Ulua were standing too. The place was crowded. Everyone was looking at her. Hira stood amongst her acolytes, arms folded, shrugging away when one of them patted her shoulder.

Ori spat out more blood, said, 'Trues have always decided what we should do, and we have always done what the Trues have told us to do. We have always served. But now we're on our own. For the first time in our lives, we have to decide what to do. It's hard. It's frightening. But we must face up to it.'

'She wants you to hand yourselves to the enemy,' Hira said.

'The enemy is already here,' Ori said. Feeling her sliced cheek part with each word. 'We found some kind of disease inside the hole made by the thing that hit us. It's spreading. Changing the fabric of the ship.'

Aata put up a window, showing the leprous rim of the hole, the thready infection pulsing in the hull plates, dividing, spreading.

Hira laughed. 'This is a trick. Got up so she can take over.'

Ori said, 'Go outside. Look for yourselves. But don't take long, because it's growing fast.'

'What do we have to do?' someone said.

'How can we help?' someone else said.

Hira pushed through them, stood face to face with Ori. 'I won't allow this,' she said, and suddenly swung her fist, hitting Ori under her eye.

Ori stumbled backwards, gripped the back of her chair, faced Hira. 'This isn't our way,' she said.

Hira stepped forward and struck Ori again, and this time Ori lost her footing and went down to her knees. She pushed up, faced Hira. Saying, 'This isn't how we decide things.'

Hira would have hit her again, but two people closed on her and hauled her backwards. She struggled for a moment, then subsided. Glaring at Ori, saying, 'Your lies will kill us all.'

And then she was pulled away. Ori felt the room turn around her and she sat down. Her whole face was throbbing to the quick pulse of her heart. Someone pressed a wet cloth to her cheek. Tane, the leader of the maker crew, said, 'Tell us what to do.'

Ori realised that everyone was looking at her. Waiting for her to speak. She said, 'We need to go back outside and deal with the enemy. And I think we'll need explosives. Can you spin some?'

The black necrosis had spread a good two metres around the hole now. Deltas and streaks, feathers and curlicues. Ori and the rest of her crew deployed a small flock of drones that surveyed the infection from every angle, used the data to map where to plant the shaped charges that the maker crew had spun, then walked their bots to the underside of the ship and began to cut through the skin at the rear of the hangar, through plates and deep layers of insulation and pressure tanking, into the structural elements beneath. They worked with feverish haste, knowing that if they cut away too little, the infection wouldn't be cauterised, but if they cut away too much, the ship's integrity would be compromised.

When they had finished, they retreated to the stern and clamped down, and without any ceremony Ori set off the charges.

Ripples pulsed through the skin of the ship. At the prow, debris flew out in a long line and a cylindrical section dropped clean away, dwindling into the bright gulf of air. Ori's heart lifted when she saw that. Saw it fall straight down, shedding shards and flecks of debris, dwindling to a mote, a speck. The ship lurched, swung back, rocked to and fro, but it held together.

Ori led the others to the long and ragged edge of the cut to make sure that all the infection had been flensed away. It was unsettling to see the cavernous hole punched clean through the ship, exposing the truncated remains of the garage.

'It seems we aren't quite done,' Hereata said, and pointed to a chunk of internal wall that hung from a ropy cable at the edge of the gap, black with infection and rocking to and fro on the wind.

Ori and Hereata took what was left of the shaped charges and climbed down into the truncated remains of the hangar. Just two predator cradles were left. Strange to see them in sunlight and open air, half-buried in a mash of floor mesh and railings and broken machinery. There could be bodies in there. Leto and her crew. Ori hoped that when they'd died it had been instant. Painless. She pictured the gale that must have punched through the hangar when its integrity had been breached and the external pressure of twenty atmospheres had equalised with the ship's internal pressure, ripping out walkways and machinery, flinging everything against the far end of the garage . . .

She and Hereata X-rayed the ceiling around the cable spun by the infection, found that it had gone deeper and further than they had reckoned. They climbed up a wall and edged out across the ceiling, hanging over a gap bitten in the floor, with a view straight down to the cloud deck more than twenty kilometres below. Working on either side of the cable's attachment point, they pulled out access plates, clambered into narrow inspection spaces and placed explosive charges against structural spars, then climbed out and repeated the process over and again, laying two lines of charges that angled towards each other in a vee shape.

Probes hovered around them, transmitting everything they did to the rest of the crew. Wind whistled, whirled up twisters of dust that glinted in slanting beams of sunlight, rocking the section of infected plating that dangled from the cable. The cable was definitely thinner, and thin black tentacles were spreading out across the ceiling, dividing and diving at their tips, sending out runs towards the edges of the vee that Ori and Hereata had defined.

They pulled out the last of the access plates, at the point of the vee. Ori swung her bot into the narrow space and saw black threads laced across on a structural spar, scarcely a metre away. She picted the view to Hereata and said, 'It's as if it knows what we're doing. Trying to grow around us.'

'Perhaps it does,' Hereata said.

Her bot passed the last of the explosive charges to Ori's drone, and Ori fitted them against the infected spar and activated the radio trigger.

As she backed away across the ceiling, she felt an odd and unsettling whisper of static across the comms.

'Did you hear that?'

'The wind?'

'Interference,' Ori said.

It was louder. A staccato arrhythmic pulsing. Hereata said something, but her words were garbled by the interference.

'My bot is infected,' Ori said. 'Get out now.'

The pulse drumming, staggering, lopsided. A fluttering in the video feed, and a kind of pressure or surge in the downlink, something trying to cut its way through the filters, probing, pushing.

It was like being enfolded by someone else's heart. Squeezed down to a dot by muscular pumping. Ori reached for the command that would trip the explosives, but it was like trying to insert her hand down a pipe that was being crushed and constricted out of existence. As she flailed and pushed, Hereata reached past her.

Ori felt a hard thump beneath her bot, saw narrow blades of brief fire define the two sides of the vee. For a moment, nothing else happened. Then a big wedge of the ceiling dropped away, falling straight through the gap in the floor. The ship bucked and surged, and Ori went with it, galloping out across the ceiling and dropping into the void, reaching out as she fell and gathering up control of the probes and sending them spinning out into the air.

Wind snatched at the bot, sent it tumbling. She glimpsed the ship receding into the blue sky, saw a speck falling away from it: Hereata's bot. Sky and the long distant horizon and the cloudscape below tumbled around and around. A roaring of wind buffeting splayed limbs and manipulators. She could feel something making its way towards her, moving into the core of the bot, and she cut the link and was thrown back into herself. In the immersion chair in the jockeys' hutch, her pulse pounding in her head, pounding red and black in her eyes, in the stapled wound in her cheek, cramps ripping at the muscles of her arms and legs.

Someone helped her sit up, fed her sips of chilled water from a pouch. Someone else said, 'What do we do next?'

It was a good question.

4

Despite the long drought, a shallow lake some ten kilometres long spread under the open sky behind the dam and common lodge of the River Folk, its margins lost in the tall trees on either side, its broad calm surface clogged everywhere with the rimmed circles of giant water-lily pads. Some pads were so big that the Child could lie on their waxy surfaces – beds that conformed to the shape of her body and gently rocked on the face of the water. The air was cool at night, and perfumed with the giant blossom spikes of the lilies, which thrust up like swords between the pads and were attended by bats and giant moths. Above, the starscape swept from horizon to horizon, spanned by a hazily luminous arch somewhat like the Milky Way, except that it was narrower and more diffuse, and intermittent showers of meteors fell, and the red and green hairy stars chased each other down towards dawn.

The River Folk browsed on the lily pads for much of the night, ploughing ledes of black silky water through the floating fields. During the day, they lay on their backs under the shade of the largest pads and slopped mud on their bellies and dozed or meditated, talking each to each in voices that boomed across the lake. Slow, ponderous conversations with long pauses between sentences and phrases. Their thoughts ran deep and were intricately braided. Mostly they were mathematicians, engaged in unravelling the eleven-dimensional geometry of hyper-Riemann space-time that enclosed the multiverse.

Three families shared the lake. According to Jaguar Boy they had been working on the same problem for centuries. A great collective achievement that had constructed a gigantic and supremely elegant cathedral of thought. The Child asked how this could be true. Because if it was, the River Folk must have diverged from common stock long before the development of any genetic science capable of reshaping the human form – long before the Industrial Revolution, in fact.

Jaguar Boy shrugged. 'There is more history than you yet know.'

'Conspiracies that used advanced sciences in secret?'

'No, it's simpler than that.'

'Are they aliens, fallen to Earth centuries ago, living in secret all this time?'

She was wondering if Jaguar Boy was an alien, or perhaps descended from people who had been captured and reshaped by aliens. Her ama had often told her about flying saucers and cigar-shaped craft that cruised the skies above the forest, searching for human specimens.

'Be patient,' Jaguar Boy said. 'You'll soon understand everything.'

'Why can't you tell me now?'

He shrugged again, said, 'You still have much to learn.'

The adult River Folk were as large and fat as cows; like cows, their barrel-shaped bodies were bioreactors that fermented and digested the vast amounts of vegetation they ate every day. They had loose black skin that was velvety to the touch, legs shrunken and broadened into flippers, truncated arms with small hands, delicate fingers with pearlescent fingernails. Their faces were broad, with large, mournful brown eyes and wide, mobile mouths.

Their children were much smaller, about the Child's size, agile and playful. They fed and groomed and generally indulged a little school of infants, maintained the dam and the broad dome of the common lodge with the help of snake-like machines that also gardened the floating fields of lily pads, scared off would-be predators, and collected from the fringes of the forest leaves, rocks, dirt and other materials which they fed into their maker. This was a fat black cube packed with microscopic machines that broke down into atoms the stuff that it was fed, and used them to make more snake-machines, the beads and ribbons which the River Folk children used to decorate their hair (they were covered in a fine pelt that thickened into crest-like stripes on top of their heads), the drug that the adult River Folk used to deepen their meditations, and many other things. It produced shorts, sandals, and a short-sleeved shirt for the Child, any kind of food she requested, and a small coracle as light as a soap bubble and as strong as steel.

The Child slept during the day. At sunset, when the children of the River Folk grew lively and playful, she swam with them, and later, after

236

sunset and her evening meal, she lay on one of the giant lily pads, talking to any who came by. At the beginning of every evening there would be six or seven River Folk children fringing her pad, combing and braiding each other's crests while they talked and told stories and sang songs (they loved to sing, usually ballads in three-part harmony, chronicling their long and strange history). But they grew distracted as darkness fell, and swam off to play games of tag or experiment with sex, and long before midnight the Child would be left alone, to think about what she had learned. In this fashion, over the days and evenings, she was told fantastic stories of how the River Folk and people like them had come to dominate the human race as it spread out into the Solar System.

It was not uncommon for the moons of the outer planets to possess oceans or inclusions of liquid water beneath their icy shells. Jupiter's moon Europa had the largest, an ocean a hundred kilometres deep wrapped around a core of silicates that was molten at its centre, heated by tidal friction as the moon was pulled this way and that by the gravity wells of the inner moon Io and the outer moon Ganymede, and it was stretched and kneaded by Jupiter's gravity. In the deep rifts of its floor, bacterial colonies grew around hydrothermal vents that pumped out superheated water rich in sulphides and iron and other nutrients. The bacteria were the only extraterrestrial life known in the Solar System, but shared the same genetic code as life on Earth, and had most likely arrived on Europa via a rock knocked off the Earth by some massive impact.

When humans had begun to colonise Europa, the ocean had been lightless and lacked oxygen. At first, the Europans had lived in settlements carved into the underside of the moon's thick icy rind, but at last they had begun to reshape their children, and construct self-replicating bubbles containing rafts of lights and photosynthetic weed that had spread out in great chains across the upper waters. Some of the children were air-breathers like the River Folk, and swam and dived but always returned to their labyrinthine ice cities. Others were truly aquatic, with external gills that trailed in long frills on either side of their smooth bodies.

And as in Europa's ocean, so in the oceans of other moons in the Solar System – Jupiter's Ganymede and Callisto, Saturn's Titan (the subsurface pockets of liquid water that powered tiny Enceladus' geysers were too small to sustain anything other than bacteria), Uranus'

237

Umbriel and Ariel, Neptune's Triton, Pluto's Charon. Many of these subsurface seas, and the artificial seas created on other icy moons and in the larger of the planetoids in the Kuiper belt, initially melted by guided asteroid strikes and maintained by fusion reactors, were freezing mixes of ammonia and water, but colonising them required only a few simple metabolic adaptations.

Natural seas under the surfaces of icy moons and planetoids were very common, more than twenty for every rocky exoplanet occupying the habitable zone of its star. As humanity spread out through the systems of the near stars River Folk, deep swimmers, and clades of other aquatic posthumans began to outnumber every other kind of human and posthuman. Some, like the River Folk, returned to Earth's oceans and rivers, and there were several aquatic clades that had taken to living in spaceships or orbital habitats containing tiny seas of oxygen-bearing fluorosilicone fluids, free-fall nymphs that were smaller than the Child and pursued long trading orbits between moons and planetoids. But most lived under the frozen surfaces of icy moons. And so the human race shaped itself to inhabit seas like those from which its distant lungfish ancestors had crawled, and to which the ancestors of whales and dolphins and manatees had already returned.

'Life is change,' Jaguar Boy said. 'Change is life. The human race diverged from its ancestral hominin form in less than a million years, driven only by Darwinian selection. Divergence of clades from the base form was much faster than that, driven by genetic engineering that can shape a new clade in only a few generations.'

The Child said that this must surely be a fairy story. She knew that the Outers had settled several of the moons of Jupiter and Saturn, but the tweaks they'd made to their genomes were no more than minor adaptations to life in microgravity; basically, they weren't much different from people on Earth.

'In your time they are still more or less base-line human. But we are talking about the time after your time. The human race as you know it still exists, but in small and stubborn pockets of barbarism. Perhaps they will rise again, after the clades have gone. And if they do, it is likely that the cycle will repeat itself. The human species is characterised by nonspecialist intelligence. Which will shape its future as surely as it shaped its past.'

'Who are you? Are you from this future?'

'I hope I am a friend.'

They were talking while sharing supper. One of the few long conversations that the Child had with Jaguar Boy during her stay with the River Folk. He spent most of his time asleep, stretched out on the broad branch of a tree close to the dam. Once, she'd tried to sneak away, and he'd been there, standing in a shaft of sunlight with a halo of butterflies orbiting his head, smiling his fearsome smile. He was her guide, and he was also her guardian; she was both pupil and prisoner.

'I mean, are you like them? From a clade?'

'I am what you wanted me to be. You wanted freedom. I am here to help you explore it.'

'I don't think you're real.'

'I'm as real as you are. As the River Folk are.'

'That's what I mean. They're a story told by my ama. She told me a story about you, too, once upon a time. I'm dreaming about you, and I'm dreaming about them, and I'll wake up . . .'

The Child lost track of the time she spent with the River Folk, but at last Jaguar Boy said it was time to leave. They had other people to visit, much more to learn. And so, early one evening, all of the River Folk, young and old, gathered by the dam and sang a long song that stayed with the Child and Jaguar Boy as they walked through the forest. When they could hear it no more they set up camp between two prop roots of a massive tree, and slept like two lost innocents.

5

We left Avalon, Prem Singleton, the Horse, and I, in a bucket rocket that was little more than a big motor with a few lifepods bolted to it, each just big enough for a crash couch and a single passenger. I spent most of the trip crushed by over one g of acceleration or deceleration – more than five times steeper than Thule's gravity – with only a little relief when the rocket swung around at the midpoint. It was a crude and brutal way of travelling, but much faster than the freighters I was used to riding, which generally followed long, minimum-energy orbits amongst the worldlets of the Archipelago. Speed was of the essence now. We'd spent far too long, almost half a megasecond, waiting in Avalon's port while Prem's mysterious friends tracked down Yakob Singleton.

He and his companion had travelled under false identities created with tools and skills acquired during his work for the Department for Repression of Wreckers, and their route had not been a direct one. They'd returned to Thule and immediately caught a freighter bound for an industrial worldlet, Wayland's Smithy, and there they'd changed identities again before hopping to Ull, a garden worldlet made over into a hunting ground for scions. Where they had disappeared into the wilderness and where they were still, unless they had adopted new identities that Prem's friends had been unable to uncover.

Both Prem and I were by now convinced that Yakob's companion was Bree Sixsmith, but we were unable to agree whether he had been turned by her, or whether he was playing some elaborate game of doublethink. I favoured the former theory; Prem the latter. She believed that her cousin was pretending to help the traitor so that he could uncover others who'd been turned by demons or had for whatever reason allied themselves with the enemy. She thought that he could be redeemed, and I did not try to disabuse her because I quickly realised that it was more a matter of faith than of logic.

I blacked out when acceleration peaked during the trip to Ull, and the rest of the journey was scarcely more comfortable, with the iron toad of gravity squatting on my chest and blood swimming in my eyes. It was hard to imagine how the ancestors of human beings could have developed the ability to walk upright in that gravity; hard to imagine how the first amphibious fish could have chosen to leave the support of the sea to crawl about on land.

There was no time to recover from the rigours of the journey. Upon arrival at Ull's orbital station, we immediately transferred to an elevator the size of a small freighter. Riding inside a hollow cable with a transparent diamond sheath, it took some eight thousand seconds to fall from the station to the surface of the worldlet. We were masquerading as two scions of a minor family come to hunt with their trusted bodyservant – disguises constructed by Prem's friends. As we fell towards the glistening bubble of the worldlet's halflife shell, I tried again to find out who those friends were, and grew angry when Prem told me that now wasn't the time to discuss such matters.

'If you knew who they are, it could put you in danger,' she said.

'I seem to have been co-opted by a conspiracy with questionable methods and unclear and possibly seditious aims.'

'You are working towards clearing your name by helping me find my cousin. Everything else is my concern, not yours.'

Prem seemed calm, but she couldn't stand still for long. Sitting in the couch before the big window of the compartment, jumping up and pacing around, studying the trencher's menu, turning back to the window. She stepped close to me now, took hold of my hand, and said that she envied me and the rest of the Sixsmith clan.

The Horse, perched on a low stool in one corner of the capsule, pretending to be asleep, half-opened one eye and smiled his sly smile.

'You have certain advantages,' Prem said. 'Not just because you're clever, although you are. Most of my people may not be as clever as most of you, but they are cunning and ruthless, they have a wealth of experience to draw on, and they are schooled to make the best use of any talents they possess. Those without power think powerful people are stupid and complacent because they have everything they want and are insulated from the troubles that ordinary people must face every day. But it isn't true. We have learned hard lessons about surviving in a world where everyone else wants what we have, and are prepared to do anything to get it. No, the troubles of ordinary people are nothing to ours. In their world, a mistake can cost you a meal, or a job. In my world, it costs you everything. So we must be clever and cunning simply to survive. But your people, Isak, can move unnoticed through every layer of society. You have power, and custody of a great treasure, but no one wants to or dares to try to take it from you because only you know how to make proper use of it. I envy the freedom that gives you.'

I thought that most of what she said was wrong, but it wasn't the place or time to start an argument about power and privilege. Instead, I asked her what would happen if she failed to find her cousin.

'Thanks to that malicious fool on Avalon, we've begun to attract the attention of the wrong people. They don't know what Yakob is chasing, not yet. But if they do . . . Well, let's say that most outcomes are bad.'

'Which is why, Majistra, I would like to know what is at stake here.'

'Victory. Freedom. Everything Our Thing claims we're fighting for.' Prem let go of my hand and stepped up to the window and looked out at the half-globe of the worldlet below, white and dun inside the shell of its halflife bubble, which glistered with bloody highlights in the glare of its damaged microsun. 'It's down there, Isak,' she said. 'The secret of the starship and its passenger. The thing Yakob has been chasing. The thing we need. The end of the war, or the beginning of something far worse.'

Ull was one of the hundreds of dwarf planets that had accreted out of the debris left over from Fomalhaut's formation and survived the early violent period of the system's history. A roughly spherical ball of water, methane, and ammonia ices wrapped around a silicate core, marked everywhere with impact craters, and rifts and wrinkle ridges caused by the slow contraction of its outer layers as it cooled. Captured like half a hundred other bodies by the 2:3 orbital resonance with Cthuga, elevated above the plane of the dust ring. Then the Quick seedship had arrived, and Quick machines had diverted chunks of ice and silicates to intersect with Ull's orbit, glancing impacts that removed most of its volatiles and exposed its core. Some of the hydrogen and helium blown off by those impacts had been collected by the steep gravity well of a superstring placed in orbit, creating a microsun; the small percentage remaining on the surface had been used to synthesise an atmosphere, provide enough water for a hydrological cycle, and synthesise a halflife bubble to keep in the atmosphere and exclude cosmic rays. The machines had dropped a superstring into the centre of the worldlet to give it a pull of around 0.2 g, had sculpted the surface, creating ranges of bare, shaly hills fretted with canyons and arches of rock, and buttes standing up amongst fields of tall crescent dunes, and had added a sparse scattering of life. Tough grasses and cacti, creosote bush and yuccas. Dwarf forests along the tops of the hills, where climate machinery created fogs. One of many garden worlds of every description scattered through the Archipelago, some with gravity and some without, some rocks enclosed in a halflife shell, some hollow shells with free-fall forests or grasslands on their inner surfaces and little suns in their centres.

In this fashion the busy, powerful, tireless machines had transformed several tens of planetoids and dwarf planets. Later, the Quick would abandon most of these early creations, saying that their machines had built and gardened worlds because they had been gifted with the desire and need for creation by those who had sent out the seedship. The machines had the best of intentions, the Quick said, but they had been wrong to try to impose an alien standard of beauty on their new home. Better to embrace the worldlets of Fomalhaut as they were, not use them to create pocket versions of Earth. Better to find new ways of living. So they'd abandoned the garden worldlets, choosing instead lives of solitary or communal contemplation in ships and habitats that were extensively and exotically designed and decorated. Only a few holy or crazy people made their homes on the worldlets, contemplating whatever it was they contemplated. Guardians or gardeners, each plugged into the ecology and climate of their home, recording every detail of its uneventful days.

And then we True had arrived, and had taken possession of everything, including the garden worldlets. And proceeded to wreck most of them through carelessness, ignorance and misplaced confidence in our ability to shape them to suit our needs. One of the first clans had taken a shine to Ull, had manoeuvred it closer to the worldlet where they'd set up their home. It had lost its microsun during the move and everything on it had died and it had grown so cold that the carbon dioxide in its atmosphere had snowed out. The clan had recaptured the microsun and tried to fix up a new ecosystem, planning to turn it into some kind of arena where young bucks could show off their prowess by hunting top predators, but it hadn't really worked. They had broken an intricate mechanism that they didn't really understand. Eventually they had given up on trying to rebuild or fix it, and sold the wreckage to Our Thing.

It was a patchwork of private and public hunting grounds now. Prem's friends had rented a place for us in one of the public estates, a base where we could search for Yakob Singleton and Bree Sixsmith. It was no easy task. Although Ull was just two hundred kilometres in diameter across its major axis, it had a surface area of more than a hundred thousand square kilometres.

When we arrived on the surface, we were met by an antique open-top half-track vehicle driven by one of the Quick housekeepers of the estate's lodge. It immediately set out across the broad valley where the elevator cable was anchored, and climbed a long switchback that snaked up one of the steep sides, where tree stumps stood amongst loose rock and tongues of rotten ice.

The weakened insolation of its damaged minisun meant that it was always winter on Ull. Grey and white and black. We crossed a field of dunes capped with frost that gave way to stony scrub and the fretwork skeletons of long-dead tree-sized cacti. Hanging forests of dwarf dragonblood trees had once grown along fretted scarps, but they had died when the worldlet was moved, and most of the birch and pine trees planted amongst their stout smooth-skinned stumps had also died, standing in sere and leafless clumps against the iron sky. By some quirk or mismanagement of the worldlet's climate control, the fogs that had once sustained them now filled canyons and valleys. Streams ran out of the foggy canyons, smoking in the cold, spilling into marshlands and strings of small lakes. The lakes were fringed with ice and stands of giant rushes. A small population of 'native' Quicks hunted fungi and lichens that had psychotropic properties prized by True scions. Jack sheep and deer with bladed antlers and humped shoulders taller than a man grazed the mosses and lichens that grew in the foggy valleys, and jaguars and sabre-toothed mountain lions preyed on sheep and deer and elk, and scions hunted the jaguars and lions and everything else.

Prem Singleton had rifled a dressing chest in the elevator terminus. Wearing a sheepskin jacket with a fur collar, thick black tights and riding boots, she looked the very image of a hunter, and grew animated as we trundled along. She pointed out animal trails, good spots to set up hides, a salt lick where animals would come at night.

'If this were another time, I could take you on a trek, Isak. Can you ride a horse?'

I told her that I did not know, for I had never tried; for some reason that amused her.

'They're small, and very docile and sure-footed. The best way to travel through country like this. There are bikes, too, but they don't connect you to nature the way a living mount does.'

'You enjoy getting in touch with your wild side.'

'All Trues should experience this. Not just scions. One day, when the war is over, it may be possible.'

'Yes, and we'll live in a paradise where everyone can rule their own worldlet, and can pluck fruit and tame birds from the trees. Except that whenever we try to establish some kind of utopia we wreck it. As we wrecked this world. That's how we are, Majistra. We won't change because if we did we would no longer be Trues.'

'Some believe that we have already changed. That we have absorbed some of the traits and habits of the Quick,' Prem said.

(Beside me, the Horse, who was once again pretending to doze, stirred and opened his eyes; I gave him a look and he shrugged and shut them again.)

'We changed the Quick when we made them our servants,' Prem said. 'And by doing so, we changed ourselves. There are hardliners who say that we should let the Quick die out, when the war is over. That we are True, and should make sure that our proud heritage is not con-taminated by posthuman decadence. Are you a hardliner, Isak?'

'I am a servant of the Library,' I said, and asked her which side she chose.

'Most in my clan are hardliners,' she said. 'Like all the old clans.'

'I understand they are not monolithic in their beliefs.'

'They aren't democracies, either. Scions must respect the beliefs of their elders and betters, and subdue their own beliefs for the greater good. It's dangerous to have ideas that clash with the ideas of those above your rank. I'm sure it's the same with your clan.'

'We all try to do what is best for the Library. But we also like to talk, so there's often little agreement over what that might be.'

There were two benches in the back of the half-track, hard against either side. Prem was sitting in the middle of one and the Horse and I sat on the other, facing her. Now she turned away, her profile keen in the wintry light as she looked out at the landscape, lost in some reverie.

245

After a while, she said, 'This is like one of the sagas, isn't it? We're on a kind of quest, and we are bound together by ties of blood and betrayal. You by Bree Sixsmith; me by Yakob. I suppose you librarians know all about those old, old stories.'

'I know that all too many of them were tragedies.'

Prem's smile was like a starburst in the wintry gloom. It occurred to me that if this really was like one of the old sagas, then she must be the heroine, fierce and beautiful and wild. And more than a little frightening to those who knew how dangerous such heroines were to those around them.

'We'll find him,' she said. 'I can feel it in my core. The same feeling I get on a hunt. I know it may seem foolish, to pin your hopes on something as abstract and subjective as a feeling. But if you had ever hunted, you'd know that you quickly learn to trust your instincts as much as your reasoning.'

'I think I understand. After all, I hunt in my own small way,' I said.

'In hells and other virons. This is the real world, Isak, with real consequences. It's completely different.'

'I can assure you that actions in hells all too often have real consequences,' I said. 'Isn't that why we're here?'

Prem didn't seem to hear me. 'We come to places like this to renew our ties with the world in blood and death,' she said. 'And not always the death of our quarry. Scions are sometimes killed on hunts.'

'Then let us hope this is no hunt, but instead our prize will fall into our hands as easily as one of those birds in the fabulous paradises of the future.'

Prem laughed, and pointed past the cabin of the half-track, towards a low cliff that rose against the iron sky. 'We'll find out soon enough. There's the lodge.'

It was a rambling single-storey stone building that clung to the edge of the cliff and bridged a small river that plunged in a short waterfall to a deep pool below. Prem said that she wanted to interrogate and instruct the lodge's staff, and left the Horse and me in a long, low-ceilinged room. Its curved wall-window gave a view of the river's course scribbled across a rumpled plain of open scrub towards the close horizon, which had already swallowed Fomalhaut and was now rising towards the crimson spark of the minisun. The room was filled with the minisun's cold and bloody light.

I was taking in the view and thinking that Lathi Singleton's tier high in the thistledown city of Thule was the summer aspect of this little worldlet's winter, and that both were as fake as any viron and far more sentimental, when movement off to one side of the pool directly below caught my eye. A quartet of riders – Prem Singleton and three Quick – on shaggy-pelted ponies, cutting away from the river and vanishing into the deep shadows at the edge of a stand of dark green conifers.

'I hope that isn't what it looks like,' the Horse said.

He had come up behind me. Like Prem, he'd raided the dressing chest of the terminus, exchanging his colourful motley for a plain tunic and leggings worn under a fur coat that reached to his ankles.

'What does it look like to you?' I said.

'Betrayal.'

That was what I had immediately thought, but I didn't want to believe it. 'Perhaps she wants some exercise after the rigours of the journey,' I said.

'Or perhaps she knows where her cousin is, and has gone to make some kind of bargain with him.'

'If you believe I have been too trusting, you should say so plainly.'

The Horse shrugged inside his oversized fur coat. 'She has a deal with you. And she also has a deal with those mysterious friends of hers. I can't help wondering which she considers more important.'

'You are welcome to follow her.'

The Horse struck a pose. 'If you command it, I'll do my best. Despite my complete – and completely ironic – lack of experience riding my totemic animal. Not to mention my utter ignorance of the territory. But I have another idea. That is, if you are in any way worried about your friend's fidelity.'

'You want to talk to the house servants. Exactly what I was about to suggest.'

'Then I should do it at once,' the Horse said.

'Have them bring me something to eat, too,' I said, as he walked off down the length of the room.

I turned back to the window and studied the stand of trees under which Prem and the Quicks had ridden. It was growing dark. Shadows lengthened and merged as the horizon rose up and obscured the minisun. Shells of light refracted by the worldlet's halflife bubble slowly died away and stars stood everywhere in the black sky, shining hard and bright above an inky panorama.

247

More agitated by Prem's disappearance than I cared to admit even to myself, I prowled the margins of the long room. It was carpeted with red halflife grass, and the few pieces of furniture were handmade, expensive, and shabby, in the fashion of places that are infrequently used and owned by no one in particular. The wall at the rear was of naked olivine, polished to reveal the glittering swirls of shock inclusions. There was an odd, small, square cave in the centre with a stuffed lion head mounted above it, eyes of black and gold glass and skin gone brittle and cracked and moulting. To one side was a rack of antique weaponry. Knives with long and variously shaped blades, crossbows, and rifles with long muzzles and mechanical firing pans. All of them handcrafted, all showing the wear of much use and the polish of much care.

I was examining a knife with a serrated blade as long as my forearm when the Horse returned. Carrying a tray covered with a cloth, he stalked down the length of the room, saying, 'That was a fool's errand. There's no one here.'

'No one at all?'

The Horse set the tray on a side table. 'They must have left with your friend.'

'A place like this must have more than three servants.'

'Then three left with your friend, and the rest fled. Or they're incarcerated in some place I can't find. Or murdered. That's a big knife. I hope you aren't considering self-harm.'

'I was marvelling at the inlay,' I said, displaying the haft to the Horse. 'It's bone, carved so cleverly that it induces a strange and very fine emotion when you pass your fingers over it. A mingling of regret and happiness a little like nostalgia, if one can be nostalgic for something one has never experienced. The fakes sold in the Permanent Floating Market are as crude a kick as raw sugar compared to this exquisite confection. Try it.'

But the Horse flinched back when I attempted to hand the knife to him. 'It isn't for me,' he said.

'It was made by a master craftsman from your glorious past. Carved, I believe, from bone grown in a culture of his own oocytes.'

'That's why it isn't for me,' the Horse said. 'Your nervous system and mine, they are tuned differently. You feel only a small portion of what I would experience.'

'Your loss,' I said, and sheathed the knife in the rack.

'Yes, it is.' The Horse had a strange look that almost exactly mirrored the sensation I'd felt when I'd passed my thumb across the delicate ridges of the ancient sliver of bone. Then he shook his head and forced a smile and with a flourish whipped the cloth from the tray, revealing a plate of bread and cheese, pickles and curls of dried fish, and a bowl of white tea that steamed in the cold air. Saying, 'I failed to find the servants, but I did manage to loot some provisions. In a crisis, it's always good to eat when you can.'

'This isn't a crisis. Is it?'

'I suppose that depends on whether or not she comes back.'

I warmed my hands on the bowl of tea. 'She'll come back. She needs my skills. But I admit that the manner of her departure is . . . odd.'

'You're wondering why she didn't explain that she had an errand. Why she didn't take us. Seeing as she needs our skills, and so on.'

'I am wondering if some of her friends might be close by. After all, they arranged our travel, our disguises, and these accommodations.'

'I've been wondering about them too,' the Horse said. 'And I've been wondering about a question she asked you on the ride here. About whether you side with the hardliners who believe that we Quick should be allowed to die out once the war has been won.'

'What about it?'

'I've been wondering if she left because she wasn't satisfied by your answer.'

I sipped my tea. 'I told her that I served the Library.'

'I know. But you didn't tell her that you weren't a hardliner.'

'That goes without saying, surely.'

'Only if you are familiar with the customs and history of your clan. You assume that everyone you meet knows about them, even though most people don't have the first idea about the way the Library works.'

'Why should what I believe concern her?'

'Because of what *she* believes.'

'And what is that?'

'This one is not sure that he should presume to hazard a guess at what a True might think.'

'I'll allow you an opinion about it. You have enough opinions about everything else.'

The Horse smiled. 'Will you allow me two opinions?'

'If I must.'

'The first is about you. You have many admirable qualities, and there's no doubting your skill in harrowing hells and dispatching demons. Which allied with my own small talents makes us such a formidable team.'

'Is this about you or me?'

'This one is your kholop. He is nothing without you.'

'Spare me.'

'The Library is your world. Perhaps that is why you do not realise that few people in the wider world know or care about it. Perhaps that is why you know much less about the wider world than you think.'

'I know that I know enough, and no more.'

'Exactly.'

'I hope this has something to do with Prem's disappearance.'

'She asked you whether or not you were a hardliner.'

'And I gave an unsatisfactory answer, according to you.'

'You gave an answer that was clear to you and to anyone in the Library, and obscure to almost everyone else. I don't think she realised that it was the answer she had been hoping for.'

'Of course we are not hardliners. After all, the Library is based on Quick knowledge.'

'And this worldlet was shaped by Quick machines. But look at it now: a half-ruined wilderness where yahoos hunt animals and various kinds of Quick cut into animal form.'

'Yet we are remaking the Library, not destroying or perverting it.'

'My point is that a familiarity or even a dependence on Quick technology does not always imply a sympathy with its creators. Librarians are different from most scions, yes, but most scions don't know that.'

'Prem may be smarter than you think.'

'Let's hope so, for I believe that you and she have much in common. Like librarians, some scions not only respect Quick culture, they also respect Quicks.'

'You think Prem is one such.'

'I told you I had two opinions to share with you. This is the second.'

'And how do you know this?'

'She has no servants. She was upset when that brute of a prefect massacred the workers in the hatchery. And most of all, she has at all times treated me with a touching courtesy and respect. You may think that isn't much, but it means a lot to me. In short, she's the very opposite of a hardliner,' the Horse said, and explained exactly what he meant.

We talked about it a long time. At last, when it became clear that Prem might not soon return, I asked the lights in the room to dim and settled on a low couch covered in a worn and much-patched tapestry that depicted the exodus of our seedship from our last redoubt in the Solar System's asteroid belt amidst a hectic and fanciful battle between ships and droids and drones, and slept. And woke when someone shook my shoulder, and turned over and saw Prem silhouetted against the flat pinkish light of dawn.

'I know where he went,' she said.

6

The battle for Cthuga was far from over. Ori and the rest of the surviving crew of *The Eye of the Righteous* had made no contact with the enemy since the falling star had struck their ship, but they had seen signs and wonders in the sky by day and by night. High contrails crossing and curling around each other. Sheets of lightning that flickered and danced across significant segments of the immense horizon. Deep pulsing heartbeats from far below. Screams and squawks, wails and unsettling, near-human cries in the radio spectrum. Rippling curtains of auroras. There were disturbances in the usually placid equatorial weather, too. Hazy streaks of cloud laid across thousands of kilometres high in the stratosphere. Little archipelagos of oval storms whirling around spikes of infrared energy rooted far below the upper cloud decks; thunderheads as big as continents boiling up, so tall that the station was forced to make long detours to avoid vast hailstorms and displays of thunder and lightning like the birth of something new and terrible in the world. Once, the ranging crew spotted something bright moving with great speed at approximately their level in the atmosphere, but whether it was a friendly or hostile craft was impossible to determine.

Perhaps *The Eye of the Righteous* was lost to enemy sight in the immensities of the planet. Or perhaps the enemy believed that it had been fully converted; or perhaps they had more important targets to deal with first. In any case, the ship sailed on unharmed, creeping slowly and uncertainly above the cloud deck, its crew always watchful, always fearful. Their ship a small world entire in itself, riding the winds ever westward, finding its way home through the signs and portents and detritus of vast battles.

There were seventeen of the crew left alive and, as was the way of

Quicks, no clear leader had emerged. They preferred to talk everything through, several overlapping conversations that gradually merged into a single voice, as if coalescing around a strange attractor. It was soothing to reach that point where everyone, more or less, was thinking like everyone else, and it helped to bind them together.

Ori politely deflected suggestions that she should take control. She felt that the surviving Quick should not emulate the True now that they were, for the moment, free, masters of their own fate. No, they should revert to the old ways as much as possible, and because the old ways were known to them only by rumour and myth, they were in truth forging a new way of living. A democracy in which agreement was not won by appealing to logic or emotion or self-interest, but by a kind of mutual meditation. And besides, she did not want the responsibility of leadership. She did not ever again want to stand out from the crowd, to become the target of someone else's enmity. She was content to be no more important than anyone else, and to abide by whatever was decided by consensus.

Hereata pointed out the inconvenient truth that Ori wasn't like everyone else because she alone could refuse to take command. Hira, or anyone else who dissented from the majority, would have to seize control by main force, but it was Ori's to take if she wanted. All she had to do was reach out, and it would be placed in the palm of her hand.

'You took charge in the moment of crisis,' Hereata said. 'Only you knew what to do to save the station. After that, the station was yours. The station, and everyone on it.'

'Except Hira and Lani,' Ori said.

'They have no power over you,' Hereata said. 'Everyone knows that they made the wrong choice.'

'I didn't know that what I did was right until I did it,' Ori said.

'Of course you did,' Hereata said. 'You were right to forgive them, too.'

'What else could I do? If I was a True I suppose I would have had them whipped and beaten, or given the long drop. But we are not Trues, and we should not behave like them. And besides, we have to fix up this poor old wreck before the enemy finds it again, and we need all the help we can get.'

For the moment, Ori and Hira had settled on frosty politeness and exaggerated observation of every small courtesy, and as in all things Lani followed her bunky's example. But Ori knew that this truce could not last for ever. Hira was a danger to everyone because she refused to accept the reality of their situation. At every meeting, she argued that they should chase down and engage with the enemy because that had been Commander Tenkiller's last order, and that they should also attempt to make contact with other stations where Trues would be able to tell them what to do; their debates on how to survive from day to day were, according to her, tantamount to mutiny. Ori tolerated this nonsense as best she could, but privately believed that Hira should have remained in custody so that she couldn't poison the consensual process with her dangerous ideas. Sooner or later, the woman would attempt to assert herself again, and Ori would have to intervene.

But as far as day-to-day survival was concerned, Hira was the least of their problems. A crew led by Ulua cut down the wrecked hangar and sealed the gaping hole with foam, but discarding so much mass at the leading edge of *The Eye of the Righteous* had altered its trim, and because of the damage its crew couldn't alter its configuration to correct for the imbalance, so it flew with an eccentric corkscrewing list that limited its speed and at every moment threatened to become uncontrollably chaotic. They were short of water because more than half the ship's supply had been lost when the impact of the falling star had ruptured tanks and pipework; one of the air-recycling plants had been lost, too, so the surviving plant had to be run at maximum capacity and watched carefully; food was rationed; and because almost every system had to be rerouted around the damage caused by the falling star and the growth of the seed it had carried, nothing worked as well as it should.

In short, they would have been in deep trouble even if they weren't caught in the middle of a planet-wide battle. So when the ranging crew reported that a steady blip that appeared on the long-range radar was definitely a pelagic station, it took a long time to decide what to do. They couldn't inspect the intruder remotely because most of the drones had been destroyed by the enemy, and the rest had been garaged in the forward hangar and lost with everything else. A sizeable minority of the crew wanted to avoid the intruder by tacking south, but for once Ori and Hira were in agreement: they both hoped that the station and its crew had survived or avoided contact with the enemy. Ori and her supporters hoped that it would be a useful ally, and might even have news of the progress of the battle for control of Cthuga; even if it was damaged or deserted, it might have supplies of water and food and air, and equipment that they could salvage. Hira hoped that Trues were aboard, that they would take charge and eradicate all uncertainties. So after several hours the crew voted to turn towards the blip, and within a day it was finally in optical range.

It hung in silhouette against the sunrise that banded the broad horizon, a few degrees north of the bright point of Fomalhaut. A stack of circular platforms each about three hundred metres across, set around a central shaft and hung beneath a cluster of tall balloons: one of the chain of resupply stations that girdled the planet, with hydroponic farms on the upper decks that supplied fresh food, and manufactories below. It should have been much deeper down, trawling the depths for carbon and other essential elements, but here it was in the upper air.

As *The Eye of the Righteous* drew nearer, its crew saw that the winches for the station's dew-catcher nets and much of its lower deck had been torn away. Infrared imaging revealed that none of its decks were significantly warmer than the freezing atmosphere. If anyone was alive, they must be huddled in pressure suits or an emergency capsule and either weren't keeping watch or were scared that *The Eye of the Righteous* had been converted by the enemy. None of the signals sent by radio or microwave were answered. It hung there in the sky under its cluster of silvery balloons, quiet and serene, slowly revolving. One of the hatches of the garages was open, and there was the truncated wreckage of its lower deck, but no sign of the kind of growths that had sprung from the enemy seed that had struck *The Eye of the Righteous*.

At last, with less than ten kilometres separating it from the resupply station, *The Eye of the Righteous*' motors were turned off. Ori found the absence of their vibration alarming. They were adrift again. Beginning to turn as the resupply station was turning, caught in a gyre in the atmosphere.

Ori plugged into one of the maintenance bots and walked it to the edge of the sheared-off hangar and studied the station as it moved past. After a little while, a bot ridden by Hereata came across the deck and stood beside Ori's.

'Well, here we are,' Hereata said. 'What do we do now?'

'It certainly looks deserted. If no one answers our signals, I suppose we'll have to go aboard and find out what happened to them.'

'It looks like something took a bite out of it. As if they ran into the same kind of trouble we had.'

'I was wondering about that.'

'My passenger is quiet, if it means anything.'

'Mine too,' Ori said. 'And I don't think it means anything.'

'So anything could be inside.'

'Anything we can imagine. Not to mention a few things we can't.'

'And it won't be easy, getting aboard.'

'I have an idea about that,' Ori said, and explained her plan.

Hereata was silent for a little while. The resupply station revolved into view once more. *The Eye of the Righteous* hung a kilometre away, its upper deck at about the same level as the station's smashed lower deck.

'I suppose we should put it to the democratic process,' Hereata said. 'I know one thing: Hira won't like it.'

'Hira is the least of our problems.'

As soon as the meeting was convened, Hira took the floor, claiming that because the resupply station was most likely a trap set by the enemy. They should use the railguns to punch holes in its balloons, send it straight down, and sail on.

'Either there's no one on the station, or they don't want to make themselves known,' she said. 'And that means they can't be friends, for they must know who we are. Either way, we must destroy it. If it's unoccupied, we'll have made sure that it doesn't fall into the hands of the enemy. If it's a trap, then we'll have saved ourselves.'

Several members of the environmental crew chipped in, pointing out what had been pointed out many times before: they were critically low on food and water and the other station was their first and perhaps only chance at resupply. This devolved into a long and unfocused discussion about what they lacked and what they needed to do, if they were going to complete their voyage around the world. Finally, Ori lost the last of her patience and stood up.

'We are here,' she said. Her mouth was dry and her heart was beating quickly, but she felt quite calm. Looking around at the others all packed together, looking at her. Like children, waiting for their orders. Was this how Trues felt? Probably not. They were used to giving orders, and expected them to be obeyed because the Quicks were, to them, a lower order. Slaves. But these were her sisters. She wanted to help them. To save them from themselves. Even if it meant taking charge and breaking her promise to herself.

'We are here,' she said again. 'And we have only two real choices. To leave at once, or to go aboard the resupply station. Well, I can see that we have not left, so I think that we must do the other thing.'

Some laughed at this. Hira and Lani did not. Lani was staring hard at Ori, and Ori stared back until Lani looked away, a flush rising in her face.

Ori said, 'Are we agreed?'

Hira stood up, not bothering to hide her anger. 'What is there to agree about? You have decided.'

Tane, the senior member of the maker crew, said, 'It's easy to decide to go aboard. But how are we going to do it?'

'And who will go?' Hira said. 'You've all decided that Ori will decide for us. By your silence if not by spoken assent. Will you let her choose who to send? Will you agree to go if she chooses you?'

'If I have to choose anyone, I choose myself,' Ori said.

Hereata, who rarely spoke during the debates, stood now, and said that she would go too. One by one, the other Quicks stood and volunteered, until only Hira, Lani, and a handful of their supporters were left.

Ori was glad and unhappy. Glad that the others had backed her, that they knew they had to risk everything to save themselves. Unhappy because she was by no means sure that her plan would work. That she might well have condemned herself to the long drop.

Hira looked all around, her face set in a grim and angry expression. 'You're all of you fools,' she said. 'If you go ahead with this thing you put everyone's lives at risk. I will ready the railguns and do my best to defend you from your foolishness, but if it is not enough you have only yourselves to blame.'

She turned and pushed through the little crowd, and Lani and the rest of her supporters followed, a few with embarrassed and backwards glances.

'Someone should stop her,' Tane said. 'In case she gets it into her head to fire on that station before we can take a proper look at it.'

Wirimu, the senior member of the environmental crew, flourished her slate and said that she could make sure there and then that the railguns didn't get any power until Ori allowed it. There was a murmur of assent.

Ori said, 'One railgun will have to remain operational. How else am I going to cross to the other station?'

✽

Tane took charge of manufacturing several kilometres of monofilament cable and balls of strong but resilient plastic that exfoliated thousands of microscopic filaments and hooks when it struck any surface. Bunched into a holdfast, these would grip with enough tensile strength to hold the weight of the cable and of a Quick combined, Tane said, but would in no way provide a permanent anchor. If the resupply station and *The Eye of the Righteous* started to revolve in different directions or to pull apart, the holdfast would shear.

'That's why we'll have to fit a collar of polarised explosive behind it,' Tane said. 'Also, why we'll have to make more than one rig. If there's any kind of problem after you ride across, we can cut the cable and fire off another one to bring you back.'

'Just don't cut it while I'm halfway across,' Ori said.

'We'll do our best. But if the worst comes to the worst, the sling's brakes should be able to clamp you fast, and we'll reel you in.'

Everyone worked through the night. Soon after dawn, *The Eye of the Righteous* began to judder and sway as the program rigged by the motor crew began to fire short bursts to correct the ship's rotation and match it as closely as possible with that of the resupply station, using lasers aimed at a specific part of the station's superstructure as a guidance system. It would work as long as no significant turbulence was encountered, the motor crew said. If that happened, all bets were off.

Ori and Hereata pulled on unfamiliar skinsuits and helmets and rebreathers, checking each other's equipment before passing through an airlock to the upper surface of the station. It was the first time Ori had been outside since a safety drill more than a year ago, on the Whale. The padding of the helmet chafed the half-healed wound in her cheek. Strange and frightening to stand under the open sky, to feel gusts of wind plucking at her as she and Hereata clomped across to the comb of railguns, where half a dozen bots were working with speed and precision, dancing around each other as they loaded the coiled ball of monofilament cable on to the sled of the single operational railgun. Two bots stood off in the distance, ridden by Hira's supporters, watching everything. It occurred to Ori that she was especially vulnerable out here: a bot could run her down or scoop her up and throw her off the edge before she could begin to react.

At last, the final checks were made and she and Hereata hunkered down with the bots. The railgun was aimed at the lower deck of the resupply station, which swung to and fro in short arcs as *The Eye of the*

Righteous struggled to keep orientated towards it in the capricious wind. The railgun fired with a sharp crack and the sled rebounded on its stop as the ball soared out into empty air, trailing unravelling loops of cable, and struck a bulkhead at the back of the truncated remains of a big room. The holdfast at the end of the cable held firm, and there was a long delay while Tane and her crew checked its attachment, fitted the cable to a winch and reeled in excess length, and then mounted a simple cradle. When everything was ready, *The Eye of the Righteous* rose a little way so that the tethered cable slanted down at an angle of some thirty degrees, the winch running backwards and forward as the crew attempted to keep it as taut as possible.

Ori clambered into the L-shaped sling. Hereata buckled her in and leaned in and touched helmets and wished her luck and then stepped back.

With a sudden jolt, Ori was lifted into the air and was suddenly sliding down, swinging out across a gulf of air, rocking to and fro as she shot towards the resupply station, her whole skin tingling, cold air hissing against her face inside the helmet, a metallic taste in her mouth. Hands and feet freezing. A sudden jolt of panic as the sling jerked to a halt, Hereata's voice in her ear, saying that they were taking up slack, she'd be moving again in a moment.

Ori felt the cable jerk upward, clung tight to the frame of the sling as it rocked from side to side. A glimpse of the cloud deck far, far below. If she fell, she wouldn't climb off her couch and try to shrug it off as best she could. This was this. If she fell, she fell. All the way down until velocity ripped open her skinsuit or heat and pressure fried her.

Then she was moving again. The curved flank of the resupply station slammed towards her and she passed beneath a ragged arch torn in it and on into shadow, using a squeeze-grip control to brake herself, coming down towards the shell of the hangar, a strong wave of relief washing through her as her boots touched the deck. She hit the release clip of the harness and fell to her hands and knees, and after a moment was able to push up and tell Hereata that she was all right, she was down.

She followed the taut cable past empty maintenance frames to the edge of the ruin, where wind roared past a bulkhead cleanly sliced in half, and looked up at *The Eye of the Righteous*, a small island in a big sky, and semaphored with her arms.

Hereata said, 'We're waving back. I'm ready to join you.'

'I'm going to look for a way in first. Wait until I find something.'

As Ori plodded back into the room, something stirred in the shadows at the far end and she felt her heart freeze in a moment of fright. But it was only tools, swinging to and fro on their rack. Beyond them was a short stairway with an access hatch at the top. Ori asked the hatch to open, and it dilated at once and lights came on inside a short length of tubular passageway that was stopped by another door at the far end.

She reported what she'd found. 'It's a rough-and-ready airlock. Shut the access hatch, ask the inner door to open, and we're inside.'

'Don't go in until I'm down,' Hereata said in her ear.

'I won't.'

'I'm about ready to go.'

'It wasn't as bad as I thought it would be.'

'If it's only half as bad as I think it will be, it'll still be the worst thing I've ever done,' Hereata said.

Ori shut the access hatch and walked to the edge of the truncated room. The cable had slackened and fallen on the floor; now it rose up, curving away towards the top of *The Eye of the Righteous*. The helmet's visor had a magnification feature, and she could just make out bots at the edge of the upper deck, fussing around a small figure. After a few moments, something dropped away in a long swoop: Hereata riding a sling chair down, pausing about halfway because the cable had slackened again, forming a U-shape in the air.

Hereata was caught in the dip of the U. She asked what was going on, sounding calm and unflustered.

Ulua cut in and said there was a minor comms problem with the motor crew.

'I thought the stability system was automatic.'

'That's why I'm trying to talk to them,' Ulua said. 'We appear to be sinking relative to the station. Don't worry. If we keep falling it will take up the slack and you'll run back down to us.'

'I'd rather you let me get to where I'm supposed to be. I don't fancy trying this twice.'

Ori could see that *The Eye of the Righteous* was definitely sinking. When she'd touched down, its keel had been level with the balloons from which the resupply station hung. Now it was about level with her viewpoint, and the cable running through the room had dropped to the floor and was sliding sideways, bending sharply against the cut bulkhead. *The Eye of the Righteous* was not only sinking; it had lost synchrony with the resupply station and was beginning to turn in the opposite direction.

Hereata said, 'I'd like to join Ori before nightfall.'

Silence.

Ori said, 'Ulua, tell me what's happening with the motor crew.'

No one replied. The link was down.

Ori braced herself against a chopped cable duct and leaned out into the wind as far as she dared, trying to spot Hereata. The U of slack cable was bending sideways and Hereata was still stranded in the middle of the dip. She was only five hundred metres away, but might as well have been on another planet.

Ori told Hereata that she could see her, told her to hold on. No reply. All the comms channels were down now. Ori searched the menu for a line-of-sight-option, and there was a bang behind her and the cable snaked across the floor and its end whipped out past her and was gone. Someone had cut it at the anchor point, and the other end was falling away from *The Eye of the Righteous*, writhing like something mortally wounded. As it dwindled away towards the cloud deck, Ori screamed Hereata's name. But her friend was gone.

The Eye of the Righteous was turning faster now, and beginning to move away. Ori could see its upper deck, where bots were working around the railguns. Then its motor lit with a flare of white light, and it began to accelerate. Ori watched, heartsick. Her suit was still scanning channels, trying to pick up live comms. Finally, one channel lit up and Hira leaned into the little window in Ori's visor.

Saying, 'It was a trap. You led us into a trap.'

'You killed Hereata.'

'To save the rest of us. The station is a trap. Set to lure fools like you. We're under attack right now. Look.'

The window cut to a view of sky stretching away to the horizon. Something small and black slanted across it, skipping and shuddering through the air. The view zoomed in, showed a flattened oval with swept-back wings.

'The enemy,' Hira said. 'You delivered us into the hands of the enemy.'

'Run, then,' Ori said. 'Run as far and as fast as you can.'

'We're going to engage and destroy it. And then I'll come back and deal with you,' Hira said, and the channel shut off.

7

A little before sunrise, the Child woke to hear a deep voice booming above the treetops. It was calling her name.

Sri Hong-*Ow*en. Sri Hong-*Ow*en. Sri Hong-*Ow*en.

The sky was beginning to lighten in the east, but the darkness beneath the trees was as yet unbroken. The Child climbed a young tree and sat in its forked bole and scanned the little patches of sky visible here and there in the layered ceiling of the canopy, and at last saw a fat shape drift past about a kilometre away. It was the cargo blimp of the weather wranglers who had tried and failed to bring rain to the little town. It was tricked out in green and gold livery now, the flag of Greater Brazil decorating the tall vane of its rudder, the first light of the rising sun starring a row of portholes in the long cabin slung under its belly as it turned away, trailing its mournful song.

Sri Hong-*Ow*en. Sri Hong-*Ow*en. Sri Hong-*Ow*en.

'You could call back,' Jaguar Boy said, and the Child realised that he was squatting on a branch of the tree that stood next to hers.

'They wouldn't hear me.'

'Wouldn't they?'

'Did my mother send them?'

'Not exactly.'

'Vidal Francisca, then.'

Jaguar Boy shrugged.

'What happens if I call to them?'

'They would take you home.'

'Would you let them do that?'

'I'm not holding you prisoner.'

'You wouldn't let me leave the lake.'

'You wouldn't have been able to find your way home by yourself. But the weather wranglers will help you, if you call them. They'll take you home in a split second, and you'll forget all this.'

'I'll wake up, you mean.'

'You aren't ready for that. Not yet.'

The Child studied him through a scrim of drought-scorched leaves. 'You're very talkative, all of a sudden.'

'When it's important.'

'Tell me where we're going next.'

'The Sloth People.'

'My ama told me about them, too.'

'They were preparing you, in their own way.'

'Preparing me for what?'

Jaguar Boy regarded her for a moment, then yawned and flung himself backwards, hanging from the branch by his crooked knees, swinging to and fro before flinging himself across the air to a branch below the Child and dropping from one to the next to the forest floor. He looked up at her, caught in a long shaft of golden light that set a halo around his small furred head.

'Are you coming with me?'

You are no doubt wondering why we didn't end this pilgrimage. Why we allowed the interloper to seduce the Child and divert her from her preordained path. The simple fact is that we had been locked out of the virtual recreation of her childhood home when the drones had been killed on the bank of the river at São Gabriel da Cachoeira. And in that same moment the clockspeed of the viron had been altered, too. Ever since the accident, our resources had been limited. We had been forced to choose between detail and clockspeed, and we had chosen detail, running the viron at much less than one second per second so that we could make it and the agents that inhabited it as realistic and detailed as possible, providing the Child with a rich environment whose physics simulated as closely as possible the real world (there was an editing attachment that ensured that she did not remember any missing detail, continuity problems, lags in refresh time, and so on).

But now control had been taken away from us, and the viron was no longer a broad scape but a narrow section, and running at a much faster speed. We could not rewrite it from the outside because there was no code to rewrite. It was a holographic totality. Unpick one random thread and everything could unravel. Nor could we halt it until we found out how to regain control. The only option left to us was to shut it down completely. And because we did not have the facility to take a snapshot of its entire state at any particular moment, shutting it down would have been the end of the reborn Child. She would have been lost to us, and there was not enough time to start over. Besides, we were no more than her handmaidens, her humble daughters dedicated to her survival. We could no more kill her than monotheists could murder the avatar of their creator. We could only hope to find her, delete her kidnapper, and restore her to her mother. And to do that, we had to interfere directly with the viron.

In the hours that it took us to find a way into it, many days had passed inside, and we were having great difficulty maintaining synchrony. In short, our view of the Child's world was no longer as complete as it had once been. It had acquired an independent agenda, and we had completely lost sight of its most important inhabitant. We can tell you her story now only because of what we found out about it, afterwards. At the time, we could only peer through a keyhole and hiss directions to a few onstage characters.

In this fashion, we had brought back the weather wranglers, and planted in the mind of its chief pilot detailed memories of meeting with the self-important little cane-sugar grower, Vidal Francisca, who paid a considerable sum of credit up front to search for the kidnapped daughter of his fiancée, with an equal sum promised for her safe return. And while the weather wranglers sailed above patches of forest, shrunken rivers, hills and mountains and dead zones around and about the little town, searching for any trace of the Child, we began to search the interior and the hull of our ancient ship for evidence of sabotage. And in less than a day (far longer, by the clock of the viron) we discovered it.

8

Prem told the Horse and me about her nocturnal adventure while we ate breakfast at a low table near the square little cave, filled now by warm yellow flames, in the rock wall of the lodge's long room. How she'd ridden out into the wilderness and in a secret location had met with a convocation of lichen hunters, and convinced them to reveal the location of an ancient Quick machine which Yakob Singleton and Bree Sixsmith had discovered.

'I don't know what it is,' she said. 'My new friends say it's dangerous, and I believe them.'

I said that it would be prudent to call on the prefect of Ull for reinforcements, or perhaps to ask for the help of Prem's mysterious friends. But Prem was adamant that we had to move now rather than wait for her friends, who were in any case thinly stretched, and that to use troopers would attract the attention of the wrong kind of people.

'The lichen hunters have already helped me find Yakob,' she said. 'They know this world better than any trooper, and they will watch our backs. That's all we need. That and a little courage. We are almost at the end, Isak.'

She was tired and dirty, and in a grim mood. She had not said as much, but I believed that she knew now that when she confronted Yakob it would not be a happy reunion.

'I am ready to harrow any hell and fight any demon,' I said. 'But I am not sure that I will be able to subdue Bree.'

'I'm sure you're better than her.'

'But not, perhaps, better than what she may have become.'

'When my master makes an admission like that,' the Horse said, 'you should take it seriously.'

'Here it is,' Prem said. 'I'll go with you or without you.'

'I'll come, of course,' I said. 'And do all I can. But I want you to know that it may not be enough.'

'It will have to do,' Prem said.

We set out from the lodge within the hour. I had refused Prem's offer of pistols, telling her that our algorithms gave us sufficient protection, but the Horse and I both wore armoured corselets and rode bikes – little platforms with T-shaped control yokes and fan motors at each corner that easily kept pace with the horses of Prem and her guide, an old lichen hunter named Akoni.

He was a strange, hierophantic figure, at once ridiculous and alarming, small and skinny as a starveling child, cheeks seamed with spiral welts, long grey hair drawn up in an elaborate topknot. He wore a ragged vest and trews under a robe stitched from the pelt of a jaguar; a necklace of jaguar claws encircled his bony throat; his ears were pegged with yellow incisors as long and stout as my thumb; a short hollow length of bone pierced with holes hung on his chest from a sinew loop. He told the Horse that he had killed the jaguar himself, with a spear he'd carved from oak wood and tipped with a point of flaked stone, after stalking it for half a hundred of Ull's short days. He rode beside Prem with a lordly ease, as if he was her equal. As if he was the secret prefect of the world.

It was a place that I should have understood, being a True, complete with a set of unaltered and primitive psychological templates formed (so we are told) by the hardships of living in wild and dangerous landscapes, but as far as I was concerned it was a cemetery of endless shifting shadow and cold monochrome light. A death world. Akoni and his brothers were free spirits of this cold tomb world. They mostly lived off the land and visited the terminus only to deposit the lichens they'd collected.

The bikes were easy to fly, but the terrain was difficult, and as spooky as the Ciborium Quarter. We picked our way through a dark conifer forest, climbed a long stony ridge where the pale shells of ancient Quick towers, shaped like spaceships of the long-ago, reared up amongst graveyards of dead trees and cacti taller than men. Beyond, the crescents of barchan dunes filled the floor of a broad valley like a flock of sleeping animals, and then the land dropped in a maze of deep canyons and rifts brimming with fog, where mosses and lichens grew in sodden carpets on boulders and dripped from overhangs. We were still in this maze when night overtook us, and we ate and slept on a damp ledge in a bubble of light and heat cast by a small radiant stove. Akoni played a strange slow mournful music by blowing through the hollow bone that he wore on his chest. I slept fitfully, worried that fierce animals and desperate escapees armed with home-made and improvised weapons might at any time sneak up on us. As dawnlight curdled the mist we ate a scant breakfast and went on. The Horse was as jumpy as me. Half expecting to be led into an ambush or a trap. Half expecting to be engaged in a firefight at any moment. I'm not trying to excuse what happened when we finally discovered what had happened to Yakob Singleton. I'm trying to explain why what happened happened.

Our destination was a steep-sided rift that cut the side of a wrinkle ridge. Fog hung in heavy sodden billows between bare rock walls, and snow fell through the fog, driven to and fro by strong and erratic winds. Akoni claimed that this wasn't normal, said that someone was playing with the weather.

'I can't locate any machines or points of energy flow,' the Horse said.

'I know this world better than you, I think,' Akoni said with lordly calm, and for once the Horse didn't essay a retort.

We travelled past the margin of a narrow lake caught between high cliffs, with a cluster of towers standing half-drowned in its centre. Our destination lay beyond its far end, a steep climb up a path that wound up a slope of shaly stone to a little hanging valley where black mosses made fat pillows amongst boulders fallen from tall cliffs.

There was a crevice under an overhang, where half a dozen lichen hunters and their horses waited in the freezing mist. Akoni conferred with them, and told us that there had been no sign of any activity.

'Are you sure they're still in there?' Prem said. 'They could have found another way through the caves.'

'The watchers on the rim have seen no sign of any movement,' Akoni said, and shook out a sheet of paper that showed a pict of a tower standing up from the flooded floor of a deep and steep-sided shaft. Lights showed in the tower's narrow windows, reflected in the dark water all around it.

Prem had already explained how Akoni and his brothers had discovered where her cousin and Bree Sixsmith had gone to ground. It had not been difficult. The lichen hunters knew of three places where fragments of the Library were lodged on Ull. They were wary of the old machines, but knew that they were curated by several house servants who were almost certainly members of the cult, and also knew that those servants had killed themselves some one point eight megaseconds ago (when Prem had told us this, the Horse had given me a knowing look). Prem, or her friends, had reached out to the lichen hunters when Yakob Singleton and Bree Sixsmith had been tracked to Ull; the lichen hunters had checked each location, and found activity only in this one.

Prem studied the pict, spinning the view all the way around the tower, and said, 'Has anyone gone down there?'

'A few of the young ones wanted to prove their courage,' Akoni said. 'But none have broken discipline. I am certain your targets do not suspect they are being watched.'

'I'm not so sure,' Prem said. 'That's why we'll take the back route.'

I took her aside as the lichen hunters struck their little camp, and told her that I knew who her friends were, and why she was doing this.

'You do, do you?'

'You asked me whether I was a hardliner. I am not. But that doesn't mean I agree with what you want. You and your friends.'

'Say what you need to say, Isak. Don't dance around it. There isn't time, and I don't have the patience. What exactly don't you agree with?'

'Overthrowing centuries of consensus about the Quick. Restoring their freedom. Taking control of Our Thing to achieve that. Directly opposing hardliners who want an end to the Quick. In short, revolution.'

'You worked all this out yourself.'

'I may be naive, Majistra. But I am not stupid. My clan has a deep and abiding respect for Quick achievements because of our work. We look after our kholops and the other servants as best we can. We do not abuse them. Sometimes some form of correction is necessary, but it is never excessive. We're often criticised for this by outsiders, but it is an ethos we cherish. But we have never tried to impose it on others. Nor will we. But I know that there are many young scions who want to impose their ideas on everyone else. Young scions like yourself, Majistra, who have served and fought alongside Quicks in the war.'

Prem stared at me with a mixture of contempt and exasperation. Her eye sockets were bruised from lack of sleep and her wet hair straggled across her forehead. 'That's an astonishingly simplistic view.'

'Yet you do not deny it.'

'All I ever expected from you was to harrow any hells I uncovered while looking for Yakob. No more, no less. What I do after that is my business. And you have your own reason for helping me, don't you? Those back doors you're so scared of, and the forgiveness of your clan you hope to win by locating them. When this is over, you can go your way and I'll go mine. Why don't we leave it that?'

I was as tired, and as unreasonably angry as Prem. And scared, too. Of what we were about to face. Of what might happen if we failed, and the consequences if we succeeded. I said, 'We agreed to be equal partners, but you have not held your end of the bargain. You have never told me the whole truth. Perhaps you didn't trust me. Perhaps because you thought I would not follow or help you if I knew your real intentions. It doesn't matter. I've been led into something deep and dark and dangerous. And that means my clan is implicated too.'

'If you don't like this, you should go,' Prem said.

She turned from me and walked to the edge of the steep drop down to the lake. A small, defiant figure, half-lost in blowing scarves of mist. When I came up behind her, she did not turn.

'You should have trusted me,' I said.

'This isn't about your wounded dignity.'

'When you lack power or wealth, dignity is important. Not just because it is hard-won, but because you have little else by which to measure your status.'

'You think too much about what other people think about you, Isak. You worry that they think you insignificant. I can assure you that I don't.' She turned then. Droplets of water starred the fur of the collar she'd raised about her face, and clung to her wet hair. 'I could say that I didn't tell you the whole truth because I was trying to protect you. But it would be a lie. I did it because I didn't entirely trust you. Because, I suppose, I underestimated you. Because I need you, Isak, and I was frightened that if I told you the truth you'd quit the search.'

Her small cold hands found mine. 'You think we'll fail, my friends and I. You're worried that you'll be implicated in that failure. That you'll be unfairly punished. Don't worry. This is a very small part of something very much larger. It's so insignificant, in fact, that I'm pursuing it contrary to all counsel and advice. Most of my friends don't think it's very important. The Quick do. They know. They understand. But almost everyone else . . . Well, I won't deny that I'll be in trouble if I'm caught, but I promise I'll do my best to convince everyone that you were a fool I led astray. Someone who had no idea about what I was really chasing. That's more or less the truth, after all. And think about this. What if we succeed?'

I would be lying if I told you that I didn't think of returning to the Library in glory, of elevating my clan to a central place in a new order, but I was mostly aware of Prem's hands in mine, her dark and solemn gaze.

'You're free to go back right now,' she said. 'But I hope you'll be true to your promise, and help me finish this. For whatever reason.'

Akoni and two of the other lichen hunters followed us into the crevice; the rest stayed behind to keep watch in case the prefect's troopers worked out where we were and what we were about. A long gullet of rough rock sloped down and down, a ragged and irregular passage so narrow that we had to go in single file, sometimes climbing over rockfalls, sometimes stooping where the ceiling dipped or the floor rose. A handful of drones moved with us, shedding an envelope of bluish light, and several more flew ahead, searching for traps and sensors. All around lay a lightless universe of rock. Masses balanced precariously, ready to shift and crush us out of existence. We picked our way over and around fallen rocks, squatted and shuffled crabwise through a long low passage and emerged at the top of a slope that ran down to the floor of a cathedral void. Behind us was a bulging wall sheened with wet pink and purple mineral deposits. Water dripped from the ends of stalactites high above and fell into cold pools, like so many clocks ticking away eternity.

We stood bunched together as the drones shone tight beams of light here and there. I felt that I was being watched; felt that I had committed to a very bad idea and now I had reached the irrevocable point where there was only a way forward, into a world of trouble.

Prem told the lichen hunters to move out to the left and right and the Horse and I followed her as she started down the slide of rocks. The drones glided through the air ahead of her, pencils of sharp blue light flickering in every direction, and she was suddenly silhouetted by a flash of red light, and a sharp deafening crack filled the black space and echoed back to us in overlapping percussion.

The lichen hunters called to each other and the Horse and I crouched down, our securities searching the darkness for movement, finding it overhead. Small pale winged things were dropping from perches amongst stalactites that hung down from the roof, passing back and forth overhead, swooping lower and lower.

'Don't do anything,' Prem said calmly. 'They're only bats.'

The animals whirled around us, fluttering, darting past, somehow aware of our presence in what to them must have been absolute darkness, spattering us with sharp-smelling dung. Naked bird-things with translucent skin and faces like horrorshow masks, whirling past and gone like smoke sucked up through a flue, the cave absolutely still again. Too still, and too dark: the drones were down.

Prem said, 'It was an EMP grenade rigged to some kind of flash-bang. No doubt designed to frighten away the natives.'

'We are not frightened,' Akoni said.

'They underestimated you,' Prem said. 'Isak, are your algorithms and other tricks still working?'

My mouth was dry and there was grit on my tongue. I had to work up a measure of saliva before I could speak. 'They are hardened against all kinds of attacks.'

'Then get up, both of you. We're not turning back. Not now.'

Prem was standing downslope, pale and slim in the ghostlight of my security's enhanced vision. Stepping now over stones, moving from one to the next with a smooth and certain gait. She had taken out her pistol, and the Horse and I exchanged glances and started after her, crabbing down the slope, crossing an uneven floor littered with fallen rocks, the lumpy glistening spikes of stalagmites, brimming pools rimmed with slick dripstone. The hunters discovered another explosive device, and another. The Horse destroyed their tiny intelligences with an unnecessarily extravagant gesture, and I stepped close and quietly chided him for showing off.

'I thought it would be a good idea to display some flair to remind them that we're an important part of this,' he said.

'I have a feeling that we may be too late to do any good,' I said.

'But we will do our best, just the same.'

The cavern narrowed at its far end, funnelling into a passage that twisted and turned much like the one by which we'd entered, until at last a star appeared in the darkness, growing into a wedge of pale glow as we approached it. While the Horse and I waited with the other lichen hunters, Prem and Akoni went ahead, returning after some six hundred seconds.

'No more traps that we can find,' Prem said. 'Follow me and keep close.'

We emerged in a cleft where part of the cave system had collapsed, leaving a winding gash caught between steep walls that led to a lake as round as an ancient coin. The tower stood at its centre, light shining from window slits at various heights; a slender bridge made of some translucent halflife polymer arched above the still black water of the lake and descended to kiss a small oval doorway at the base of the tower. It was very cold, and a few flakes of snow drifted down from the circle of gunmetal sky pinched between the high cliffs.

The Horse and I parsed the tower and the bridge and found nothing active.

'That doesn't mean there aren't any more traps,' I said. 'They may be too stupid or too sophisticated for us to detect.'

Prem called out Yakob's name, her clear voice echoing back across the dark water. I thought it incredibly foolish, and braced for some kind of cataclysmic reply, but nothing happened. She called several times, and stood with her arms folded, her head moving up and down as she scanned the tower from bottom to top and back again. At last she told all of us to wait, and walked up the arch of the bridge to the oval doorway, ducking under its low lip.

A moment later her scream cut the air.

I sprinted across the narrow span of the bridge, my security wrapping tight and hard around me, the Horse and the lichen hunters following at my heels. Usually, the old towers left by the ancestral Quick are more or less empty, open chimneys with platforms of different sizes jutting from the inner walls at random heights and linked by a spiralling ramp (the Redactor Svern based the public entrance of the Library on this design, in homage to the creators of the Library's virons). But when I ducked through the entrance of this tower, I threw up my arm to protect my eyes at once, because it was full of flame. Huge flames beating with white light and heat, and Prem on fire at my feet, writhing as she burned.

Or so it seemed. The entrance had been rigged as a translation frame that opened on to a pocket hell. The flames and heat weren't real, but Prem's agony was. My security reached out and enveloped her; as I stooped to pick her up, something coalesced from the flames all around and shot towards me like a runaway star. I threw a string at it and the string shrivelled and flared out like a comet, and then the thing was on me in a furious rush that knocked me over. Something punched at my torso, a sharp point plunging over and again. It didn't penetrate the armoured corselet that Prem had made me wear, but it knocked the wind out of me, and a moment later hard fingers were clawing at my face, at my eyes.

My attacker was no ordinary demon; it was a demon cloaking a human being, as my security cloaked me. Stabbing and punching at me while the furnace fire raged at my security, burning its way in past layer after layer of futile-cycle algorithms and deadlock traps.

Violent action has a strange effect on memory. Moments are preserved with perfect fidelity, but the connections between them are lost. I remember grasping a sharp blade that stung my palm. I remember a blow that jarred my cheekbone, and my sight going black for a long moment. I remember finding a warm human mouth and wrenching at it, and the shocking pain as teeth clamped on my fingers. I have no idea what I was thinking; most likely I wasn't thinking at all. And I remember a dark shadow emerging from the furnace light raging all around, and I have a memory that may be true and may be false of a bee flying past my face and shattering into an angry swarm that struck my adversary and hurled him away.

Somehow, I was outside, lying on cold stone in dull pewter light, the Horse kneeling beside me. The lichen hunter, Akoni, emerged from the doorway, Prem limp in his arms. He staggered towards me and knelt and half-lowered, half-dropped her. I remember the hollow thump her head made when it struck the stone.

I managed to push to my feet. My chest was tattooed with points of pain and blood dripped from the fingers of my gashed hand and one eye was hot and half-closed, but my mind was growing clear as thoughts knitted each to each.

'She's in shock but I think she'll live,' Akoni said. He was kneeling by Prem, looking up at me.

'Who attacked me?'

'I shot him. I picked up Prem's pistol and shot him,' the Horse said, and burst into tears.

There's not much left to tell of the debacle. I used my security to engage with the translation frame, and after a few tens of seconds worked my way into its kernel and shut it down, and the tower stood as it had always stood. The body of a Quick lichen hunter lay just inside the entrance. It wasn't one of our party; he must have been caught and turned by Bree Sixsmith, and left to guard the place.

The Horse and I found Yakob's body on a platform at the top of the tower, beside an array of comms equipment. The top of his skull was gone and thousands of fine threads had pierced the membrane that wrapped his brain, and had grown through its meat. A bush robot that had been used to interrogate him.

There was no sign of Bree Sixsmith, and we could find no trace of the kernel of the hell that had been lodged here. We were still searching when two flitters dropped out of the mists and discharged troopers who'd come to investigate a strange signal, transmitted when Prem had sprung the trap that Bree Sixsmith had left behind. That was when we discovered that the lichen hunters had left, and had taken Prem with them.

9

Ori entered the resupply station through the hatch in the rear of the hangar and searched corridors and rooms until she found a helical ramp that climbed around the core to the diamond-paned dome at the top. There were no traces of any kind of fighting or struggle, and the motion detector of her suit registered no movement anywhere, but she walked warily, watching shadows and doorways, spinning around every ten steps. She was still wearing her helmet because she was afraid that the station's air might be laced with subtle poisons, biologics, or psychotropics, and she carried a welding pistol she'd found in the hangar, an improvised weapon useful only at close range but comforting to hold as she stalked the deserted station.

Under the skylight dome, she skirted an abstract sculpture woven from thorny loops, threaded between hydroponic beds of banana plants and fruit bushes, vibrant green under bright suspensor lamps. Because the station was slowly rotating it took her a little while to locate *The Eye of the Righteous*: a bright star flaring away towards the enemy craft, which was suddenly close to it and suddenly far away again, skipping to and fro as if playing some deadly game of tag. It was much smaller than the ship but much quicker, and Ori was certain that the ship's lashed-up railguns would be no match for it.

Run, she thought. Run.

And felt, at the back of her head, for the first time in days, the passenger stir in her personal dark. Felt it moving forward.

The Eye of the Righteous was beginning to yaw now, a ponderous attempt to turn broadside. The enemy craft was below it, then off to one side. There were tiny puffs of vapour and white contrails shot past the black craft: the railguns had fired.

The enemy craft slid backwards very quickly and came to a sudden stop. A tiny mote hung way out across the sky. *The Eye of the Righteous* was still turning towards it when it drove forward. Ori saw what was going to happen and shouted *No!* and the enemy craft plunged straight through *The Eye of the Righteous*, punching through the upper surface and ripping out through the keel in a shower of debris that twinkled away towards the cloud deck as the enemy craft described a graceful circle and halted in the air again as if to survey the damage it had done.

The Eye of the Righteous wallowed in the air. Another set of contrails raked out from its starboard side, aimed at nothing in particular. It was tilted downwards, stern first. Then a chunk of superstructure dropped away and the rest shot up, unbalanced. The motors flared and died, and then the ship was sinking, nose tipping up as it fell with increasing velocity towards the cloud deck.

Ori watched, paralysed by horror, as the enemy craft skipped and slid towards the resupply station. When something rustled behind her, she blinked and shuddered and swung around, raising the welding pistol, pointing it at something vaguely human-shaped, woven from black loops and twice her height. It was the statue, reconfigured. An enemy drone. It had a tiny head of loops constricted around a single eye, and two pairs of arms. Three terminated in long saw-toothed blades, the fourth in a broad plate that it held towards Ori. The plate buzzed and gargled, and a deep, pleasant voice asked her to put up her weapon.

'We are your friend. Do no harm and no harm will be done to you.'

Ori held out the welding pistol, and the drone snatched it away with a flick of one of its arms.

'Wait there. We are coming.'

The enemy swarmed into the domed garden like guests arriving at a party, full of energy and curiosity, laughing, calling to each other in piping voices, speaking a clacking language that Ori didn't recognise. They wore hard-shell pressure suits decorated with swirling patterns or stripes or spots, some in black and white, others in bright clashing colours. They were smaller than her, so slender that she reckoned she could snap any one of them over her knee. Most had taken off their helmets, revealing round heads that seemed too big for their slender frames, and large eyes and skin paler than the palms of her hands.

Translucent skin tinted pink with the blood beneath. Blond or brown or black hair shaved close to their scalps in patterns of swirls and dots and dashes that echoed the decoration of their pressure suits.

Ori, who'd been indoctrinated with the idea that the enemy were soulless hive creatures, all alike, all slaved to a central authority, was amazed and alarmed. They were no more than children, running around the aisles of plants in a happy and noisy chaos, tearing off leaves, sniffing them, tasting them.

Several gathered in front of her and spoke in careful, stilted Portuga one after the other, telling her that she was not their prisoner. No, they had rescued her from bondage. She had been a slave, and now she was free. Free to choose. Free to decide her fate.

It wasn't much of a choice, it turned out. Join them, or be worked to death as a prisoner. But it was more than Ori had expected.

She told them she was with them. What else could she do? They laughed and clapped, and the machine let her go and stepped back as she fell to her knees. The enemy were all around her, helping her up, patting at the visor of her helmet, smiling at her.

'You have joined the company of heroes.'

'You and your companion.'

'The little intelligence that has made its home in your head.'

'Yes, we know about that.'

'We know everything about you. Commissar Doctor Pentangel is one of ours, now.'

'What do you want me to do?' Ori said.

'First, you must choose a name.'

'You must shed your slave name. Here. Choose.'

A list scrolled in the air. She chose a name at random. 'Janejean.'

'That's good.'

'That's wonderful.'

'An old name.'

'A good name.'

'One of the first martyrs.'

'Come with us now. There's so much to be done.'

They flowed out of the domed garden at the top of the station, taking Ori with them, carrying samples of plants and dirt in sealed cases. Out through an opening cut in the outer skin of the station, into a transparent bubble divided by a mesh floor at its equator into an open space above and a motor below. The bubble detached and skittered out across the gulf of empty air towards the enemy's ship, and that was it: Ori had become a Ghost.

PART FOUR
CTHUGA

1

We searched long and hard for evidence of sabotage and at last it was found by one of the small robots crawling across the pitted sheath of ice and fullerene that had protected our ship during its voyage: a tiny, complex probe embedded deep in the centre of a small crater marked by a sunburst of bright rays, scarcely larger than an old-fashioned bullet of the kind fired by the ancient rifles carried by some of the wildsiders, weapons handcrafted by their great-grandparents and handed down from father to son, mother to daughter. This, though, was a very subtle bullet. It was sheathed in layers of diamond alloy interleaved with layers of impact gel; its interior was packed with microscopic machinery; there was a ring of tiny one-shot motors around its waist.

Although it had been built to withstand tremendous acceleration and deceleration, the impact had killed it. It had registered on the ship's log, but had not been checked: the frequency of small collisions had begun to increase as we approached Fomalhaut, even though we were travelling above the plane of the system. Now we sent out robots to check the site of every similar impact, and presently we found another probe. Or rather, what was left of it. This one had survived, and split open like a seed. The machinery inside had spun threads that had sunk into the icy sheath of our ship, mining it for elements used to grow a fractal microwave aerial and a complex pseudohyphal network that had spread through the sheath and interfaced with the ship's nervous system.

We had no doubt that this parasitic system had spawned the intruder and inserted him into the viron, and at once began to map and analyse it. We wanted to reconstruct the matrix from which he'd sprung. We wanted to understand his origin so that we could find him, and the Child. And then we wanted to use that knowledge to destroy him.

What we failed to see was that we were being manipulated by something more powerful and subtle than the intruder. We failed to detect another network that went deep into the nexus of our interfaces with the systems of the ship. We failed to understand that we were as blind to our true situation as the Child was to hers. And while we were deconstructing the intruder, atom by atom, the Child and Jaguar Boy were walking away from the burrows and galleries of the Sloth People, crossing trackless swales of iron-hard caliche in a dead zone created by deforestation and climate change, when it began to rain.

They'd lived with the Sloth People for so many days that the Child had lost count of them. They were a gentle, slow, small race, the Sloth People, none taller than the Child's waist. They spent much of their time sleeping, and most of the rest grooming each other or singing long plaintive songs that could take days to complete, as singer after singer took up the thread of the melody. The songs were all they had of their history, a much degraded mythos that described the cosmos outside their burrows (which they never left) and where they had come from. Songs of a distant Earth.

There were no children. The Sloth People were born fully formed after a gestation of two years in ectogenetic tanks, and lived on average a little over twice that. The tanks were maintained by bots, as were the gardens of fungi that grew in low galleries on mulches of wood chips collected from the distant forest by roving machines. In real life, Jaguar Boy told the Child, the fungi were vacuum organisms, growing on carbonaceous material collected from the surfaces of the asteroids into which the Sloth People had burrowed. The Child said that she knew about vacuum organisms – the Outers had developed many kinds, to generate power from the faint sunlight at Jupiter and Saturn, to mine carbon and other elements from the silicates and ice of the gas giants' moons, to manufacture edible plastic and CHON food, and so on, and so forth.

'Vacuum organisms went everywhere humans went in the Solar System and beyond,' Jaguar Boy said. 'They are genuine commensals. As rats and cockroaches and fleas once were, in the ships that sailed the oceans of Earth in the long-ago. The genetic templates of all kinds of organisms were carried in seedships, but few were used, and most of those died out in places like this.'

The Sloth People were slow and small because theirs was a low-energy ecosystem. Carbon and nitrogen were plentiful, but many other essential nutrients were not. Their machines had adapted them to their circumstances, and over time they had lost all curiosity and much of their intellect. All they had was their past, celebrated in song and in murals they daubed on the walls of their burrows. Recycling was not perfect, so essential elements were slowly lost and had to be replenished from dwindling sources. And as the resources of their chosen home became rarer and harder to mine, the Sloth People grew smaller still, and their numbers further declined: a meagre tribe huddling against the encroaching cold and dark.

After Jaguar Boy had explained this long, slow attrition, the Child said that it must have taken millions of years. She had the floating feeling that this was a dream. A calm acceptance of the impossible. She'd had it ever since she'd first met the River Folk. The feeling that Jaguar Boy had drugged her and was controlling her dreams. Or perhaps she'd been dreaming when she'd first met Jaguar Boy in the strip of forest in the ruined city, and was dreaming still, and would wake up to find that her mother wasn't engaged to Vidal Francisca, that she wasn't going to be sent away . . .

Jaguar Boy said that the human race had split into dozens of clades as it spread through the Solar System, and dozens more as it spread through the systems of other stars, but most evolved in only two directions. Some became highly intelligent sybarites who dedicated themselves to the study of esoteric philosophies and mathematics, but the pursuit of knowledge was too often a trap. The River Folk had already become neotenous; their children reproduced before they transformed into sexless, big-brained scholar-adults. If evolutionary pressure caused the loss of the ability to make the transformation from child to adult, the intelligence of the clade would diminish until they became only a little smarter than seals. Other clades became so obsessed by their abstract philosophies that they gave up the messy business of reproduction altogether, choosing instead various kinds of amortality, flickering out one by one like stars in some ancient galaxy. And other clades, trapped like the Sloth People in resource-poor environments, began to evolve away from intelligence.

'Most histories converge on one or another of these strong attractors,' Jaguar Boy told the Child. 'Only a few escape.'

'What happens to them?' the Child said.

'Some develop or stumble upon a philosophy that engulfs them in a moment of transcendence so marvellously advanced that no one left behind understands where they went, or the manner of their passing.'

'They become gods?'

The idea was strangely exciting, resonating with the stuff of her own dreams and fantasies.

'No one knows what they become,' Jaguar Boy said. 'But most often, as with the River Folk and many others, philosophical investigation leads only to decadence and decline. Sometimes, clades engineer limits on their intelligence to avoid that fate. They celebrate and imitate the fierce and terrible past when most human beings were no more than human. The consequences are never very happy, as you'll soon see.'

'We're moving on to another fairy tale.'

Jaguar Boy shook his head. 'It's time you learned about where you will soon arrive, and the kind of people you will meet.'

They set out one cloudless night, the sky spanned by the dust belt and the two burning stars rising in the east: the Child and Jaguar Boy each cast green and red shadows as they walked north across the ruined land of the dead zone. But they had not been walking for very long when clouds boiled up in the west and spread out across the sky and the air grew warmer and heavy with moisture. The Child wondered if the long drought was going to break; Jaguar Boy said this wasn't an ordinary storm.

Lightning cracked at the horizon and lit the stark landscape in fitful strobes. Rain fell with a sudden fierce intensity, as if the sky had been the bottom of an ocean and had inverted. The Child was drenched in an instant, her hair flattened to her skull, her cotton dress flattened against her body. Jaguar Boy caught hold of her arm and pulled her up a slope already turning to mud. The Child shouted that it was very definitely a storm, hardly able to hear herself; Jaguar Boy said no, it was a pathetic fallacy.

'We must hurry,' he said. 'I've already given you more time than you should have had. There's only a little left.'

There was a motorcycle at the top of the slope, a lean black machine with a bubble shell. Jaguar Boy lifted the Child on to the back seat and swung up in front of her and told her to hold on to his waist and not to let go. The motorcycle kicked into life with a terrific roar and they shot into rain and darkness. Rain drummed on the bubble and rain streaked past on either side, each drop seeming to elongate and grow brighter, suddenly frozen in mid-air. The raindrops ahead were blue and those behind were red, either end of a rainbow that enclosed the roaring motorcycle.

'Time slows when you speed up,' Jaguar Boy said.

'Where exactly are we going?'

'To meet the True People. You need to see them because they are about to become part of your story. Also, they might be able to defend us against those who want you back.'

The rain stopped as abruptly as a curtain being raised. They had outrun the storm and were travelling alongside a vast river that spread out to the horizon. The Child supposed that it was the Amazon. The dark sky was cloudless once more, packed with stars and spanned by the bridge of luminous dust.

There were islands on the great river, and this was where the True People lived. Like the Sloth People, they were conceived by crossing genetic templates in virtual matrices, and grew to term in ectogenetic tanks. They were divided into clans whose rivalries sometimes broke out into open warfare, and they had enslaved the descendants of a posthuman clade, the Quick, that had first settled the islands. For many years the Quick had lived in peace, setting out on the road down which the River Folk had travelled, losing themselves in contemplation of infinitely complex philosophies. So that when the True People had finally reached the islands, they'd had no difficulty conquering the Quick and altering their descendants. Making them stupider, short-lived, and obedient. Turning them into slaves.

The Child was greeted with much ceremony. It seemed that she was an important figure from the mythic past of the True People, and her return was believed to herald a new Golden Age. The clans made her their queen and promptly began quarrelling over who should have access to her. Jaguar Boy told her that they hated and feared and loved her in equal measure because of who she was and what she would do.

'You did not begin the divergence between humans and posthumans, but you played an important role in its development. You became a great and powerful gene wizard. You helped to win the war against the Outers, and then you helped to win a second war, which freed the Outers and began the great expansion out into the Solar System and beyond. The True People love you because you gave ordinary human beings more influence than they deserved, and they fear you because of what you became, and hate you because they need you still.'

'Will I become as great as Avernus?'

'Greater.'

'And will I meet her?'

'No. But one of your sons will.'

'I don't plan to have any children.'

'You'll find it necessary and useful. Besides, the Quick are your children, in a sense,' Jaguar Boy said. 'Their genomes contain sequences that you designed.'

'For all the good it did them,' the Child said.

She'd had several clandestine meetings with Quick slaves, learning about their history and the long years of suffering under the Trues. They were melancholy and defiant. Resigned to their fate, yet still carrying a spark of the original fire of curiosity and creativity that had carried them across the big dark of interstellar space to a place where they had, briefly, reached the full flower of their potential.

'They could rise again if they were freed,' Jaguar Boy said.

'Is that why you brought me here? To change this part of the story?'

'I want to help you to learn something of the worlds in which you will soon awake. What you do with that knowledge is up to you. I wish I could have shown you more, but there wasn't enough time.'

It was night. The same night on which she'd reached the archipelago of the True People. A very long night. So long it seemed to the Child that she had been living in it all her life. They were standing on a terrace of her palace at the summit of the hill that dominated the central island. Below, the hill stepped down in terraced tiers, each owned by a different clan, each a home and a hunting ground. Apart from the scattered and isolated stars of campfires, the tiers were dark, but the base of the hill was ringed with a small crowded town where Trues unaffiliated with any of the clans lived cheek by jowl with posthuman slaves. Beyond were other islands afloat on the black water of the great river, dark silhouettes limned by the lights of towns and the solitary stars of hunting camps.

And in the distance, like a sunrise, was a sudden conflagration where the clans of the True People had encountered and begun to fight a common enemy. The weather wranglers had arrived, and were advancing towards the Child. The islands of the True People sparkled with the discharges of every kind of weapon and arcs of tracers and the blades of energy beams split the night, but all fell short.

'They will be here soon,' Jaguar Boy said. 'You will have a choice to make then. I cannot advise you what to do. All I can ask is that you choose wisely.'

An especially large flash lit the horizon, seeming to circle half the world. The Child laughed in terror and awe. 'This isn't real! None of this is real!'

'It is the only reality you know. You were born into it, and those who have raised you have made sure that it was as similar to your childhood as possible.'

'Who? Who raised me?'

'Your children. Descendants of servants you clipped from your own genome when you started on the long process of change that led you here. Driven by love and duty, they attempted to recreate you as you once were, but they are blind to certain facts. They do not understand that it isn't possible to remake someone out of old and partial stories of the long-ago. And they do not understand that they are no longer free agents. That they have been captured. They are about to destroy this avatar because they believe I am manipulating you, but they do not realise that they are being manipulated by an old enemy of yours. Remember all I told you. Remember the various fates of humankind. Remember that nothing is inevitable. Above all, remember who you are.'

There was another terrific explosion. It lit up the river and the forest on either side, and whited out the sky. As its light died away, the Child saw that most of the islands were gone. The cargo blimp of the weather wranglers floated high above the river, making directly towards the hilltop palace. She turned to Jaguar Boy and discovered that he had vanished.

The blimp ploughed on, unharmed by the furious displays of the Fierce People, occluding the starry sky. It was very low now, very close. The Child could see rows of lighted windows in the cabin slung beneath the blimp, could see people moving inside or staring down at her. She did not have time to feel afraid. She wondered briefly if she was going to wake up, and then searchlights sprang on along the margins of the cabin, overlapping beams that pinned her like a moth. A rope ladder dropped and an imposingly tall, pale-skinned woman dressed in a black spidersilk blouson and khaki trousers climbed down.

The Child looked up at her and asked if she was going to take her home.

'You have been found just in time,' the woman said. Her face was shaded by the bill of her cap; only her wide white smile showed. 'We thought you would be late.'

'Late? Late for what?'

'Your wedding, of course,' the woman said, and held out her hand.

2

The Horse and I were taken back to Thule aboard a bottle rocket, and separated at the orbital station. He was returned to the Library, looking small and forlorn as he was led away amongst an escort of armoured troopers; I was taken to the Office of Public Safety, where I was interviewed by a grey little man with a parched voice, a perfect memory, and seemingly infinite patience. Although I insisted on making a formal protest about the violation of my right to be tried by my own clan, I was eager to cooperate. I wanted the truth to be placed on record. I wanted to make it clear that my clan and I had been tricked into working for Lathi and Prem Singleton.

And so I recounted every detail of our adventures, from my meeting with Lathi Singleton to the discovery of Yakob's decerebrated body in the ruined tower, with especial emphasis on my theory that Bree Sixsmith had been possessed by a demon that was using her to further the cause of the enemy. When I finished there was a long silence before my interrogator told me that he was interested only in facts, and started to take my story apart. No detail was too fine, no discrepancy too small, to escape his attention. He pounced on what he believed to be faults and contradictions and explored them so thoroughly that I soon began to have trouble remembering what had actually happened and what he said I'd said had happened. He showed me select clips of the field interrogations of Quicks on Ull – the housekeepers of the lodge, stoic lichen hunters I did not recognise. He implied that I had caused their suffering. He told me that others would suffer as badly as the investigation proceeded. He told me that I deserved to be treated no better.

He was only doing his job, but it was not a job any sane man would have chosen, and it was hard not to hate him. In the long and intense kiloseconds of my interrogation, I grew to believe that he enjoyed tormenting me. That he had a fine contempt for everyone he met, seeing them as imperfect vessels that he had been born to test to destruction.

At last he told me that he was done with me for now. And as he stood up I told him what I wanted, speaking quickly and clearly and fixing my gaze on his in the manner of a pitchman in the Permanent Floating Market.

'I must reconsider my analysis of you,' he said. 'I believed that you were a simple fool. Now I must wonder if you are insane.'

'Tell your masters what I told you,' I said. 'That is, if they aren't listening to this conversation.'

'I am their servant, not yours,' he said, and turned his back on me and walked out.

I was relieved to be rid of him, happy to be left alone in the small room with my fantasy that everything would work out for the best. After a few hundred seconds, two troopers came in, and I rose, smiling, believing I would be taken to someone who would discuss my proposition. Instead, I was promptly blindfolded and transported to a high, bare cell near the top of one of the spines of the thistledown city, and left there.

It was shaped like a trumpet flower, with a circular floor and a seamless wall of slippery ceramic that was three times my height and angled inwards. There was a soft patch of the floor where I slept, another patch that absorbed my wastes, and a third that extruded basic food pellets. I had no connection to the outside world except a view of the sky whose skin was less than a hundred metres above my head, and the cell was open to the vagaries of Thule's climate conditioning. I was exposed to the naked light and heat of the thistledown city's minisun, and the freezing fogs of its clouds. Once, it rained so long and so hard that I thought I might drown, because the floor could not absorb the water fast enough: by the time the rain stopped I was up to my knees in it. It rained at other times, too, but never again so fiercely. Apart from the weather and the usual cycle of night and day, there was no variation in the dreary kiloseconds of my isolation except once, when a small bird perched briefly on the rim high above me.

It was an unremarkable dun little creature, hardly bigger than my cupped palm, with a blunt beak the colour of old bone and a short tail cocked above its back and wings barred with black and white, like the rank stripe of a trooper. The kind I had seen a hundred times in the park beyond the Permanent Floating Market and scarcely noticed. Now, intruding on my involuntary solitude, it seemed like a celestial messenger. I hardly dared breathe as it perched above me, unreachable, cocking its head and fixing me for a moment with its unblinking gaze. Then it looked away and its beak opened and it sang a brief song like pure cold water bubbling over silvery pebbles, and with a quick flick of its wings it flew away.

I sang its song to myself, over and again. I cannot explain why, but it gave me the strength to believe that my position was not hopeless, that my proposal had not been rejected outright but was still being considered, that I would not be imprisoned for ever. I remember it still.

Despite my initial bravado, I quickly lost count of how long I had been there. I started to mark the beginning of each diurn by making scratches on my thigh, but I'd been infected with theriacae to treat the various small wounds and injuries I'd acquired during my struggle with the possessed lichen hunter, and they quickly healed the marks I made on my skin, so that I had to remake all the previous scratches at the beginning of each day as well as adding a fresh one. It wasn't easy, keeping count.

At last, a round hole puckered open in the floor and a voice spoke out of empty air, telling me to climb down into the flitter that waited below. There were no troopers to blindfold or bind me, and the flitter's canopy was left transparent. I saw the pale trumpet-shapes of my cell and others like it clustered around a black spine that dwindled down through sunlit air. I saw other spines in every direction, angling towards the skin of the sky. I saw, beyond flocks of fluffy white clouds far below, a loose patchwork of square and circular and rectangular platforms that curved away in every direction, the whole pierced by the spines from which individual platforms jutted. A second layer of platforms was visible in some of the gaps between the upper layer, and another layer was visible beyond that. Somewhere far below, near the core where the spines converged, was the platform that supported the Permanent Floating Market and the Library of the Homesun.

For a moment, I hung above the city entire. Then the flitter shot away from the spire in a wild swoop. I yelled with exultation as it cut through the streaming whiteness of a cloud, and the upper platforms of the city rose up and the little craft decelerated with sudden and brutal force that squeezed me into my seat and took away my breath. It hovered in the air for a moment, then dropped straight down towards a platform covered with dark green trees from edge to edge. White pyramids stood here and there amongst the trees; the flitter fell towards the largest and touched down, as gently as a fallen leaf, on the wide lawn of flower-starred turf that surrounded it.

Two troopers and a marshal caparisoned in a glistening white breastplate escorted me into the lowest level of the pyramid. The marshal told me that I was to meet with Yenna Singleton, but would not say why. I did my best to suppress my hope that my offer had been accepted, and asked the marshal how long I had been imprisoned. It had been just one and a quarter megaseconds after the incident at the tower on Avalon. Roughly fifteen diurnal cycles.

I said that I had thought it much longer.

'All prisoners do,' the marshal said. 'You were fed a drug to keep you compliant and to stop you killing yourself. It also affected your sense of time. Don't worry. The drug was removed from your food yesterday. We need you to be sober and alert.'

I was allowed to shower and shave, and to dress in my own clothes. My security had been shut down and I could not unlock it; I felt naked as the troopers and the marshal took me to a disc that promptly shot up a transparent tube, rising through floor after floor to a windowless atrium whose walls, floor and vaulted ceiling were constructed of seamless, polished black stone, with the badge of the Singleton clan set in silver in the centre of the floor.

The Horse was waiting at the far end of the atrium, sitting cross-legged on the floor beside a tall double door.

After I had stood before the college of Redactors and had been tried for causing the deaths of Arden and Van through culpable negligence and then had been sentenced to exile, after I had been led through the Alexandrian Gate in disgrace and the great double doors had clanged shut behind me, I had seen a small figure standing at the foot of the bridge that arched across the moat. It was the Horse, who had chosen to stand by me. My heart had leaped with gladness then, and it leaped again now, as the marshal marched me across the atrium, her boot heels ringing on stone.

The Horse stood up to meet me and said, 'I thought I would never see you again.'

'I had the same thought about you.'

'It seems we were both misinformed.'

'Do you know why we have been brought here?'

'The Redactor Svern sent me here. He didn't trouble to explain why.'

'I may have an idea,' I said, and told the Horse about the deal I had tried to make with the Office of Public Safety. 'I was given to understand they had no interest in it. Hence my imprisonment. But perhaps they have changed their minds. Or perhaps the Redactor Svern has intervened.'

'I hope you know what you're doing.'

'As much as I always do.'

'Then we're still in trouble.'

'As much as we always are.'

'At least you still have your sense of humour,' the Horse said.

'And you still have your cynicism.'

The Horse had no news of Prem Singleton. He was telling me how badly the war was going when at last the marshal commanded the doors to open. They swung apart in ponderous silence, exposing a dark space beyond.

'Walk through,' the marshal said. 'Majistra Yenna is waiting for you.'

She did not follow us, and it immediately became apparent why. As in the ruined tower on Ull, the door was a translation frame. In a single step, the Horse and I were transported to a place I hadn't dared to believe I would ever see again – the chamber in the Redactor Svern's memory palace where he received visitors.

I knew then that I had won the attention of the right people, but instead of triumph a cold shrinking feeling washed through me. Dread. The realisation that I was at the threshold of something truly important, something life-changing. The fear of failing to measure up to the test I had set myself. It was deeper than the nervousness I'd felt at my final examination before I'd passed from novice to practitioner. Then, the course of the rest of my life had been at hazard; now, everything I had ever done or ever would do was in the balance, and I was scared that it had already been judged, and found wanting. If so, I thought, there was nothing I could do except meet my fate with dignity, so I straightened my back and told the Horse to keep quiet unless spoken to, and walked forward.

As before, an immersive simulation of the Fomalhaut system filled the chamber edge to edge, with the bright point of Fomalhaut in its centre and the broad but paper-thin dust ring circling the walls. A thick thread of blue punched through the diffuse red oval of the Ghosts' territory, and Ghost forces were retreating from it. Abandoning long-established positions, moving towards the edge of the dust ring in the direction of Cthuga. The thready pathways I'd seen before had thickened and joined in a kind of pseudopod or tentacle that angled across the dust ring; its tip had engulfed the gas giant, and the mass of the main body was beginning to flow along it.

The Horse was looking all around with avid curiosity. When I told him to pay attention, he said that someone was coming, and pointed across the chamber, a little to the left of Fomalhaut's spark.

An old woman walked through the simulation of the dust ring, hip deep in dust clouds and comets and planetoids. Her white hair was done up in a helmet of little plaits and she wore the black one-piece uniform of an army trierarch, with a silver starburst on her right breast. I supposed that she must be Yenna Singleton, the matriarch of the clan, dead for more than two centuries. The Redactor Svern materialised from the shadows behind her, the hem of his black duster trailing behind him as he followed her across the chamber.

'It's good to see you again, Isak,' he said. 'Even if the circumstances are unfortunate.'

I told him that I was sorry that I had failed him, and he dismissed my apology with a flick of his hand.

'I have a small confession to make,' he said. 'An apology of my own. You see, I knew when I gave you the task that it was almost inevitable that you would fail. Not because you lacked skill or courage, but because it was the kind of problem that no one could solve. And that's why I chose you, Isak. You had already fallen so far that neither our clan nor you would be hurt if you fell a little further.'

'You sacrificed me for the greater good.'

'And I could not tell you at the time, because you might have refused. I am sorry.'

'I am sorry you doubted my loyalty.'

'I do not blame you for being angry. But everything has worked out. You have done better than I believed possible, and you have returned.'

'I survived, yes. And returned as a prisoner.'

The old woman, Yenna Singleton, said, 'Because you were associated with the traitors Lathi and Prem. Because you were a threat to the security and safety of my clan.'

'And that has been resolved,' the Redactor Svern said.

'Lathi tried to gain power over the senior members of my clan. For

that crime she has been arrested and tried and executed,' Yenna Singleton said. 'Prem is still at large, but we will capture her soon enough.'

'And I have forged an agreement with the Singleton clan, and you
have been returned to us as part of that agreement,' the Redactor Svern
said.

'Forgive me, Majister, if I don't share your happiness. For I fear that
I still have some way to fall.'

'We may yet all fall,' Yenna Singleton said. 'The Ghosts have changed
their tactics and thrown everything they have at Cthuga. We are
retaking positions they took from us out in the ring, but Cthuga has
been overwhelmed. Its defences have been destroyed or compromised.
Most of its pelagic stations are lost, and its communications net has
fallen over, so little is known about the survivors. We have twice tried
and failed to punch a hole through the Ghosts' forces and we are
readying a third wave, but we do so with little hope.'

The Redactor Svern said, 'It's always been my belief that we have
been fighting the war for the wrong reason. We have been defending
our territory, but the enemy don't care about us and our worldlets,
except that we stand between them and Cthuga's Mind. They call
themselves Ghosts because they believe that their reality will not be
validated until they reach back in time and change history to ensure
that they become the only posthuman species. If they do that, we will
become no more than ghosts. Haunting rare timelines separated from
each other by the many in which the enemy has been victorious.'

Yenna Singleton said, 'We have always suspected that they wanted to
win the help of Cthuga's Mind. They tried and failed to make contact
with their probes. Now they have flung every resource at the planet.
And, at the same time, a starship that departed from the Solar System
some fifteen centuries ago is approaching Fomalhaut.'

The Redactor Svern said, 'And that is why you are here, Isak.
Because what you have discovered may have some bearing on the
matter of this starship.'

'With respect,' I said, 'I believe I'm here because you failed to find
what you were looking for in my security.'

'You wanted to bargain with my clan, for the good of your clan,'
Yenna Singleton said. 'But as you can see, the two are united.'

'There's no more need for subterfuge,' the Redactor Svern said.

'There is only a small chance that we may be able to retake Cthuga,'

Yenna Singleton said. 'But we have a much better chance of capturing the starship.'

'It is our last chance to foil the enemy's plan,' the Redactor Svern said. 'And you can play an important part in it, Isak.'

A window opened in front of me, showing a bright lumpy shape composed of no more than a dozen pixels.

'We got that from the deep-space array that's usually pointed at beta Hydri,' Yenna Singleton said. 'It took a great deal of persuasion to convince Our Thing to look for it, and it took some time, too. It's very small, not much bigger than an ordinary lighter, and it has deviated from the optimal course between the Homesun and Fomalhaut.'

The Redactor Svern gestured; the lumpy mote in the window shrank to a bright dot as the view widened and tilted to show that the dot was slanting in above the plane of the dust ring. It was not heading towards Cthuga, as I had supposed, but towards Fomalhaut. In fact, it had already passed the inner edge of the dust ring and Cthuga's orbit.

'According to my clan's philosophers, it will swing close in around Fomalhaut,' Yenna Singleton said. 'A manoeuvre that will exchange a great deal of its delta vee with the rotational energy of our star, and also bring it into the plane of the system. Then it will deploy a braking sail. It is an ancient, reliable technique that was used by our seedship and by the seedship of the Quick. Both sent a package ahead of themselves which took root in an asteroid and manufactured a solar-powered laser array. If the starship has done the same thing, then we must find out where its laser array is sited, and take control of it.'

'And here is the crux, Isak,' the Redactor Svern said. 'You claim that certain cultists have opened back doors into the Library. Back doors that lead to information about the ship. It's a serious claim, and we are taking it seriously, as you can see.'

'Our two clans have joined in common cause,' Yenna Singleton said. 'We are working together to capture the starship, deprive the enemy of a valuable resource, and begin a final battle to eliminate them from the Fomalhaut system.'

I looked across the glowing plane at the two revenants, light and dizzy with relief and elation. I was certain that Prem was chasing the same thing as me, but only I had the means to track down the information she needed. I could hand my clan a great victory, and reclaim my place amongst my peers.

'You failed to find what you were looking for in my security not because it is hidden, but because it isn't there,' I said. 'It isn't in the security of my assistant, either. I removed all trace of it. But if you want to know about the back doors, and where they lead to, and what they have to do with the ship, I'll lead you to them. I ask only that my kholop and I be returned to our former position.'

'Oh, I think that we can do better than that,' the Redactor Svern said.

And so I returned to the Library of the Homesun. Not as a lone and penitent exile who had succeeded in the small task given to him, but at the head of a small army of officers and troopers. We were met at the entrance hall by the living Redactors, and the journeymen and women I had asked to volunteer to help me, and their kholops. The Redactor Miriam stepped forward to meet the splendidly caparisoned myrmidon who was the chief of the delegation from the Singleton clan. He bowed so low that the crest of tall plumes on top of his helmet almost brushed the floor, and then straightened and held up his hand, and shot the formal request to the Redactor Miriam's security. She accepted it without comment, and turned to me and looked me up and down with cold contempt.

'Don't think this will absolve you,' she said. 'In fact, you're doubly damned now.'

I met her gaze and said, 'You always wanted me to join the army. And so I have, and so has everyone who serves the Library.'

She slapped my face, spat on the ground between us, and turned and stalked away. The other Redactors and the journeymen and women and their assistants, all clad in the plain black of our clan, parted to let her through. There was a long moment of silence. Everyone was looking at me. I felt the blood beat in my cheek.

'Let's get to work,' I said.

Within three kiloseconds, I was standing on an elevated highway that swept between the glass and steel towers of the Brutal Quarter. The sky was the blank white of a dead slate, shedding an even and directionless light. Dry weeds grew here and there in cracks between the concrete blocks that paved the roadway, and around the concrete posts of the railings on either side. There were no shadows, and everything stood out with stark particularity, vivid as anything in reality, far more real than the low-resolution simulacrum of Yakob Singleton's data miner.

The Horse stood beside me, wearing a sealed recording algorithm that manifested in the viron as mirrored goggles strapped around his head and fastened at the back with a padlock. The eight volunteers, selected because they'd all had experience in shutting down powerful demons, rode skycycles of an antique design, hovering in pairs at the cardinal points around the blocks of the Brutal Quarter. If anything manifested, they would engage it as best they could, without scrupling to save either the Horse or me.

'Even if we survive this,' the Horse said, as we walked along the centre of the elevated highway, 'what makes you think that they'll let us live after we return with what they want?'

'The Redactor Svern gave his word.'

'You always were a hopeless romantic.'

'And you an unredeemable cynic.'

The Horse looked up at me, the blank sky blankly reflected in the round lenses of his goggles. 'At least one of us knows how the world works.'

'Don't worry,' I said. 'This is just another exorcism. Nothing we haven't done a hundred times before.'

'I remember the last time we encountered a demon in the Library,' the Horse said. 'First we screamed. Then we ran.'

'There may not be any demon. There's no reason why the cultists would have protected their back doors. They hid them well.'

'You know who has been here,' the Horse said. 'And you must remember what we found when we last visited one of the places where she got ahead of us.'

The highway passed between two towers of identical height, one faced with mirror glass and the other with glass as black as obsidian, and we followed the curve of an off-ramp down an empty eight-lane street, crossed an empty plaza. Our securities sent enquiries darting away in every direction, returning reports of nothing more than the normal low-level cycling activity required to maintain the texture and physics of the viron. Every hundred seconds the journeymen and women in the perimeter reported that they had nothing to report.

'If it wasn't bad luck to say it's too quiet, I'd say it's too quiet,' the Horse said.

We passed a flock of metal tables and chairs. We skirted the edge of a square planted with a waist-high labyrinth of neatly trimmed thorn bushes. We passed a row of empty storefronts that lined the ground floor of one of the towers. We passed a giant bronze sculpture with three fat lobes, like an internal organ extracted from some alien behemoth. We passed the dry basin of a fountain, where a disarticulated human skeleton lay, its skull grinning at the white sky.

'Oh-ho,' the Horse said, with a grim smile.

'We've seen skeletons elsewhere. They didn't signify.'

'In the Chapel of Skulls and in the Catacomb Gardens, as part of the viron design. Does this look like it's part of any design?'

We entered a wide plaza, that stretched away, punctuated only by a gigantic fretted globe balanced on a plinth, towards a tower with narrow windows set in a honeycomb of white concrete. I told the Horse that it wasn't far to the gate now; a few moments later, he held up a hand and looked all around, turning in a complete circle.

I felt it too, a granulation in the fabric of reality, and unzipped my kit a picosecond before a hundred little mouths opened in the air around us and disgorged a hundred flapping things that flew at us in stuttering stop-start trajectories like trash blown on errant winds. The nearest recoiled from the perimeter of our securities and we loosed algorithms that chased them down and devoured them on the spot, dissipating their little loads of computational energy in bright fizzes of random calculations.

'That was easy,' the Horse said.

He was still turning in slow clockwise circles. I turned widdershins, and on my second revolution spotted and zeroed in on motion at the far end of the plaza, low down inside the tall building. It had a double-height lobby, empty but for a pair of tall stairways hooked at either end like integral signs. Their stepped treads were rising and falling past each other, and someone rode the descending staircase. It was Prem, walking across the lobby, through glass doors that slid apart in front of her.

'It isn't really her,' the Horse said.

'I know.'

But it looked so very much like her. She walked out across the plaza, slender and strong, her dark eyes steady and serious under the straight-cut fringe of her helmet of black hair. Part of me wanted to run towards her, but the impulse was overshadowed by my fear. As she skirted the plinth of the big, fretted globe, she began to grow and lose definition, fading into shadow that grew darker as she expanded. Already taller than the globe, growing taller still with every step, her footfalls thundering across the plaza and echoing from the tall buildings on every side, slabs of stone cracking under her weight and turning black as if charred as she sucked energy from them, their husks splintering away into little whirlwinds of ash.

The demon was ten storeys high, twenty. Sucking all light from the plaza, stooping over us, reaching out towards our perimeter. Energy moves from a hotter to a cooler place, yet the demon was so cold that it seemed to radiate a chthonic chill as if its absolutely black shape was a gateway on to some place colder than absolute zero: a region of negative energy where atoms had not merely stopped moving, but had lost all integrity and shrivelled into the strings that composed their basic particles, and the strings themselves had frozen and ceased singing.

The volunteers at the perimeter of the Brutal Quarter were asking what they should do. I told them to hold their positions. The demon towered above, filling the plaza with its darkness. It was huge, and it was stupid. It reached towards the Horse and me, and we threw algorithms that meshed in mid-air and grew a net fashioned from Riemann geometry that snapped shut around the demon's hand and raced up its arm in an exotic frothing lace that fixed parts of it inside deeply folded dimensions. Its other hand reached up to its shoulder and broke off the infected arm and with a tremendous wrenching motion tossed it backwards. It spun out propeller-wise, shedding fragments of its fabric, and smashed into the tower at the end of the plaza and evaporated. The shock exploded a thousand panes of glass from their concrete sockets and glass and concrete rained down and fell apart into ash and less than ash before hitting the ground.

One-armed but still growing, the cold black giant reared back and lifted a gigantic foot. It loomed above our feeble protective perimeter like an enemy battleship. And then algorithms spun out of the air all around it, a tangle of thorns and briars that sank into the giant's flesh. It staggered backward and roared and threshed, but the briars were strong and doubled and redoubled with each blink of the Library's checksum clock. They bound the giant on the spot in a thorny casing that began to shrink inwards, narrowing to a cable that hung in the air above the shattered plaza and shrank again, at right angles to reality, and vanished.

The eight journeymen and women hung above us on their skycycles, their kholops clinging behind. One dipped lower. It was Li, the partner of Arden. She had gone in, after the demon had killed him, at the head of the crew that had destroyed it. She stood in the saddle of her skycycle, looking down at the Horse and me with grim amusement, saying, 'Next time you stand against a demon, bring better mathe-matics.'

'I did,' I said. 'You are carrying them.'

At the far end of the plaza, there was a tinkling crash as the last of the tall building's glass fell.

Li turned to look, looked all around. 'The demon was guarding the gate. Where is it?'

It was just two blocks away. I recognised the originals of the buildings in the data miner's sketchy simulacrum, and in the basement garage of the mirror-clad tower the Horse and I located the collapsed traces of the back door gateway. In the simulacrum it had been no more than a place marker; here, it still retained certain properties that, by use of a simple root kit, could be read and reconstructed from the matrix in which it had been embedded.

Within minutes, we had the locations of all the back doors in the Library. There were not as many as I had expected, but as Li pointed out, even one back door was one too many. I wasn't surprised to see that one was located in the undistinguished quarter where the demon had killed Arden and Van and destroyed my reputation; the demon that had ridden the poor data miner at the ruined tower on Avalon had been a low-grade copy of that same demon.

It would have taken several gigaseconds to explore and make safe all of them, and track down the information which those who had used the back doors had been sampling and copying. I chose instead to go to the one that had been used most recently.

It was in the Grey Havens. A quarter of docks and shipyards that stretched either side of a reach of water where waves patched from a simple equation rolled endlessly past every kind of ship at anchor. There was a demon here, too. It came roaring out of a warehouse like a comet set on fire and the Horse and I took it down together, binding its raging decoherence into a cube of pure iron scarcely larger than a crystal of salt.

I had been expecting it, or something like it. If we could track all the back doors using a root kit, so could Bree – or the thing that rode her – and it was inevitable that she would have set guardians at each one. Even so, I was badly shaken.

'Just like any exorcism,' the Horse said. He was shaken too. And, like me, smudged with carbon soot.

All around us was a circle of devastation. A wooden trireme on fire from stem to stern on one side; two mangled and half-melted travelling cranes and the smashed ruin of a warehouse on the other. Above us, the riders of the skycycles were scouting the rest of the territory for demon traces, questing in a grid pattern over the roofs of warehouses, amongst the beaks of cranes and the masts and superstructures of ships. Tiny shapes against the vast sunset that bloodied the waves endlessly rolling up the reach of water.

'I think we're getting better at this,' I said.

'We'd better be, if it's going to be like this at every back door,' the Horse said.

'I think we can find what we want here.'

'They're probably dead, the people who used it. Either Bree reached them, or they didn't realise she'd turned their back door into a trap. Anyone who came through would have been possessed, and then the screaming and the stabbing would have started. Just like the cultists Yakob Singleton found, and all the others.'

'That's why we have to find any survivors as soon as possible.'

While the volunteers tracked the back door's connection through the Archipelago's network, the Horse and I set to work uncovering the footprints and fingerprints of its users. They led us to an antique office in a low building that overlooked the hulk of a half-built ship in dry dock. On a drafting table were diagrams hand-drawn in white ink on blue paper: information about construction of a laser array and its orbital dynamics, and tiny drones that were, according to Yenna Singleton and the Redactor Svern, when I showed them what we'd discovered, the kind used to scout enemy territory.

'They can withstand tremendous accelerations, so can be fired by railguns for fast fly-bys,' the Redactor Svern said.

I said, 'Could they intercept a ship travelling at high speed?'

'Hit it, you mean? Of course.'

'You're wondering if the cultists tried to contact the ship,' Yenna Singleton said.

'He has a point,' the Redactor Svern said. 'If the probes can survive the high acceleration caused by a railgun, they could survive high decelera-tion, too. And deliver some kind of message, or establish a comms node.'

'It's a trivial question, and one that will be answered soon enough,' Yenna Singleton said. 'Once we take control of the laser array, we will have control of the ship. We'll know everything about it then.'

'As for that, I have another task for you, Isak,' the Redactor Svern said. 'I want you to join the assault force.'

'For the greater good of the clan, I suppose.'

'For the greater good of everyone,' Yenna Singleton said.

3

The enemy ship punched out of the atmosphere in an arc that took it halfway around the waist of Cthuga before it re-entered, shedding shells of superheated plasma, gliding towards the calm atmospheric layer where the Whale hung. Ori watched all this on one of the windows set before her face. She was wrapped in a cocoon that not only protected her from abrupt changes in gravity but also effectively imprisoned her, but she was allowed access to the vertiginous indices of the ship's knowledge base and a zoo of blobjects that conveyed the status of various systems by their shapes and changes in colour, pulsations, and the pitch of their simple songs. She could trace links with other ships, too. Ships in orbit and ships trawling and transiting the atmosphere, and stations and rocks spread across the dust belt. So many of them. The enemy seemed to have moved everything they had to Cthuga.

Her captors were monitoring her all the while. Explaining that everything was open to all, that nothing was hidden. Guiding her to places and things they wanted her to see. Showing off their favourites with the innocent open pride of young children to whom everything is precious because everything is new, and everything is true. Streaming a dizzy kaleidoscope of vids and picts that gave Ori a headache and a kind of oceanic state of fear. Individually, each of the enemy was little more than a child. Collectively, knit by this open-access thing of theirs, united by a common purpose focused on a single goal, they were a Power. Ruthless. Implacable.

They wanted her to know the truth, they said. They wanted her to understand the true history of the human species. Where it had come from, what it had become, where it had gone wrong and how they were going to fix that. Once she understood all of this, she would know that she had made the right choice.

As the ship glided in towards the Whale, Ori saw how foolish she'd been, thinking that somehow she could contribute to its defence. For it had been taken and was being transformed. Hung at the centre of a great flock of platforms and towers and other structures floating under clusters of balloons, and swarms of ships and smaller craft that moved between them, it seemed superficially intact, and the cable still hung below it, dwindling away to the cloud deck. Ori could even see a train moving up the cable towards the inverted tree of the marshalling yard, returning for a fresh load of material to feed the never-ending work of construction and repair far below. But as the ship in which she rode skittered towards the upper flank of the Whale, she saw areas where the skin had been peeled back by explosions, and gaping holes burned into it, and black patches and scabs mottling it, growing into each other.

The ship docked above one such patch. It extended for a kilometre down the skin of the Whale, flat in some places, erupting in clusters of latticework spires in others. Some of the spires were several hundred metres long, and small lightnings stuttered around their tips. Then the window shut and the cocoon around Ori relaxed. She clambered out of its slick embrace. All around her the enemy were twittering and laughing as if at the end of some hugely entertaining joyride. Most ignored her, and for a moment she wondered what she was supposed to do, and was more afraid than ever, as if she was exposed on a high pinnacle, where a single misstep could send her plunging down in a long, long drop.

Then someone touched her elbow, told her that she shouldn't be afraid.

'You're with us now. You're free.'

The way they spoke, it was as if they were sight-reading unfamiliar words. Perhaps they were – perhaps some AI function was translating for them, putting up what they needed to say to her.

She said, 'What do you want me to do?'

The enemy studied her. A grave little thing, with olive skin and dark brown eyes and a spray of pigmented spots over its snub nose. Ori realised that she didn't know if it was male or female or something else. It smiled, and said, 'Why don't you find your friends first? They'll help you understand what you need to do.'

'My friends?'

'In what used to be called the commons of jockey crew #87.'

It was a strange, heartbreaking homecoming. The interior of the Whale was hardly changed at all, apart from the enemy swarming cheerfully and purposefully down the main companionways. They made a tremendous noise, talking to each other, exchanging greetings, taking up snatches of wordless songs – high weird ululations, chanted streams of nonsense syllables with simple rhyming schemes – and there were so many of them. If the Whale was as crowded everywhere else as here, Ori thought, its captors easily outnumbered the original crew by at least ten to one.

Ori was taller than any of them and slower than most, and wondered if this was what Trues felt like, in a crowd of Quick. She found her way to one of the elevator shafts and descended past the docking areas and got off and rode another elevator down past the manufactory levels and got off again, and took a third elevator down to the zone of the crew commons. She saw a few Quicks on the way, clumping along amidst the slight figures of the enemy, no Trues. She supposed that all the Trues had died in the fighting, or had committed suicide rather than be captured, or had been given the long drop.

The crowds thinned out as she made her way through familiar companionways towards the commons, passing murals she remembered being painted, a big mobile sculpture made from old tools strung on wire below an airshaft, turning in the faint breeze of the air conditioning. The commons was empty. Everyone was on shift, she supposed, as the rush of recognition hit her. A blow to the heart. It was as if she had stepped out just a few minutes before. The tubular space lit by the yellowish glow of panels in the low ceiling. The soft, scuffed black floor. Niches in offset rows down either side. Low tables, seatpads, the casual detritus of living.

Something salty slid down the back of Ori's throat and she realised that she was crying. She snuffled, wiped tears with the back of her hand. She'd come all the way around the world, had lost good companions, had been captured and told she'd been freed, and now she was back, and she had no idea what to do next.

Someone was standing behind her and she turned but no one was there. It was the sprite, of course. The passenger in her head. Her silent sharer.

She climbed into the niche she'd shared with Inas, into the old familiar smell, the double groove in the temperfoam, and although she didn't think it would be possible, she fell asleep. And when she woke, people were watching her. A small group, standing back as she swung out of the niche. She recognised them all. There were far fewer than there had been, but she was glad to see them, and there was Inas, and they fell into each other's arms, and Ori started to cry all over again.

Inas touched the half-healed wound in her cheek; Ori said it was nothing.

'I underestimated the malice of someone who disagreed with me. She's dead, now. They're all dead, Inas. Only I survived . . .'

Emere, the oldest of the crew, said, 'You can't stay here. I'm sorry, but there it is.'

'They told me to come here,' Ori said, looking at her across Inas' shoulder.

'That's why you can't stay,' Emere said. She had a strained expression that was mirrored in the faces of the others. Anxiety. Disapproval.

'I'm not one of them.'

'That's what everyone says,' one of the others, Ahe, said.

'You shouldn't have come here,' Emere said. 'It's too dangerous.'

'Where else would she go?' Inas said. 'Aren't we her friends and comrades?'

'Are we?' Ahe said.

'I'll go.' Ori uncoupled from Inas' embrace. She was upset and angry at this naked rejection, but resigned too. She should have realised how different things were, now. That there was no going home again. She said, 'I'm sorry. I didn't realise that I was putting you in danger. If I did, I wouldn't have come here.'

She hadn't gone far when she heard someone hurrying after her, heard Inas calling her name. 'We agreed that you need to know what happened here,' Inas said. 'I can tell you that, and I think I can tell you what the Ghosts want from you, too. But don't ask any questions. Even if I know the answers, I can't deal with them.'

'I understand. You're afraid that I'm a spy.'

'We're all of us afraid all of the time,' Inas said. 'You'll see why, soon enough.'

They talked in a crowded commons where Quicks and Ghosts ate at long tables, the Ghosts noisy and ebullient, the Quicks hunched and subdued. The food was strange. Smoky or bitter gruels, bowls of tasteless, slippery red ribbons, little nodules that crumbled to a grainy sweetness on the tongue. Ghost food.

307

Ori told Inas about her sojourn in the station down below, her transfer to *The Eye of the Righteous* and the terror of the invasion and the long voyage that had ended at the pelagic station, where she'd been captured and brought here. Inas told her about how she and the other jockeys had been riding their bots out on the skin of the Whale when the enemy had invested it, so they'd had a grandstand view of the battle. The loss of the raptors, enemy ships settling all around the Whale, Trues flying sleds and flitters loaded with explosives at the ships, Trues and the enemy fighting in hand-to-hand combat after the enemy broke into the Whale's modules and compartments, how a gang of Trues had attempted to blow most of the ballonets and send the Whale plunging down, and how some Quicks had rebelled against them.

'They killed the Trues and saved the Whale,' Inas said. 'Not because they were in league with the Ghosts, but because they wanted to save their sisters. They wanted to save us. And they did. Most died fighting the Trues. The rest died fighting the Ghosts. Some say that they're heroes. I'm not so sure.'

Inas had changed. She'd been spiky, confident, outgoing, and now she was troubled and vague and confused. As if she was ashamed that she had survived. She told Ori about the flocks of tiny enemy machines that had settled in huge patches that had disintegrated into black nanostuff that spread and transformed the Whale's skin. They'd been ordered to contain the infection, Inas said, and although it had been like trying to bail out a reservoir with a cup, they'd kept at it until their connections had been cut and they'd found themselves back in their immersion chairs with the enemy crowding around, helping them up, telling them that it was all right, it was all over. Some of the crew had refused to cooperate and they'd been taken away. Everyone else had been converted.

'Most of the Trues were dead by then,' she said. 'We didn't know what to do, so we did as we were told.'

'Did they make you take a new name?' Ori said.

Inas nodded. 'One of their saints. Janejean.'

'I chose that name too!'

Inas' smile was weak, there and gone. 'Don't think it means anything. There weren't that many to choose from. Apart from the thing with the names, they've mostly left us alone. We still work out on the skin, although we aren't dispatching probes any more. Mostly, we help to load hoppers, help keep the cable growing. Can't let that stop. Nothing's really changed. Except, of course, we're free now. According to the Ghosts, anyway.'

'Do they watch you?'

Inas took Ori's hands in her own. 'You mean, are we being watched now? No. That's not how it is.'

But Inas' fingers were moving on Ori's palms, shaping the signs they used to pass on gossip and jokes about Trues while riding bots out on the skin of the Whale.

They say they don't watch us, but we can't be sure.

'We have our work,' she said. 'Only now we are responsible for it. We organise ourselves, do what we think we're supposed to do. It's challenging.'

And on Ori's palms, she tapped out: *Some fought back. They all died. A few went crazy, started killing the nearest of the enemy. They died. None of them had a plan. We do.*

'I guess I should join you,' Ori said.

'Word is, you're marked for something higher.'

It could be useful to us.

'How do you know?'

'Anyone can know anything. I suppose that's a difference. The Ghosts, they talk to each other all the time. They're all linked in this big network. Sharing everything,' Inas said, tapping the side of her head.

'And you?'

'I suppose we'll be linked in too, eventually. Meanwhile, we can use windows, look at everything and anything. And we have to, to make sure that we're doing what we're supposed to be doing. No one tells us. We're free to choose. But if you don't make the right choice, you get the long drop.'

'Some things haven't changed, then,' Ori said.

The small joke died in the air.

'What has changed, the Ghosts don't tell you what you should do,' Inas said. 'You have to work it out for yourself. And if you don't, if you make the wrong choices all the time, you're gone. They don't want to do it. They just don't have any way of dealing with people who don't or won't do what's best for everyone else. They expect us to be like them, but they don't tell us how. It doesn't occur to them to explain anything. They've been united in a single cause for so long that it doesn't occur to them that other people might not understand what they are doing. As far as they're concerned, either you're part of the programme, or you're a problem.'

Ori learned that the enemy had no leaders, and none were needed because they were united in a common purpose, and had been for over fifteen hundred years. Tasks weren't assigned to individuals; individuals volunteered to help according to ability and proximity to the work at hand. And when the work was completed, the group dissolved, so that someone could be directing a fleet of attack ships one day and loading shit into a recycler the next. But while their self-organising society resembled that of one of the anthills of Earth, the enemy were not mindless drones. Each was an individual, with their own talents and weaknesses, desires and dislikes. The only thing they lacked was any trace of sexual desire. They were children, male and female, and because their life span was short, like Quicks, they did not live long enough to become sexually mature, and they lacked all curiosity about it. Their love was universal and unconditional, but it was platonic.

'That's the worst thing,' Inas told Ori. 'Their love. They love us because we joined them. They love those who fail to make the right choices, too. They love everyone. They even love the Trues. They call them their cousins in combat. They say that struggling against the Trues helps them to define themselves. They love to talk about the fight for the Whale, and all the glorious deaths. They say the Trues who died are heroes because they fought for what they believed in. The Trues were wrong, the Ghosts say, but they were sincere. That's what counts, for them. Sincerity. Truth.'

'I'm beginning to understand what they want from me,' Ori said.

And tapped out on Inas' palm: *I think that they think I can help them contact the Mind. Because of what happened, back in the quake.*

'They bring all the Quicks they've captured here,' Inas said. 'They turn them loose, and if they don't get with the programme . . .'

'I understand.'

'We survived because we can ride bots,' Inas said. 'That gives us a purpose. It makes us useful. We try to keep out of their way. We stay down here. We work at what we've always worked at. Not the probes now. They have no use for the probes. We found that out the hard way . . . But they need the cable, and so the cable must be fed. And that's what we do. Even so, if you stray outside the commons you can get caught up in some tide or other, and if you don't know what it's for, that's it for you. It happened to Hahana. She was caught up in one of those tides, she tried to resist, and they . . .'

Inas looked away for a moment, above the heads of the Ghosts and Quicks at the other tables. When she looked back, tears stood in her eyes.

'They're so sorry, so sad, when they have to do someone that way. Because the person has failed, and so has become an unperson. They mourn that, even as they kill you. They don't kill you because they hate you. They kill you because they love you.'

'One of them told me to come here,' Ori said. 'I didn't think anything of it at the time because I didn't understand what they're like. But I see now that it was a kindness. An extraordinary kindness. They wanted me to know as quickly as possibly how to survive here.'

Inas said, 'If they need you so badly they should have told you everything themselves.'

I'd like to know everything, she tapped. *It could be useful.*

I'll come back and tell you, Ori tapped back. And said, 'I've changed, Inas. I've been changed. They know that. They told me.'

'I kept a watch for your name,' Inas said. 'I shouldn't have, but I did.'

She looked away again. Ori took her hands in hers.

Inas said at last, 'I knew you were almost certainly dead, but I hadn't given up hope. So I asked one of the AIs in their system to keep watch for you, and it pinged me when you were taken. And it gave me the names of others interested in you, and the tags associated with you, too. They definitely want you for special work. Most people don't have anything associated with them. If they did, we'd know what we were supposed to be doing by looking up our own names. But most of us, and most of them, we're like general-purpose labourers. Doing whatever's needed wherever it's needed whenever it's needed.'

'Who is interested in me?'

'Some of the Ghosts. And someone you know. Commissar Doctor Wilm Pentangel.'

Ori felt a chill. 'I thought all the Trues had been killed.'

'Not him,' Inas said. 'He crossed over. He became one with the enemy.'

Inas helped Ori use the enemy's data-base to find out where the commissar was working – a workshop down at the base of the Whale, beneath the repurposed hangar where Ori and all the other Quick touched by sprites had trained. It wasn't too far from the commons, but it took Ori a long time to reach it because she knew now what she hadn't known when she'd recklessly ridden the elevators, knew that she'd been lucky not to be caught up in one of the groups that wedged their way through the crowds, or suddenly appeared in the middle of them, forming around a notion or a need as a raindrop forms around a speck of dust, gaining mass and direction and sweeping up everyone in its path. And because she didn't know and had no intention of finding out if the special interest the enemy had in her would protect her from being caught up, she kept to the minor companionways as much as possible, avoiding the main arteries and the serviceways where the enemy scampered along in their customised pressure-suits, laughing and singing. A press of exultant faces like the flowers in Commissar Doctor Pentangel's garden.

The worst thing wasn't the hike down more than a dozen levels. It was the anticipation of seeing the commissar again. Of becoming a possession again, after her brief spell of freedom. Of remembering every detail of what he'd done to her.

The workshop, where damaged hoppers and freight cars had been repaired and new ones manufactured, along with the rails and switches and track-control gear and all the other stuff associated with the transport of raw materials down the length of the cable, was a tall, annular space set around the upper part of the cable's collar, with two sets of rail tracks circling it and big airlocks that led to flying buttresses that swooped down to the tracks that ran the length of the cable. There were open spaces where large makers, spinners, tanks, and other machinery associated with fabrication stood. Heavy lifting gear hung overhead, and smaller workspaces clung to the circular cliff of the interior wall in rows and tiers, where finer work was carried out.

It was in one of these that Ori found Commissar Doctor Pentangel. The long dim room had worktables down one side and several windows hung in the air at the far end; the commissar stood behind the largest, studying diagrams of what looked like energy flows. The shock of seeing him was worse than she thought it would be, and she had to brace herself, had to repress an urge to run, strong as nausea, as he walked, tick-tock, tick-tock, towards her.

He knelt stiffly in front of her, his exoskeleton's motors whirring; his face twisted in what seemed to be genuine anguish when she stepped back.

'I used you, cruelly,' he said. 'I attempted to dominate you because you possessed something I could never have. It was wrong. It was a crime. I ask forgiveness so that we can put it in the past and move forward together on this great and glorious project.'

Ori, surprised and frightened and confused, fell back on formal speech. 'This one regrets that she does not have the power to forgive you.'

'Oh but you do, you do!'

The commissar shuffled forward on his knees, grabbing at Ori's hands, his gaze imploring, wretched. She backed away, but he kept coming, until at last her spine was pressed against a wall and she had nowhere to go. He took her hands in his, his grip hot and clammy, and said again that she must forgive him.

What she wanted to do was hit him, or laugh, or scream. Do something to shock him. Show him that he wasn't in charge any more. Because that was what this was all about. He was still asserting his authority. Ordering her to forgive him for crimes he no doubt had been forced to confess, so that he could dismiss them. Well, she wouldn't let him. And she wouldn't run, either. She was going to see this through, even though she did not yet have any idea what she was going to do.

Ori took a breath, took another. Managed to meet his gaze, and the madness behind it. Said, 'This one will try her best to do what is required of her. But she fears it will not be good enough.'

'You don't need slave speech. Not with me, or anyone else,' Commissar Doctor Pentangel said, and let go of her hands and ponderously got to his feet. 'You are free, and you have been recruited into a great work of science. Because of what happened to you, during my experiments, you are an essential part of it. You and others like you, you have the templates in your heads.'

'This one . . .'

'You don't understand. Of course you don't,' the commissar said. 'They never explain. They expect you to know everything. It's very challenging. One must adapt to new ways of thinking, and it's no small thing. I'm one of the few who could do it. As soon as I was captured, I began to study my captors. I realised how they thought, and how their behaviour is organised. I tried to tell the others that we weren't prisoners. That we were free to choose. They didn't understand. And so they refused the freedom they'd been given, and their refusal condemned them, until at last only I was left alive. And once again I am working on what I've always been working on. It was taken away from me by short-sighted fools who didn't understand its significance. *You* were taken away from me, and all the others like you. But you're back now. And I am here to work with you.'

There was something manic in the commissar's gaze, a sly brightness that Ori hadn't seen before and didn't like or trust.

'They are trying to contact the Mind,' she said. 'I think they want me to help.'

'They need me, and I need them. And we need you, yes. You and others like you. But this isn't about contacting the Mind, not exactly. No no no. This,' the commissar said, with a flourish that reminded Ori of his old ways, 'is about *making* the Mind.'

4

And so the Child came back to São Gabriel da Cachoeira, standing between the captain and the chief pilot in the little transparent bubble of the bridge of the weather wranglers' cargo blimp. The green sea of the renewed forest flowing below, and then the sinuous dark channel of the river and the famous profile of the Serra da Bela Adormecida mountains rising against the shimmering blue sky, and the grid of the little town on its promontory coming into view.

The blimp slowed, came to a halt above the futbol field. People crowded the touchlines. The whole town was there, applauding as dozens of wranglers slid down dangling lines and pegged them to the hard clay with simultaneous blurts of power jacks. The blimp wound itself towards the ground like an ungainly cloud and a long ramp unfolded from a square hatch in the centre of the gondola's underside and the Child followed the captain of the wranglers down it. There was another wave of applause and cheers; the town's little band struck up the national anthem as it accompanied the small delegation, led by Maria Hong-Owen, that came out to meet the Child. Ama Paulinho was there, pushing her father in a wheelchair, and Vidal-Francisca, Father Caetano, the head of the hospital, the chief of police, and the colonel who commanded the army base.

We were there, too. Posing as children, for children were running around everywhere, unnoticed by adults. We were so very glad to see the Child again, and foolishly believed that we had regained control of her story, that the entity that the Child called Jaguar Boy was our only enemy, and that all would be well now that he had been deleted.

But there were other watchers in the crowd, cool intelligences who were manipulating and guiding us, who were about to make themselves known.

A few of us followed the small welcoming committee out on to the field, watching as Maria hugged her daughter, lifted her up, whirled her around. Then the Child was set on to a chair and the chair was raised by four soldiers who each held a leg, and she was paraded around the edge of the futbol field in the midst of wild music, cheers and applause, and the crackle of fireworks exploding in the bright sky beyond the looming bulk of the blimp.

The Child looked all around, dazed and confused. She was searching for Jaguar Boy, expecting him to step from the people pressing all around, feeling a profound disappointment when he did not. Feeling as if she was the only real person in a great crowd of ghosts.

She was driven to the hospital in an army jeep and given a brisk medical examination by her mother, ending with a scan of her brain activity that her mother and several of the other doctors studied with grave intensity.

At last, the Child and Maria were alone. Maria gave her clean clothes, underwear and a white dress with a flounced skirt that dropped to her ankles. Red slippers. Telling her that they had much to talk about, and much to do.

They were shy and awkward with each other. The Child wanted to tell her mother about her adventures, but the great flood of words was dammed by a prickling caution. Everything was familiar, and everything seemed unreal.

Her mother said that she understood. 'You think that your captor was your friend. You don't want to betray him. That will change. Tomorrow we'll explain everything. It will all become clear to you. And then you'll know the true nature and intentions of your so-called friend, and the true nature of those who truly care for you. But first you need to sleep. You need to remember who you really are.'

'He said that, too.'

'Jaguar Boy. Don't look so surprised. We know his name, and we know how he lied to you and how he wanted to use you, and a lot more besides.'

'Everyone says they know what I want and what I should do. But they don't.'

'Hush now. Sleep.'

And then, somehow, the Child was in her bed, and a great wave of exhaustion was rolling through her, carrying her away. Her last thought was that the stars stuck to the ceiling had been rearranged into new and unfamiliar constellations.

5

'It's splendid,' the Horse said. 'But it isn't war.'

'It seems to fit every definition,' I said.

'That's the point. It looks like war, but it isn't. Or at least, it is not the main event. It's a sideshow. It's distraction. It's bait-and-switch.'

'Bait-and-switch?'

'A trick shills use in the Permanent Floating Market. It's older than the market, older than the Quick or the True for that matter. Shills on Old Earth used it before the first ships hit vacuum. They were probably using it in the first cities. You and your partner show the marks a fancy box and open it to show something desirable inside. Nepenthe, fine tea, a handwrought pistola . . . Any old goods at a bargain price. You show it round, you let them handle it, sniff it, taste it, and then you start them bidding on it. You get the patter flowing, and you and your partner throw the box back and forth between you. Distraction, you see? The patter confuses the marks; the hand is faster than the eye. You get the marks to bid against each other and drive up that bargain price. That's one thing. The other, when the hammer comes down on the bidding, you throw the lucky winner a box containing dodgy goods. Like but not like the stuff you showed them at the start. Cheaper stuff. Shoddy stuff.'

'What happens when your customers finds out they've been cheated?'

'The odd one that comes back looking for restitution gets a refund, of course. But most don't come back. They don't like to admit they've been fooled. Or they think it's all part of the entertainment, the price for the thrill they had outbidding everyone else. But that's not the point. The point is that even the cleverest mark can be fooled. And that's what's this is,' the Horse said. 'Bait-and-switch.'

We were strapped in facing crash seats in a niche deep inside the cramped quarters of an assault ship. Windows hung between us showed various views of the laser array. It was the first time we'd been able to talk in private since we'd harrowed the back door in the Library. We'd been taken aboard the assault ship separately, had spent the journey – a straight slam across some two hundred million kilometres – doped up and breathing an oxygen-rich silicone liquid inside coffins packed with gel to protect us from the worst of the brutal acceleration and deceleration.

The assault ship was part of a wing that was standing off at a distance of more than three million kilometres, behind spinning mirrored sails designed to deflect any energy beams. Spy drones sent zipping past the array at tremendous velocities were transmitting updates and there were multiple views from the third wave of combat drones that was sweeping towards the enemy defences. Several windows gave views at different distances and angles of the five laser-cannon assemblies in the array, silvery ship-sized cylinders forming the points of a pentagon that orbited a small planetoid. Another window mapped the clouds of aggressive machines that defended them. Two waves of combat drones had attacked these defences while we still slept, opening up holes through which the third wave would manoeuvre towards the planetoid at the centre of the array. And when the planetoid was secure, we would be sent in to harrow the machines that controlled the laser array, so that Yenna Singleton's philosophers could take command and guide the starship to a safe harbour in the Archipelago.

That was the plan according to the Redactor Svern and Yenna Singleton, but although I had done my best to seem eager for action when they had explained it to me, in truth I'd felt anxious and resentful, realising that I would be no more than a small component of a scheme whose architects I did not entirely trust. I had enjoyed being a free agent more than I cared to admit. I'd thought that I had been the hero of my story; the discovery that I was instead a pawn, that the Redactor Svern had used and manipulated me, even if it was for the greater good of the clan and the Library, had cut deeper than Prem's casual betrayal. And I feared and disliked Yenna Singleton, and was worried that she was using and deceiving the Redactor Svern as he had used and deceived me.

So I wasn't angered by the Horse's impertinent ridicule of the plan to capture the array. No, I was intrigued, because it chimed with my own feelings.

I asked him if by bait-and-switch he meant that there might be another laser array. 'One more powerful than this?'

The Horse shook his head. 'There could be a hundred arrays. A thousand. It wouldn't make any difference. Yenna Singleton and her generals think that whoever controls the array controls the ship. They're wrong.'

'And you know this because?'

'Why were we able to find out about the array in the first place?'

'We defeated a demon and secured the locations of the back doors—'

'Aside from our guile and cunning,' the Horse said.

'If you interrupt me like that in front of anyone who counts, I'll have to punish you,' I said. 'The Singleton clan is very old-fashioned, and this is a ship of the line besides.'

'This one would like to explain that his presumption is motivated by his desire to protect his master.'

The Horse didn't look especially scared. Defiant, certainly. A shine in his eyes, his expression grim and eager. We sat face to face amongst the windows inside the little niche, like equals.

I said, 'Your master would like you to break the habit of a lifetime, and speak plainly for once.'

'We followed Bree Sixsmith from hell to hell,' the Horse said. 'Each was collapsed to a minimum size and data was erased. But the data about the array and the probes was not only left intact, all of it was left in plain sight.'

'She couldn't erase that data because it was in the Library. She could only attempt to prevent access to it. And she underestimated the speed at which we were able to unravel her traps.'

'Or perhaps we were meant to find it,' the Horse said. 'Because it's sham masquerading as quality.'

'All right. Let's suppose Bree led us here. To what end?'

'The demon riding her wanted us to come here because it works for the enemy. The enemy wants us to come here because it wastes our time and resources. Because it distracts us from what is really going on. There is no point capturing the laser array because it does not control the trajectory of the starship. It doesn't control the starship because the enemy already has it.'

'I see. And what about the ship imaged by Yenna Singleton's philosophers?'

'Also a sham. A clever duplicate carved from some icy rock and powered by a drone.'

'And yet, despite your amazing insight, you are not even a trooper, let alone a general.'

The Horse ducked his head. 'I had help,' he said.

'I think you had better tell me everything.'

'Back on T, I got out of that treehouse where we were being held in custody, and I came back with a flitter and fresh clothes—'

'That was my plan.'

'And very good it was. But after I got out, I was intercepted by two Quicks. They knew why we were there, and what we were searching for.'

'Let me guess. They were cultists.'

'They did not admit it, but yes, I am certain that they were. They told me that Yakob Singleton's quest had something to do with the ancient starship and its passenger. As I told you, later on. But I didn't tell you everything—'

'No, you didn't. To begin with, you didn't tell me who told you.'

The Horse ducked his head again. 'I also didn't tell you that the cultists had made direct contact with the starship's passenger.'

'I assume you had a good reason.'

I was angry now.

'This one believed that you would be endangered if you knew too much. Also, like the laser array, that you would provide a useful distraction.'

'I see.'

'There's more.'

The Horse threw a package at me and said it would explain everything.

'It appears to come from Prem,' I said.

He nodded.

'She gave it to you? When?'

'One of the techs slipped it to me while I was being prepped for the voyage,' the Horse said.

'And you opened it.'

'It is addressed to both of us.'

'It probably isn't from Prem at all, but from some clique inside her clan that wants to use or confuse me to further some petty intrigue.'

'If it is, I'm sure you'll see through it.'

Deep inside my security, I watched as Prem walked out of the shadows between two black cypresses into bright sunlight, stepping beside a small stream that ran down a dusty slope towards a mud-rimmed pool. I recognised the place immediately: the platform owned by Lathi Single-ton. Prem was wearing the same white shirt that she'd worn when we'd first met, its hem clinging to her bare thighs. Her gaze was cool and steady. She looked imperious and infinitely desirable.

'If I'm talking to you now, it's because things have gone wrong,' she said, and I realised at once that she had recorded this message before we had met. That she had prepared for this moment.

'It means,' she said, 'that poor Yakob is dead, and Yenna Singleton has found out about our quest. You're in her power; I've had to flee. But I must be alive because you're listening to this message, and not the other one. So there's still a chance, Isak. We can still make something good from this.

'I have friends. And they are your friends, too. One of them made sure you received this message. He's ready to take you to me.' She smiled. 'Wherever I am. I can't tell you that, because I don't know. But if you're watching this, it means that my future self knows what Yakob found, and what to do about it. But I need your help. So come to me, Isak. Please. Any conditions you like. Any precautions. Any price. My friends will agree to them all. But I hope you'll come to me because you know it's the right thing to do.'

The final assault on the enemy position began like most engagements in the war: flocks of insensate killing machines zipping past each other at high relative velocities, each using microsecond windows of opportunity to try to destroy the other. Views of the array began to flicker and jump as the enemy locked on to camera drones and took them out with kinetic weapons, or blinded them with X-ray or gamma pulses. But there were more drones behind them, and more behind that. The planetoid and the five cannon of the laser array were each enclosed in loose shells of brilliant flashes and sheets of raw lightnings. Tiny novae blinked as antimatter bomblets let go. Expanding clouds of debris were pierced by the violet or red threads of particle beams.

Deep inside the energetic displays, microscopic Q-drones were attaching to each of the cannon. Most died before they could hatch their nanoassemblers, zapped or poisoned by the equally small machines of the cannons' immune system. The few survivors grew networks that pierced the integuments of the cannons and shook hands with their nervous systems and attempted to subvert them.

Every attempt failed. One after the other, the cannon self-destructed in fierce blinks of raw light as antimatter batteries yielded all their stored energy at once, scorching the surface of the planetoid and washing past the first wave of assault ships and killing everyone on board.

Slamships carrying the second wave were fired from railgun launchers and crossed two million kilometres of void in less than three kiloseconds, dumping velocity in a fraction of that time, blasting straight down to the planetoid's lumpy, cratered surface.

Electromagnetic pulses and sleets of gamma rays and exotic particles had killed everything unshielded, and the thermal pulses of the cannons' deaths had shocked the deep-frozen regolith. Minor quakes sent boulders tumbling down slopes, opened cracks and vents. Jagged lines of geysers, fed by pockets of frozen methane and nitrogen that had undergone explosive phase changes, were shooting columns of vapour tens of kilometres high. Some of it fell back as nitrogen snow; the rest achieved escape velocity, and views of the planetoid were blurred by a thickening haze that was slashed everywhere by the flares of slamship drives.

Even as they fell, the ships fired off packages that exploded and loosed a rain of combat machines. Multi-limbed things that looked like squashed crabs or engorged snowflakes, each clinging to a crash balloon that absorbed the kinetic energy of impact and instantly deflated. In the diffused and dimming light of five new stars – the slagged cores of the laser cannon – the machines skittered away in every direction, across the floors and inner slopes of craters, across dusty intercrater plains, searching for any sign of enemy activity.

Pods of elite troops followed in slower slamships, falling away as the ships went into orbit, riding T-bar rocket bikes down to the surface. Quicks modified for low-gravity combat, with arms where their legs should be or legs fused into muscular coils, utterly lacking any notion of fear or forgiveness. Rangers, all of them women, all of them pregnant, their embryos arrested at three months' development and heavily modified: implanted nervous systems loaded with reflexive subroutines; endocrine systems pumping combinations of combat drugs into their mothers' bloodstreams.

Squads zeroed in on entrances to subsurface tunnels and voids mapped by fly-by drones. As soon as they touched the surface, enemy machines and child-sized troops erupted from dust pools and engaged in vicious firefights with rangers, Quick soldiers, and combat machines.

There was nothing noble or glorious about the battle. It was a slaughter. It was like trying to put out a fire by throwing people on it. And it continued remorselessly even though there was no point in capturing the planetoid after the destruction of the laser array. But we were Trues, and nothing less than full and outright victory would satisfy us.

The Horse refused to watch. He was hunched inside the blanket of his security, turned inwards, until at last he flashed a message to me. It was time to go.

Two of Prem's cousins shepherded us to the garages under the outer skin of the ship and loaded us into a slamship that was being readied with fifty others for the next stage of the assault on the planetoid. We were seized, stripped, pumped full of drugs, and dumped in the coffins. Facemasks displaced the air in our lungs with fluorosilicone fluid. Dozily, happy and stupid thanks to the cocktail of muscle relaxants, soporifics, and neurosuppressors in my bloodstream, I watched on a tiny window as the slamship was swung out of the line waiting to be shunted through the forward railguns and was lowered into a big, cubic airlock. The double doors above shut; those below opened. The slamship dropped into black vacuum and shot away, powered by strap-on fusion motors, accelerating at a steady 3 g towards Cthuga.

6

Several of the jockey-crew commons were empty and unused, and there were plenty of spare bots. So it was easy, once Ori had slipped away from the workshops during one of her rest periods, to walk one out on to the skin of the Whale, and flash a tag to Inas. Strange to be riding a bot again, to stalk through the marshalling yard. It seemed mostly unchanged and was as busy as ever, but the upper parts of the Whale were blotched with dark growths and enemy craft darted and jerked amongst spires and platforms hung up there in the sky, their shadows flowing and flitting everywhere.

At one point on her short journey Ori felt her passenger move forward and stand behind her eyes, and she wondered if it realised they were close to the place where they'd first met. And wondered too if it might leave her, push all the way out into the clear freezing air and become a sprite again. Fly out, she thought. Fly, fly. And something inside her head relaxed like a muscle unclenching and the sense of double vision faded. Whatever it wanted from her, it wasn't yet ready to leave.

She and Inas met by one of the tipplers where freight cars were loaded with raw materials, and they spoke in gesture talk.

I feel horribly exposed out here, Ori signed.

It's safer than meeting face to face, Inas signed back.

For me, or for you?

The others have good reason to be scared.

I know. And I'm sorry. I'm scared too. Do they know you're talking to me?

It's better that they don't. And that's all I can say. Now, before someone spots us, tell me everything.

It broke Ori's heart that the war and the Ghosts stood between them, but she did her best to tell Inas about her work with the commissar, and passed on the data and specifications she'd gathered, and answered all of Inas' questions.

Ori had been assigned to a group of Quicks being tested by Commissar Doctor Pentangel and a crew of Ghosts. Like her, the other Quicks had all experienced close encounters with sprites; had all been imprinted with a passenger. The Ghosts were intensely interested in this, and Ori and the others were subjected to all kinds of tests designed to probe and map the handful of affected neurons that, according to the commissar, mirrored the information-processing capacities of the sprites.

The tests were not difficult or unpleasant, but the regime was rigorous and repetitive, and Ori and the others had been tasked with learning techniques of 'unthinking', of completely clearing their minds to minimise activity that would interfere with measurements of the little clusters of mirror neurons. It was also exhausting, because the Ghosts did not sleep. Or rather, they were able to function in a reduced capacity with either the left or right halves of their brains asleep – what they called down time. Commissar Doctor Pentangel and Quicks he had recruited to work under him got by on catnaps and the drugs that True pilots had used to enhance their performance. She should be asleep now, Ori told Inas.

We can sleep when we're dead and the enemy is defeated, Inas signed. *Tell me why the Ghosts are so interested in sprites.*

They don't tell us anything. We're supposed to know, I guess. And we don't dare ask. All I can tell you is what the commissar told me.

According to the commissar, the Ghosts wanted to change history. They believed that the history they inhabited was the wrong history. That it had taken a wrong turning in the distant past that had led them to this point, where they could begin to correct it. To do that, they had to send a message into the past, to their founder, Levi. He had already received such a message, but according to them it was the wrong message. They wanted to send back a different one, one that told Levi what to do to avoid the path they had already taken. A message that would enable him to set out on a new path.

'History will be changed,' Commissar Doctor Pentangel had told Ori. 'Our present, which is far in their founder's future, will not be erased, but it will become unreachable. He will move away from it and create a new future in which the Ghosts dominate the history of the human species from the beginning.'

'What will happen to us?'

'We will continue as before. But we will not be part of the dominant sheaf of timelines rising from Levi's present, our past. We will be a rare example of a deviance. That is, if you believe that the classic Many Worlds interpretation is the literal truth. If it isn't, then everything we know will be unmade. That's why the Ghosts call themselves Ghosts. Because they believe themselves to be ghosts. The restless dead, striving to correct a great wrong in their past.'

The Ghosts believed that the so-called Mind lurking at the core of Cthuga was key to sending this message. And so was an ancient starship that they had captured. The starship contained what remained of a passenger who had been alive at the time when things had gone wrong, when history had switched to the wrong path. In fact, she had been at the centre of events that had changed history, a major player in the so-called Quiet War that had briefly given Earth hegemony over the cities and settlements on the moons of the outer planets. According to Commissar Doctor Pentangel, this meant that her light cone extended back to the crucial moment when Levi had received his message, so the Ghosts could use it to send *their* message and force history on to the correct path.

'They have others from that era,' the commissar said. 'Heroes who, like her, live on in virtualities. And their minds will be entangled with the Mind of Cthuga, in due course. But there is a major problem.'

He looked at Ori, his apt pupil.

She said dutifully, 'The Mind does not exist.'

'Not yet. It will, it will. I will see to that. All of us here will see to that, by hard and clever work. Especially you, Ori, and the others like you.'

Is that what they're doing? Inas signed, after Ori told her all this. *Making the Mind?*

Yes. But first they have to make sprites.

Commissar Doctor Pentangel had explained this too, in his manic way. Saying that he'd been a fool, an idiot. Saying that he had seen everything front to back. Saying that now he understood how to see things properly because the Ghosts had opened his eyes. And how marvellously simple it was!

'Your ancestors misled me. They misled everyone. At the last, when they knew they were done for, they dropped their seedship into

Cthuga, claiming that its mind would unite with the Mind in the core of the world. But there is no Mind. It was a great and glorious deception. A lie that kept us busy for centuries.

'The Mind does not yet exist. And when it does, it will not live in the core of the world. There are quantum effects at the core, yes. But they are both too uniform and too random. Uniform because the core is amazingly uniform. A solid sphere of metallic hydrogen generating everywhere the same effects. And those effects are randomly generated and transient because the core is so hot. Nothing lasts. I had thought that helium raining out of the atmosphere and falling through the core to the planet's centre of mass would perturb those quantum effects in ways that could be used to support an information-generating network. I spent years investigating this, in theory and in practice. Every failure spurred me to greater effort. For I knew that there must be a Mind, and lacked only an explanation and evidence. And why did I know? Why was I so certain? Because your ancestors lied!'

The commissar pacing up and down in his long dark room, his exoskeleton clicking and creaking. Telling Ori that sprites were not manifestations of the Mind's activity, or side-effects of the activity that sustained it. No, he said, they were the components of what would become the Mind.

'Cthuga's magnetic field is very strong, created by the rotation of its core, which is made entirely of metallic hydrogen leavened with a little helium. And where the field lines intersect with the solar wind of Fomalhaut, knots and vortices are created that propagate backwards, and create knots and vortices deep inside the planetary field. That is what creates the sprites. Millions of them. Billions. We do not know how many because we are still trying to pin down the parameters on which we can base our estimates. In any case, there are huge numbers of them, and they have the capacity to process information. In the wild, they decay because they are unstable. But we are creating stable sprites.'

They are making these things? Inas signed.

They are trying to. Down in the deeps. At the base of the troposphere, below the water zone.

So that's why they still need the cable.

That's why they need us, Ori signed. *We interacted with sprites, and some of their properties were imprinted on us. They are using us as templates to make sprites that will somehow form the Mind. And the*

Mind will be shaped by their heroes, and this old star traveller. And that's all I know.

Activity was increasing in the workshop, hour upon hour. There were more and more Ghosts busy there, and they were tireless and unsleeping. Making small pressure-shells packed with all kinds of intricate machinery that were sent down the cable to the inception points where sprites were being created. Testing Ori and the others. Modelling their altered state in virtual neuronal systems. Testing some kind of wide-pipe upload system that was supposed to plug virtual models of human consciousness into a flock of sprites; two of Commissar Doctor Pentangel's Quicks had been taken away and their brains had been stripped neuron by neuron by bush robots, to upload alternative models into virtuality.

The commissar showed Ori and the other Quicks the spiky construction or growth that wrapped around the terminus of the cable in the hot dark far below, the way it bent and constricted magnetic lines and tangled them into self-sustaining knots sent whirling off like particles on a flood. Soon, he said, their templates would be used to give those sprites intelligence and volition. The first step in the creation of the Mind.

He claims that once intelligent sprites have been created, the Ghosts will bring one of their ancient heroes to the Whale, Ori told Inas, after she'd flicked several fat data packages from her bot to the bot ridden by her bunky. *She will be the seed for the Mind itself.*

How long? Days? Hours?

I don't know. Days, maybe. They have to create these intelligent sprites before they can move to the next step.

It was their third meeting out on the skin of the Whale. Bot signalling to bot in a quiet corner of the bustling marshalling yard.

There's talk that Our Thing are planning a counterstrike, Inas said. *That they will try to destroy the Whale. Perhaps the Ghosts are taking that seriously.*

I heard that too. Do you think they can do it? Destroy the Whale?

We can't count on it.

I know you're planning some kind of sabotage, Inas. I want to help.

Inas didn't reply. Her bot sat very still with both its forward manipulators raised, the signal that the operator was thinking or otherwise engaged off-line. Ori wondered if – despite her claim that they didn't know about these conversations – Inas was talking to the rest of the crew. Deciding what to do about the information that Ori had given her. About what to do about Ori.

Below, streams of hoppers were jostling down rack-and-pinion lines to the big tipplers that loaded the freight cars or climbing back up the skin of the Whale to fetch more construction material from the processors. All over the vertical freight yard the same actions were mirrored, hoppers unloading into freight cars at tipplers, loaded freight cars creeping forward and forming strings that rumbled away towards the flying bridges that led to the main tracks down the cable. High above, the hard bright point of Fomalhaut shone close to the apex of the ring-arch; below, the deck of white ammonia-ice clouds stretched out towards the distant horizon.

Yes, just another day out on the skin of the Whale . . .

It was so familiar, and yet different somehow. Thin, insubstantial, like the backdrop for a pageant. An idealised approximation of reality. The world we see is not the world that is, the commissar had once said. Our minds conjure it moment to moment from imperfect and fractional sensory impressions. We are unable to truly comprehend what is because our minds aren't capable of processing sufficient information. So we inhabit a world of shadows and guesses and fictions. But the Mind will be able to process so much more. Its internalised world will be so much closer to the real world; it will be able to manipulate the raw stuff of reality as we are able to shove around crude blocks of atoms. It will seem to us like one of the gods of the long-ago. In the moment it is kindled, it will change everything. We will become no more than ghosts and shadows, he'd whispered. In fact, because what it will do will echo backwards through the abyss of time, we are already no more than ghosts and shadows . . .

Inas' bot was signing again. Telling Ori that her information was useful, and there was much that needed to be processed.

I think you need to meet someone.

Who?

You'll see.

What are you planning, Inas? Why don't you trust me?

But Inas' bot had gone off-line. After a moment, it spun around and marched away towards the garage. Ori set her own bot to auto and cut the link, and sat up in the immersion chair. Several people stood around it, people from her crew. Two seized her arms.

'What's this?' Ori said.

Emere said, 'Inas says that we can trust you. Now it's time to test that trust.'

Ahe raised a hand, a patch caught between thumb and forefinger. 'But we don't completely trust you,' she said. 'I'm sorry.'

She slapped the patch against Ori's cheek. Ori's face went numb in an instant, and darkness crowded in and everything turned over and slid away, and then she was somewhere else. A small, dimly lit space that stank of piss and blood and old sweat. Someone helped her sit up – it was Inas.

'You told me that our conversations were private,' Ori said. 'You lied.'

'We weren't sure if you'd be entirely candid if you knew that everyone knew about them,' Inas said, and touched a finger to Ori's lips when she started to ask another question.

Emere and Ahe and the others crouched on either side, all of them looking towards, but not directly at, a person who lay in a kind of nest of blankets. A True. His right arm was wrapped in a halflife bandage and held across his bare chest by a sling around his neck. His head was bandaged too, and one eye was obscured by a crust of blood and there was a livid burn on his cheek. A sack of clear fluid was taped to the wall above him and a line ran from it to the crook of the elbow of his left arm.

He looked at Ori, who tried and failed to meet his gaze. 'The enemy has the Whale for now, but that's a temporary set back,' he said. 'You understand?'

Ori nodded. She realised now what had kept the crew together, and felt a bitter disappointment. The True was badly injured and survived only because of their care, and yet he commanded them.

'Tell me you understand!'

Inas nudged Ori, who said dutifully, 'This one is yours to command.'

'I'm told I can trust you,' the True said. 'I'd like to be certain of it.'

'She was one of us before,' Inas said. 'She came back to find us, and she gave us the information I gave you.'

'But she works—'

The True began to cough and couldn't seem to stop. A racking retching that darkened his face and convulsed his entire body. Emere smoothed a patch on to his chest. As the convulsions began to ease, she dabbed blood from his mouth and nose, and Ahe held a cup to his lips.

He drank greedily, pushed Emere and Ahe away. 'I need better drugs,' he said.

'Yes, Majister,' everyone said.

'What I was saying, she works for them,' he said. 'And who knows what they did to her, before they brought her back.'

'She works for Commissar Doctor Pentangel so that she can tell us everything he is doing,' Inas said.

'Yes, the traitor. She was one of his before it all went to shit, and she's still one of his. That's what I mean about trust. I don't like this. If you let her go she could tell them about you, and if the enemy put you to the question, one of you would talk. I know you would.'

Everyone around Ori denied it.

'Or they'd watch you, find out about me that way,' the True said. 'Easiest way of dealing with this problem, you kill your little friend.'

Ori said, 'What do you want?'

The True looked at her.

She said, 'Do you want to regain control of the Whale, or do you want to destroy it?'

'If you know of a way of killing all the enemy without destroying the Whale, I'd like to hear it.'

'I know what the enemy wants to do. They want to create a Mind. That's the only reason they came to Cthuga. Suppose I can help you stop that?'

It was pure bravado. She felt her pulse behind her eyes as she met the True's bloodshot gaze and waited for judgement.

At last, the True laughed. 'At least one of you has a spine.'

Emere said, 'Our lives are yours, Majister.'

The True ignored her, saying to Ori, 'How closely do you work with the traitor?'

'He talks to me from time to time.'

'Then you can prove your loyalty, and sabotage their plans, all at once,' the True said. 'Kill the traitor. Kill Commissar Doctor Pentangel. Do it by the end of today. If you don't, I'll have your friends kill you.'

7

The Child dreamed while she slept. A dream inside her dream of becoming. A dream of what she had once been and what she would be once more.

It was not our doing. Yet again, we had been shut out of full access to the viron, this time by those who had been lurking at the margins of our mother's story while they developed deep links with the systems that controlled the ship and subtly influenced every kind of sensor, so that we saw only what they wanted us to see. Now they made their presence known because they needed our mother to complete their project and their enemy was mounting a counterattack on the vital facility they had captured and they feared that they would lose it. As far as they were concerned, there was no time left for any kind of instruction but a brutal and swift force-feeding.

And so the Child dreamed her way back into her adult self. A great flickering download of information. An entire library opening inside her head. Scenes from the life of her first iteration, strung together by emotional cues. If a caterpillar dreams of becoming a butterfly, that was the kind of dream she had. Of leaving São Gabriel da Cachoeira and travelling downriver to take up a menial position at a minor agricultural research facility. The bitter revelation that talent and ambition counted for less than accidents of birth. And worse, that she was a woman in a patriarchal society where women were considered most useful as the servants of men and the bearers of their children. And then her lucky break. Her discovery by the green saint Oscar Finnegan Ramos, who gifted her with a scholarship that gave her the time and resources to elaborate her first truly original ideas, and to understand how she must shape herself and her career so that she could win from the world her heart's desire.

In a flicker of images culled from the archives we had so painstakingly reconstructed, she dreamed of her growing success. Of developing a novel artificial photosynthesis system more efficient than any other then known, including those created by the greatest gene wizard of all, the Outer, Avernus. Of running a research facility that designed biological weapons; of taking Oscar Finnegan Ramos' place when he retired, and becoming the Peixoto family's chief gene wizard. Of her brief liaison with Stamount Horne, a one-eighth-consanguineous member of the Peixoto family and second-in-command of their security service, who before they could consummate their relationship in marriage had been killed in one of the interminable brush wars with bandits. Sri had allowed Stamount's son to come to term, a companion for her firstborn, Alder, who'd been cloned from her own flesh. The two growing up together in her private Antarctic research facility. Alder and Berry. Alder brilliant and resourceful; Berry sullen and troubled. She dreamed of them playing in a forest of dwarf beech trees. Blond head by dark.

And she dreamed of the war between Earth's three great power blocs and the city states of the moons of Jupiter and Saturn. The Quiet War. A war of stealth and sabotage, infiltration, economic destabilisation, diplomatic manoeuvres. A war with no real beginning, developing in a cascade of consequences as the symptoms of a genetic syndrome unfold from a single misplaced base. A war that had determined the future of the entire human species. A war to which she had contributed so much, and which had entangled her, almost fatally, in the internal politics of the Peixoto family: she'd been forced to murder her old mentor and flee Greater Brazil, and Earth, taking Berry with her, leaving Alder behind.

The war had ended in the defeat of the Outers and the escape of their great gene wizard, Avernus. And Sri had grown ever more powerful, synthesising new wonders based on techniques harvested from Outer knowledge bases and her discoveries in gardens created and abandoned by Avernus. She dreamed of her first attempt at becoming more than human. Her withdrawal from all the worlds on which she had influence; a retreat to Janus, one of Saturn's icy little moons, where she built a unique habitat and spent most of her time trying to learn how to outwit death. An experiment had backfired. She'd grown vast because of an incurable cancer, and then she'd become that cancer – or perhaps it had become her. For many years she'd been confined in a vat in her secret garden, beneath the surface of Janus. Estranged from her sons, from the rest of humanity. Dependent on the kindness of her new children: children she'd grown using her own genome as a template.

She dreamed of how the Outers in the Saturn system had taken advantage of a revolution in Greater Brazil to free themselves. But there'd been a faction of Outers who had wanted revenge. Yes. The Ghosts. Who'd believed that they were being directed by a future that their actions would create. Who'd built a small fleet of ships on Neptune's big moon, Triton, and had returned to Saturn to destroy the occupiers and take control of the rest of the Outers. Sri's home on Janus had been threatened by the Ghosts, too, so she'd retaliated. Yes. She and her children had already manufactured the seeds of ten thousand gardens, and they'd flung some of those at the incoming Ghosts ships. Destroyed them. Yes. And they'd aimed the rest of the seeds out into the Solar System, gifting the human species with hundreds of oases of life. Gardens of the Sun. After that, during the long peace following that last spasm of war and a reconciliation between Earth and Outers (brokered in part by Avernus, who'd fled to Earth, and later died there), Sri had retreated further from humanity. Cut all remaining contacts. And as groups of people had begun to light out for the planetary systems of other stars, she'd done the same. Converted part of Janus into a starship. Set out on the long voyage, some twenty-five light years, to the star Fomalhaut and its huge circumstellar disc.

But it had not turned out as she had expected. Another ship had overtaken hers: a seedship that had arrived at Fomalhaut and grown machines that had built cities and settlements, and ectogenetic tank farms where the first Quick colonists had been born. And then her ship had been badly damaged, and her original had been killed, along with most of her children. The survivors had rebuilt what was left of the ship and revived their mother as best they could, as a construct inside a detailed viron. And so she had been reborn, and had begun to dream her life all over again while her grievously damaged ship fell towards Fomalhaut. Where a second seed-ship had meanwhile quickened the True clade, and a third had arrived from the Ghost settlements around nearby beta Hydri and begun a war for control of the gas giant, Cthuga. Where the Trues believed that a vast Mind existed in the quantum strangeness of its metallic hydrogen core. Where entities known as sprites, possible agents of the Mind, were created from vortices in its intense magnetic fields. Where Ghosts were constructing an apparatus capable of pumping immense amounts of data into the magnetosphere via stabilised electromagnetic packages that imitated the sprites . . .

Sri understood what she had to do, if she was to survive.

And now the Child was grown.

The dream was gone.

The gene wizard Sri Hong-Owen woke in the bedroom of her childhood. Everything achingly familiar and yet so strange and vivid. Her appearance had not changed; she was still a pale and slender girl-child on the cusp of menarche. But she was no longer a child. Nor was she what she once had been, before the so-called accident. She had detailed memories of growing up in the old garrison town of São Gabriel da Cachoeira, but everywhere else there were great gaps. A life learned rather than experienced.

She lay still for a little while. Minutes, hours, days. She thought about what had recently happened, in her long dream of becoming. She thought about what she knew and what she needed to know. She thought about how she had changed, and what she should do next.

A hot breeze rattled the blinds and shards of sunlight advanced and retreated across the sheet contoured over her body and legs. The mosquito trap whined its one-note song up in one corner of the ceiling. She was aware of her body and the room, and she was becoming aware of everything beyond it as her consciousness extended into every part of the viron and into a much larger and more complex external volume beyond. It was a little like taking on the god-view in one of Ama Paulinho's immersive sagas. Slowly, she began to understand the matrices of information and algorithms that defined her, began to understand the limitations of the viron that contained her and the obstacles and obstructions that impeded her access to her rebuilt starship.

At last, her reverie was disturbed by sounds outside. A distant crackle and pop. A deep thump that shook her bed. Another. She rose and put on the white dress and red slippers that her mother had given her, and went out.

Her mother was waiting for her on the broad lawn outside the bungalow, standing there in front of a small deputation. Vidal Francisca in a hunting jacket and riding breeches and polished boots, pistols holstered at his hips. Father Caetano and Ama Paulinho. Her friend Roberto, taller than everyone else, smiling at her shyly. Sara, the red-haired mercenary from the north. The chief pilot of the weather wranglers. Three small and ragged children.

Her mother said, 'Well, you're awake at last.'

'And just in time,' the mercenary, Sara, said. 'The enemy is at the gates.'

Sri Hong-Owen ignored them. She smiled at the children and said, 'You must be my daughters. It's time you gave me control of my ship.'

8

When I woke from a deep and dreamless sleep, the slamship was drawing close to Prem's ship, matching its delta vee. The pilot wished us good luck, and the next moment the gig in which the Horse and I were cocooned shot out of a launch tube. A net glittered out of the dark, wrapped around us, drew us in towards the black shadow of Prem's ship.

Groggy, aching, coughing up globs of fluorosilicone, the Horse and I were hauled out of the gig by a couple of Quick sailors, rode up a vertical companionway in a kind of bucket that ratcheted along a rail to a cramped bubble drowned in red shadows. The ship's crew lay in five immersion couches set in a star pattern. Prem sat in the centre of the star, in a high-back chair that cupped her like a giant's hand. She wore a blue navy uniform with captain's bars on her shoulders. Her head had been shaved clean; red highlights gleamed on her bare scalp. Akoni, the leader of the lichen hunters, sat cross-legged on a cushion beside her chair, like some revenant of a lost age in his ragged homespun tunic and leggings.

'The uniform completes you,' I told Prem. 'Is it the one you wore when you fought the enemy, or is this a fresh promotion, in anticipation of your success?'

I was torn between wanting to hug and kiss her or punch her in the throat, but the ship's deceleration was so steep that walking a few steps to a chair that skittered out from the curved wall was like wading uphill at the bottom of a pool of mercury. As I lowered myself into the chair, sweating hard, breathless, the Horse folded himself neatly at my feet.

Prem said, 'This isn't the kind of task where you win promotion, Isak.'

'I thought as much.'

'And yet you came. I'm more pleased than I can say.'

'This one would like to speak plainly,' the Horse said.

'Why not?' Prem said. 'I suppose you've earned the right.'

'I am wondering why you brought Akoni with you. Is he one of the cultists?'

'I had to flee my home after the prefect discovered how I helped Prem,' Akoni said. 'Also, I am here as a witness for our people.'

'Most of the cultists are dead,' Prem said. 'There were never very many, and the enemy did its best to hunt them down. And even if any are still alive, they would not ally themselves with any True. After all, they wanted to overthrow us.'

'It seems to me that we've come here by different roads,' I said. 'And for different reasons. We are here to save the reputation of the Library. You are here because you're part of an army within the army. You want to bring down Our Thing. That is why you wear that uniform. That is why you command this ship.'

'Bring down Our Thing?' Prem said. 'No. Like many who fought, or who are still fighting, I am one of its champions. For many years, it was no more than an arena where blood feuds could be resolved and grievances and grudges could be aired before they blew up into feuds. But the war gave it additional powers, and increased autonomy. Some of us have worked from the inside to change it. We have shed the freight of history – all the old grievances that must be aired and weighed every time one clan wants to speak with another. We have developed new ways of doing things. Cooperation. Democratic discussion and decision-making. We're smarter and quicker, and over the years and decades of the war we've begun to loosen the grip of the elders.

'We don't want to bring down or destroy Our Thing, Isak. We want to remake it. But first, we must defeat the Ghosts. Everything follows from that. If we succeed, the enemy will lose a great prize. The focus of its efforts; the reason why it came to Fomalhaut. Not only that, but my clan will be put on the right path. Yenna will be disgraced. Newer, younger scions will take her place. The clan will be renewed. As will yours. Isn't that why you're here?'

'I am here to finish the task I was assigned.'

I couldn't tell her that when I had first seen her I had realised that the Library was no longer all I cared about. I couldn't tell her that I would follow her anywhere, for she would think less of me for harbouring such a foolish weakness. And so I hid my true feelings behind my pride, and the rectitude of my profession.

'And I'm glad you came, for whatever reason,' Prem said. 'I admit that it was Lathi's idea to hire you, not mine. I also admit that it was one of the few sensible things she did, towards the end. But then it became complicated, once we realised what Yakob had stumbled into. We had thought it was at most a conspiracy between the enemy and renegade Quick, and most likely some fantasy of a few Quick about conspiracy. But it's so much more than that, and here we are, you and me, at the centre of things.'

'If you need me, why did you abandon me on Ull?' I said.

'Because I did not know that I needed you then,' Prem said.

'You did not know that at least one of the cultists had infiltrated the starship, but had been discovered when the ship was captured by the enemy. You did not know that you would need me to help you get aboard.'

I had guessed where this was going – I had come here in the full knowledge of where it was going – but I still felt a chill grip my spine.

'The cultists dispatched several probes, but only one survived contact,' Prem said. 'Its passenger sent a brief message saying that he had discovered a viron inside the starship and that he was preparing to enter it. As far as we've been able to discover, they heard no more.'

I said, 'Was this before or after the enemy captured the starship?'

'It was still falling towards Fomalhaut. Now, of course, it is in orbit around Cthuga.'

'The gene wizard Sri Hong-Owen inhabits that viron,' I said. 'Perhaps she surrendered to the enemy. Or made an alliance.'

Prem smiled. 'We can't know until we ask her, can we?'

'There's no need for you to come with me,' I said. 'That is, if you trust me to do the right thing.'

'It isn't a matter of trust, Isak. It's a matter of honour. How could I ask you to do what needs to be done without making the same sacrifice?'

'I'll go too,' the Horse said. 'I've seen the plans of the probes. I know what it entails. But I'll go with you, master.'

'No,' I said. 'For once, I will do this myself.'

'You couldn't harrow a nursery without my help,' the Horse said.

'We'll have to take that risk,' Prem said.

'You talk about overthrowing the old order and freeing Quicks,' the Horse said. 'And yet you presume to act for us. As if we were children.'

'I'm doing this to help right all the wrongs done by my people to yours,' Prem said.

'You can start by trusting me,' the Horse said.

'If Isak and I fail, you can follow us, and do your best to win what we could not,' Prem said. 'Until then, like Akoni, you will best serve as a witness.'

Akoni raised his bone tube to his lips and blew a single high clear note. The Horse slapped at his neck, then slumped sideways.

I stooped over him and turned him on his side so he could breathe easily. The dart in his neck was as small as a pin, tailed with a tiny black feather. When I plucked it out, a bead of blood swelled in the tiny puncture wound.

Akoni said, 'He'll sleep a few hours and wake unharmed.'

'You shouldn't have presumed,' I told Prem.

'It was necessary. I trust you, Isak, but I don't entirely trust your kholop.'

'He is also my friend,' I said.

'I know. It's one of the reasons I like you.'

For a moment our gazes met and something flowed between us and I felt my heart double in size.

Prem said, 'I trust you. Will you trust me?'

'I know what we have to do.'

'Ah. I wondered if you did.'

'We'll do it together,' I said. 'As equals. I'm not your prisoner or servant. I'm your partner.'

'If we survive this, you will be a hero,' Prem said. 'You will help your clan shake off the past, as I'll help mine.'

'It's a lovely idea,' I said. 'A pity it involves dying first.'

Being dead takes no time at all, because you aren't aware of being dead. I remember the first stages of being prepared for my encounter with the bush robot that would whittle me down to a simulation. I remembered lying on a table with two technicians and their Quick assistants working on either side, remembered looking up at a window that showed my vital signs, wondering if it was the last thing I would ever see. And then, without any kind of transition, I was somewhere else.

I was standing on a broad stone bridge, looking out over a low parapet at an island in the centre of a broad slow river and a huge orange sun setting beyond the prickly roofline of a city. I recognised it at once. It was one of the ancient quarters of the Library where knowledge from Earth was stored.

A stone cathedral with flying buttresses and two square towers squatted at the prow of the island, and along its banks tall houses roofed with red tile crowded together like the walls of a fortress. The rest of the quarter should have spread along the river shore beyond the far side of the island; instead there was a vivid green jungle of palms and other trees. Threads of white and black smoke rose here and there amongst the trees and there were red flashes of explosions in the darkness beneath them and sharp thumps and the crackle of gunfire echoed across the river.

'As above, so below,' someone said.

I turned, saw a boy walking towards me. He was dressed in ragged trousers and shirt, a rifle of ancient design was slung over one shoulder, and his head was the head of one of the big cats that are grown and matched against each other in the fighting arenas. He was strange and heraldic, and yet I knew without doubt that he was Prem.

I said, 'Did you send soldiers ahead of us?'

Something exploded inside the trees beyond the far end of the bridge and sent up a column of white smoke.

'They are the creations of the cultists' infiltrator. I have control of them, and I'm wearing his shape, too. The passenger should recognise me.'

'Where is she? Is she a prisoner?'

We were walking across the bridge towards the jungle shore. I was checking my cache of tools: everything seemed to be present and in full working order. Prem had unslung her rifle and was holding it at a slant. Her small head, with its yellow and black fur and pricked ears, turned to and fro as she scanned the shore.

She said, 'All we have to do is bring her out. Allow her to cross over. But she'll have to want to come, and we'll have to block any attempt to prevent her. By her crew, or by the enemy.'

'So they're here too. I wondered about that.'

'Who do you think we're fighting? First we have to find her. Then we have to extract her. The bridge is as fat as we could make it, but she's very large. We'll have to protect it until she's done. How are you feeling, Isak? Are you ready for the fight?'

I conjured pinch traps in the air, snapped them shut, and said that I was more than ready. I was dead, a simulation inside a simulation, yet I had never felt so alive.

The philosopher who had prepared me for the crossing had told me that I would feel no different afterwards. As in life, he'd said, my sense of self would be limited by my perceptions and my ability to process information. But although I would feel the same, I would be changed in all kinds of ways. I would no longer be truly self-aware; I would instead be a simulation, based not on the complex indeterminancy of the architecture and activity of my brain's neural pathways but on algorithms that were approximations rather than accurate replicas. A bundle of best guesses that differed in a myriad subtle ways from reality and would have to constantly refer back to the baseline measurements made by the bush robot, because tiny inaccuracies in models of individual neurons quickly snowballed into gross errors when summed across the activity of the entire simulation. My consciousness would not only be less rich and less complex than the original; it would also be fixed at the point of transition, unable to change in any significant way.

Fortunately, I did not have time to worry about that as I advanced across the bridge that acted as a back door into the starship's viron. I barely had enough time to prepare myself for the fight ahead.

On the other side of the bridge, a rutted dirt road cut away through the jungle. Prem and I followed it, walking along the margin, stepping around fresh craters and the splintered remnants of palm trees knocked down by shellfire. Low buildings appeared on either side, most of them on fire, and smaller roads cut across the one we were following. A flying vehicle shaped like a giant fish drifted across the white sky, probing the little town with threads of blue laser light that cut through the smoke layering over burning buildings. The air was thick with the stink of burning. Small, angry things cracked past me; I tried to slow one down and Prem grabbed me by the hand and pulled me to the cover of a burned-out vehicle.

'We're being shot at. You can die here. The physics allow it. And if you do, there won't be time to send in another copy down the pipe. So behave as if this was real.'

We crouched face to face. Her grin was furnished with stout white fangs. Her eyes, reflecting light from a burning building, were blank orange discs.

'I can change the physics,' I said, and used an algorithm to draw a circle around us. Inside, time was fractionally out of step with time outside. When I stood, three stars flashed in front of my face and three little metal spikes fell out of the air.

So protected, we walked through the town. Past burning buildings and burning vehicles. Past the bodies of men and women and chimeras – creatures with shaggy pelts and small heads, weapons still clutched in their human hands.

Ahead was a two-storey building with a flat roof that stood at one end of a compound or yard enclosed by a white wall. All of it gleaming with sharp irreality amongst the phantoms of war. There was a door in the wall, half-hidden by flowering bushes. Prem pointed to it, told me the passenger was beyond.

'So are the crew of her ship. And the enemy, too.'

Suddenly, it was night, and the sky was the sky of the Archipelago, with one huge dim world rising beyond distant mountains whose peaks were shaped like the profile of a sleeping woman. Cthuga, half-full, mistily banded, hung inside the broad tilted plane of its rings.

I said, 'Did you do that?'

'It wasn't me.' Prem had raised her rifle and was looking all around, ears pricked.

I cut the algorithm that had been protecting us, and which also protected the rest of the viron from us. We would need to engage with it now. High above, silhouetted against Cthuga's vast bland disc, the flying vehicle began to slew around, turning towards us. Ghosts plucked at my attention, little probes trying and failing to take measure of my algorithms and other tools. I slapped them away.

'Something's coming,' Prem said.

'I know. Stand behind me.'

The gate in the wall opened, and a woman stepped out to meet us. I recognised her at once.

It was the traitor, Bree Sixsmith.

9

It should have been simple. Ori had been given a direct order to kill a traitor who was openly collaborating with the enemy. Not as a slave, like Ori and the rest of the Quicks, who had changed one master for another, but as a free man, in selfish pursuit of knowledge and power without any thought for the consequences. Not only that, he'd violated her. Used her cruelly. Now that he had been brought down to her level because of his cowardice, she had every right to take her revenge.

Yes, by any measure Commissar Doctor Pentangel deserved to die, but the very idea filled Ori with nauseous dread because it violated every principle and precept that she had been raised to obey. She had learned a degree of independence during the voyage of *The Eye of the Righteous*, had discovered in herself vital strength and determination, but it was not easy to shrug off generations of breeding and genetic tampering and tweaking, and a lifetime of discipline, education, and custom. She had been born a slave and had spent almost all of her life as a slave. Servitude was engraved in her genome. Quicks grumbled and bitched about their True masters, but none ever dared answer back to them, let alone think about harming them in any way.

And apart from revenge, there wasn't much point in killing the commissar. He had infiltrated the heart of the Ghosts' project to create a Mind, but he was in no way essential to it. The Ghosts knew everything he knew, and more besides. They had been making plans for centuries. His death would be less than a speck of grit in the slow and sure grinding of their gears. And besides all that, Ori knew that even if she could bring herself to do it by whatever means she could find, it would be hard to kill him unobserved; she would be killed immediately afterwards, and the Ghosts might make the connection between her and the crew, and kill them too. And that would be a grievous waste, for she believed that she was valuable in her own way. A conduit of useful information. An insider who might be able to find a way to sabotage the project or at least delay it, prevent it reaching completion before the rumoured counterattack.

In short, she knew that the True was wrong, and the order he'd given her was wrong. Inas and the others obeyed him because they didn't know how not to obey, but Ori had won a small measure of freedom. She had learned that she could control her own life, make her own decisions. She could see that his order was irrational, that he didn't want the commissar killed because it would hinder the enemy, but because it would avenge and erase a disgraceful blot on the honour of the Trues. But she also knew that if she didn't find a way to kill the commissar, the True would send someone to kill her. And given that he was crazy and malicious, he'd probably order Inas to do it.

Ori had a sudden, vivid and horribly graphic image of the two of them grappling to the death and her stomach clenched and she threw up in the gutter of the corridor. She leaned her forehead against the wall's smooth, cool plastic, ignored by Quicks and Ghosts hustling past, gripped by the dismal knowledge that she had no choice. That the one thing that would cause the least harm and the most good was to try to get the commissar on his own, kill him as quickly and silently as possible, and either hide his body or dispose of it. Disable his exoskeleton somehow, so he'd be helpless. Poison him. Bludgeon him. Cut his throat. Give him the long drop he'd so often threatened to give her and the other Quicks he'd recruited. It wouldn't be easy, and she didn't know if she could go through with it, but she would try her best.

And so, sick to her stomach, burdened with dread, Ori returned to the workshop. Standing on a high gantry, she scanned the knots and flows of Ghosts amongst the printers, makers and other machinery down on the floor, and at last saw the commissar tick-tocking stiffly up a spiral stairway towards one of the rooms that jutted from the wall that encircled the chamber.

Follow him, she thought. Wait until he is alone and unaware. Wait until he takes one of his catnaps in some corner. Sneak up. Do it.

She descended to the floor of the workshop and started around it, searching for a useful weapon. A boltgun, a hot-wire saw, a hammer. But almost immediately she was caught up in a small crowd of Ghosts that coalesced out of the busy swirl and surge of the crowd. Hands

345

grasped her arms, voices sang out, telling her that her time had come, and she was whirled away and carried up the curve of a walkway to a cold white room that stank of blood and burned meat.

Half a dozen Quicks, all of them the commissar's recruits, sat side by side against one wall. The bodies of two Quicks lay a few metres away, their skulls open, scooped clean. Ghosts twittered around a table where another Quick lay, her head obscured by a squat device. Ori recognised it at once: the commissar had shown it to Ori and the others a few days ago. It was a bush robot. Inside the Quick's head, a cloud of micro-manipulators were dividing and dividing and dividing, mapping hundreds of thousands of neurons and axial and glial cells every second, recording the data, stripping back another layer of her cortex. Destroying her mind even as it built a replica inside a data bank. A great and holy translation, according to the commissar. A sacrifice and a rebirth. Ori had believed that it wouldn't happen for days and days, but here it was, with Ghosts throwing windows crammed with indices back and forth, Ghosts chanting solemnly in counterpoint to the bush robot's buzzing song.

Ghosts pushed Ori forward and forced her to sit. She didn't struggle; there were too many of them. She was afraid and angry, and felt something stirring behind her eyes. Her passenger. Coming out to look. You'll be free soon, she told it. Free to fly back to where you belong.

She nudged the Quick next to her, a slight young person named Ewe, asked her why this was happening now, without warning. Ewe shook her head. Ori leaned out, asked the others. No one would look at her; no one replied. All of them settled in passive resignation. Only Ori watched as Ghosts swung the bush robot away from its victim and tipped the table sideways, so the slack body slid to the floor. The Quick at the end of the row stood up and climbed on to the table and lay down as Ghosts surrounded her. A buzzing sound: a stink of burned blood and bone: a bowl-shaped piece of skull, covered in skin and hair, falling to the floor, kicked away by one of the Ghosts.

Ori wondered why she didn't stand up. Walk out of there. Would the Ghosts stop her? She had a brief fantasy of opening one of the big airlocks. A freezing poison hurricane slamming through the workshop, Ghosts choking and dying. But first she would find Commissar Doctor Pentangel . . .

The floor jolted under her. A quick lift and fall. And then another. Everything shaking with a grinding roar that drilled through Ori's body.

346

Then the room tilted some five degrees and the buzzing song of the bush robot faltered. Ghosts chanted louder; Ghosts wiped out windows, pulled down new ones. It seemed that the interruption had fatally compromised the transfer. Some of the Ghosts were disengaging the bush robot from its victim; the rest turned and left the room.

Ori stood up and followed them, stepping carefully along the tilted floor. Just like that. She had a giddy airy feeling. As if she had become a ghost herself. A ghost amongst Ghosts. Her entire skin tingled. She expected to be challenged at every moment, but she was not.

The worst part was crossing the floor of the workshop, walking with the tilt, downhill. It was crowded with Ghosts, some working around makers and the big pressure shell, others splitting into small groups and heading off in different directions with purposeful strides. Ori saw her chance and followed one group as it cut through the agitated crowd. Head bowed, trying her best to keep her expression blank, she walked right out of the workshop and broke away and dodged into a serviceway. Ten minutes later, she was in the nearest jockey commons, prepping an immersion chair, and then she was riding a bot, out on the skin of the Whale.

10

The three children looked at each other, and then one stepped forward. A boy of eight or nine with light brown skin, dressed in a futbol shirt and shorts. Barefoot. Crew-cut hair dyed wheat-blond. Hands twisting around each other, his gaze averted in fear and respect, he told Sri, 'We cannot give you control of the ship because we have lost it. The Ghosts have it now.'

'We are so sorry,' the other two children, both young girls, said as one.

'You thought you could hide me from the war,' Sri said. 'Sneak in, settle on some anonymous rock, keep me safe. Change the way I thought so I'd *want* to hide. But it didn't work out, did it?'

'We did what we thought was best,' the boy said.

He and the two girls were pictures of abject misery. As if awaiting punishment for some crime they couldn't quite comprehend. But Sri couldn't blame them for their foolishness and failures. After all, their faults were hers: she'd made errors in some part of their design; she'd made them too protective, too loyal.

She told the children that she knew everything. That she knew the accident which had wrecked her starship had been no accident; that it had been badly damaged in a civil war between two factions of its crew over what to do after they discovered that the Fomalhaut system had been colonised by the Quick. The conservative faction had defeated those who'd wanted to wake their mother, but during the fierce fighting the coldcoffin which contained Sri's vastly altered body had been comprehensively wrecked. The surviving children had constructed a viron, quickened a kernel of Sri's consciousness ripped from her highly distributed nervous system, and tried to reconstruct her by guiding her through a simulacrum of her childhood. They'd downloaded themselves into the viron too, because by that time the starship's lifesystem was failing and its drive system was hopelessly crippled, greatly extending the time it would take to reach Fomalhaut.

'You deleted much, but there was much that you couldn't delete. But it doesn't matter. I forgive you because you brought me back to life and kept me safe. I forgive you even though you have entangled me in the war you hoped to avoid, and delivered me into the hands of my enemies. Because, without knowing it, you have brought me within reach of a place where I can at last become truly posthuman.'

The red-haired mercenary told Sri that now she understood what she had once been, now she had been given the first glimpse of what she could be, it was time to move on. 'You have the potential to become so much more than you are. We will help you fulfil that potential.'

'And who are you?'

'You know me from another life, as I know you. I am Sada Selene.'

Sri rifled through slabs of memory, came up blank. 'You have an advantage over me,' she said. 'A very small one, so don't think it's useful.'

'I am a Ghost,' Sada Selene said. 'Long dead, like you. Kept alive in a viron, like you. I helped to start the Quiet War. Later, I led the crusade to drive Earth's so-called Three Powers from the Saturn system—'

'And I defeated you,' Sri said.

'You helped wreck the first and best chance of setting humanity on the right path,' Sada said. 'It was a mistake. History went badly wrong after it. But still, that wrong turning led us here, to this point. Where we have forgiven you. Where we will go forward together, and become so powerful that we can reach back, and erase all mistakes. You say you don't remember me, but you will. One way or another.'

Sri knew that the Ghosts neither forgave nor forgot. After all, how could you spend centuries plotting to change the course of the past without dreaming of the triumphant moment when every defeat, every betrayal, every slight, would be erased? Without hoping that your enemies would feel a moment of abject desperation before they, too, completely and irrevocably disappeared? And she was most definitely one of their enemies.

She gestured towards her mother, Ama Paulinho, her friend Roberto, and the others. 'And these. They are Ghosts, too.'

'We are many,' her mother said.

'More than you can imagine,' Father Caetano said.

'I'm surprised to see any of you here,' Sri said. 'I remember that most of you were destroyed at Saturn. And most of the rest ran away.'

'And here we both are, light years and centuries later,' Sada said. 'Can you say honestly that you didn't run away, too?'

'I grew bored,' Sri said. 'The Solar System was becoming too crowded with little utopias. My fault. I gave them the oases, the gardens. I don't regret that. But it all became so stiflingly *nice*. One of those pauses in history without wars or any serious conflict. Without anything really interesting going on. So I lit out for the territories, to start over. One of the first to do so.'

'And the last to arrive,' Sada said. 'Badly damaged and in dire need of aid.'

'Is this where we begin to bargain?'

'You have nothing to bargain with,' Sada said coolly. 'Only an ancient ship that's coming apart at every seam. So badly damaged by its long voyage that we had to rescue it, take it under our command. Certainly you have no future without our help. Because the future's overtaken you. And it's ours. We have reached out and taken it. The future is ours, and soon the past will be ours, too.'

Sri laughed. 'You're like every religion that ever was. Claiming that only you know the truth. Claiming that you have access to ultimate power. Failing in every respect to demonstrate that those claims are backed by any semblance of truth.'

Sada flared with anger. 'Enough! You are in our power. You've been trying to gain control of your ship, but it isn't working, is it?'

It was true. Sri had been trying to extend herself into her ship, but it was like the bad time when she'd woken in the vat and tried to mesh the image of her body in her brain with the monstrous growth her body had become.

She said, 'You want to send a message into the past to your prophet. A message that he will use to change the future. His future, our present. It happened once, according to you, but it didn't work out. And now you want to try again. And you need me because my timeline extends further back than anyone else's. I'm your best chance of doing what you need to do. So, let's make a deal.'

'You're not much older than me,' Sada said. 'So don't attach too much importance to an accident of birth.'

'I attach precisely as much importance to it as you do,' Sri said, calling the woman's bluff.

'It doesn't much matter what you think,' Sada said.

'We're here to encourage you to take the right path,' Ama Paulinho said.

'One way or another,' Vidal Francisca said.

'It's hard, watching a child grow, knowing that she will leave you,' her mother said. 'But there is also the joy of watching her become all she can be.'

Sri said, 'If you wanted to force me to do this thing for you, you would have already done it.'

'We'll give you eternal life,' Father Caetano said. 'Just to begin with.'

'Eternal life as your servant,' Sri said.

'We are all servants of a higher power,' Father Caetano said.

'Does anyone else have anything to offer?'

Roberto shrugged and smiled and said, 'All life is change.'

There was a familiar yellow flash in his gaze and he threw something at Sri. A package of information swift and unstoppable as a bullet, piercing her, unfolding.

All the Ghosts howled in anger. Sada Selene and Vidal Francisca suddenly had pistols in their hands, and they shot Roberto and he fell as gunshots echoed off the walls of the compound.

Sada rounded on Sri. 'What did he do? What did he give you?'

Sri tried to ignore the woman's pistol. She wasn't certain that she could be killed, truly killed, in the viron, but Roberto definitely seemed dead. Lying face down in blood pooling around his head, blood spreading across the back of his shirt from a cratered wound the size of her fist. She believed that she knew who he was – who he really was. And felt, for the first time since she'd woken, a cool measure of hope.

She said, 'He wasn't one of you, and you didn't know it. That's interesting.'

'What did he give you?'

'Nothing important.'

She wasn't quite ready to run the package, not while the Ghosts were watching her so closely. She was pretty sure that she knew what it would do, and she didn't want to give them a chance to block it.

She said, 'Don't worry. Even if I had control of my ship, I couldn't outrun any of yours. And besides, where would I go?'

'That's true,' Vidal Francisca said.

'We brought you here to do the right thing,' her mother said. 'That's what's important.'

'Help me understand something,' Sri said. 'You believe that you are doing what is right, but you felt that you had to lie to my children.'

'It was necessary,' Sada said. 'It was easy to take physical control of your ship, but it took some time to take control of the viron.'

'You let them believe that they were still in charge. Still falling towards Fomalhaut. Still guiding me. You let them do your work for you.'

'And it has worked out very well,' Sada said. 'Here you are. Here I am. Together, we will go forward—'

'You have no power over me,' Sri said. She spoke quietly, staring straight at Sada. 'This is my house. I may have been asleep, enchanted by my children, who themselves were enchanted, or suffering from an unfortunate delusion. But I'm awake now. Beware.'

She had just enough control of the ship – the equivalent of being able to wriggle her big toe – to see beyond the walls of the compound. To see what was happening in the viron, and beyond. And she also had enough control for a simple trick. The hot tropical sky and sun vanished. It was night, and a giant planet dominated the sky, dimly banded in yellows and whites, circled by a ring system wider than Saturn's rings. They were tilted about ten degrees at the edge of the rings, and across the ring plane was a scattering of minuscule flashes, and the quick bright flares of fusion and antimatter explosions.

'Cthuga,' Sri told her children. 'We're not falling towards Fomalhaut, and the braking manouevre. We're already in orbit around Cthuga. And I believe that there's some kind of battle going on. Can it be about me, I wonder?'

Sada Selene would not back down. She was crazy, but she did not lack courage. She said, 'You are awake because I woke you. You are awake because your role in our great task is at hand. And this is no longer your house. I have the keys.'

'You do not have full control of my ship, and you do not have full control of Cthuga, either. If only you had told me the truth, Sada, things might have gone differently. I am always amenable to rational argument. To logic. It is how I have lived my life. To always do the right thing, the logical thing. No matter how difficult. No matter how much it might cost me. And it has cost me almost everything. My sons. The green saint who first saw my talent. You might even say it has cost me my humanity.'

'Yet you have not lost your delusions of grandeur,' Sada said.

Sri turned to the avatars of her children, costumed as children from her own childhood, and to the others. Ghosts of ghosts, inflated from shreds of memory. They'd meant so much to the child she'd been, and so little to her now. Still, she felt a pang of pity for them. For her dead. The long-lost.

'I am old,' she said. 'I am displaced in time. Yet you brought me here because you need me. And you lied to my children and you lied to me. So don't pretend you are my friend, or that you have my best interests in mind. I know you don't. If I do this thing, I will do it my way.'

Sada laughed. 'Show us what the intruder gave you. See if it will help you.'

'No. But I will show you something else.'

'And that would be?'

Sri smiled. Living in the moment. Watching dismay rise inside the avatar of the self-styled hero-saint and the avatars of the other Ghosts. All of them turning to watch as Sri walked towards the little gate in the wall of the compound.

'There are visitors you should meet,' she said, and grasped the iron lock of the gate as if grasping a gun, thumb on the latch, and swung the gate open.

Two people stood beyond it. One was a funny kind of monk with a look of quizzical alarm on his face. The other wore the shape of her friend, Jaguar Boy.

Sada screamed, and changed, and ran at them.

11

As Bree Sixsmith burst out of the gate, I felt everything around us change. Like all Librarians, I indulged in no narcotic stronger than white tea, but once, when I was very young and running some errand in the Permanent Floating Market, I had been slipped a dose of a psychotropic by one of the jaded young scions who found amusement in the discomfort of others. I'd spent several hours feeling that my body was randomly increasing and decreasing in size, clumsily crashing into stalls I thought I could step over when at my largest, marvelling at the intricacy of the weave of a piece of cloth or the interlocking fibres of a nut hull or empires in the dusty ground when at my smallest. When I had at last recovered enough sense to remember who I was, I returned to the Library and was soundly whipped by the Redactor Miriam. Not for forgetting my errand, but for having disgraced the Library by becoming the victim of a crude practical joke.

I felt something like the effects of that psychotropic now, as the demon clad in the form of Bree Sixsmith halted her headlong charge directly in front of us. She wore an odd uniform blotched with random shapes of various hues of brown and green, and she rested one hand on an ancient pistol holstered at her hip as she stared at us, as if trying to scry the marrows of our bones and the shapes of our thoughts. All around, there was an alteration in the quality of the ghost light of the vast planet that dominated the night sky, a shift in perception of scale, a heightening of resolution. And as every element of the viron gained in quiddity, I seemed to lose substance, to become as unconstrained, unbounded, and insubstantial as smoke.

Prem felt the change, too. She had raised her rifle and was looking

354

from side to side over its sight. That was when I realised that she could not see the demon.

'It's directly in front of us,' I said.

Prem aimed her rifle past my shoulder. Its muzzle made little circles in the air. 'There?' she said. 'There?'

'Do nothing for the moment. It's mine.'

'I have a magic bullet.'

'So do I.'

The demon's avatar took a step towards us. And another. And another. It was human in size and shape, enveloped in a chilly computational cocoon. I felt a shiver of premonition. The demon that the Horse and I had destroyed in the Brutal Quarter had been powerful but stupid. This one was powerful and crammed with intelligence. When I told it to stand still it laughed, and it was a human laugh.

'Poor little Librarian,' it said. 'You don't even know who I am.'

I drew a perimeter around Prem and myself. It crackled with the thorns and snares of futile-cycle algorithms, each tipped with viruses and prions eager to replicate in the demon's information space. At once, the sense of zooming and rebounding perspective vanished. I was centred again. The tools of my trade hung at my fingertips.

'I know I've already dealt with one like you,' I told it. 'I can do it again.'

'I'm like nothing you've ever seen before!'

The demon was at the perimeter now. In one beat of the viron's clock, an ornate architecture of briars and thorns reached out and wrapped around it, forming a tightly woven woman-shaped cage.

'I see it,' Prem said in my ear.

The cage held for several beats of the clock, its interior a fury of computation that leeched power from the viron around us. Everything lost sharpness and focus; it was as if we were standing in a badly pixilated image composed of just eight shades of grey. And then colour and form began to return and the briars began to shrivel. Loosening their hold on each other. Flaking away into dust that lost its shape to an impalpable wind, blowing away, vanishing.

The demon smiled in my face.

I displaced us at once into a pocket viron of my own design: a replica of the Permanent Floating Market crowded with copies of myself and Prem. But before I could ambush it, the demon whirled through the stalls and walkways, trashing subroutines and algorithms, growing into a toppling tower of debris that stooped down to snatch us up with braided filaments. I displaced us again and again, attempting to gain distance through distraction. The pitted surface of a worldlet naked to black vacuum, where the demon was a coalescence of shadows reaching for us. Bright space above the granulated surface of Fomalhaut, where a white-hot prominence arched towards us like an elongated hand. The blank blue sphere of a water-worldlet, where bubbles whirled up towards us. A flatland, where Prem and I were two triangles suddenly sucked towards a gaping pit. The road before the gate again, in a blowing snowstorm of viruses that flashed into sparks of light when they touched the demon.

'Enough,' the demon said

The snowstorm blew sideways and vanished. Prem and I were still inside the perimeter I'd drawn. Cthuga loomed in the night sky, its pale light glimmering on the road and the white wall. The air tasted of smoke; gunfire crackled in the distance. The demon stood just outside the perimeter, arms folded, its expression cool and amused.

I showed it the Klein trap I'd opened while bouncing from pocket viron to pocket viron. Its matrix packed with dizzy perspectives and lush nodes of computational power, opening up like a flower, exploding to dust in my hands.

'Is that the best you can do? How disappointing,' the demon said.

I reached up, grasped the barrel of Prem's rifle, and told her to fire.

The noise of the discharge deafened me. The barrel kicked out of my grip and a star-shaped hole appeared in the demon's forehead and wept a single black tear. The demon went cross-eyed, as if trying to look inside its skull, and then an intense look of concentration appeared on its face. It coughed and gargled, opened its mouth, showed me the bright bullet resting on its tongue. And closed its mouth and swallowed the bullet and reached towards me, brushing aside the busy algorithms of the perimeter as if they were cobwebs.

Its hand plunged into me and its look of triumph changed to one of consternation. It grabbed at me again, with both hands this time. They swept through me and I didn't even feel them. Prem asked me what was happening; I told her that I didn't know.

And now someone else walked out of the gate in the white wall. A girl-child in an antique white dress whose hem brushed her ankles. She walked with a queenly confidence, and I knew that she must be the ship's passenger. Sri Hong-Owen. She did not pause or waver when the demon in the shape of Bree Sixsmith turned and screamed at her. She walked up and took hold of the demon's hand and told it to be quiet.

The demon, amazingly, obeyed. Looking off into the distance with a stupid expression, as if distracted by something it wanted but couldn't understand.

Sri Hong-Owen looked at Prem and me. 'Thank you for the diversion. It allowed me to run the gift of another visitor. I have full control of my ship now.'

'Your ship is still owned by the Ghosts,' Prem said. 'Surrounded by their ships, the target of heavy weaponry that will blow it apart if it tries to get away. But we can help you escape.'

'I left home once before, in another life,' Sri Hong-Owen said. 'I wanted to find the secret of eternal life, but things didn't quite work out as I hoped. Change is life, and I have changed a great deal since then. This time around, I think I'll stay.'

'Show her,' Prem said, and I threw up a window that displayed aspects of the Library.

'There's plenty of room in it,' I said. 'For you and your ship, and your crew.'

Sri Hong-Owen studied the window for a moment, head cocked, eyes shining with secret amusement. 'It *is* very large. And there are some interesting things in it. But it's also very old, and it needs a lot of work. And, forgive me for saying so, but it's seriously lacking in possibility. In the capacity for change.'

'Perhaps you could help us,' I said.

'All you have to do is walk across the bridge with us,' Prem said.

'You'll find it's badly damaged,' Sri Hong-Owen said. 'Your friends fought well, but some of the Ghost avatars almost broke through.'

I called up an image of the bridge, and felt a cold dismay. I was only a copy of a copy, had known from the start that there was little chance of surviving my mission, but now that I was confronted with the hard truth of my imminent death I wanted so very much to live.

'You can't stay here,' Prem said. 'If we go right now there's a good chance that we can get you across.'

'Even if the bridge was whole, I couldn't cross it in my present form. I'm too vast. I'm part of everything now.'

'I don't think so,' Prem said, and raised her rifle. 'Let's put that to the test.'

'Are you trying to threaten me? In my viron? In my ship?' For a

357

moment, Sri Hong-Owen towered above us, a dark storm cloud that eclipsed Cthuga's swollen globe. And then she stood before us again, a young girl in a white dress. Saying, 'If you're worried that I will form an alliance with the Ghosts, I promise to be no kind of friend to them. And as you can see, they've lost whatever power they had over me. I'm free. Free at last.'

'You are still their prisoner.'

'They can destroy me, but they can't control me. And they won't destroy me as long as I control the avatar of their champion, because she'll tell anyone who asks that she's in control. I'm taking my ship out of orbit right now. Stay or try to leave, it's your choice.'

Prem looked as if she wanted to argue the point. I took her hand and said, 'We must try to go back. Our people need to know what we learned.'

Sri Hong-Owen said to Prem, 'If you ever meet an old friend of mine – the one whose form you've borrowed? Tell him that I'm grateful for the time I spent with him. Tell him that I hope to repay him and his people one day.'

She turned in a neat quick pirouette that made her white skirt flare out, and walked back towards the gate in the wall. The avatar of the demon followed her like a house pet. Prem and I looked at each other, and then we ran.

The little town was crumbling all around us. Burning buildings fell to ashes and less than ashes. Roofs and walls shivered into billions of discrete bits that sketched ghostly outlines for a moment before evaporating, as the information that had given them order turned into random noise. Prem and I ran full tilt down a narrowing road through this great vanishing, hand in hand, breathless. We passed through a stretch of forest that fell away to blank barrens on either side, and there was the bridge, arched across the river, and the lights of the Library heaped on the far side.

The island and its cathedral and crowded ranks of houses were crumbling and a long section of the bridge had fallen away at the point where it met the island's prow. Prem and I walked to the edge of the broken roadway, looking out across the churning flow of the river's repetitive cycles, saw two figures run out along the other side of the broken bridge, shouting and waving to us across the gap.

'This is a very bad metaphor,' Prem said.

'It's too late to construct another,' I said, and threw a packet of information to my twin. It turned into a bird and flew across the river as swift as thought and my twin caught it deftly in one hand and held up the other, palm out, in salute and benediction.

The remnants of the island subsided in a dust storm of shattered information that rolled out across the river. And now the bridge on which Prem and I stood began to dissolve.

'I think—' Prem said.

'I know,' I said.

We clasped each other in each other's arms. A moment later, everything fell away.

12

When Ori walked her bot out of its garage, she discovered that the sky all around the Whale was threaded with hectic motion. Sleek raptors – so fine to see! – stooped down from zenith, twisting and turning as they chased Ghost craft that jittered in erratic orbits near and far. Drones flared from the raptors' truncated wings, spiralling away towards their targets. Beam and particle weapons burned sooty threads through the methane-rich air. The percussive flares of explosions, bright blinks vanishing inside black clouds of vapour that were ripped to shreds by wind shear.

Ori's passenger moved out of the darkness at the back of her skull. You watch this, she told it, and wondered if it could feel the exhilaration and hope that surged through her and lifted her heart. Watch and learn.

Other raptors shot past the tangled contrails and explosions of the dogfights, aiming their weapons at the cable that hung from the Whale. A boxy Ghost machine jerked across the path of one of them and they met and vanished in a shatter of tumbling fragments. Then the wave of raptors had passed, and the survivors were pulling out in hard turns far below, specks fleeing out across the dirty white cloud deck.

Ori watched them go. So few of them left, and flocks of Ghost craft still circled in every quarter of the sky. But now a second wave of raptors drove down amongst a flicker of hard white stars and raking fans of black threads as Ghosts fired off countermeasures. Many of the raptors were destroyed before they reached the Whale; most of the rest were destroyed in brief fierce dogfights; the few survivors chased away after the survivors of the first wave. Behind them, clouds of tiny drones spread out, some shooting towards Ghost craft, the rest falling in long arcs towards the cable, flaring in chains of tiny explosions along its length.

High above, a bright star was descending.

Ori watched as it went past, about twenty kilometres out. A teardrop of dark, raddled water ice riding a tongue of fusion flame. The old, old starship. Ghost craft of every shape and size made way for it, and far below a carnival of tiny lights rose up to meet it. Sprites. A host of sprites dancing around it, enveloping it, following it as it fell.

The Ghosts' prize had come to Cthuga.

Ori turned her bot to look straight down the length of the Whale as the starship dwindled away, falling parallel with the cable, vanishing into the cloud deck. Her passenger watched too, pressing against the back of her eyeballs. You should go with the ship, Ori told it. Fly away. Fly away. Get ready for the big moment when everything changes.

But, as always, there was no reply.

She remembered now why she had come out here in the first place and put out a call to Inas, waited out a long, long silence, called again. Nothing. Not even the ping of acknowledgement. Perhaps the comms were jammed because of the attack; perhaps they were about some business of their True master. Ori hoped it was the former rather than the latter. She hoped that Inas and the rest of her former crewmates weren't enacting some stupid and no doubt suicidal plan of their True master.

She disengaged from the bot, levered herself off the immersion couch, set out towards the commons of jockey crew #87. She'd have to confront them face to face, tell them she'd killed the commissar. And wondered why she hadn't thought of that before. Thought to lie. Maybe it was because she didn't know how; because it was a last desperate chance to get close to the True. She'd have to find some way of brazening it out, of pretending that she'd done what had been asked of her. And if Inas and the others fell for it, they'd take her to the True, and she'd tell him about the descent of the Ghosts' champion, and find some way of convincing him of its importance, of what had to be done.

And if he didn't believe her . . . But that was unthinkable.

She was no longer afraid. She knew that death was just around the corner but she was no longer afraid. In that moment, she was free. Fully awake, fully aware. Every sense sharp. Feeling a weird exultation, in this hour of her death. Her passenger still rode behind her eyes. A funny kind of pressure, like a word she couldn't say or an image she couldn't see, that was beginning to turn into a headache. She wondered if it understood what she wanted to do. She wondered if it would be freed when she died, or if it would die with her.

It should have been a straight run to the commons. Back to the elevator ring, up three floors, and out towards the rim. Ten minutes at the most. But when Ori reached the concourse in front of the elevators she discovered that it was crowded with knots of Ghosts that swept back and forth. After a moment, she realised that they were fighting. Slashing and bludgeoning each other in furious silence. One wielded a cutting tool, waving its spike back and forth, scorching lines of black char across the faces and chests of his attackers. Another swung a whip of monofilament wire, clearing a wide space in front of her. Two gangs ran at each other, merged in a wild flurry of fists and feet. The wounded and dying and dead curled up as if asleep, sprawled in spreading pools of blood.

As Ori hung back, trying to work out how she could safely cross this battlefield, wondering if she could find an alternative route, she heard a strange ululating chant coming towards her. Within moments, it doubled in volume, doubled again. And then a wedge of Ghosts came around the corner and she was swept along in the flood as it battered and smashed its way across the concourse. A few Quicks were caught amongst the crowd and when the wedge stalled in front of the freight elevators Ori fought her way to the nearest Quick and asked her what was happening.

'War!'

'Between the Ghosts?'

'I think so!'

They were leaning into each other and shouting, but they could barely hear each other over the whooping chants of the Ghosts crowding all around.

'Why?' Ori yelled.

'I don't know!'

'Where are they going?'

'I don't know!'

And then Ori and the other Quick were pulled apart and a tide of Ghosts drove Ori into a freight elevator and it slammed upwards. She was jammed in one corner. The noise of the chants was colossal in the confined space and two windows showing images of the starship shed a ghastly light over the tight scrum. A teardrop of radiation-blackened ice, scarred and pitted, indescribably ancient. She wondered what it was going to do, down there. Whether its passenger really could pass from her viron, move out into sprites, and what would happen if she did. What she would become . . .

Then the elevator doors slammed open and she was swept out into one of the hangars. A big chilly brightly lit space into which the crowd around her quickly dispersed, breaking up into small groups that set out in different directions. Ghosts and Quicks and autonomous bots were working on small, boxy craft parked in rows. Hauling them up, fitting pressure shells around them, filling the shells with impact gel. It looked to Ori very much like they were preparing for a mass evacuation. She picked amongst a rack of tools, found a welding gun, and walked away. Trying to look purposeful, trying not to look directly at a drone that turned to watch her. Wondering if she could take it out if it tried to stop her.

Someone called to her. Called her name. Her heart turned over but she didn't look around and kept walking.

Footsteps behind her: Commissar Doctor Pentangel tall in his exoskeleton, his narrow smile, his gaze lit with triumph. Ori raised the welding pistol and black pain seized and unstrung her.

When she came around, she was lying on the floor. She'd pissed herself and every muscle and joint hurt and a sharp pain pulsed behind her eyes. The commissar bent stiffly so that his face was centimetres from Ori's.

'Did you forget your implant? I used it to track you down, child, because it's time! Time to be translated! Time to become part of the Mind!'

Crowds of Ghosts surged out of the elevators and across the floor of the hangar, singing and chanting. Two surges, three. And then the elevators stood empty and Commissar Doctor Pentangel pushed Ori forward, his hands on her shoulders, his implacable grip grinding her bones.

Ori was sick at heart, cursing her bad luck, cursing herself for not putting up a fight. She'd believed that she was free, but she wasn't. She was still a slave, weak at her core, giving in at the very sight of a True. There was nothing she could do. She could barely think around her splitting headache.

As the elevator plunged down, the commissar told Ori that he alone could save the day now. 'The Quicks failed, but I will not fail. We will not fail. We will create the Mind, Ori. You and me and your so-called passenger.'

'The Quicks failed?'

'Their so-called champions lost contact with the starship as it fell towards the core. And now different factions are fighting for control. They worked towards one goal in harmony, but now they've failed they can't agree what to do next. But I know! I know. I'll make the bridge to the past they want and need.'

'This one believes that many of them are preparing to leave.'

'Many already have. Let them! I don't need them. But they need me.'

Commissar Doctor Pentangel talked on, telling Ori about changing the past and erasing the present, about how he'd survive that erasure because he would be at the root of that change, and she felt the old, cold chains of submission settle on her. He was going to strip down her brain, neuron by neuron, to search for the template that he believed was imprinted there. She would die, and for what? The starship and its passenger had most likely been stamped flat by pressure and boiled away long before it reached the outer edge of the hydrogen ocean, Ori thought. And then she remembered how the sprites had rushed up to meet it. Dancing like the crewmates of bunkies who vow permanent partnership . . .

The elevator began to slow. The commissar spoke to it, told it to take him all the way down to the workshop level, but it stopped and the door slid back and would not shut when the commissar told it to.

'Nothing works properly any more,' he said, and shoved Ori forward again.

There was no fighting at this level, just small knots of Ghosts moving with swift purpose. As they crossed the wide curve of the concourse, Ori spotted a drone hung high up, silhouetted against the light panels, and wondered if the crew was looking for her. But the drone was turning, drifting away. The commissar spoke sharply, told her to look straight ahead and pushed her towards a hatch that led to the service walkways.

As they ducked through, someone stepped towards them. It was the True that Inas and her crew had rescued. He was strapped inside an exoskeleton, his face like a skull, teeth bared to the gums in a rictus grin as he swung a length of pipe and whacked the right leg of the commissar's exoskeleton at the knee joint. The commissar yelped and went down, and the True hit him again and again, swinging left and right, the crack of the pipe against the exoskeleton echoing flatly in the long column that housed the spiral walkway.

The commissar was on his back, one arm crooked over his face, the other beneath him. His right leg twitching and quivering as its motors fought to straighten the damaged joint. The True jabbed the end of the pipe at Ori's face and told her to stay right where she was – she was next.

'That's an order,' he said.

His face shone with sweat and blood stained the edges of the halflife bandage around his bare torso. His bloodshot gaze shone with a desperate craziness.

Ori jerked her head up and down and the True turned to the commissar, resting his weight on the pipe as he leaned in. Saying, 'This isn't the end you deserve, you filthy traitor. But it's what you're getting.'

And then he screamed and reared back, dropping the pipe and clapping both hands to the smoking wound that the commissar had burned into his face with the welding pistol. The commissar heaved up, right leg crooked, most of his weight on his left, and pressed the welding pistol over the True's heart and there was a thump and an awful stench of burning and the True collapsed.

Ori stepped out of the way and kept stepping, moving towards the pipe, and the commissar saw her and raised his hand and shook his forefinger back and forth. He was leaning on the rail at the edge of the ramp, breathing hard, his right leg still ticking and trembling.

'Never forget what you are,' he said. 'My best pupil. The last alive. The last best hope to change things for ever. We'll walk down. You lead.'

They started down. The commissar holding the welding pistol at Ori's back. Jabbing her with it every half-dozen steps. They were three levels above the workshop when the ramp trembled lightly. Ori hesitated, the commissar jabbed her hard in the back with the pistol, and the ramp trembled again and did not stop. Ori grabbed hold of the rail as the sloping floor bucked and jumped. Things grated and sang. Something fell past her – the True's body, moving fast. There was a tremendous muffled boom far below, everything jerked hard, and there was a feeling in the pit of Ori's stomach like riding a fast elevator.

The juddering gentled to a slow back-and-forth swing. The commissar stood upright, towering above Ori, and ordered her to move on.

'The cable must have broken,' she said. 'Can't you feel it? The Whale is rising.'

'It doesn't matter. Move!'

She sprang at him, and black pain crowded into her head and something pushed clean through the pain. A tall cool bright flame that stood between her and the commissar, bending towards him. He screamed and fired the welding pistol, and the flame winked out and Ori ran at him. She ran fast, bent low, ducking under the commissar's clumsy swipe, hitting him full force. He staggered and she gripped him around his thighs. She knew she couldn't match the strength and power of his exoskeleton, so she simply lifted him up, hearing her joints crack with the effort, and threw him bodily over the low rail.

His brief scream was cut off by a crash as he bounced off the side of the ramp several floors down, and he dropped in a loose tangle of limbs. Ori looked away and heard the hard smack when he hit bottom.

Then she started back up, running faster and faster towards Inas and her friends, to tell them that they were free.

ESEMPLASY

1

The dropship punched into Cthuga's upper atmosphere, shedding velocity as it shot comet-wise across the sky inside a shell of white-hot plasma, stooping down as gravity began to overcome its failing velocity, ejecting its heat shield, re-forming into cruise configuration.

It sailed the upper air of the equatorial band, outrunning winds, at last sighting the orphan it had come to find. The Whale, drifting free, the long section of broken cable hanging below it deformed by drag into a shallow curve. Its base was badly damaged. Ragged chunks missing. Sections of skin burned or blown away, exposing broken lattices of structural elements and collapsed tiers of floors. Higher up, scrofulous black growths mottled its flanks and hangar doors gaped like screaming mouths.

Riding their bots out on the skin of the Whale, Ori and Inas watched the little dropship approach like a minnow edging up to Leviathan. Swinging around and around the Whale in a wide slow spiral from bottom to top, blitzing the hulk with sensors and probes, launching drones that shot through rents in its skin and sent back damage reports.

'Standard scan-and-search procedure,' Ori said, as the dropship swung past at roughly the level where she and Inas were hunkered down. 'They're worried about walking into a trap. That's why they sent such a small ship. One they can afford to lose.'

'We're lucky they didn't shoot us out of the sky,' Inas said.

'They could have done that while the Ghosts were still in control,' Ori said. 'And it would have been much easier to destroy the Whale than attempt to sever the cable. But they pulled it off. They cut the link with the lower depths, screwed up the Ghosts' plans, and set the Whale drifting free.'

'And nearly killed us.'

Inas said this without any trace of bitterness or anger. That the True believed the Quick aboard the Whale to be expendable was, as far as she was concerned, a simple flat statement of fact. An inescapable property of the universe, like gravity, or inertia.

'We're still here,' Ori said. 'We saved the Whale and we saved ourselves. Everything will work out. You'll see.'

'Things have changed,' Inas said.

It was one of the mantras that Ori had adopted to bind the surviving Quick together and keep up their morale.

'Things have changed,' Ori said firmly.

After a final assault by True raptors and drones had cut the cable, it had fallen to Ori, using her experience of salvaging *The Eye of the Righteous*, to organise the surviving Quick and work out how to stabilise the Whale. And so she had, unwillingly, become their leader, and Inas had become her second-in-command. Her mainstay. Her drift-anchor. Her sounding post.

Ori had tried to put a positive spin on the arrival of the dropship, but in truth she shared Inas' sense of foreboding. She'd sent several messages to the ships in orbit around Cthuga, explaining that the Quick crew had taken charge of the Whale, explaining what the Ghosts had been trying to do and how they had failed, explaining that the Ghosts were either dead or had attempted to flee in the mass exodus that had engaged the True ships for so long. None of her messages had been acknowledged, and although Ori told herself that it was probably because the Trues believed they were some kind of Ghost trick – lures for the unwary; trojans for subtle demons – she couldn't shake the idea that the Trues didn't feel that they needed to respond to a gang of leaderless Quicks. That the dropship wasn't coming to rescue them, but to reclaim a valuable resource.

Inas said, 'It was nice while it lasted, our little republic.'

'We knew this day would come. We knew all along that we'd have to prove our worth. And what we've done here is more than worthy.'

'Do you really think they care if any of us are still alive?'

'They'll want to know what we've done. They'll want to hear our stories.'

They watched the dropship appear and disappear as it spiralled higher. At last, a gig detached from its belly and shot across the airy gap and was swallowed by the maw of a hangar. After several minutes, the hangar door irised shut.

'Well,' Ori said, 'I suppose we'd better get ready to meet them.'

The surviving Quick inhabited two farm decks close to the waist of the Whale. They'd sealed the bulkheads and kept the decks warm and lighted, ran air- and water-recycling units with power from fusion batteries wired in series and makeshift windmills they'd erected on the Whale's skin. Only one fission reactor was still online, and all its output went to the control systems and to heating the surviving ballonets to provide the lift that kept the Whale in the high, thin, relatively stable stream of air beneath the boundary between the troposphere and the stratosphere.

Ori and the others lacked the equipment to make any real inroads on the damage the Whale had suffered during the brief fierce civil war between Ghost factions. Most of it was dark, littered with debris, and depressurised. Gales of frigid hydrogen blew down passages and walk-ways, howled around hangars and factory decks. Ori had organised corpse-parties that had cleared out the dead and given them all, True or Ghost or Quick, a proper farewell before entrusting them to the long drop. The handful of Ghosts who had survived their civil war had either died of their wounds or had willed themselves to die; isolated from their companions, they had turned inwards and shut down like so many defective machines. After Ori's crews had patched up the Whale's altitude- and attitude-control systems and secured the two farm decks, there had been little else they could do but conserve their dwindling reserves of power and food, air and potable water, and wait for rescue.

Now Ori, Inas, and all the others gathered before the airlocks they'd rigged. The farm stretching away behind them, a quilt of greenery spread out under brilliant rows of lights. Windows hung in the air showed views of the boarding party stalking down passages and service-ways. Jerky shots captured by static cams that kept blinking out as they were discovered and neutralised. All but one of the party were troopers, clad in bulky armoured pressure suits and armed with pulse and glaser rifles. A variety of combat drones sharked alongside them. The ex-ception was half the height of the others, and dressed in a plain blue p-suit with a gold-filmed visor. Ori hoped that was a good sign, that the boarding party included a Quick. She hoped that it was a sign of respect. She hoped that they wanted to parlay.

At last, the boarding party reached the far side of the bulkhead. Drones scanned the airlocks; troopers assumed defensive positions; the small person in the blue p-suit conferred with a trooper badged as a cornet, then stepped up to the central airlock and spread its empty gloved hands in the universal gesture.

'They know we're watching. We'd better let her in before the troopers decide to blast their way in,' Ori said.

There was a small tense pause as the airlock chuntered through its cycle. Ori ran her palms over her scalp, sucked spit into her dry mouth. It was at times like this that she missed her passenger. The way it would push forward from her innner dark into the centre of her attention. Its simple presence. It hadn't returned to her after it had confronted Commissar Doctor Pentangel; no doubt it had fled after the other sprites, joined their dance in the chthonic depths. Ori often wondered if it had taken anything of herself with it. She hoped so. She hoped there was still some kind of connection, no matter how tenuous. Not merely out of sentiment: she wanted to tell the Trues that they had a good reason to keep her and her crews alive.

Behind her, the others shuffled and murmured. Beside her, Inas reached out, took her hand.

The door slammed up with a bell-like clang of counterweights and the person in the blue p-suit stepped over the lip, hands raised to shoulder height, then reaching higher, turning the bubble of its helmet with a sharp click, lifting it off, shaking out a bush of flame-coloured hair as she looked about. She was definitely a Quick, but she had an odd, crooked smile, and her face was thinner and more angular than any that Ori had seen.

'My name is Faia op (8,9 cis 15) Laepe-Nulit,' the strange Quick said. 'But you can call me the Horse. Who's in charge here?'

2

I was reborn, of course. So was Prem. That's one of the few advantages of being dead. You can die all over again, and come right back.

We've made our home in a house in the ancient quarter of the Library, on the island in the middle of the river. A tall narrow place, small rooms with whitewashed walls and striped rugs and simple wooden furniture. Some of its windows overlook the cathedral square, and the bridge. Others look elsewhere.

Much has changed in the Library since the end of the war, but there is still a great deal of work to be done. One of my first tasks when I ascended to the office of Redactor was to turn the far end of the bridge into a portal to the information cloud of Our Thing. I've opened up many others since, connecting various parts of the Archipelago to all the quarters of the Library that have been made safe. We are Librarians still, conserving data and driving out demons and making good, but we no longer control access as we once did. True and Quick come and go as they please.

'People will suspect you're hiding something, living in such ostentatious simplicity,' the Horse said, the first time he visited me after my death. 'They'll wonder where you're hiding your wealth, and fantasise about great treasures and strange and terrible secrets, and plan how to steal them.'

'They are welcome to try. Perhaps they will find something I've overlooked.'

'And meanwhile the Redactor Svern squats next door in that temple. Another magnet for trouble.'

'It's not a temple. It's a cathedral. And he needs the space for his memory palace.'

'Does he understand that he's a prisoner?'

'I'm not sure that he does. But there he is.'

I had tasked the Redactor Miriam to look after him, to catalogue his memory palace, and to discover the truth about his entanglement with the Singleton clan. I doubted that she would ever find anything useful, and do not think me petty if I confess that it gave me a small, thin pleasure to see her come and go each day, and to accept her reports. She had failed or refused to see the danger that the Library had faced, and it was a kinder punishment than exile.

'Both of them in the past,' the Horse said. 'Reliving past glories and failures without being able to change any one of them. You, on the other hand, *have* changed. You've grown up.'

'It would be nice to think so, but I'm under no illusions about my limitations. Still, I hope that I have been able to change the Library for the better. I hope, one day, when all repairs and reparations have been made, that I will be able to hand it over to your people.'

'Oh, we're not interested in the past,' the Horse said. 'We look to the future, now that we have one.'

My old friend does not visit as often as he once did. He's busy, out there in the worlds. Spending most of his time on the Whale, which has been repaired and repurposed, engaged now in monitoring and trying to understand the changes that Sri Hong-Owen is undergoing, and what she is creating at the boundary of Cthuga's sea of metallic hydrogen.

I try to keep track, but there's still much to be done here in the Library, and Prem is entangled with truth-and-reconciliation hearings that may last another generation. There are so many crimes for which we Trues must ask forgiveness, and there are so many of us who refuse to answer for all that we have done. Change does not come easily to us, who have made a point of refusing it for so long. There were many atrocities and massacres in the megaseconds immediately after the end of the war. Scattered rebellions against Prem and her allies, as they used the power they'd gained in victory to impose a new order on things, almost coalesced into outright civil war, and it was the Quicks who suffered the most, for they had the most to gain and we had the most to lose. And then there is everything before that, beginning with the arrival of the True seedship in the Fomalhaut system, and the murders committed on first contact with the Quick.

It is no easy task, and there may be no good or happy or neat ending to it. Already, many Quick are moving away from the Archipelago and

374

establishing new settlements and cities everywhere in the dust belt. And Sri Hong-Owen continues to change, at an ever-increasing rate. We do not know what she is becoming. Perhaps we will never know. Perhaps she is already beyond our comprehension.

So I'm grateful that every so often the Horse spares the time to come down the pipe and walk across the bridge and tell me the latest speculations about Sri's transformation, and swap rumours and gossip. The last time he came, he brought his son. A delightful young thing full of energy and random enthusiasms, amazed that he could run and run and never grow tired or breathless, demanding to be taken for a walk through the old quarter. And so we did. The child running ahead and running back to tell us about the wonders he'd found, the Horse and I talking about the grind of making good, and the latest changes in the depths of Cthuga.

The Horse's son was born after randomly crossing his genetic files with those of his partner, who before everything changed had been working in the Permanent Floating Market – he and the Horse had pledged themselves to each other long ago, all unknown to me and anyone else in the Library, and he had been the source of much of the information that the Horse relayed to me.

'And so for him at least it was a happy ending,' I told Prem, later.

'We could have children, you know. We may be dead, but our genetic files are still extant.'

'What kind of child would want ghosts for parents?'

'You had no parents at all, and turned out fine.'

'I had foster parents, like all Librarians.'

'Our children could have foster parents too, if they needed them. But I doubt that they would.'

'It would be a poor fantasy to think that we could live through our children,' I said.

'Perhaps we can live because of them,' Prem said.

I thought about that, and said, 'Do you think it would change us?'

And we talked about it for a long time.

3

We live in the little town of São Gabriel da Cachoeira, on a bend in the Rio Negro, with mountains to the west and the renewed and trackless forest all around. These are the steadfast walls of our prison; the happening world is hidden beyond their close horizons. But sometimes she returns to us. Our mother. She walks up the green breast of the Fortaleza hill in a cloud of bees and butterflies, and we follow her through the tall sunstruck grass, and she tells us stories of her Becoming.

We do not know everything about her. We never will. But we want to know and understand as much as possible, and that's why we've made this. A virtual model of what happened when we arrived at Fomalhaut and met some people there, presented from our limited and distorted point of view, and that of two of the people who contributed to our mother's triumph.

This is our story, and theirs. But it is not, of course, the whole story. No one can know everything.

And meanwhile our mother grows in strange ways, blazing with holy candescence as she expands into the great unknown. We live and love in the terror of her beauty.

Fomalhaut is still the brightest star in our sky. But not, we think, for much longer.